getting mad,
getting even

getting mad, getting even

Annie Sanders

First published in Great Britain in 2009 by Orion Books,
an imprint of The Orion Publishing Group Ltd
Orion House, 5 Upper Saint Martin's Lane
London WC2H 9EA

An Hachette UK Company

1 3 5 7 9 10 8 6 4 2

A CIP catalogue record for this book is
available from the British Library.

ISBN (Hardback) 978 0 7528 8972 6
ISBN (Trade Paperback) 978 0 7528 8973 3

Typeset by Deltatype Ltd, Birkenhead, Merseyside

Printed and bound in Great Britain
by Clays Ltd, St Ives plc

The Orion Publishing Group's policy is to use papers
that are natural, renewable and recyclable products and
made from wood grown in sustainable forests. The logging
and manufacturing processes are expected to conform to
the environmental regulations of the country of origin.

www.orionbooks.co.uk

To the unknown woman
who left the prawns hidden inside the curtain poles
before leaving the house to her faithless husband.
Attagirl!

'Revenge is a dish best served cold.'
Mario Puzo, *The Godfather*

Chapter One

'Right, I see. I understand completely, Mrs Cooper-Adams. It has to be perfect. Well, we'll need a sample to analyse for the closest possible match.' Pulling a pencil from the pot in front of her, Georgie tucked the phone under her chin and started to note down the details in the planner in front of her on the desk. The weak autumn sunshine was streaming through the windows, making the whole room glow like the inside of a jewellery box but the voice in her ear was unhappy and tense.

'... it's a matter of life and death, you do understand that?'

'Of course I do,' Georgie soothed. 'It's a delicate operation, naturally, but here at the agency we've dealt with this kind of ... er, emergency before, many times. Our specialists are the best. Now obviously they do have a waiting list for this kind of procedure, but given how urgent this is, I think we can get André an appointment today.'

The sigh of relief from the other end of the phone was almost as much of a reward as the hefty fee would be. 'But can you send someone straightaway?' Mrs C-A pressed. 'I want to be here with him when you take him away. Will he have to stay in overnight?'

Georgie tried hard to keep a straight face. 'Why don't you pack an overnight bag for him, just in case. Now, someone will be with you within ...' a quick scan of Flick's schedule on the wall-planner showed she'd soon be finished with the appointment in Balham, so if Georgie diverted her to Chelsea and put the later clients on hold, it would just be possible, '... forty minutes.

I

Has André eaten this morning? No? Probably just as well. Now, let me double-check the details.' Georgie looked back at the notes she'd just taken, then clicked on the relevant details on the computer screen.

'André is four and a half now, I see. How time flies. Is he his natural colour at the moment? Excellent. So – he's a pedigree Bichon Frisé, and the colour you're looking for is to match the accessories for your Armani outfit.' Georgie shook her head. Had all those years of education led her to this? She bit the inside of her cheek so it didn't sound as if she was about to snort with laughter. 'Well, if you could leave your shoes and handbag out, we'll do our best to get an exact match. Lovely. We'll keep you informed every step of the way. And we'll certainly have him ready for your party.'

Once she'd reassured Mrs C-A again, Georgie hung up with a sigh, rubbing her eyes. It was only eleven o'clock and already she'd dealt with a complaint about a babysitter who had used the family computer to access bebo and an emergency with a bath that had overflowed through a ceiling. She speed-dialled Flick's mobile. Seemingly from nowhere, a cup of coffee had appeared at her elbow, with a couple of those gorgeous German cinnamon biscuits balanced on the saucer. Somehow, once again, their trusty Girl Friday, Joanna, had discreetly anticipated just what was wanted. Georgie mouthed her thanks and took a grateful sip while she waited for Flick to answer.

Flick was on one of their regular appointments – Genevieve McKinnon, pampered wife of an unreconstructed but very wealthy City lawyer, who wanted to create the illusion (despite living in Balham) that she was an accomplished rural Châtelaine as a means of justifying her arduous schedule of shopping and girlie lunches now that their twins were away at school. She'd been one of Domestic Angels' first clients. For the last few years, since Flick and George had set up the agency, and apart from when the McKinnons were on holidays in St Barts or skiing in Verbier, they'd swooped in twice a week, filled the freezer with home-cooking, done the flowers, and arranged artful baskets of lavender-scented ironing around the place, all to complete the artifice. So far, Genevieve's husband seemed quite happy in the belief that his wife spent her days toiling to make a perfect home for them all. He was happy. She was happy. And Flick and Georgie were more than happy with the retainer she paid.

'Yup?' Flick sounded her usual brisk self. Georgie could picture her, towering and efficient in her stonewashed jeans and T-shirt, in the McKinnon's pristine kitchen, packing neatly labelled caterers' dishes into the huge American fridge. Cleaning up the kitchen was never an issue, except on a Monday, because Mr City-Banker McKinnon would insist on a breakfast cooked by his loving wife on a Sunday morning and the place would be splattered with grease. Fortunately, frying sausages was within her capabilities. Apart from that, she only ever used the microwave.

'Hi, how's it going?' It sounded as if Flick was taking the basket of neatly folded white towels upstairs to the marble bathrooms – a job Georgie had done many times. Somehow they'd fallen into a routine of alternating office days with action days so they both knew the routines for all of the clients.

'Fine, nearly done here. I've just got to muddy up her gardening boots and leave them by the back door. The landscapers have finished and the planters look tremendous. We must use them again. Put them in the master file, will you?'

'Will do.' Georgie stuck a fluorescent note in the diary to remind herself. 'Bit of a change of plan. I've just had Mrs Cooper-Adams on.'

She could hear a groan as Flick recalled the last dye job they'd had done on André. 'What is it this time? Vermilion and puce? Urgent as usual, I suppose?'

'But of course. She's leaving her outfit for you to match. Have you got the dye swatches?'

'No. They're in the desk drawer. Have I got time to call back at the office? I've got another job to squeeze in.'

'Not really. I said you could be there in …' Georgie checked her watch. 'About half an hour from now.'

'Oh God!' Flick tutted. 'She's so fussy too. What shall I do … ? Aha! I know. I've got the Kelly Hoppen paint samples for the Selbys' guest bedroom for this afternoon. I can match him up with those.'

'Fantastic! I've booked him into the usual place.'

'"Doggie Style"? Yuck. Vile name. What *would* Mrs C-A say if she knew?'

Georgie laughed. 'Well, that's just one of the many secrets of our success.'

'That and the fact that we've absolutely no shame. Hang on. I'm just putting the alarm on.'

Georgie could hear Flick rapidly tap the code in, and the awful beeping sound as she made her way to the door. 'Phew, that's better!' she sighed as she pulled the door closed. 'I'll call you if there are any problems, but I'll skip lunch so I should be able to get to the Selbys' on time.'

'Flick, you are a star!'

'You know it!'

'Listen, I meant to ask, do you fancy coming round for supper on Friday?' Georgie asked casually. She could hear Flick start the engine of the discreet and well-stocked 4 x 4, perfectly camou-flaged for the mean streets of south-west London, but Flick's answer, before she pulled away, made it clear she'd rumbled her. 'If it's just supper, I'd love to. But if this is another attempt to set me up with a bloke, forget it. It almost took me a change of mobile number to shake off the last one!'

'OK OK, point taken,' Georgie reassured her. 'It'll just be us, once I've got Libby to bed.'

'In that case, I'd be delighted. Eight o'clock OK?'

Georgie peeled off another Post-it note and started to write. 'Perfect! It's a date. See you later.' Georgie stuck the note care-fully in her diary. It read, 'Tell Ed to cancel Simon'.

*

Little André despatched for a respray, and paint samples delivered to Ellerton Road, Flick eased into the parking space right outside number thirty-four. This had to be the only good thing about Mrs Halliman: it was usually possible to park outside her house. But then, why *would* anyone want to park on this street, with its unremarkable row of terraced houses on one side, two a penny in this part of south London, interspersed occasionally with the odd flat-roofed block, filling gaps where wartime bombs had fallen and left holes like missing teeth. Opposite was a scrappy piece of land, grandly called a park according to the graffitied council sign but, to all intents, a canine toilet. Remarkably, a few trees pushed their way through the dry and barren grass, strewn with litter and neglect.

Flick sighed and clambered out of the car, wrapping her coat about her against the wind and reaching back inside for her shoulder bag. Mrs Halliman had been one of the first clients to sign up to the all-service agency, responding to the ad they took out in the local paper four years ago, and they'd been too insecure to turn her away, even though the smell of her should have been a warning. Two of their cleaning teams had flatly refused to spring-clean her house and Flick and Georgie had had to don Marigolds and go in, pegs on noses, like a SWAT team. But only once. Now they did very little for her except supply plumbers and do the regular cat feed whenever Mrs Halliman went on her annual bus tour to Spain. It never ceased to amaze Flick how their client list covered such a motley crew. It spanned the full social spectrum, from the fat-bonus crowd with their personal trainers and personalised number plates, to the likes of Mrs H. who'd lived in this part of London for ever and who'd seen new money ramping up the property market.

Digging out the key – numbered, never named – from her pocket, Flick carefully pushed it into the lock, then nearly jumped out of her skin as Mrs Halliman's ginger cat wrapped itself round her leg, meowing flirtatiously. 'You can bugger off,' Flick shook her leg vigorously. 'Scoot, flea-ridden mog!' The cat yelped, but slithered ahead of her through the front door as it opened.

Flick was a cat woman, but this was a feline too far. It was the smell that made Flick want to gag every time. It was hard to describe as an olfactory experience. A mixture of cat urine, food and stale air. How could any human being tolerate it? Didn't the woman *notice*? 'So where's your buggery food, you skanky thing,' she purred at the ginger cat, who was meowing fervently now, and eased her way through the narrow hallway, stacked with newspapers and boxes. Tripping over the wheel of a bicycle hidden behind a long coat, Flick was propelled headlong into the kitchen, kicking the cat bowl with staggering accuracy under the sink. The sink itself was full of filthy plates, with more piled up on the drainer. It seemed more likely that Mrs Halliman had died than gone on holiday.

'Oh God! You bloody owe me one, Georgie.' Flick crouched down and retrieved the bowl. 'You, my girl, are doing this next time.'

Thankfully the cat food was the dry type – opening a can of rank-smelling meat in this revolting kitchen would have been just too much – and she shook some into the bowl, trying not to breathe. The cat darted forward and was eating it before she could pull the box away. 'Don't say thank you, will you? Now, where's the rodent?'

Flick gently pushed open the utility-room door off the kitchen, but 'utility' had nothing to do with it. Dump was nearer the mark. Unwashed laundry and sheets were shoved into a basket, carrier bags with things Flick dared not imagine hung from the ceiling, and there were jars with mouldy contents on shelves above a rusting freezer. Perched on top of this carnage was a small cage, a box of pegs balanced on top of that.

'Cooee.' Flick peered inside, trying to make out the shape of a hamster in amongst the shredded bedding. Nothing stirred.

Flick tried to see into the bedding box, but saw nothing except a pile of shredded paper. Checking the cat was still engrossed in its dinner behind her, she carefully opened the cage and tentatively shook the box. Nope, there was definitely nothing there.

Flick paused for a moment. Hamsters did not just disappear. The cat, replete now, came and wound itself around her ankle again. 'Where is it?' she asked, hearing the concern in her voice, and, feeling ridiculous, she peered behind the cage. To see the door of the cage open.

'Oh fuck, fuckity fuck,' she gasped and turned the cage around as if it would solve the problem. Frantic now, Flick started to push boxes out of the way, moving boots, wellies and bags full of more bags and coats – or were they rags? – that had been left on the floor so long they'd grown stiff and crusty and were covered in a layer of dirt. She pulled them aside with one hand, not sure what was worse, the muck or the prospect of having to pick up a furry rodent if she found it.

There was nothing there of course, dead or alive, and, after looking along a shelf filled to bowing with paint cans and flower pots, Flick made her way at speed back into the kitchen, peeping into the box of cornflakes she found on the sideboard and lifting the bucket she found upright in the corner.

The cat joined her, licking his lips. 'Oh God, you haven't, have you?' Flick desperately delved into her pocket for her phone and held down '1' on the speed-dial.

'Domestic Angels,' Joanna answered crisply.

Flick gulped. 'Houston, we have a problem.'

After half an hour and a sensible let's-not-panic call from Joanna, Flick gave up. There was clearly no hamster in the house, dead or alive. Figuring that something with legs that short was unlikely to have been able to tackle the stairs, she had restricted her search to the ground floor, which was a good thing because the sight of depraved devastation that met her when she pushed open the living-room door, had persuaded her that Mrs Halliman was going to be removed from their books the second she set foot back on British soil.

'I think there were chairs under there somewhere, but there was so much junk it was hard to tell,' Flick ranted, back at the office, as she peeled off her jacket and shoved it into a carrier bag. 'That's got to go in the wash. I swear I'm never going to get the smell out of it.' She sniffed her hands. 'Can I rub Flash straight into them?'

Georgie smiled. 'Might not be a great idea.'

'But what about the hamster?' Joanna asked, deep concern in her voice.

'Well, I, for one, am not going back to have a look.' Flick picked up the pile of post on her desk. 'What the hell are we going to do?' She pulled off her boots and wiggled her toes to ease them, 'Mrs H. will go ape.'

The phone jangled again and Georgie reached for it. 'I think I know why—' she said as she picked it up. 'Domestic Angels?'

'Well, I'm glad you do,' Flick mumbled. She was fed up now. The ridiculous set-up with the dyed dog this morning had been bad enough, but she hadn't slept well, and the whole day had been destined to be a catastrophe before she started, capped off by John cancelling on her, again, via text.

She sighed and padded over to the kettle. The office, a converted corner shop, had seemed so palatial when they'd moved here from their headquarters in Georgie's spare room, but it now seemed cramped with the three of them in it and she felt like the Big Friendly Giant. Perhaps she was the only one who felt it. Joanna, although stocky, was small, whereas Georgie was a shrimp. Looking across the office at her dark curls and slim figure, Flick asked herself how she made a habit of having friends who made her feel Amazonian. She glanced at her own reflection in the mirror above the sink. Was the red lipstick too much? She'd read somewhere that dark eye make-up and red lips suited blondes, but had she overdone it? She was never quite sure. Another downside of not having a regular bloke to hint you were verging on the tarty.

Braced now with a steaming cup of coffee, she knuckled down to her messages, including a reply to John that it didn't matter, she was busy anyway. Didn't texting make lying so much easier? Face saved. No desperate clinging tone she wouldn't be able to keep out of her voice if she'd had to call. The three of them plodded on with work as darkness fell outside, taking calls, sending out invoices and chasing up tradesmen who hadn't turned up to jobs when they said they would, until Joanna shrugged on her coat and declared it a day.

'See you tomorrow,' Georgie called distractedly, as she finished whatever she was doing on the computer, and glanced at her watch. 'I'd better shove off too. Libby's at a party and I've got to get to the shops before I pick her up.' She pushed back her chair and stood up, closing her desk drawer.

The idea of rushing here and there to collect children, and having her time tied up appalled Flick, but she wasn't too chuffed with the prospect of an evening alone ahead of her either, and she shoved away a brief feeling of despondency. 'You coming?' Georgie asked, wrapping her coat around her. It did nothing for her.

'Nah. I'll have a butchers on eBay to see if there are any nice new shoes going cheap. Though there's not much competition with my shoe size, except from the odd transvestite.'

'Flick,' Georgie gave her the admonishing look Flick had seen her give her daughter when she ran her fingers over a plate to soak up the last bits of gravy. 'Stop talking yourself down.'

'What's to talk up?' Flick hoped her attempt to sound witty and up-beat would be a good cover-up.

'Mmmm.' Georgie came and rubbed her hand over Flick's shoulder. 'See ya in the morning, mate. I've got to stop off at the Bridges' first thing to see in that new painter.' She picked up her bag and was heading for the door when it burst open and in the doorway stood a tall man with dark, wet hair. Flick looked at the windows to see if it was raining. It wasn't. He was dressed in a dinner suit, his shirt white and stark against his tanned skin, and it was open at the neck. In his hand he was holding a bow tie.

'Sorry to bother you,' he said breathlessly. 'It says on the door "We'll take care of it". I assume you mean domestic-type things.' He scratched his head. 'But I wondered how you were with bow ties. I can't get the sodding thing done up and I'm due at a dinner in the City in ...' He looked at his watch. 'Half an hour.'

Flick looked over at Georgie, who had already put her bag back down. 'I haven't got a clue. Your department, I think?'

Chapter Two

It was still dark when the alarm clock went off. Ed had set it early because it was one of his gym days and Georgie wriggled over to snuggle into his warm back, hoping to delay the moment when he hauled himself out of bed to get ready. Encouraged by his sigh of contentment, she eased her feet towards his legs but he flinched away. 'Oh no you don't,' he growled. 'Keep those ice blocks on your side of the bed.' But he turned round and pulled her to him for a brief cuddle until the alarm insisted its way into their snooze again.

With one eye open, Georgie looked at him sitting on the side of the bed, his head in his hands, silhouetted against the light from the bathroom, left on in case Libby should stir. 'God, you're a masochist. I wish I had your will-power,' she murmured.

He turned and smiled sleepily. 'No you don't. You wish you had another hour in bed. And, guess what?' He patted her rump through the goosedown duvet. 'You do.'

She watched him get dressed in the half-light, pulling on Nike track pants and a T-shirt. His silhouette revealed a softening round his shoulders and what looked worryingly like a paunch. Best not to mention it. 'Are you coming back to change before Lib's assembly or shall I meet you there?'

He turned round to stare for a moment, then slapped his forehead in annoyance. 'Dammit, I'd completely forgotten. I've got a site visit today and I'll have to go straight on from the gym.' He shook his head in irritation. 'Was it in the diary?'

'You bet! Lib wrote it with glitter pen. Oh, Ed, she's going to be ever so disappointed. She's reading her own prayer and I think she's even doing a dance.'

Shrugging helplessly, he opened a drawer and took out an ironed shirt, laying it carefully in his holdall. 'Oh God! My fault. I'm so sorry. Can you tell her ... tell her something came up. And will you take the Digicam so I can watch tonight? Tell you what – I'll come home early and we can have a sushi takeaway. All right?'

Georgie sighed. She'd have a major strop to deal with when Lib found out her dad had other plans but by the time Ed came home, any resentment would be smoothed over and he'd make a big fuss of her. She wondered if Patsy, the First Wife, had had the same tussle with him over the boys. It was one the many questions she'd never be able to ask Ed – and she sure as hell wasn't going to ask the chilly Patsy. He still loyally went to all the boys' hockey tournaments, even on the weekends when he wasn't in charge, but then that was his thing. Ballet classes and scratchy violins, understandably, weren't.

She smiled sympathetically. 'Oh well. Maybe next time, eh? I'll make sure to give you a bit more notice. There probably won't be many of the other dads there, so I hope she won't be too upset.'

Ed turned and continued to add the rest of his work clothes from the dressing room he'd incorporated into their extension. Georgie watched his progress with fascination. He was always so painstaking – with everything – and she admired it, being so slapdash herself. Today he was looking to project an air of respectability with a sharply tailored suit. Just right for an architect meeting clients at the site of a huge city development.

Georgie felt a surge of tenderness as she watched him deliberate over his ties. There was something touching about his serious approach to his work. And didn't she reap the benefits! Even after maintenance payments to Patsy, their standard of living was far beyond anything she could have hoped to provide as a dance teacher – her feeble source of income before she and Flick got the agency going. And, in all fairness, she'd known he was obsessed with work before she'd got involved with him. That had been clear from the first date – a meeting at the ICA followed by a stroll in St James's Park. He'd talked so intensely about design and form, pointing out buildings as they walked. He'd even dissected the menu at the restaurant where they'd eaten, commenting on the juxtaposition of the ingredients. He was so different from the unreliable, arty-types she'd dated before and Georgie had been blown away by the analytical mind that drove this intense, ambitious man. She couldn't resist him.

'Tell you what.' Georgie swung out of bed. 'How about I make the ultimate sacrifice and bring us both some tea?'

Ed turned and smiled at her, his eyes crinkling at the corners, knowing he was forgiven. 'You'd do that for me? You really are the ideal woman.'

Georgie smiled to herself as she padded downstairs into the kitchen.

By the time Libby had uncurled from the cocoon of her cosy bed, Ed was long gone. She took the news of him not being present at her assembly with surprising equanimity, merely shrugging and cuddling her bear a little closer. But then again, so many things about Libby were surprising for an eight-year-old. Her self-possession, her amazingly mature pronouncements about current affairs that sometimes made them both laugh. Where did she get it all from? Presumably from watching the news with Ed at night, curled up on the sofa in her pyjamas with him while Georgie rustled up supper for them all. Maybe it was to do with being an only child – something Georgie had no experience of, coming from a happy tribe of five.

At the breakfast table, Libby smiled quietly as Georgie presented her with a bowl of porridge with a heart traced in maple syrup on top. 'Daddy says you should always eat it from round the sides because it's cooler but I do it anyway, to keep the heart looking nice.' She took a tiny spoonful and popped it thoughtfully into her mouth. 'Sometimes babies get burns in their mouths because their mummies heat up their milk in the microwave. That would be horrid wouldn't it, Mummy? A poor little baby wouldn't be able to say its milk was too hot. It would just cry and no one would know what was wrong.'

Georgie placed a glass of milk next to Libby's bowl. 'Yes, that would be horrid. You should always test anything a baby is going to eat first so you know it's the right temperature. And you have to test the bathwater before you put the baby in. I had a special thermometer for yours. We've still got it, actually.'

Libby took a sip of milk, leaving a little white moustache on her upper lip. 'Yes, but we don't need it now, do we?'

'Well, no. But we might need it, say, if a baby came to visit.'

'Or if you and Daddy have another baby.'

'Yes,' Georgie answered slowly, suppressing the familiar ache that came up every time the subject did. 'I don't want to just throw it out. So let's keep it, just in case. He doesn't take up much space, old Temperature Ted, does he?'

Libby giggled and took another spoonful of porridge. 'Oh no – I've made the heart go all funny. Look at it.' She frowned at the bowl.

Georgie took the spoon from her hand and stirred the remaining syrup into the cooling porridge. 'Now it's disappeared. Hey, I never knew I was a magician! Now, can you be as clever as me and make all the porridge disappear, 'cos it's time to go and I'll be late for work!'

Libby took her spoon back. 'Turn your back, Mummy, and when you look again it will all be gone.'

Georgie obligingly turned around, wiping the brushed steel work surface carefully, watching Libby's reflection in the shining dark glass front of the built-in oven as she quickly gobbled up the rest of her breakfast and drained her milk. 'Look! All gone. I'm magic too. Let's go. Oh, Mummy, don't forget the Digicam. Poor Daddy will be so sad if he doesn't see me do my prayer.'

Flick could sense John wasn't beside her before she opened her eyes. She knew he had to get to work early but she was disappointed that he never touched her in the morning, preferring to slip out of the bed and get dressed without a word. She could hear the rain on the window and turned, snuggling into the duvet, knowing she had a few precious moments before she had to face the day.

'Bye,' he whispered loudly from the doorway a while later. 'I'll call.'

'Yeah,' she croaked. Would he, though?

Flick waited until she heard the flat door close before swinging her legs out of bed. His wife in Sunderland would be doling out something delicious and nourishing to the brood, no doubt. Did she ever wonder what he did on his work trips down to London? Did she imagine he ate alone, reading a novel, then went to bed early in a cheap hotel after watching the news on CNN? Or had she guessed that he called his mistress – lover? – on the off-chance that she was free and, after a few drinks in a bar, took her to bed. Lover? Flick snorted softly. She wasn't sure what she was to him. He never said, and she never dared ask.

She climbed into the shower and scrubbed herself vigorously to wash it all away. This was a side of her Georgie wasn't going to see. Lovely, naive Georgie, who was always casting about for a man for her, bemoaning the fact that the gorgeous ones had always been nabbed and the ones that were on their own were usually saddos with baggage. Ain't that the truth.

Picking up a takeout coffee from Nino's – he always had it ready for her with a round of toast and the latest update on his wife's prolapse issues – Flick headed for the office. She was always the first in, jotting down the answer machine messages that came in late at night or first thing in the morning. The late night ones were usually speculative. Could they send over a builder because they'd been talking about a loft conversion over supper and would like a quote? The morning ones were the more urgent. A ballcock had got jammed. There was water pouring in from the roof or, and this one was legendary, did they know where they could buy organic Swiss muesli, because it was needed for breakfast.

Flick was putting her key in the door when she remembered the hamster. Another little issue that had to be dealt with.

'You missed a nice bit of eye candy last night,' Flick called over to Joanna later, once the three of them were ensconced and the day had got going. 'Breezed in here smelling of something delicious and spicy and demanded we dress him.'

'Bloody hell. Why did I go and leave on time?' Joanna groaned.

'That'll teach you to be a part-timer.'

'Lime and basil.'

'Pardon?'

'Lime and basil,' Georgie said, a bit louder, without taking her eyes off her screen. 'That's what he smelled of.'

Flick looked over at Joanna and raised an eyebrow. 'Well, I suppose you did get closer than I did.'

Georgie had a little twinkle in her eye. 'You see, you should have learned these skills from your mother like I did, then you could have swung into action and netted yourself a gorgeous City gent. Must be single with no wifey to tie his tie.'

'Or gay. The only things my mother taught me are how to stop the room spinning when you're drunk and other things too rude to mention in front of you ladies. Oh, and how, if you spit on your mascara wand it goes further.'

'You are one class act.'

'Sure am.' Flick picked up her bag as Georgie took another call. 'Right, Jo, I'm off to cater to the every whim of the population of south London, but first I have a date at the pet shop.'

The shop, imaginatively called 'Great and Small', smelled of the barrels of colourful, and vile-looking rabbit food that were on display. 'Can I help?' The woman behind the counter looked brassy, with giant gold earrings that swung as she talked.

'I need a hamster.'

'You *need* a hamster?'

'Yes,' Flick replied defiantly.

'Well,' the woman came around the counter, 'I've got a couple left.' Flick followed her wide backside into the back of the shop where there were a range of cages full of a variety of rodents, including what Flick strongly suspected were rats.

'Here.'

Flick crouched down and peered at the little furry hamsters, who looked sleepily back at her. 'Can you hang on a moment?' She flipped open her phone and called the office. 'Jo, is George there? Bugger. What time is she back? Oh. Do you happen to know what colour Mrs H.'s hamster was? Sort of *brown*? Well that's helpful!' Flick laughed. 'OK.' She flicked the phone shut again. 'Which one would you say was the browner brown?' she asked the shopkeeper.

Fifteen minutes later, Flick pulled up outside Mrs Halliman's and carefully climbed out of the car, holding the hamster box high so the cat, who was once again wrapped round her legs, couldn't sniff out the contents. Pushing open the door, and trying once again not to breathe, she shimmied through the hallway and deposited the contents into the cage, firmly securing the cage door behind her.

'There, mog, she'll never know the other one went AWOL.'

Behind now with her appointments, Flick had to race. The afternoon amounted to massive frustration when the dry-cleaning Mr Grafton had asked her to pick up for an event that night wasn't ready and she had to make a curtailed dash to the Dixons' house in Mountville Road to check the carpenter, who was building shelves for Mr Dixon's massive toy soldier collection, hadn't left too much mess – the Dixons being holed up onboard a friend's private yacht in the BVI. It took her half an hour to find the hoover and clean up after him, and by the time she got back to the office she was ready to chew off her own arm with hunger.

'Have a few of my almonds,' Georgie offered.

'That's not going to fill the stomach of a six-foot woman who's spent the day rushing round like a blue-arsed fly, including doing a hamster match to fool the lovely Mrs Halliman.'

'Ah.' Georgie stopped, mug halfway to her mouth.

'Ah, what?'

'Ah. I meant to say last night, but Mr Bow Tie made me forget.' Georgie looked sheepish and then her eyes crinkled with mirth. Flick felt a sense of foreboding.

'I meant to say ...' Georgie started slowly biting her lip. 'I remembered ... er, Mrs H. billeted the hamster out to a friend while she was away.'

'You are, of course, bloody joking?'

'Er, no.'

'Do you know how much trouble I've gone to? Do you? Well,' Flick leaned over Georgie's desk, using her full height to intimidate her, 'as a forfeit for not telling me and putting me in direct contact with vermin, YOU are going to collect the effing thing, YOU are going to take it back to the shop and YOU are feeding that revolting cat in that revolting house until Mrs H. comes home. And, in the meantime, you're making me a cup of tea.'

Georgie sniggered on and off for the rest of the afternoon, in between a deluge of calls – almost all pre-Christmas panic. A common request was for presents to be collected from shops and stored so they wouldn't be discovered before the Big Day. Last year Georgie had had to find house room for a four-thousand-pound wooden rocking horse and then had to deal with the fall-out when her daughter found it and had the news broken to her that it wasn't *actually* for her.

'Have you managed to find the burgundy baubles for Mrs Goldberg?' Jo asked Georgie.

'Yup,' she smiled back, triumphant. 'A little place in Henley-on-Thames. Plus just the right ribbon from VV Rouleaux. It will be a sublime Christmas round the Goldbergs'.'

'Which is an odd concept when they're Jewish.' Flick muttered.

It was 6.30 p.m. and Joanna was long gone before Flick felt she had staved off the day's emergencies. Georgie, who'd had to call on a friend to collect and take care of Libby while she finished up, was beginning to close down her PC when Flick heard the door of the office open. Flick sighed. Perhaps it was Mr Bow Tie man again, wanting his shoe laces done up this time.

The woman who came through the door, however, was about Flick's age, maybe older, with a blonde bob and an expensive-looking brown wool coat. She was tall and striking, her pearl and gold earrings caught the light and around her neck was a wide scarf of interwoven threads in greens, pinks and browns.

'Can I help you? We're actually closed.' Flick hoped she didn't sound too sharp but it was Friday, she was tired and wanted to go home.

'Yes, I'm terribly sorry to bother you. I realise it's late.' Her accent was a clipped South African. 'Only it says on your door that you "can take care of it".' She pulled herself up as she said it.

'Yes,' Georgie came round her desk. 'It works like this. You pay to be a member and then you can call on our services. Domestic things, mainly.'

'This is domestic,' the woman said softly.

'Right. Would you like to fill out a membership form or you can go to our website?' Georgie pulled a form out of the display box.

'It's a bit more delicate than that, really.'

Flick offered her a chair. What was this? Did she need something embarrassing sorting out? It wouldn't be the first time they'd had to make a dash to someone's flat to secrete the spoils of a Bond Street shopping trip so they weren't found out.

'Can you really handle anything?'

Flick and Georgie looked at each other. 'We'll have a go. What did you have in mind?'

There was a long pause. 'Thing is, I need your help getting my own back on my lying bastard of a husband.'

Chapter Three

Saturday morning saw Ed up early for a hockey match his older son was playing in. Georgie didn't point out that he hadn't written it into the diary and she was pretty sure he hadn't mentioned it, either. Perhaps it was a last-minute three-line-whip from Patsy.

With Libby at her ballet lesson, Georgie popped into the supermarket to get some flowers to take to Mike and Amy's that night. She'd let Ed choose some wine from their own collection once she'd checked with Amy what they were going to be eating, although she hoped he wouldn't go on about it too much at dinner. She loved his passion, but it was doubtful any of Amy's arty friends would be interested in which side of the vineyard the grapes had come from. The mingled scent of fresh newspapers and potted plants greeted her as she stepped inside and away from the blustery wind, and she browsed the display with interest. The forced hyacinths were tempting, but such a cliché at this time of year, although the white ones might do. She rejected lilies because of the pollen and eventually settled on a jasmine covered in tight, white buds that would open to perfume the whole house by Christmas. She then selected some tempting-looking berries that she could add to the cheesecake she would make that afternoon. The rest of the shopping for the week could wait until she had more time.

That evening, getting ready to go out, she could tell that Ed was tired by his rather muted conversation and she tried to draw him out. 'So, did Charlie's team play well?' It was a vague question, but she had no ideas of the intricacies of hockey.

'Yes, well enough. They won but they didn't really deserve to. Charlie did all right but I don't think he'll make the first team. What time are we due at Amy's?'

'Eight, but we won't be eating till late – you know the score.'

Ed sighed theatrically. 'I'll be paralytic by the time she serves up and then it will be something that looks like cat sick. Anything I could have to keep me going, and soak up the wine?'

Georgie laughed. Ed's suspicion of vegetarian food was legendary. 'There's some quiche left in the fridge.'

He rolled his eyes. 'Quiche? That's almost as bad. I'll raid the bread bin. We don't have to stay too late, do we?'

'No, we can't anyway. We'll have to be back for the baby-sitter. Will you drop her home or shall I?'

Ed looked pleadingly. 'If you drive, I'll do it next time.'

'Agreed. But not too much vino, eh?' She patted his back gently. 'We don't need another argument about developers and capitalism and all that – OK?'

Ed looked sheepish. 'If I hear bollocks being spoken I can't just let it go, can I?'

Georgie handed him her necklace and turned her back to him while he did it up round her neck. 'I'll make it worth your while if you do,' she purred suggestively.

He kissed the nape of her neck. 'Then Mike can talk all the bollocks he likes,' he murmured. 'I won't say a thing!'

By the time she'd settled Libby and had ten minutes about GCSE coursework from the babysitter, they were late leaving, and Georgie was relieved that the meal seemed to be at least partly cooked by the time they arrived.

'Mmm, that smells yummy! Is it Moroccan?'

Amy returned her hug warmly. 'Yeah – Mike got me a tagine and we've been using it all the time. Probably won't last though. It'll be like the wok and the bread-maker, and all the other stuff we've got at the back of the kitchen cupboards.'

Ed's laughter rumbled behind her in the hallway as he waited for the congestion to ease up and Georgie felt herself relax. It was a good start. She squeezed past Amy into the cosy, candlelit kitchen where Mike was cautiously prodding at a steaming colander of couscous, and introduced herself to the other couple there while he fretted. Lydia, dressed in multi-layered woollens, was wedged into a corner and her partner, Alan, was crooning over their tiny new baby, held in a faded blue sling across his chest. Both were sufficiently wrapped up in each other and the baby to pay only the most passing interest in the newcomers and Georgie sat right opposite, where she could shamelessly feast her eyes on the little scrap.

'Oh! And who's this?' Ed asked as he clambered over the banquette to sit beside her. 'What type? Pink or blue?'

'She's called Evie,' Lydia smiled tiredly. 'This is the first time we've been out since she was born.'

'Well, congratulations. Your first?'

Alan and Lydia nodded at Ed in unison, smiling with shy pride and Georgie slipped her arm through Ed's.

'Knackering, isn't it?' Ed laughed. 'Still, console yourselves, it won't last long. Then it gets really serious doesn't it, darling?' He smiled knowingly at Georgie. 'And expensive! Better start saving now. Glass of wine? I've got some white Bordeaux here. Where's your glass?'

Georgie untucked her arm and stood up, neatly swivelling round on the bench. She had the awful feeling that the dream she cherished was ebbing away. Every time Ed made even the mildest joke about babies, it chipped away at her hopes. She knew he was right about the cost and the energy children sucked from you, but she couldn't help feeling something was missing. Their family wasn't complete. 'Can I help?' she asked Amy briskly, who was sorting through the cutlery drawer, squinting at the knives.

'Well, if you can see in this semi-darkness, six matching everythings. Honestly, Mike, did we have to use the lanterns?

I can't tell whether the tagine is done or not. Here, Georgie, have a chickpea and tell me what you think.'

Georgie tasted the sludge-coloured mixture on the spoon Amy thrust at her and chewed on it for some considerable time before answering, 'Maybe a bit longer.'

Amy replaced the ceramic lid and slid the pot back into the oven while Georgie rummaged in the drawer. 'Let's start with some mezze then. George, could you plonk these olives over there? Mike, for goodness sake, leave it alone. It has to steam and it can't do that if you keep taking the lid off. Just stick some more boiling water in the pan underneath and, er, slice up that pitta bread, will you?'

Georgie listened in amusement to the banter. The affection between the couple shone through the barbed comments and teasing. And certainly, nothing was left unsaid between them. She thought again about the woman who had called into the agency on Friday night with her tale of marital woe. Caroline Knightly, she had said her name was, but neither Flick nor Georgie was convinced it was her real one. Something had stopped her mentioning any of it to Ed, especially as she and Flick hadn't had time to discuss it yet.

By the time the couscous was served, Georgie was already stuffed with stuffed vine leaves, carrot sticks and hummus. Ed had mellowed under the influence of his Aligoté and the New Zealand red he was now sampling and Alan had handed over the baby, somewhat reluctantly it seemed to Georgie, to Mike, who was holding it slightly awkwardly.

'See, Mike? You're a natural,' Amy teased. 'Far better than I'd be. Maybe we should wait until they have the technology and *you* can get pregnant.'

Mike jiggled the baby gently and lowered his head to drop a kiss on her forehead, then sniffed once or twice.

'Uh-oh,' laughed Ed. 'Is it happy nappy time? I thought I could detect a whiff.'

'No, it's not that. It's just that her head smells of … I don't know. It's really nice.'

Georgie felt a wave of longing. 'Mmm, it's like baby powder, isn't it? I've always thought if you could bottle that scent it would sell a million. Could I?' She looked questioningly at Lydia, who nodded and smiled and, carefully, she lifted the baby from Mike's arms. 'Hello, Evie, you are a beautiful girl, aren't you?' Georgie gazed at the unfocused eyes and red puckered lips. 'Oh, she's gorgeous. She's just perfect.'

Ed looked sideways at her, smiling wryly. 'Oh dear. I know that look. I've seen it before, three times. I shall have to be very careful indeed. Could I have a refill of that red, Mike? It's really quite drinkable, y'know, and another glass of it will render me incapable anyway.'

Everyone laughed and Georgie smiled gamely. She knew it was looking increasingly unlikely. The timing never seemed quite right, but she could still hope, couldn't she?

Flick had been late for her friend Camilla's dinner party on Saturday evening, but she more than made up for lost time with an assault on the Rioja, and then she woke on Sunday morning feeling as if a tank had been driven through her head. She dared not open her eyes – the rain on the window told her it probably wasn't worth it anyway – because she really couldn't remember much about what had happened. The dark-haired futures trader Camilla had seated her next to – and who she'd flirted with outrageously all evening – they hadn't, had they …? He had certainly been cute.

Then she remembered through the fug that she'd come home alone in a taxi and fumbled to fit the key in her door. She felt a wave of relief and shame flood over her.

'God, Flick, girl, you'd better get a grip.'

The second reason for not opening her eyes was the prospect of going to see her mother. She'd already delayed it for two weekends, and she wouldn't get away with it again. Tentatively opening one eye she squinted at the clock. Nine-thirty. Slowly, as if getting up for the first time after a serious illness and bed confinement, she swung her legs out and sat up, clutching her head in her hands until the throbbing subsided.

Fortified by coffee so strong that few of her friends were able to cope with it – Georgie likened it to engine oil – she headed off in the car towards Mitcham. Now Flick knew that Mitcham was considered the poor man's Wimbledon. It wasn't even the Surrey of moneyed Richmond or golf club Guilford. Many of the agency's clients had bought up what they considered bargains in Mitcham, unable to afford the sunny avenues of Wimbledon with its common, its quaint shops in the village and the air of entitlement earned by two short weeks in the spotlight once a year. Flick's Mitcham was a whole different story. She'd grown up here and, to her, it was row upon row of uninspiring post-war housing in street after uninspiring street of urban sprawl.

As if in her sleep, which it practically was, she swung past buses and slow drivers heading south-west for a trip out for the day – shopping no doubt, the great British pastime – and tutted as people held her up. Her windscreen wipers made the best of sudden sprays from passing traffic. The day was icy and grey, and she drummed her hands on the steering wheel as she waited at the lights. Beside her was a large and battered estate car, and out of the back window gazed a sullen-looking small boy. Unable to stop herself, Flick stuck out her tongue and crossed her eyes.

The child smiled broadly and, checking that his parents in the front weren't looking, gurned back at her, pulling down his bottom eyelids and sticking his fingers up his nose. Flick laughed and, as she burned off at the lights, she thumbed her nose at him. Poor sod. It might liven up a day which would probably be spent being dragged around a shopping mall and being subjected to canned Christmas muszak and having his hand slapped every time he touched anything.

Squeezing into a tight space on her mother's road, Flick looked at herself in the mirror and sighed deeply. Then, tentatively, she climbed out of the car, convinced that the older you get the harder it is to shake off a hangover. Or perhaps it was just all the cheap wine.

'Yoo-hoo.' Flick tried to push open the front door but had to lean in and round to move the bag that was wedged behind it, evidence of her mother's latest cause, in a long line of causes. A list that included women's rights, CND, the Poll Tax, saving the whale, the panda, the rainforest. For years Flick had been dragged to rallies or dragooned into delivering leaflets through letter boxes each and every weekend. Now her mother was saving the planet, single-handed, but Flick had managed to escape the crusade. Except, that is, for the inevitable shuffle around piles of recycling which crowded the hallway and every corner of the little house, ready to be put into the ancient Volvo outside.

'Just upstairs.'

'I'll put the kettle on,' Flick called.

'Don't fill it too full.' Flick muttered the words at the same time as her mother trilled them from her bedroom. 'Yeah, yeah.'

Tiptoeing around various boxes filled with cartons or cardboard, peelings and empty bottles of (organic) wine, Flick filled the kettle up to the mark her mother had made on the side. She then spooned into two mugs some of the powder her mother insisted on drinking because it involved no possibility of the exploitation of foreign workers.

'Darling!' Her mother came through the kitchen door like a whirlwind, preceded by the cat. Small and plump, Flick's mother had the sort of face that benefited from make-up, which was a shame because she refused to wear any on political grounds. 'You look like shit.'

'I love you too,' muttered Flick.

'Have you been burning the candle at both ends again?' Her mother poured boiling water into the mugs. 'Having milk today?'

'Only if it's not goats' and improves the taste.'

'Now. Christmas.' Flick's heart sank as her mother plonked the steaming mugs down on the table in front of them and sat down heavily on a kitchen chair. She knew she couldn't avoid the discussion indefinitely, and it wasn't as if she or her mother were particularly enamoured by the whole festive thing, but, scared to be the first to quit, they kept up the pretence of making it a celebration. 'What are your plans?' Same question as always.

Flick sighed. 'I'll go to the pub on Christmas Eve, have too much mulled wine, wake up with a sore head, then I'll come over here and we'll munch our way through some falafel and watch a re-run of *Only Fools and Horses*, a film starring Harrison Ford, and round it all off with the *Eastenders* omnibus in which someone will walk out on someone else, dramatically saying they're having an affair with their son, daughter, cat, just as the turkey is about to be carved.'

Flick's mother tutted. 'You are a very cynical person, young lady. It's not healthy.'

'Oh come on, Mum, it's all bollocks and you know it is. Since Dad left it's never been any fun, has it?' Flick watched a flash of pain shoot across her mother's face before she looked down into her cup.

'No, no it hasn't and I'm sorry about that.'

Flick knew she'd been too harsh. 'It's not your fault. Christmas brings out the bastard in everyone.'

'Why's that, do you suppose?' Her mother looked up, her soft brown eyes wide with innocence. She'd never quite understood how people could be less than wonderful all the time. A bit like Georgie. Flick must have inherited her cynicism, like she had her height, from her father, for whom everyone was an idiot until proven otherwise. How these two diverse personalities could ever have come together was beyond Flick. Perhaps her father had fallen for the optimistic innocence her mother carried with her. Perhaps he'd been transported by her hippy kaftans and the urge to save the world from itself. Whatever, he'd quickly got bored and left one miserable November evening to shack up with a woman from Catford who promised reality and a half-share in the pub she ran.

'Who knows the vagaries of a man's mind?' Flick played with some crumbs on the table top. 'They certainly don't function on the same level as we do.'

'Sylvia Derens. Remember her? I worked at the Oxfam shop with her for a while. Lovely husband. Cared for her and the garden. They always holidayed in Wales every year, just like clockwork. Turns out he's been having it away with the receptionist at work. *And* he wears socks with his sandals.'

Flick laughed at the revolting image that popped up in her head. 'Perhaps that floats the receptionist's boat. I wonder if he keeps them on in bed.'

'They're odd though, aren't they?' her mother pressed on. 'I mean, they woo you, tell you that you are marvellous and that they'd die for you, but the minute things get domestic and life becomes discussions about dripping taps and "have you put the cat out", their eyes start to rove to anything in a skirt.'

Flick raised her eyebrows. 'And I'm the cynical one, am I?'

Her mother waved away her comment. 'Oh, just me getting old. Do you remember that thing that man said about mistresses?'

'Er, can you be more specific?'

'That man who named the nightclub after his wife.' Her mother rubbed her forehead, frustrated at not being able to remember.

'James Goldsmith – Annabel's?'

'That's the one! I think he said that when you marry your mistress, you create a job vacancy or something like that. It sort of sums it up.'

Flick thought about John and the one very brief text she'd had from him yesterday. At weekends there was always radio silence as he embedded in domestic life. So that's what it was.

The best of all possible worlds. Flick suddenly felt very lonely.

'Come on,' she stood up suddenly, making her mother start. 'Let's go and do what the whole sodding nation is doing today.' Her mother stood up too, expectantly, her eyes a bit suspicious. 'Let's go shopping. Let's go and waste the day wandering round shops, buy each other some bit of nonsense, and have lunch in a café. No excuses now. Coat on and we're off.'

Her mother hesitated for a moment, then a smile spread across her face, and Flick realised how precious she was, with her campaigns and her hope for all things to be good and safe. She leaned forward and planted a kiss on her cheek.

'What a lovely idea, darling. Let me get a warmer jumper on.' She left the room, dodging the boxes and bags, and made her way upstairs. 'Oh,' she shouted down a moment later. 'Can we stop at the recycling plant on the way? Only, I've a few things to drop off.'

By the time she had delivered her mother home and headed back to her place, Flick felt exhausted but elated. They'd headed for Kingston (via the council dump) and, with no particular agenda, had mooched about trying on scarves and hats, making silly faces in the mirror, and she'd even persuaded her mother to buy a new handbag. Fabric, of course. She'd failed to persuade her that the cow that had been sacrificed to make the lovely black one with the big clip fastening had probably had a long and happy life.

Fuelled up with a sandwich and a cup of hot chocolate, they'd bought a few bits for Flick's aunt and cousin Deborah, and had treated each other to some hand cream and foot balm, and it felt good to have spent the day in such an unexpected way.

Flick, freshly showered, curled up on the sofa with a glass of wine and the TV on quietly in the background. She was always a bit worried about calling Georgie in the evening in case it wasn't convenient and she was interrupting family time. 'Hiya, good moment?'

'Yes, fine thanks. Libby's watching something and Ed's in the study. Had a nice weekend?'

'Yes, not bad at all,' Flick replied, glad that she could honestly say she had. 'Have you had any thoughts about our Friday night visitor?'

'Yes. Lots.' She could hear Georgie moving around the kitchen and the plink of cutlery. 'It's a bit odd to come to us with something like that.'

'She was so confident, don't you think? All beautifully turned out. Even her accent was clipped and neat, like a box-hedge.'

'I thought she was quite scary, to be honest. Mind you, she has every reason to be.' They were both silent for a minute, reflecting on Caroline Knightly's revelations about her husband's infidelities and chronic roving eye. 'How far would she want us to go?' Georgie lowered her voice to a whisper. 'I'm not doing anything illegal.'

''Course not,' Flick replied, not quite sure why she was whispering back. 'She just wanted to put the willies up him, didn't she?' Flick tried out her best Johannesburg twang to imitate the woman. 'Show the bastard to keep his todger inside his trousers in futcha!'

Georgie laughed deeply, then said nothing for a moment. 'Do you suppose he deserves it?' she asked eventually.

'Any man who screws waitresses behind his wife's back deserves what's coming to him,' replied Flick, more determinedly than she meant to. 'And how stupid to have them call him on his mobile.'

'S'pose you're right.' Georgie didn't sound too sure. 'OK, just this once, but it wasn't my idea.'

Chapter Four

'Whose stupid idea was this?' Flick whispered to Georgie, who she could just about make out beside her in the dark. The wind was searingly cold, stirring the bushes around them and creating shadows to startle them. Flick pulled her beanie further down over her head.

'God knows. I'm sure it was yours. Whatever Caroline Knightly is paying us isn't enough. And besides, that can't be her real name.'

'Who cares?' Flick looked around her. 'She paid cash upfront and that's what matters.'

There had to be better way to spend a Thursday evening than standing outside a public loo on the edge of Hampstead Heath. They'd barely spoken in the car on the way up, both of them focused on the job ahead, Ed's comment that they were both dressed very strangely for a Christmas night out still ringing in their ears as they drove away from Georgie's house. Flick giggled now. 'I feel like Cagney and Lacey.'

'Bags I be the blonde one. She was prettier. The other one was dumpy.' Georgie shivered. 'Have you got the pen?'

'Yup.' Flick fished into her jacket pocket and handed over the permanent marker. 'Sure you don't want me to do it?'

'No, I'll be OK. You just keep watch. If anyone comes, you go into the ladies and I'll lock my cubicle door.' She paused. 'Oh God,' she moaned, 'What'll I do if two you-knows come in and …'

'In this weather? They'd have to be mad or desperate.' They

looked at each other. 'Oh, just be quick, will you?'

'Shall I misspell his name?'

'Just put Kevin.'

'And shall I say, you know, what he'll *do*?'

Flick laughed at Georgie's discomfort. 'Shall I do it? I've seen more of the world than you have.'

'Perhaps you'd better. Here's his mobile number. Now *quick*,' Georgie whispered.

The smell inside the gents was hideous and Flick tried not to breathe. It was obvious she wasn't the first here with a pen and she had to look behind the doors of three cubicles before she found space, six inches or so, between other graffiti. She pulled the lid off the pen and started to write, quite certain that she had never actually written such words down, let alone on a toilet door, though she'd probably said them. It was the sort of language that turned John on, but she never felt comfortable when he asked her to talk like that.

'Come on, I can hear something,' Georgie hissed from the doorway of the toilets.

'OK, OK,' Flick checked and double-checked the mobile number Caroline had given them and put the lid back on the pen, admiring her artwork. The little drawing had been an inspiration.

'Thank God, you were ages,' Georgie grabbed her arm and they ran out of the door, squealing all the way back to the car, and collapsing inside, out of breath from fear and excitement. Six toilets later, even Georgie had plucked up the courage to do the artwork, once Flick had given her some idea of the words to use, and they congratulated themselves with a drink in a pub in Battersea.

'Never again,' Georgie said after taking a deep swig from her glass of wine. 'The cash will be great for Christmas but that's it. Too scary.'

Flick, convinced they'd broken the record for visits to public gents in one night, felt vaguely grubby and changed her mind about eating the peanuts Georgie had bought. 'Oh well, it was a laugh. Let's hope it works and he gets some custom. What did she say he was? A headhunter? Not sure that's the sort of head he was hunting!' They both shrieked with laughter, causing most of the pub to turn and stare at them. 'Still, that'll serve him right for giving out his mobile number to random waitresses.'

The next few days were very busy at Domestic Angels. As always towards Christmas, female clients went into overdrive about cleaning arrangements, convinced mother-in-laws who were coming to stay would run their fingers over skirting boards as a measure of the quality of the women their sons had married. Flick spent the usual amount of time advising callers on where to buy the best turkeys, Claret and hyacinths that would come into bloom on Christmas Eve. And she spent the usual amount of time in wonder at the stress and expectation people had about it all. Suddenly falafel with her mum and the afternoon in front of the TV in Mitcham sounded like heaven.

'Can you collect Mrs Ambrose's dry-cleaning?' Joanna asked, logging something onto the computer. 'And, while you are out, Mr Fisher wondered if we could pick up a package from D'Alton's for his wife and he'll collect it on his way past tonight.'

'His wife?'

'So he says.'

Flick snorted and picked up her bag. 'What time is Georgie back?'

'She's helping with the nativity play dress rehearsal,' Joanna made a face. 'Libby's an angel apparently. Sounds like hell to me.'

'Me too. See you later.' Flick headed out of the door and down the road. She'd leave the dry-cleaning till last. It was curtains (who needed clean curtains for Christmas, for crying out loud?) and she wasn't going to lug them further than was necessary. It was already beginning to get dark, even though it was only just past three, and lights from the shops flooded out onto the street. She glanced in at the windows, full of sparkle and glitter. Even the butchers looked Dickensian with plucked geese hung upside down outside. That would make a nice change this year. It had been years since she'd had a proper Christmas dinner, one that didn't involve beansprouts.

The warmth of D'Alton's hit her as she opened the door. By far the most delicious shop in the street, and a regular haunt for both she and Georgie when they wanted cheering up, D'Alton's sold everything you could live without but shouldn't. Necklaces and bracelets in the colours of boiled sweets hung on displays, and glass cabinets mesmerised with glittering earrings and glass ornaments. Shelves were filled with handbags and beautifully shaped vases, mugs with pretty patterns and scarves in every colour you could imagine. With its relaxed air and smooth background music, D'Alton's elicited an avarice that was almost overwhelming, and it made Flick's mouth water.

'Hi, Sally,' Flick greeted the owner, who'd just finished serving a customer. There were plenty of people in the shop. 'You look busy.'

'God, it's non-stop, but it'll pay for my February skiing trip,' she said quietly.

'I've come to collect something for George Fisher?' Sally looked under the counter, and came back up with a package all wrapped in D'Alton's signature paper and ribbon. 'He's paid for it, I hope?'

'Yup, all done.'

'Right, see you soon, until I can't keep away,' Flick laughed and headed for the door. As she was about to open it, she spotted a familiar figure behind a display to her left. 'Hi, Ed, how are you?'

He'd obviously been in a world of his own because he looked up, startled, then broke into a smile, greeting her with a kiss on both cheeks. He smelt of an expensive aftershave. 'Flick, lovely to see you.' They both looked down at the necklace he was holding, Ed as if he hadn't seen it before. It was big and exaggerated, very contemporary even for D'Alton's, with abstract shapes made from brown and orange plastic.

'Is that for Georgie?' Flick asked.

'Yes, yes,' Ed said brightly. 'I thought I'd get it for her for Christmas. What do you think?'

Flick paused. 'Honest answer?' she asked apologetically.

'Would you give anything else?' he laughed.

'It's not really her thing. Georgie's more greens and pinks, isn't she? With that lovely colouring she wants something soft.' Flick glanced at the display and picked up a bracelet made from delicate enamel flowers. There was a necklace to match and Flick held them out, her head on one side. 'Yes, this is definitely more her thing.' Something came into her head. 'Oh, I remember now, she did mention a scarf that she saw and loved. She showed me last time we came in. Let me see if it's still here.' She handed Ed the jewellery, and parted the scarves that Sally had hung over a ladder display. There it was, a shimmering soft silk in pearl pink that would look beautiful next to Georgie's pale skin and dark hair.

'Ed, it's here,' she took it back to him, delighted it hadn't been sold. How pleased Georgie would be. 'I hope it's not more than you were going to spend – but she deserves it,' she nudged him knowing he never took a dig without umbrage, but unable to resist, 'almost as much as you deserved that new car of yours, hey?' She'd rather die than say anything to Georgie, but she felt Ed had Ed firmly at the centre of his universe, and there wasn't much love lost between them. She thought him pompous. He clearly disapproved of her and the odd comment showed just how much. But now Ed shot her a glance and she knew that this time her barb had struck home. Fifteen–love.

'Yes, yes. I'm sure she'll love it,' he muttered. He headed towards the counter. 'Must hurry. See you soon, Flick.'

Flick, glad to have done her mate a favour, left the shop and went down the road to the dry-cleaners.

*

'Star of wonder, star of light. Fill yer pants with dynamite,' sang Libby at the top of her voice. 'Light the fuse and off you go, around the world to Mexico.'

Georgie suppressed a smile – oh, the joys of being eight – and reversed into a slightly too small parking space a little way from the school. 'Don't keep singing that. You won't be able to do it right when the time comes and you'll end up embarrassing yourself in front of the whole school, not to mention all the mummies and daddies. Come on now, we'd better hurry up.'

On the damp pavement, glistening under the street lights, Libby danced from foot to foot while Georgie fished around in the boot for the bag containing the fairy – no, strike that – angel wings, the dressing gown and coat-hanger halo that would transform her into one of the angelic host. They held hands, Libby's tiny, squirmy, warm one in Georgie's as they trotted through the car park towards the brightly lit school. They were late, of course, and all the best parking spaces must have been nabbed while they were still waiting for Ed to get home. Then he'd called to say he'd been delayed and would have to meet them there. Georgie had had to rush, although trying hard not to panic Libby. There was still plenty of time, of course, by any normal standards, but the obsessive headteacher wanted all the children *in situ* with three-quarters of an hour to spare. Georgie glanced at her watch. Fifteen minutes to go.

She hustled Libby through the school hall, hot and crowded, and round to the changing rooms filled with diminutive shepherds, stars, oxen, and sundry other angels, trying not to clonk any of them on the head with her shoulder bag as she struggled through.

'There you are, Libby. What kind of time is this to be turning up? Come on, get changed. Get changed!' Red-faced and agitated, Mrs Cadney shot an indignant look at Georgie before ushering Libby into a corner with some dozen other angels in various states of readiness.

'Shall I help her?' Georgie asked, still holding the costume in its carrier bag. 'Might be easier if I do.'

'Mmm, yes perhaps.' Mrs Cadney looked slightly mollified. 'But I doubt if you'll get a seat. It'll be standing room only. It's quite against health and safety, but what can you do? Parents turn up without tickets and you can hardly turn them away. Theo! Don't put the head on until just before you go on for the stable scene. You'll get far too hot. What? Stuck? Oh, for goodness sake!'

She bustled off and Georgie set about getting Libby ready, no easy matter when she had so much to say to her co-stars. By the time the halo was rammed onto her head firmly enough to ensure it wouldn't fall off during the performance, Georgie was hot and red-faced. Libby looked delectable. After a final kiss, barely tolerated by her daughter, she made her way back into the hall which, as predicted, was full to bursting. She searched the serried ranks of dads, all jockeying for position like paparazzi with their camcorders, for a sign of Ed but couldn't spot him, so tucked herself in beside the PE vaulting horse from where she could keep an eye on both the door and the stage. How her mum would have loved this, but Lincoln was a bit far to come for a play, especially when her parents had to split their time fairly between ten grandchildren.

Then the lights were switched off and a single wavering spotlight trained on the stage as the play began. Georgie, in spite of herself, was suddenly lost in the stumbling retelling of the Christmas story, eyes raking the stage for Libby, following her every movement and filling up with unexpected tears at the strains of *Away in a Manger*.

At last, applause rang out. Georgie clapped until her hands were hot and sore and, as the lights came up, and the children started to file off the stage and the lengthy vote of thanks was read out by a dutiful governor, she saw him near the door, dishevelled and apologetic-looking, and she felt a surge of love for him. They worked their way towards each other, dodging chair-stackers, small knots of chatting parents and pre-schoolers seizing the opportunity to dash around unchecked, and hugged, both talking at the same time.

'I'm so sorry, darling. Bloody meetings ran on and on. I just couldn't get away.'

'Did you see her? Wasn't she gorgeous? Did you manage to film her?'

Ed pulled a rueful face. 'I only just made it. I got the last bit on my phone – oh, darling, don't look like that, it just couldn't be helped. I'm sure someone else will have got it all – look, I'll ask.'

Georgie shook her head in resignation. 'No point. Everyone only films their own. Oh, Ed.'

He pulled her into a hug. 'I'm so sorry, honey, I just couldn't get away. You know I'd have been here if I could.' He looked over her shoulder. '*There* you are, baby. You were fantastic. The very best angel of all.'

'Daddy! You're here!' Libby launched herself into Ed's open arms and he hugged her tight. Georgie stood back for a moment, unsure of how she felt as her disappointment with Ed was replaced by a slight resentment. Had he turned up for his sons' Christmas plays? If Libby played hockey (God forbid) would he rush to every match? Or was she just being a bitch?

Her thoughts got no further, however, after Libby turned and flopped against her. 'Mummy, can we get chips on the way home? I'm hungry again after all that acting.'

Ed's eyes crinkled with amusement, met hers, and her annoyance ebbed away. 'You girls go on ahead,' he said. 'I'll go to the chip shop and see you back at the ranch, OK?' And he ruffled Libby's hair and dropped a kiss on Georgie's cheek.

Christmas seemed to rush in on them once term had ended. Fortunately, Georgie had prepared everything for their own celebration well in advance, including filling the freezer and buying the presents for Ed's boys along with Libby's, her nieces' and nephews', all on the same trawl around the toy shops – a task that had somehow devolved to her, even though she felt unqualified. But with Ross and Charlie now in their early teens, she had found little among the remote-control robots and construction toys to inspire her. With Libby's doll's house safely wrapped and tucked away, she roamed the relatively unknown territory of the computer and electronics shops, looking for games that were compatible with the handheld consoles the boys were getting, but wouldn't turn them into axe-murderers.

With everything wrapped and safely tucked away, the house tastefully decorated in the leftovers from a client's house in south Wimbledon, the halls of which she and Flick had decked, Georgie felt justifiably smug as she looked around at her handiwork.

The revenge work she and Flick had done for Caroline Knightly – Operation WC they'd called it – paid for in cash, had given Georgie a little more scope for extravagance than she would normally have. She still hadn't mentioned it to Ed, and she wasn't sure she ever would. As it was only a one-off there seemed little point in telling him, but the Eames chair she'd bought him made it all worthwhile. She hoped she'd made the right choice – he was so discerning.

The only highlight in the frantic countdown to Christmas was the arrival in the office doorway one evening – luckily after Joanna had left to go late-night shopping – of Caroline herself. She reported back, gleefully, to Georgie and Flick, 'It was fantastic! The phone started ringing late the evening after you did it, and he obviously thought it was La Waitress so he went out and took the call in the conservatory. You should have seen his face! And when he listened to his messages the next morning! I didn't think anything could put him off his cooked breakfast, but he didn't even touch his sausage! What was so funny was that he had no idea how his number had got out – he didn't suspect a thing. Apparently he had meetings that morning and he had to turn his phone off because it was ringing all the time. When he turned it on again there were over fifty calls! He eventually sent his secretary out to get him a new phone, and that was that, but he came home with his tail between his legs, I can tell you.' Her eyes glittered. 'I was so understanding too. I said, "I wonder how those awful people got hold of your number – I mean, it's not like you give it out to just *anyone*, is it?"' She shrieked with laughter. 'His expression as the penny dropped! And look what I'm getting for Christmas!' She held out a slender, tanned hand to show off an exquisite band of what looked like platinum studded with emeralds and diamonds. 'Of course, he doesn't know yet. But he's hardly going to argue, is he?'

Georgie felt vaguely guilty, but it had been a lark. It wasn't until the day before Ed stopped work for the holiday that her plans started to unravel. He called from the office, tension making his voice sound almost hysterical.

'Look, erm. You're going to hate me.'

'What?' she said cautiously. 'You're not working over Christmas, are you?'

'Oh good Lord, no. It's just – well, you know how Ross and Charlie were coming for Christmas Day?'

'Ye-e-e-s?'

'Well, bloody Patsy's only gone and booked a last-minute trip to some country house hotel with that bloke she's been seeing and she wants me – us – to have the boys from Christmas Eve until the day after Boxing Day.'

Mingled with satisfied outrage at this new example of Patsy's selfishness was irritation. Yet Georgie couldn't help feeling for the boys, awkward and spotty and growing almost visibly. What a time to be abandoned by their mother. And here, also, she had to admit to herself, was a chance to shine. She took a deep breath. 'Don't worry, darling. Of course the boys are welcome.'

Georgie could almost hear Ed's brow unwrinkling as he sighed. 'Darling, you are the very, very best. I'll make it up to you, I promise. And just you make a shopping list and I'll get everything we need.'

She smiled wryly as he went on. Yeah, right. On past experience it was her that would end up in Sainsbury's with a teetering mountain of extra groceries. But if she was honest, she'd rather do it herself anyway than risk the addition of rollmops, every flavour of stuffed olives, and expensive Claret that would end up in her trolley if he came with her. Exquisite taste came at a hefty price. She blew him a kiss, replaced the phone and started on a list.

Chapter Five

January saw itself out in a sluggish grey chill which didn't seem to lift. Everywhere Flick went, people were gritty and fed up, longing for the crocuses to push through on the common to give some indication that spring was on its way. The agency was busier than ever, of course, watering plants and feeding cats whilst their owners enjoyed Courcheval and, for the lucky few, the Caribbean.

Flick, who turned off ITV whenever the holiday ads came on, tried to ignore the imperious wording of the instructions that she found left on the side in each house she visited. The unique tone the English use to talk to the lower orders – the staff – seemed innate in the breed. No wonder we had an empire, she thought to herself. The only break in the constant pressure of the days was the resignation of two of their cleaners, a major blow when they were two of the most reliable – poached by a cleaning business in Streatham – and Joanna's announcement one Friday lunchtime that she had to have a little 'op' on her varicose veins on the Monday.

'I'll be off for a few days.' She hadn't given them very much notice and Georgie had to admonish Flick with a stern look when she'd growled about her leaving them in the lurch. 'Poor love. It must be horrid. I'm bound to get them. My mum's got them really badly and they're terribly genetic.'

Flick started to plan out how the two of them were going to cover for Joanna and the two cleaners. Later that afternoon she headed out in the car to a job, cranking up the heating to try to warm up a chill which seemed to have entered her very bones.

The chill set in even harder on Saturday and by Sunday night she felt stiff and achy. The heating in the flat was on full and she curled up on the sofa in a large fleece and PJ bottoms, moving only to take another paracetamol and make herself a cup of tea. She'd tried to get sympathy via text from John, but he'd come back a few hours later with a 'bad luck'. Flick chucked the phone onto the other chair. His mood since she'd last seen him before Christmas was even chillier than she felt. Perhaps The Wife had spoiled him with turkey and stuffing, and the rosy cheeks of his children as they gathered around the sparkling Christmas tree had shown him the error of his ways. Flick groaned, pulled the duvet around her, and sank into even deeper self-pity.

On Monday morning she couldn't be sure she hadn't died, and was about to reach for the phone and tell Georgie she wouldn't be in and to call an undertaker, when she remembered Joanna's absence. 'Bloody hell,' she howled and gingerly raised herself from her bed, her head throbbing, to totter to the shower.

Georgie was no better. Flick could barely see her face when she came through the office door after dropping Libby at school, and when she unravelled her scarf her face was pale, her eyes a pool of brown with dark shadows beneath.

'Oh God, not you too?'

'I feel like shit. Can we just go home?' Georgie was about to take her jacket off but changed her mind, and sat down heavily at her desk, hunched up and incapable even of reaching down and turning on the computer.

'I've already had three calls before you came in,' replied Flick, 'and that bloody new Polish girl smashed one of the Deakins' ornaments yesterday so I'm going to have to find another one. And Beryl's called in with the flu so she won't be able to do the Grettons' cleaning today, and—'

'Oh, enough!' Georgie put her hands up to her head. 'Can't they just go away?'

' – and we need to write a cheque for the tax bill.'

'Bollocks.' Georgie laid her head on her desk. 'And Libby was completely vile this morning. And it's her that's given me this cold. And Ed can't help. He's off to Cardiff so he can't pick Lib up. '

'And the rent for this place has gone up. The bastard landlord said he'd keep it the same, do you remember, but he must have overspent at Christmas.'

'More like he just wants a new Mercedes.' Georgie groaned and sniffed. 'I just want to die.'

'Coffee?'

'Oh, please can we have a hot choc?'

There was a pause. 'It means we'll have to go out for one.' They both sat for a moment in silence, weighing up the magnitude of the task that faced them.

'I'll go,' Georgie sighed.

'Nah, I will.'

'But I've still got my coat on. And besides, you look worse than I do. So, at huge personal sacrifice and putting my life in danger, I shall brave the elements.'

'Thanks. You're a doll.'

Georgie pulled herself up and slowly put her bag over her shoulder. Flick noticed the bracelet on her wrist – it was the one she had persuaded Ed to buy Georgie for Christmas and which she seemed to wear every day. Flick had been right. The colours did suit her, and out of somewhere she felt a wave of loneliness, wishing for a moment that she had someone special to give her gifts and spoil her. Her mother's present – a sponsored goat in Namibia – was sweet but you couldn't really wear it to go out on the town. It wasn't even cashmere.

'Back in a mo. If I don't return in fifteen minutes it's 'cos I've stopped off at the bed shop on the corner for a kip!'

The door clicked shut behind Georgie and Flick forced herself to open the file of invoices in front of her. All things monetary were not Georgie's forte. Long ago, they'd settled on a pattern

45

of responsibilities that involved Flick keeping them solvent and Georgie being the 'face' of the agency, schmoozing clients and pouring oil on frayed tempers. Flick had no tolerance for that.

For the next few minutes she wrote cheques and filled in counterfoils, her head telling her that the benefits of the paracetamol were beginning to wear off. She felt shivery and her throat hurt. The phone suddenly shrilling in her ear didn't help.

'Domestic Angels,' she practically whispered.

'Hello,' said a faltering female voice. 'Is that Domestic Angels?'

'Er ... yes.'

'I wonder if you can help. A friend of mine recommended you.'

'Oh, that's nice. That's how we work really – word of mouth,' Flick croaked, trying to assume her best sales patter. 'What sort of service were you looking for? Full membership gives you access to cleaners, home care and access to our vetted trades database.' There was a pause.

'My friend's called Caroline Knightly. You might remember her?'

Realisation dawned. 'Ah.' At that moment Georgie shouldered through the door, two cardboard cups of hot chocolate in her hands. Seeing the expression on Flick's face, she raised an eyebrow questioningly at Flick, who replied with a quizzical look. 'I see. And ... ?'

'Well,' the woman went on, her voice soft and well spoken. 'She said you had done a very good job for her. Very thorough.' She paused, a gentle chuckle in her voice. 'In fact, she said it had worked a treat and her husband is very attentive these days.'

'So I hear.' Flick smiled to herself.

Georgie put down the cup on Flick's desk and strained to read 'friend of Caroline Knightly' that Flick had scrawled on the pad in front of her.

'The thing is, I wondered if you'd do the same for me. My

husband seems to be away a lot – if you get my drift. He does a lot of business in Eastern Europe and I'm fairly convinced that it's not always the kind of business he should be doing.'

Flick felt a moment of morality. What if the poor man was innocent and doing what he should be in Ljubljana or wherever. 'Do you have any evidence?'

'Oh yes, plenty. Even the clichéd lipstick on the collar. In fact, one little tart even answered the phone when I called his hotel. He said it was the chamber maid.' Her voice maintained its gentle tone as if she was chatting about the weather. 'I don't want anything major. Just a shot across the bows. I'll leave it up to you. Put it this way, I'm not losing everything I've worked so hard for in my marriage to some Slovenian nympho with half an eye on his credit card. Do you understand?'

'Well, yes, I'm sure we can help. We only take cash, I'm afraid.' Flick plucked a figure from the air – having glanced down at the pile of invoices and adding a couple of hundred quid. She saw Georgie's eyebrows shoot up.

'That's not a problem. Half upfront and half when you've delivered?'

'OK, that will be fine. Perhaps you can drop it round in an envelope?' Flick gave the office address and put the phone down. Georgie was standing stock still, eyebrows still raised.

'So we're doing another one, are we? Should we, though?'

Flick waived the landlord's letter in front of her. 'Decision made, my love. Besides, it sounds like her husband's a plonker. Domestic Angels? We're now the Avenging Angels!' Suddenly she felt better.

So Caroline Knightly had been gloriously indiscreet on the ladies-that-lunch circuit about her outsourced revenge. Over the next few days Flick began to wonder if she'd been a bad person in a former life, or if the relish she felt planning this latest hit came from being a bad person in this one. Georgie, however, was more reticent about dishing out revenge. 'I've always been crap at this sort of thing,' she moaned apologetically. It was seven-thirty and they were sitting in her ultra-modern kitchen, making a dent in a bottle of Sauvignon Blanc. 'I could never even bunk off school 'cos I was so terrified of being caught. I'm just a goody-goody.' Georgie, perched on a bar stool, played with the stem of her wine glass.

'You were too well brought up, that's your problem. You should have been dragged around by a born radical like I was.'

Georgie laughed. 'Don't blame your mother. We could do with more of her sort in the world. You just have the morals of the gutter, young lady.' Georgie pretended to look haughty, but Flick knew she was closer to the truth than she realised. Flick was the risk-taker, the bad girl. She'd been the one who bunked off school and went to the shops, not to class, who smoked behind the bus station, the girl who pushed the boundaries of decency with her school uniform. She was the girl who slept with other people's husbands.

Was she proud of herself? She didn't think she could help herself. She practically had an O level in finding trouble. In spotting the wrong type of man. 'But this bloke,' she went on, 'is off on the Continent, pretending to be doing business, and what he's actually doing is his bit to cement relations with the former Eastern Bloc.'

'Nice image, thanks,' said Georgie and topped up Flick's glass. In the silence Flick could hear the TV in the room next door and the patter of rain on the kitchen roof with its high glass ceiling so cleverly designed by Ed to make the most of natural daylight, the black and white minimalist units and glass sculptures. Georgie had mentioned that Ed would be out at a planning appeal meeting and it seemed like a good opportunity to talk over the latest call. And to try and persuade the reluctant Georgie. Flick leaned forward. 'We're not going to do anything illegal or dangerous. It's not the SAS, you know. It's just serving the bugger his just desserts.'

'I never understood that expression,' Georgie sighed. Flick's phone bleeped a message, and she picked it up idly. It was John. Her heart beat a bit faster with pleasure. 'Am in town Thursday. U free?'

'S'pose you're right.' Georgie continued. 'It's a miserable thing to do, isn't it? Shag a Slovenian, I mean. Mind you, his Mrs sounds like the kind of woman who plays hardball.'

'Ah,' said Flick, considering herself something of an expert on the subject. 'These women have to work damn hard to be the type of wives their husbands want. It's a full-time job, all those hours in the salon or having Botox so they look like a dish of fish at functions. After all that exhausting pressure, they get doubly pissed off when he falls into the arms of some nubile little gold-digger who doesn't even have to wear make-up.'

'What's nubile mean?' Libby wandered into the room, clean and rosy-cheeked and in top to toe pink pyjamas and dressing gown. Her hair was fairer than Georgie's, though as unruly and curly, and she had her mother's wide eyes. If it wasn't for her slightly small mouth – the mirror of her father's – she would have been an angelic-looking child.

'Flick said "mobile" didn't you, Flick?' said her mother quickly. 'Crikey, look at the time – bed, my girl. What have you been watching?' Georgie's face was racked with the guilt and horror that she'd forgotten all about Libby being in front of the TV.

'Something about STDs.'

Flick and Georgie froze, then Georgie chased her upstairs and an idea began to form in Flick's head.

The following morning she was on the phone from her flat.

'I speek with Meester Scrivener, please?' What exactly did a Slovenian accent sound like? Flick tried to think about how they spoke on the Eurovision song contest. She hoped she wasn't sounding too Spanish or – oh God – what if he talked back to her in Slovenian? She hadn't considered that he might be fluent.

'I'm afraid he won't be back till later. Can I help?'

'This is ...' Flick tried very hard to keep a straight face. 'This is the 'ospital of Infectious Diseases in Ljubljana. Slovenia, you know it? I have important message for Meester Scrivener, please.'

'Oh, I see. Well, I'm afraid he won't be in at all today. He's at a board meeting. Can I take a message?'

'Eeez very confidential, you understand?'

The voice at the other end of the phone hesitated, then rushed to reassure. 'No, that's perfectly understood. You can leave a message with me.'

'Oh thank you much. I am from the – how you say it? – department of sexually transmitting diseases.' Flick was beginning to enjoy herself. Terry Wogan, *nul points*. ' Meeester Scrivener must come to have check-up, as soon as he come back in Slovenia. It is quite very urgent. Please, he can contact?'

There was a stunned silence. 'Oh. Oh, I see. Right. I see. Erm, well can I take a number for him to contact you?'

Flick looked down at the details she'd found after a quick internet search and provided a number she'd found for a hospital in Ljubljana. With any luck, he wouldn't find anyone there with enough English to disabuse him and he'd spend several anxious days fending off leading questions from his receptionist who – given that Flick had warned it was a confidential matter – would have informed the entire office by lunchtime.

Flick put the phone down, well pleased with her morning's work, then finally replied to John's message from last night.

'OK. Usual place?'

'Look at this one, Mummy. They've got a swimming pool. And you can do acting. Look at those girls, all dressed up as witches. That one looks the best.'

Libby pushed the glossy prospectus at Georgie across the kitchen table, scattering the neatly stacked pile of other brochures they'd yet to peruse, and carried on eating her pasta.

'You've said that about all of them so far. They can't all be the best. Here, let's have a look.' Georgie peered at the photographs of the Year Ten play. 'Maybe they're not acting, though. Maybe that's the uniform. Had you thought of that? Pointy hat and a long black cloak – that would be interesting.'

Libby threw back her head and laughed. 'And stripy socks and pointy shoes. Or p'rhaps it will be like Hogwarts, and I can have my own owl.'

'Well, I'll keep an eye out for letters coming down the chimney, but I still think we should look at the other brochures. Y'know – in case you turn out to be a squid, or whatever it's called.'

'Squib, Mummy, it's squib. Like Filch, you remember.'

Georgie shook her head. Sodding Harry Potter. She watched Libby poring over another set of tempting photographs of oh-so-happy girls on grassy playing fields or in well-equipped labs. If only the entrance exams for these sought-after private schools included a paper on Harry Potter, Libby would probably get a scholarship. And that would certainly help! Georgie pulled the pencil from behind her ear and quickly wrote, 'Scholarship? Music?' on the pad in front of her. It was worth considering. The fees, even when quoted termly rather than yearly, were enough to make Georgie's already curly hair curl even more, but Ed had gone the private route with his boys so he was bound to want the same for Libby. And given the alternative – the scramble for a place at the local academy – the fees seemed more than reasonable.

Georgie looked with satisfaction at the selection of folders and brochures in front of her. With her customary thoroughness, she'd sent away for information on independent schools throughout the area. With Ed due home any moment, they could spend a couple of hours going through the booklets together, after supper. That would be nice, and it would give him and Libby some time together. He seemed to have been out so often in the evenings lately, what with meetings and site visits and trips away, but tonight he was due in at the normal time.

The smell of casserole, with just enough garlic, would welcome him as he stepped through the door. There was a bottle of Merlot ready to be opened on the side and some pavlova with kiwis and sinfully expensive raspberries. All in all, it promised to be a lovely, cosy evening.

Georgie glanced at her watch. 'Tell you what, Lib. Why don't I run your bath now, while you finish your supper and you can have a nice, long soak before Daddy gets back? Then you can come downstairs in your lovely new jim-jams and show him the schools you like the look of. How would that be?'

Libby considered for a moment, head on one side. 'Hmm, yes. That would be nice. Can I have some of those left-over profiteroles though? And some of your bubbles?'

'Not all mixed together, I hope.'

Libby giggled again. 'No, silly. That would be horrid. But I could have the profiteroles in the bath. That way it wouldn't even matter if I got the chocolate on me.'

Georgie reached over and took Libby's plate away. 'Not a bad idea, but that top's going in the wash anyway. Look at all the pesto on it! A bit of choccy won't make much difference now.'

Libby looked down in surprise and swatted at her school polo shirt in a gesture so like Ed's that Georgie had to swallow hard. What would a little boy version of her and Ed be like, she wondered once again? With Libby growing up so fast, she was thinking more and more of what it had been like when she was tiny and the hunger it awoke in her was like an ache, sad and huge. She quickly turned away to the fridge. 'Right. Let's see what we've got left. Only two. Have you been helping yourself, young lady?'

Later, with Libby splashing contentedly in the bath, Georgie got on with loading the washing machine in peace. Ed's key in the lock broke into her daydreams and she greeted him with a kiss that he returned with surprised pleasure.

'Well, hello! That's a nice welcome home. I'm glad I bought you these now.' He presented her with a bunch of statuesque Arum lilies, long and sleek, and terribly out of season.

'Oh, Ed! They're lovely. What did I do to deserve this?'

He pulled her close and sniffed her hair. 'It's that lovely perfume you're wearing – garlic, isn't it? Reminds me of my favourite casserole.'

'Oh go on,' Georgie laughed, pushing him away. 'Are you ready to eat now? I'll lay the table, while you check that Lib hasn't dissolved away to nothing, if you like. She's been splashing about for ages. If you listen, you can hear her singing. She's happy as anything, and she wants to show you her shortlist of schools. I've got all the prospecti – is that what you call them? – and I thought we could have a look together tonight.'

Ed, on his way to the stairs, stopped and turned round. 'What do you mean?'

Georgie rolled her eyes and shrugged. 'I know, I *am* a bit early, but it pays to start looking sooner rather than later. And if we make a shortlist now, we can target her coaching so she stands the best chance of getting her first choice.'

'I don't understand.'

'Oh, for goodness sake, Ed,' Georgie laughed. 'It won't be that long. Big school. You know. Year seven. I've got prospectuses from all the ones in Wimbledon and Wandsworth and a few a bit further away. I know Dulwich might not be so convenient, but Putney would be perfect and ...'

Ed shook his head slowly. 'But we've never ... George, I can't possibly take on another set of school fees, you must see that.'

Georgie stopped dead. 'What? What do you mean? You can't – you have to. We have to. The boys – you pay for them. I mean, I assumed ...'

Ed looked at her in silence, his brow creased, and his hands hanging by his sides. Georgie stared back at him, speechless as her plans and assumptions started to crumble. 'But, Ed, she's your daughter. It's not even fair when the boys ...'

Ed sighed deeply and rubbed his face hard. 'Look, the boys were already down for the prep when I left. And Patsy pushed for it as part of the settlement. But I thought that Libby – well, she's always gone to a state school. I assumed she'd just be going on. I mean, lots of her friends will go to that place, won't they? And everyone says how good it is.'

Ed came over to the table with the low-hanging lamp casting a warm pool of light, and sat down heavily, pushing aside Georgie's pile of favourites without seeming to see them. 'The thing is, work hasn't been going so well. We've had three jobs pulled this last week and another two put on indefinite hold. I tell you, Georgie, it's bloody out there at the moment.' He shook his head and stared blankly into the distance.

'There's my money too, don't forget.'

Ed looked circumspect. 'Oh come off it, darling. That's fine for holidays and treats, but it won't cover a year's fees at the rate they are now. And there's all the bloody extras, of course.'

Georgie was about to open her mouth and tell him about the new income stream Flick and she had discovered, then she changed her mind. She was not quite sure why. Outside the glow of the lamp, she shivered. Ed looked so bereft. She couldn't bring herself to make things any harder for him. It was so unfair, but she wouldn't stoop to demanding from him the same privileges for Libby that he had given to the boys. After all, Libby had him around and they didn't, and that was more important than anything else. She could have kicked herself for setting the wheels in motion without consulting him. Now she'd have to face Libby's disappointment. She felt a core of resolve forming inside her. She'd make it work, like she always did. It was just another problem to be solved. She'd find a way to make things all right for Libby, and for Ed too. She'd go and visit the local schools herself, the next chance she got. And maybe she could get involved with the PTA or something. She'd make it all right. Swallowing hard, she went over and put her arm round his shoulders, dropping a kiss on his bowed head.

'Well, shall I pour you a glass of wine? I'll put those lovely lilies in some water. Shall we have some garlic bread? I'll get Lib out of the bath. Whose turn is it to read to her tonight? Yours or mine?'

The school issue filled Georgie's head for the next few weeks – when she wasn't answering the phone at work that never ceased to ring. The new year had brought an encouraging raft of new clients, but the avenging sideline seemed to have died a death. However, one morning, just as crocuses were pushing their way through to create a carpet of colour under the trees on the common, the door of the office flew open. Flick, Georgie and Jo's heads snapped up and, shortly after, all three of their mouths dropped open as a tiny, dazzlingly pretty dark-haired woman walked in. She was dressed as though she were on her way to a party in a fantastically impractical cream trouser suit, like a miniature Bianca Jagger, and carrying a huge handbag that looked as though it ought to make her fall over. It soon became apparent that the air of fragility was deceptive.

Over steaming mugs of coffee, she started to speak in a heavy and immensely sexy accent that they later discovered was Brazilian. 'My friend, erm, Caroline, she came to see you before Christmas. You helped her with her little private problem, yes?'

Georgie coughed quickly. 'Joanna, could you possibly ... get along to Sainsbury's for me? I forgot ... something ... er, loo paper. That's it. Completely out. Would you mind?'

Joanna pulled on her duffle coat, a little surprised, and headed out of the door. Things were going to get tricky if 'Caroline' was recommending their services to her friends, and beautiful Brazilian women were going to storm into the office at all hours.

'It's my husband,' the woman continued. 'I love him. And he

adores me, I know it. But just one thing he does makes me crazy. I can't take it any more!'

She paused theatrically, sinking her face into her beautifully manicured hands. Georgie looked anxiously over at Flick, wondering if this was going to be too serious for them to take on.

'It's my parking. He makes fun of me all the time. In São Paulo, the traffic is crazy but I have a driver most of the time and so I never have to think about it. But here …!' She shook her head in disgust. 'One, two little scrapes. A bump, maybe – nothing! A few tickets. It's money, nothing more. And he has plenty of that. So why does he tell all our friends, like it's a big joke? I ask him not to tell everyone again and again, but he tells me, "Oh, it's the British sense of humour, it's because I love you". I. Can't. Stand. It! Please, help me to stop him. But he is so careful. Always doing everything just right. If, just once, he could get a ticket sometime, we would be even. He would never say it again, I know it!'

Georgie felt herself relax. This didn't sound too hard and, once their new client left, having given the highly un-Brazilian name of Moira Kennedy, they set to work on making the punishment fit the crime.

A few days later, driving out to Heathrow airport, the spare set of keys to a 7-series BMW placed carefully on the dashboard, Georgie and Flick were in high spirits. Moira's husband had gone away on business to Kuala Lumpur but was going to come back to more than he'd anticipated. The manoeuvre took them no time at all and they splashed out on a double latte with some of the money Moira had paid them upfront, with a similar amount promised once she'd seen the look on her husband's face when he eventually came home.

In the event, Moira paid them almost double, because, she related with glee, she'd had the satisfaction of him calling to beg her to pick him up because he was convinced his car had been stolen. She'd helped him search the other levels of the long-stay car park, then gently suggested he might have left it somewhere else, 'After all, you do travel such a lot'. His horrified disbelief at his own stupidity, when they eventually tracked down the car, conveniently moved to the short-term car park at fifty pounds a day, and the fact that he was five hundred pounds poorer, put an end to the teasing entirely.

'Moira' promised to recommend them and they didn't have to wait long. 'Debbie' called ahead and arranged a time to visit the agency so Flick and Georgie were able to talk to her in what they jokingly called the executive office – little more than a broom cupboard where they kept supplies and a broken office chair they kept meaning to throw out. Joanna was clearly suspicious this time and, once or twice, as Debbie haltingly explained her plight, Georgie thought she could hear her just outside the closed door.

The solution to this problem – a hedge-fund manager fiancé with a taste for nightclubs – came to Georgie while helping Libby get ready for the Valentine's Day disco at her school. The UV pen she'd bought to draw flowers on Libby and her friends' skinny little arms so that they would show up under the fluorescent disco lights, was pressed into service on a pile of beautifully ironed shirts at the house Debbie shared with her fiancé. The scantily dressed young things at the club wouldn't be too keen to consort with a man whose shirt proclaimed 'I've got herpes' in large and glowing letters, and his colleagues must have found it far too funny to bother telling him. After that, the attraction of the clubs seemed to wear off a bit and Debbie was more than satisfied. In fact, when she came back to give them the balance of the agreed sum, they'd shared a coffee and speculated on what his final night at the club must have been like.

After she'd left, though, Georgie couldn't help wondering what sort of marriage Debbie was in for. It wasn't anything she wanted to raise with Flick, of course, whose cynicism with regard to love was notorious. But why would a girl as pretty and bright as that settle for a relationship that was based on manipulation? She fiddled absently with the gorgeous bracelet Ed had given her for Christmas. That, the matching necklace and the scarf now hanging on the back of her chair, had hardly left her neck since and she could tell Ed was really pleased because he kept looking at her, sort of lingeringly, when she wore them. She shrugged, and returned to the list of approved plumbers in the area that she'd been updating.

The next case, which arrived just before Easter via an ex-wife, was a tricky one, but so rewarding. And both Georgie and Flick were in complete agreement that their victim deserved everything he got – and more. The only slight qualm they had was whether or not spraying 'I am a tight bastard' in weedkiller onto an immaculate front lawn in front of a huge ranch-style house near Virginia Water amounted to criminal damage. At the last minute, they chickened out of using a long-lasting preparation, guaranteed to prevent growth for at least four months, and went for a milder formula. Ed had been a bit hard to convince when Georgie explained she had to leave the house at midnight, dressed head to foot in black, but he'd been so tired lately, working long hours on a station refurb, that he eventually accepted with a shrug her story about a client coming home from abroad and having lost his keys, and took himself off to bed.

The wronged ex-wife made sure, on Georgie and Flick's recommendation, that she had a perfect alibi but anyway, as she explained, it could have been any one of the several ex-wives of her smooth-talking furniture importer ex-husband, so quick to promise and so slow to pay up on maintenance. 'Just imagine,' she gloated, 'when his neighbours see that lawn slowly turning yellow. He won't be so keen on inviting them round for drinks to show off his landscaping then, will he?'

Flick had a characteristic take on it. 'Well, he shouldn't keep getting married if he can't or won't afford it. Why bother, for goodness sake? My dad was as bad and I'd spray his lawn, if he had one. Honestly, men are just pathetic, aren't they? You know, I actually feel lucky that I've never got married. More fool any woman who relies on a man doing the right thing!' she snorted.

Georgie yawned. 'Oh, they're not all bad. We only get to hear about the problems, but there are plenty of happy couples out there, y'know. And plenty of decent blokes. And I bet, if you only looked in the right place, there'd be a perfect one for you.'

Flick raised a sceptical eyebrow. 'Oh, yeah? I'll stick to the slimy kind, thanks. At least you know what you're getting. No expectations.'

Chapter Six

Now Flick wasn't sure what she was getting at all. Contact from John was more and more infrequent, and she was determined she wasn't going to make all the running. That would make her seem desperate. And when they met, there seemed less and less common ground. She could hardly discuss her and Georgie's new sideline, not when the whole subject matter was so close to home. What kind of revenge would John's wife seek if she ever discovered just what he got up to when he came to London? Flick could only hope that no woman as enterprising had started up a similar service to theirs up north. How ironic would that be?

Nor did John seem very interested in the rest of her life. They followed the usual pattern. Meeting for a drink somewhere up the West End. Perhaps a meal then, by the coffee, he'd have his hand on her thigh and would whisper in her ear all the way home on the tube until he could rip her clothes off as soon as the front door of her flat was closed. Then she'd watch him as he slept, lying on his back, his mouth slightly open and wonder who exactly this person lying beside her was.

One particular evening, he hadn't even wanted to bother with the meal and had met her at nine-thirty in a cocktail bar. Now, as he slept, she watched his face in the soft light from the bedside table. Then, feeling uncomfortable and restless, she slipped from the bed and padded to the kitchen, shrugging on her dressing gown around her as she went. After perusing the near-empty fridge, she found some guacamole still in date and spread it on a few crackers. Taking her feast into the sitting room, she opened the *Standard* which she'd left on the coffee table, and had only half read whilst she'd waited for John to arrive. Her two cats, Dolce and Gabbana, wrapped themselves around her and she stroked them distractedly.

For a few moments she skim-read a theatre review of a play she'd never see, then her eyes fell on John's wallet lying on the table beside her. She nibbled the edge of the cracker before putting it down, wiping her hands on her dressing gown, and picking the wallet up. Inside were stuffed the usual receipts and about sixty pounds in cash. She slipped out a couple of credit cards: Mr John Hobday. It didn't seem like anyone she knew, this man with credit cards and business cards that had nothing to do with her. She pushed them back in again.

Slipping her fingers into another pocket of the wallet she felt some flat paper and pulled that out too. It was photographs. Three of them. The first was of a small girl wearing a blue sweatshirt with a white collar neatly poking out of the top. Her hair was tied back and she had a smattering of freckles on her nose and a broad smile revealed two missing front teeth. The second was of an older boy in a school blazer and tie. He looked about twelve, though Flick was hopeless at guessing children's ages, and he seemed geeky and square. His hair had been brushed down neatly and he had the same serious expression as the man asleep in the bedroom next door.

Flick knew what the third picture would be before she even slipped it out from behind the others. The woman, whose face looked back at her, was smiling broadly, and her short, sensibly cut brunette bob was slightly windswept, as if she was sitting on a beach. She was plain, but her smile made her seem quite pretty and her face had clearly been cut out of a photograph which had included other people.

Why were the pictures here? Did John keep them like men who had photographs of their families on their desk at the office did, as if they might forget what they looked like before they got home from work that night? Or did he look at them while he was away from home? Lots of men carried around pictures, but when he was playing away ... ? Flick slipped the photographs back into the wallet and, flipping it shut, put it slowly back down on the table. Then, after rubbing her face with hands that still smelled of him, she took her plate back into the kitchen, tipped the remaining crackers into the pedal bin, and made her way back into the bedroom.

He hadn't moved, his breath coming deep and slow with the rumblings of a snore in each exhalation. She sat on the side of the bed for a moment.

'John?' No response.

A bit louder now. 'John!' He started and lifted his head off the pillow, looking round confused, then focusing on her.

'Wha'?'

'I think you should leave.'

He didn't answer for a moment. 'What, *now*?'

'Yes, if you don't mind. I'm sure they'll have a room at the Travelodge. I'll call if you like.'

He pushed himself up on his elbows. 'Oh, come on. It's late. What's the problem all of a sudden?'

Flick sighed. 'Because we're nothing, John, and I feel like a hooker. I don't want this any more.' He looked at her face for a while.

'I thought we were OK with this arrangement. Can't we talk about this in the morning?' He rubbed his eyes.

'No.' Flick felt the resolve fill her. 'I want you to leave please.' John sighed, then swung his legs out of bed.

The next morning, as she made her way through the traffic, Flick wasn't sure how insulted to be that he had simply got dressed and left the flat with barely a word. She'd tried to say 'I'm sorry', but at the last minute had closed her mouth. What was there to be sorry about? For two days she felt a strange gap, as if a piece of furniture had been removed from the room, but when she woke up on Thursday morning she realised it was a piece of furniture she had never really liked much anyway and she was glad it was gone.

'You look chipper.' Joanna glanced up as Flick pushed her way into the office after nine, two budgies and a Persian cat fed at a client's flat on her way in. 'What you been up to?'

'Just clearing things out.'

'Oh I love doing that,' gushed Joanna. 'I did our garage last weekend. I hope you're going to recycle though?'

'No, Joanna,' Flick said gravely. 'This is one thing I'm not recycling. Now, how have those new electricians got on at the Smythes'?'

By Monday and a weekend spent half at her mother's and half alone – she'd left it too late to make arrangements with friends – her pleasure at ridding herself of John had turned to irritation and, by the time she had finished taking a leaf out of Joanna's book and filled four boxes with junk – she felt deep indignation. There was nothing in her boxes that related to him in any way, as if he had never existed. She'd been a fool, a stupid, gullible fool to make herself available to a man who had no respect for her and who kept a picture of his wife in his wallet.

So, by the time the door opened on Monday evening and framed in it was a petite blonde woman with a pink cashmere cardigan and smart grey trousers, Flick was feeling even less charitable towards the opposite sex. And there was something about this woman that was different from the other 'clients', as Georgie liked to refer to them. Her skin was soft and smooth but thin and delicate, and her petite hands looked almost too fine for the large expensive rings she wore. Her eyes were wide and almost fearful, and she even threw a look anxiously behind her before entering as if she might be being followed.

'Can I help you?' Georgie asked, getting up from her seat as if sensing too that this woman needed gentle handling.

'Yes, yes, I hope you can.' Georgie indicated the chair in front of her desk, and the woman perched on it elegantly, resting her

Prada handbag on her knee. Flick knew immediately that she wasn't looking for cleaners or plumbers; this sort of woman would have her own fleet of on-hand help. She probably had a housekeeper too. 'I think you may be just what I'm looking for.'

Georgie and Flick watched in horror as tears welled up in her eyes, and Georgie handed her a tissue from the box in her drawer. The woman took it and dabbed delicately at her nose. Flick took in the Patek Philippe watch on her slim wrist. This was class.

'I understand ... or, at least, I've heard,' she faltered, 'that you run a very discreet service. The thing is, it's my husband.'

'It often is,' muttered Flick under her breath, earning herself a sidelong admonishing look from Georgie.

'He is, or at least he can be, very cruel, and I don't know what to do.' She stopped and there was silence.

'Cruel?' Flick said slowly, trying to encourage her to go on. 'Do you mean he hurts you? Because if so, we're not the people you should be talking to.'

'No, no,' she assured them quickly, then sniffed elegantly. 'It's mental cruelty. I'm sure that in the past he has had many lovers and I'm equally sure he still has.'

'How can you be sure?' Georgie asked gently. 'I mean, do you have evidence?'

There was a tired smile. 'Oh, yes. Mobile phone messages that he quickly deletes. Women have even called our house. Our *home*,' she emphasised. 'I've found things too ... receipts from restaurants, you know. That sort of thing.' She seemed to droop under the weight of her sadness and she looked down at her hands and fell silent.

'Well,' Flick pulled the lid off her pen, suddenly uncomfortable with this woman's despair. She was tired too, and quite keen to head home for a glass of wine and a takeaway. 'We can certainly help. We've actually got quite a good track record on the bring-them-to-heel front. If you can give us some details we'll put together a plan. All totally anonymous of course, but,' she smiled her best saleswoman smile, 'guaranteed to give him a gentle reminder that he's not being nice, if you know what I mean—'

'No, I don't want a gentle reminder,' the woman had an edge to her voice now. 'What I need is proof – something he can't deny – that he's been seeing other women. I want to show the bastard that he can't treat me like this. I want concrete proof.' She began to shred the tissue in her lap, and tears spilled out of her eyes. 'He can be very difficult, and he's so clever with words. He leaves me out of my depth and ...' she opened her hands and shrugged to demonstrate her size, 'and if he got angry, what could I do against a man who is over six foot and so strong?'

Flick and Georgie were silent, Georgie's sideways glance to Flick indicating that she agreed they might be out of their depth here. 'Why don't you leave him?' Georgie asked eventually. 'I mean, you would have good grounds for divorce. Adultery – unreasonable behaviour, even – though I'm no lawyer.'

The woman looked down at the tissue in her lap again. 'He is a very important man, with influential friends. All I want is to make sure that I get what I deserve. To get some recognition for the hell I've been through. Tolerating his behaviour. And,' she leaned forward earnestly, 'I need evidence so I can clear my name when he says terrible things about me. No one would believe me without proof. I've given my all to him.' She stumbled over her words and her eyes were full of tears again. 'I'm good for nothing and no one else will want me now.'

'Bloody Nora,' sighed Georgie eloquently when they'd finally ushered Alison Houghton out of the office. She'd made her way through several more of Georgie's stock of Kleenex, sobbing through an account of years of misery. She had wanted children so much, she'd explained, and had done everything to try and persuade her husband, Ben, to have a family but he wouldn't hear of it, claiming they were fine as they were and that children would stop them being able to holiday where and when they felt like it.

'He has never understood how much it meant to me. You must understand that, as women?' she'd struggled to get the words out and had looked up beseechingly at Flick who'd muttered something she hoped sounded understanding. Georgie, though, had waded in.

'Oh God, yes,' she'd said, with an edge to her voice that startled Flick. 'Men just don't feel it, do they?'

Now Alison had left, they both sat in silence.

'Well, I think that's her real name at least,' said Georgie at last.

'It must be. I mean, she gave us all the details about where to find Ben, didn't she? So we'd have to know his name and everything. It would be easy enough to find out if she had made up an identity.'

'She's putting a lot of trust in us though,' Georgie frowned. 'I mean, getting us to trail him. That scares me a bit.'

'Me too. She really ought to just divorce him. Take him to the cleaners.'

'She's scared, Flick. Can't you see that?'

'Mmm,' Flick slipped on her coat and picked up her bag. 'Yup, I guess so. I meant to ask how she'd heard of us. She didn't mention it, did she? Anyway, off home, you, and tomorrow I'll go and see if I can find out a bit more about Mr Ben Houghton.'

Georgie got in late the following morning. They'd had to go back home to pick up Libby's PE kit which she'd left in the hall and, by the time she'd found somewhere to park and pushed in through the office door, Flick and Joanna were on the phone being busy. Flick hung up and handed over a Post-it note with a flourish. 'Here you are, Mrs Part-Timer. Brand-new client – and,' she added in a theatrical whisper, 'Not one of the revengey ones, either. This sounds strictly, and boringly, legit – *and* it's practically on your way home. He sounds rather sexy, actually – his name's Tim Rowlands. A bit distracted, though. He said he was at the airport. Anyway, he's paid by credit card upfront and he's asked for someone to be at his place to collect the keys at three so we can get in to check the phone's been connected. He's had a nightmare with BT.'

'Right. OK,' Georgie stretched out her hand for the Post-it note distractedly while attempting to concentrate on a list in front of her on the desk. 'You're sure about that? Did he say exactly what he wants? No sugar in the oil of a love rival's car or anything?'

'Nah – just the usual sort of agency member,' Flick sighed, looking through a pile of papers at her elbow. 'He's been living in Stuttgart but is moving back to London – his family too, presumably. But he's going to be away quite a bit over the next couple of months so he wants us to sort him out. All the usual stuff.' She consulted the planner in front of her and ticked off a list on her fingers. 'Overseeing builders, taking deliveries, that sort of thing. Think it's a refurb.'

'Well deduced, Sherlock!'

Flick swivelled her office chair around to face her computer and started to transcribe the notes she'd taken onto one of their new client forms. 'Don't you try to fill in the gaps about our clients? I mean, when you go into a house for the first time, you can tell a lot about the person who lives there, don't you think?'

'I suppose so,' Georgie nodded, taking a grateful sip of the tea Joanna had just put in front of her. 'I try not to, really, but I suppose we do see a side of our clients that other people don't, especially when they employ us to change how they are into what they want to be seen to be. It's like looking at the back of a tapestry.'

Flick turned to look at Georgie in surprise. 'Oh, get you, all poetic. Well, if Mrs Halliman is a tapestry, I reckon both sides are the back with her, and it's full of moth holes. I still haven't recovered from that missing hamster debacle, you cow.'

Georgie laughed, slightly guiltily and took the print-out for the new job that Flick handed to her. 'Oh yes, I know that street. It's rather nice actually. Very quiet and green. I can go on my way to pick up Lib.' She folded the sheet neatly in half and slipped it into her bag.

She'd only been waiting outside the new client's house for a couple of minutes, but she was already feeling the cold seeping from the pavement through the thin soles of her shoes. She'd scoped out the place as much as she could without alerting the attentions of Neighbourhood Watch. Three steps led up to the front door, which would have been improved by trimmed bay lollipops in Versailles tubs to frame it – although they were notorious thief magnets. Through the leaded lights she could make out a typical lay-out – a staircase straight ahead, white panelled doors leading off a hallway with what looked like the original tiles on the floor. Dark, bulky shapes leaned up against the walls but, basically, it looked like a lovely, if somewhat unloved, traditional family house. She glanced down the street and checked her watch again.

As if on cue, a courier bike skidded to a halt in the road. The rider removed a small package from a shoulder bag, unfolded a piece of paper and read it carefully, then looked at Georgie with amusement on his face. 'I've got a delivery for this address. Do you know anything about it?'

'I ... don't know, to be honest. I'm supposed to be meeting someone with a key to the house but whoever it is should be here by now and I don't have a contact number so I can't get in to accept the delivery. Hang on. I'll phone the office and see.' She took her phone from her pocket but the courier interrupted.

'I think this is for you. Can you sign for it?'

'No, I *can't* take the package because I can't get in.'

The courier laughed. 'No, I think these are the keys, and I think it's you I'm supposed to be giving them to. This is the

68

choice I've got. "Tall, curvy, long legs up to her armpits and straight blonde hair". No offence, but that doesn't sound like you. "Light-brown curly hair. Serious expression. Blue eyes. Short."' He looked her up and down appraisingly. 'Yup. That sounds more like it. Here you are. Sign here, please.'

Georgie tried to grab for the paper. 'Short?! Let me look at that!'

'You'll have to sign first!'

Georgie snatched the pen in exasperation and scribbled her name on a pad next to the address. Once he'd handed over the envelope, the courier rode off without a backward glance, leaving Georgie alone and thoughtful on the pavement

How had the courier known what they looked like? The description of Flick had been bang on, but to call her short! She tutted and, suddenly very aware of her posture, climbed the three steps leading to the front door. It must have been a personal recommendation who'd simply forgotten their names. She drew the set of keys from the envelope and compared them to the locks on the slightly chipped blue door. She selected a large brass key first, slipped it into the lock, where it turned easily, then the Yale key. Bracing herself to push the door open, she muttered a quick prayer that the mysterious owner hadn't left the burglar alarm on, then turned and pushed.

There was no ear-splitting klaxon, and Georgie felt herself relax as she closed the door behind her and looked around. The place was virtually empty – no carpet, no pictures and, from what she could see, no furniture, or at least, not any in use. The dark shapes she had seen were all bubble-wrapped parcels, waiting to be opened up and positioned. There was a smell of sawdust and something else, familiar but elusive. Something tangy and sharp. Lime? It was quiet and Georgie felt very aware of the sound of her footsteps on the tiles. Moving cautiously forward, she tried the doors leading from the hallway – a front room, cool and north-facing, with the original fireplace and large windows overlooking the road, completely bare; mirror image room on the other side of the stairs, but with no fireplace. She closed the doors behind her and moved on towards the rear of the house. A large L-shaped kitchen and family room that must have been knocked through, with three long windows letting in the late spring sunshine. There was a phone on the side and she picked it up. The dialling tone was clear as a bell. Job done.

Still half an hour until she had to pick up Libby. She wandered over to the window that looked out onto a garden and, beyond that, what looked like playing fields. Suddenly the geography made sense – these were the grounds of the school Libby would probably end up going to.

Georgie leaned against the casement in the sunshine and watched. A group of teenagers was standing around in green tracksuit bottoms, listening to a man who was gesticulating as he spoke. A couple of boys were pushing and shoving at the back but, at the man's signal, they all went off in the direction he pointed, picking up bats, cones and sashes as they went.

She shook herself and checked her watch. She really had to get on, but there was something about the atmosphere of quiet in this place that made her want to sit down with a book and a cup of tea. She turned and scanned the room. Now this, at least, appeared to have been lived in. A large, cream retro-style fridge hummed against the wall next to another door that led, on inspection, to a scullery – again almost bare apart from pasta shapes in matching glass jars and some olives. A wooden wine rack on the floor contained a selection of bottles of red. She returned to the kitchen. Like everything else she'd seen so far, this room was painted white and the smell suggested it had been fairly recently done. The house was, basically, a blank canvas but it had a homely atmosphere despite its impersonality. The other kitchen fittings were serviceable but certainly not new and must have come with the house.

A large, heavy oak table took up most of the short side of the L. So far, only two chairs, also in what looked like oak, were tucked underneath but they had a simplicity that matched the room perfectly. So far, Georgie – who, like Flick, had fun making deductions about clients – had no sense of the person who lived here, but in the corner, next to a large leather armchair, was a small table with a photograph frame on it. She went to take a closer look. A tall, dark-haired man and a brown-haired woman, wearing sunglasses, on a windy beach. She was holding a small boy, a little younger than Libby. They were all smiling – the man and woman at the camera, the boy at the woman. It could have been Cornwall. They were all wearing striped tops. Unable to stop herself, Georgie picked it up and sank into the armchair. Even more comfortable than it looked, it enveloped her, giving her a sense of safety and security that she didn't even try to analyse. The man looked vaguely familiar. Where had she seen him before? Georgie settled back into the chair and tucked her legs up underneath her, wondering about this lovely, empty, silent house and the people who would live here. She smiled, thinking what Libby would say – that she was like Goldilocks sitting on the comfy chair. But she allowed herself to relax, just for a moment, fairly confident that the bears were in Stuttgart.

Chapter Seven

Flick wasn't familiar with this part of town, it was much too posh to be her manor, and the agency had no clients at all north of the river. She pulled into a space and squirmed in her seat to find a sign that confirmed this was permit-holder parking only. She knew it would be, but it was well after eight now and she'd have time to move off quickly if a traffic warden came. Did they work this late anyway?

She killed the engine and pulled her coat further round her. The wind was cold today, coming east straight off the river and, with the engine off, the interior of the car soon cooled. She kept the radio on low, unsure of how long she'd have to wait. She felt shifty and was on the alert for anyone walking past in case they would guess she shouldn't be there. She'd be so obvious in a car that was ten years older than any parked around her. But the street, one of those delightful and exclusive Chelsea streets with rows of immaculate houses, was relatively quiet. People were shutting curtains in what seemed to Flick to be the epitome of elegance – upstairs drawing rooms. Where the odd curtains were left open, she could see sumptuous sofas and clever lighting, with large and original artwork on the walls.

This was hedge-fund manager country, she supposed, or the odd writer or aristo who'd been here since the sixties or before, and would never be able to buy here now. She thought about Mitcham and the semis – oh, to have been born with a silver spoon in your mouth.

Flick snuggled further down in her seat and thought about

the information Alison had given them. Ben Houghton was no hedge-fund manager or aristo, it seemed, but had made his money through clever and well-timed property development. Apparently Alison had met him ten years ago at a party, and Flick could imagine her looking irresistibly pretty with her big blue eyes and clear complexion. He'd lived in a bachelor pad in Chelsea Harbour in those days and she'd sketched out a life of endless partying and holidays on the Med with friends who owned yachts. They now had a *gîte* in the Dordogne and a pad in New York when she'd begged for the Hamptons. At this point Alison had welled up again and admitted how she'd just wanted to be at home, perhaps buying a place in the country and keeping chickens, creating a garden and making babies. Flick couldn't quite imagine Alison in an apron pinning nappies on the line and watching a chubby toddler tottering over the lawn, but perhaps her delicate elegance came from years of urban living. Flick yawned and looked in the rear-view mirror. What did *she* feel about chickens and nappies and country gardens? Queasy.

She glanced at the clock. Alison had texted to say Ben would be home about eight-thirty, and had told her he was going out again soon after – she knew not where – and that he had a dark-blue BMW. Their house, number seventeen, was one with the curtains still open and Flick watched the windows for a while, wondering what Alison was up to. Making dinner for her errant husband? Something delicious from the Harrods Food Hall? The long upstairs windows were framed with cream curtains held back with large tasselled tie-backs. She could see the edge of a cream sofa and a fine fireplace with ornaments laid out with military precision. Christ, if *she* had a cream sofa it would have been covered in chicken chow mein from day one.

Just at that moment Alison came to the window and peered out. She couldn't see Flick – how would she know what car to look for? – so Flick flashed her lights quickly and Alison waved before loosening the tie-backs and closing the curtains.

It was nearly eight forty-five and the *Ask the Doctor* pro-
gramme on the radio was deep into teenage pregnancy before
lights swung round the corner behind her and were caught
in her rear-view mirror. The car passed her, slowed, and she
recognised the BMW badge and the registration number that
matched the one Alison had given her. There was a space two in
front of Flick and as his reversing lights came on, she slid further down her seat, until she could only peer over the steering
wheel. He parked smoothly and with confidence and, through
the windows of the car parked between them, she could see
the back of his head as he gathered things from the passenger
seat.

Flick held her breath as eventually she heard the car door
open and he climbed out. Or rather unfolded. Alison was right
about his height. He must have been six foot three or four and
whilst she'd been expecting a city suit and even a long cashmere
coat – wasn't that what sharp property developers wore? – in
the darkness she could make out a loose shirt and jeans. She
couldn't see his face because he had his back to her until he
turned and shut the car door and, in the glow from the interior
light, she could make out a strong face with short, well-kept
hair that was brushed off a high forehead.

The indicator lights flashed to show he'd locked the car on
the remote and, picking up his briefcase, he turned to cross the
street to number seventeen. By the time he came out again at
nine-thirty, Flick needed a pee and was beginning to squirm in
her seat. She hoped to God he wasn't heading off somewhere
miles away because she didn't think her bladder would hold
out. She waited as long as was safe without losing him before
she pulled out of the parking space, and tried to keep a couple
of cars behind him, but one set of rear lights looks pretty much
like another, and her knowledge of the back end of cars was even
shakier than the front. Dangerously missing the side of a taxi
that was trying to undercut her, and being honked at by several
other cars as she navigated Sloane Square, she eventually saw

him indicate left. She slowed down, hoping that her headlights would make her unrecognisable, and then followed.

The street was narrow, narrower than she had hoped, and to her horror she saw it had a dead-end. She stopped and watched, helpless, as he parked. His car lights were turned off and he climbed out of the car, pulling a small case with him. Flick froze. Should she reverse? Then she wouldn't see where he was going to go. Clicking the remote, he locked the car and for one ridiculous moment, she thought he hadn't spotted her. Then, halfway across the narrow street, he stopped as if he'd forgotten something, turned his head and looked straight at Flick's car. Heart pounding, she slipped even further down her seat.

He stood immobile for what felt like an age, then turned on his heel briskly and rang the doorbell of a building on the other side. It wasn't until she had reversed out and was halfway down the King's Road again that she breathed out.

She couldn't tell Georgie about this mess up. Less Cagney and Lacey. More Laurel and Hardy.

To Georgie and Flick's relief, the next case that came in appeared less complicated and emotional – ground they could cope with. A City property surveyor with a penchant for naked flesh. His wife, Sara, had stumbled on his membership card for a less-than respectable 'gentleman's club', and his account with an online porn site that apparently made Readers' Wives look like the WI. He was clearly nothing but tacky, with a soft spot for cleavage and no qualms about paying for it. Sara made no bones about her distaste, but she was nothing if not pragmatic.

'Silly old sod. It's his hormones,' she explained frankly. 'Male menopause, if you like. A typical mid-life crisis and I want to bring him to his senses. Make him see how stupid he looks. Embarrass him so he daren't misbehave again. I'll leave it up to you, but let me know what you decide to do!' Her eyes had sparkled with the idea of getting her own back and, for fun, Flick had handed over their agency business card, having changed 'Domestic' to 'Avenging' with a flourish.

Flick and Georgie got through a whole bottle of wine before they came up with a suitable revenge, and the following day, after consultation with Sara about her husband's social diary, Georgie was on the phone actioning the plan.

'Yes, I realise it must be a bit unusual,' Georgie laughed nervously, her fingers clenching her mobile tightly as though she could will the manager of the pole-dancing club to agree. In the cold light of day she was now having her reservations. It had seemed such a good idea last night to use video evidence to nail Sara Jackson's lecherous husband and post it on YouTube for all the world to see – but now Georgie wasn't so sure. Even to herself she sounded unconvincing and she could virtually feel Flick cringing beside her as she drove. The voice in her ear made no effort to conceal its amusement and she had a horrible feeling she might have been put on speakerphone so he could share the joke with everyone. They'd agreed that she'd only offer money as a last resort, but she was getting nowhere fast.

Georgie glanced across at Flick, who was peering at street names, shadowed by neatly clipped and glossy laurel leaves. Even the hedges looked expensive in this part of Wimbledon, the locale of the type of *über* families with trophy children who were given the type of birthday parties Flick and she were about to prepare for.

The manager spoke again, in the accent she suspected he reserved for his clients rather than for his employees. 'Well, it might be possible. Just might I stress, Mrs – er —'

'It's Miss,' Georgie blurted. 'Miss Smith.'

Beside her, Flick shook her head. The manager laughed. 'Yes, I rather thought it would be. Look, love, can I be honest here? You say this is a long-held ambition to pole-dance and, to you, it's probably just a bit of a laugh. But it is a considerable inconvenience to me personally, you understand. For a start, it's against all my regulations. What if you was to fall over and

76

break your leg. God forbid, someone else's. What then? Not so funny now, is it?'

They hadn't considered this. 'What if we were to sign something to say we'd take all responsibility ourselves. A sort of waiver?'

There was an audible snort. 'Come off it, love. What are you going to sign? Alias Smith and Jones? I wasn't born yesterday, y'know. I'd be putting myself to a lot of trouble for you and your friend, see what I mean?'

Flick was starting to slow and indicate left. Georgie had to clinch this deal – and fast. 'OK, I can see where you're coming from. How about if we cover some of your expenses, the extra insurance and so on?'

The voice warmed up, but still tried to sound dubious. 'To be honest, there is another thing, love. This is a respectable establishment and we have a reputation to maintain. I pick my, erm, representatives with care. Hand-pick 'em. I can't let my standards drop, even for a short session. Do you see what I'm getting at?'

Georgie felt more confident here. 'I don't think you need to worry about that. I am a professional dancer and I think I can assure you that the standard of performance will be more than adequate.' Flick had stopped now in front of a gated driveway.

'Yeeees, that's all very well, but that's not all there is to it.'

Georgie tried not to sound impatient. 'Well, what else? Can you be specific? I'm a little bit pushed for time at the moment and I'd like to get this confirmed.'

'Well, I'll be perfectly frank. From your voice, I'm guessing that you're what – in your thirties? My clients are very particular. Be honest, love, you're not a minger, are you?'

Georgie spluttered, incensed. 'Minger!' Flick jerked her head round and nearly accelerated into the gate. 'No, *no*, certainly not! No one's ever said I am, anyway.'

'Well, I'll have to take your word for that, love, but I might have to make a decision on the night. I can't have any old slag turning up to dance at my club. I have my standards, y'know.'

Flick, barely able to contain her laughter, inched her way up the drive as the gates opened remotely, but the porticoed front door was already open and a slender, fair-haired girl in jeans – presumably the nanny – was waiting for them. 'Yes, all right,' Georgie replied tartly. 'We'll come in time for you to make a decision.'

'OK, and Miss … er, Smith, cash only please, but you get to keep anything the punters slip you.' Georgie shuddered at the thought and clicked off the phone.

'Bloody hell,' Georgie fumed, batting away the pink metallic helium balloon that had been bobbing at the back of her head. 'The nerve! He only wants to give me the once-over.'

Flick was rocking with silent mirth. 'Give you one, more like. You know,' she cried at last. 'I think we can finally call it quits after Mrs Halliman's hamster.'

Georgie looked at her quellingly. 'Well, you're bloody coming with me 'cos you're the camera woman.'

'Oh, believe me, I wouldn't miss it for the world!' Flick sniggered as they climbed out of the car.

The Wimbledon nanny was a piece of work. Her meek looks were deceptive and, as Georgie and Flick set to work attaching balloons and yards of pink netting to the walls of the conservatory for little Bryony's birthday party, she filled them in on the finer details of life in the family, in a broad Middlesbrough accent, while fielding a stream of calls from her employer from the bank where she worked.

'And the caterers – the trouble we've had with them! It's all gluten-free and lactose-free and gourmet and organic. And the kids won't eat any of it, y'know. My little brother – when he has a party, all me mum does is crisps, grapes and choccie fingers, and they eat the lot. This little madam and her friends, they'd look at it and turn up their snotty little noses, I'd bet you.'

The doorbell rang at the same time as the phone. The girl tutted. 'That'll be the magician or the face-painting artists or the juggler or the snake-petting zoo. Honestly, as if I didn't have enough to do!' She strolled off, answering the phone with a bright, 'Hi, Miranda – yes, the food looks lovely and the decorators have almost finished.'

Flick and Georgie exchanged glances as they attached a piñata – a huge purple unicorn – to the ceiling so that it hung at a suitable height for six-year-olds. 'Did I hear snake-petting? She's a charmer that one,' Flick observed. 'I thought all nannies came from the Eastern Bloc and were subservient, grateful and doting.'

'So did the mother, apparently. Miss Congeniality filled me in while you were out fetching the ribbons from the car. She's had a run of bad luck with foreign girls. One got banged up by the pool boy, one seemed to have her eye on Mr Miranda, and one never stopped crying so she's resorted to sturdy northern stock in desperation. Apparently, having a British nanny is a bit of a status symbol round here now, because they're so much more expensive than foreign girls and they demand more in the way of perks, so you have to be mega-rich to afford one.'

Flick laughed. 'Oh, I get it. Like the way it's posher to holiday in the Scillies now, rather than the Caribbean, since it got so common.'

'Yes, and that place in Dorset that's got the most expensive property prices in the world?'

Flick snorted and tied a bow around a standard fuchsia in a white planter. 'It's all just status though, isn't it? I mean, look at this place. Look, even the floor tiles are fabulous. Haven't these people ever heard of B&Q? And it's as if the kid is just another acquisition.' The phone shrilled and they heard the nanny soothing her employer, yet again. 'I bet you anything that woman won't be here until the very end.'

'If at all,' Georgie agreed grimly. 'I mean, what could be more important than actually being there for your kids? All the money in the world can't make up for missing your daughter's sixth birthday party. Do you remember Libby's?'

'How could I forget? I wonder if the goats at that city farm have recovered from the stress yet?'

'I doubt it – and you were no bloody help.'

Flick took a swipe at the piñata, which swung wildly to and fro. 'Well, what do I know about little girls? And come on, I did do the run for multipacks of Hula Hoops and Kit Kats from the Tesco over the road! I can wield a credit card, can't I?'

Georgie laughed. 'All right. You were indispensable. Anyway, you did better than Ed's efforts. He was too busy trying to avoid the little buggers.'

'Perhaps he was worried about getting muck on his Paul Smith.' She got a quelling look from Georgie. 'Sorry. I bet there won't be any more visits from the stork for *this* lot. Far too high-powered. That wouldn't fit in with the brilliant career, would it?'

Georgie looked down. 'Even the not-so-high-powered can't always get the stork to pay a visit on demand.'

Flick paused for a moment. 'Crikey, George. I had no idea. I mean, no idea you were having trouble conceiving. Have you been having treatment?'

Georgie busied herself with tying balloons together in bunches. 'Oh it's not that. Least, I don't think it is. We're perfectly able, it's just that Ed's not willing.'

Flick laughed. 'Men need a good nudge from what I've heard. Can't you just jump him? You know, forget your cap and just let nature take its course? He'd hardly cast you out on the streets, now would he?'

Georgie hoped she wasn't blushing. She was remembering that night last week when Ed had come in late from being away in Cardiff and she was reading in bed after a long bath. She hadn't exactly jumped him, more snuggled suggestively. He'd been tired, but after a while he'd responded, once she'd slung a leg over his thigh, breathed on his neck a bit and put her hand in strategic places. And although she was ashamed she hadn't bothered to put in her cap, it had been the wrong time of the month so it wasn't really a risk. That was a million miles away from setting about getting pregnant deliberately, as Flick was suggesting. That would just have been wrong.

'It wouldn't be fair,' Georgie shrugged. 'He's struggling to pay for the boys as it is. And I wouldn't want to have another baby if he wasn't totally committed. It wouldn't be fair on anyone. And I have got Libs.' Georgie knew she was rationalising it, but as long as she kept her head in charge of her heart, she'd be OK. 'Not like poor Alison Houghton. I can't believe that husband of hers not wanting a family. He should have told her before they even married. You know, I think that's even grounds for annulment, not agreeing to let her have any children at all. She should just ditch him, in my opinion.' Georgie glanced over at Flick, who seemed engrossed in the range of sushi the caterers had delivered, then continued slowly. 'We need to action Operation Surveillance on that one.'

The knotty problem of how to observe Ben Houghton had been looming in the background for a couple of weeks now, and Georgie was beginning to regret they'd taken it on.

Flick shrugged dismissively and stepped back to look round the decorated conservatory. 'Not bad. Not bad at all,' she nodded. 'We need to know a bit more about his movements first.'

'He sounds like a nasty piece of work, for sure.' Georgie picked up her handbag. 'Are we done here, then? Let's try to escape before the little darlings get back from school. Maybe we can talk about it in the car on the way to Tim Rowland's house. The plumbers have been at it since the start of the week and I'd like to see how they're getting on.'

'Oh, yes. The mysterious Mr Rowlands. Yes, I'd like to see his place. It obviously made an impression on you. Let's just get the nanny to check this over before we leave.'

After a short search, they found the nanny unashamedly bidding on eBay for a latex clubbing dress. They waited patiently until she'd won it – against some lively competition – and refused her offer of a glass of wine while she scrutinised their efforts. 'Honestly, don't worry about it. There's plenty more in the cellar. They get through it like nobody's business and they don't even notice when me friends come round during the day for lunch and we help ourselves.'

Georgie shuddered, torn between irritation with this mouthy girl, so ungrateful for the perks of her job, and feeling Miranda, the mother of the house, thoroughly deserved it. The only innocent in the whole sorry affair was little Bryony and it was probably only a matter of time until she was spoiled beyond all salvation. The cost of the gift bags they'd put together for the guests over the last week was far more than Georgie had paid for Lib's whole sixth birthday party, plus all her presents from her and Ed. Georgie remembered Lib at six – how little she'd been and how round – and the familiar ache came over her again. Maybe Flick was right. Maybe she should just present Ed with a done deal. But that was unrealistic. She couldn't work full-time with another baby, their income would drop and there'd be greater pressure than ever on him. She sighed deeply, grateful that Flick was taking charge of the sign-off on their party make-over.

The nanny was completely satisfied. 'It's lovely.' she shrugged. 'I just wish it was for someone who'd appreciate it. Honestly – more money than sense, this lot.'

Georgie sighed again. And I have got more sense than money, she thought.

Flick found a parking space right outside Tim Rowland's house. Once again, Georgie was struck by how quiet the road was and she could hear, quite clearly, the chirping of birds hidden among the leaves of the trees and hedges, making homes for the winter. The front door was open and dust sheets were carefully laid on the floor. Mick Hodges was Georgie and Flick's first choice of plumber from their carefully compiled list and the one they always asked to take on anything tricky.

They called their hellos, and made their way carefully up the stairs. Georgie found it particularly satisfying to see the house start to take shape. Tim had evidently been back here a few times – the place seemed more lived in – and she'd found the occasional note in strong handwriting left for her on the kitchen table, only ever signed from 'Tim'.

Ahead of her, Flick gasped. 'Mick, it's fantastic! What beautiful tiles. What stone is it? Granite?'

Georgie peeped over Flick's shoulder and her mouth fell open. Talk about smart! Even with the dust and the floorboards up, it was perfect in a way you only expect from interiors magazines and so different from the neo-Georgian vulgarity of the house they had just left. Mick straightened up, grinning. 'Fantastic, innit? It is granite, you only get it from one place in Northumberland or something. Cost a bloody fortune too. And underfloor heating, Very nice of a winter morning, I should think. And look at these taps. Grand each. Can you believe it? Italian handbasin. Delivered special this morning. I tell you what, they've got some taste, this lot. He's nice though. No side to him.'

Georgie nodded as she gazed at the newly installed wet room. It was stunning yet simple at the same time. Mick pointed out the tall heated towel rack, the lighting units, still wrapped and waiting for the electrician, and was at pains to show them how carefully he was dealing with this posh gear. Impressed, Georgie led the way back to the car, pausing on the threshold to take another look. In a way she'd be sad once this project was over and she no longer had an excuse to come here and just revel in the comforting atmosphere of the house.

Flick tutted as she did up her seatbelt. 'Nice pad. Wonder who he is.'

The question had been plaguing Georgie since that first encounter with the courier and they'd debated it many times over the intervening weeks. In a way, she'd got to the point where she'd almost rather not know, in case it was a disappointment.

They pushed through the office door with the leftover ribbons clutched in their arms and found Joanna looking unusually pink, and talking animatedly to a man sitting with his back to them and, embarrassingly, in Georgie's chair with all its photos of Libby arranged on her desk in full view. As they stumbled to a halt, the man unfolded himself and turned round expectantly.

He extended a long, strong hand to Flick. 'Hello, I just wanted to come and thank you in person for all your help.'

Suddenly, it clicked. He was the man in the photograph. 'You're bow tie man!' Georgie exclaimed.

He laughed. 'Is that how I'm known around here? Yes, that's right. I was so impressed by your skills, I had to entrust my whole house to you. I'm Tim Rowlands.'

Georgie laughed too. Now it all made sense. 'Hello. I'm the short one.'

He roared with laughter this time. 'Yes, I remember you well.'

'Well, you're clearly better at interior design than you are at dressing yourself!'

'You should see me with cuff links. You need another pair of hands to put those in.' Georgie could feel a little plan growing in her head. Wouldn't he be just perfect for Flick?

'So has your family not arrived from abroad yet?' she asked audaciously. No point in beating about the bush.

He didn't seem affronted. 'No, they'll stay out in Stuttgart. This is my base from now on, but I'll be backwards and forwards all the time.'

That plan was up the spout then. 'We love your house,' she gushed. 'I'm afraid we've been terribly nosey snooping about – but are you happy with the work so far?'

'Delighted.' He looked at them both. 'I was wondering – I deal with major refurbs all the time. I'm a designer, you see – and I wondered if you've got any spare capacity to oversee jobs I'm running, like you have with mine. Coordinating – that sort of thing. It's a bit of an unusual request, I know.'

Flick's snort was audible. 'Meat and drink to us – and believe

84

me, we've had odder requests. We'd be delighted. Wouldn't we, George?'

Encouraged by Flick's enthusiasm for Tim, Georgie smiled. 'Let's sit down and discuss it, shall we?'

Chapter Eight

Two days later, the girls were doing some serious research for the hit on Sara Jackson's husband and his penchant for scantily clad women. 'Oh bloody hell,' Georgie slumped back in her chair as she and Flick watched the video playing on her computer in silence. *Pole-Dancing For Beginners* was a jerky film of three girls demonstrating the right moves, interspersed with helpful advice about appropriate clothes and what to wear on your feet.

'Trainers! I don't think that'll go down too well at the Kasbar, do you? I suppose I'll have to dig out some outrageous heels and a bikini.' Georgie sighed in distress, and clicked on *Pole-Dancing for Intermediates*. 'The Kick-up Invert? We didn't do *that* at dancing college.'

Flick laughed. 'And there was me thinking pole-dancing involved people from Warsaw. Not very subtle, is it?' She too slumped back in her seat. 'Men, hey? You have to admire the little darlings. Direct link between their eyes and their genitals. Do Not Pass Go. Do Not Collect £200. Stick a silly slapper in front of them wearing next to nothing, wrapping herself suggestively round a giant phallic symbol, and the thrills come cheap.'

'All right, Mrs Cynical,' said Georgie eventually. 'But the only difference here is that, this time, I'm the silly slapper, and Jackson's bloody wife is going to pay through the nose for this.'

'Mum, have you got—' What are you two looking at?' As Libby came up behind her mother, Georgie was a fraction too slow closing the page on the computer. 'Oh, pole-dancing. I can do that.'

Georgie's mouth dropped open. 'What! What do you know about it?

Libby waved her hand airily. 'Oh, on MTV. Loads of videos have it. Look, I'll show you.' Before they could stop her, she belted into the kitchen and came back with a broom, then proceeded to squirm and gyrate around it clumsily, her little pot belly thrusting in and out. It was halfway between sweet and grotesque and Flick tried very hard to suppress a laugh. Georgie's face was a picture of horror.

'God, what am I raising here?'

'Trouble, from where I'm looking,' replied Flick, crossing her arms.

'Come on – in the bath pronto, before your father comes home. And don't let him see you do that!' She scooted her daughter out of the room and halfway up the stairs. 'On second thoughts, perhaps she should,' Georgie said, coming back into the room. 'He might realise stumping up for a posh school is the only salvation to keep her off the streets and falling in with a pole-dancing crowd of fallen women.'

Flick topped up her own and Georgie's glass from the side in the kitchen, picked a cold chip off the plate Libby had left and sat herself down on the sofa in the corner of the room. It was as uncomfortable as it looked, with a low back and hard seat. The ones in the sitting room were even worse. Why did Ed find it so important to place design above comfort? What the hell else was a chair for, except to relax in? This would have worked well in a dentist's waiting room.

Georgie picked up Libby's plate and scraped the leftovers into the bin that was secreted away in the sideboard and slid out with a hiss.

'Cool bin.'

'Yeah, but it's too small and I end up emptying it every five minutes.'

'Don't tell me, the dirty plate will now be whipped out of your hand into an invisible dishwasher?'

'Oh, it's all clever stuff,' Georgie smiled and shot a very quick look at Flick that Flick couldn't quite read. Georgie then wiped the side, picked up her glass and curled up next to Flick on the sofa. Perhaps that was the secret to making the damned thing comfortable enough to sit on – she was petite enough to be able to do it though. Flick would have to contort herself into some sort of yoga position.

They sat side by side in companionable silence for a moment. Despite being together so much of the day, there was rarely time to really chat and Flick had lost touch with Georgie's home life. She missed the evenings they'd spent in the early days putting the business together, poring over the business plan and spreadsheets. They'd agreed from the start that an agency to handle those little domestic chores for the money-rich, time-poor would be a winner and the hard work had paid off. But, in doing so, they'd created a monster that was taking up all their time. Georgie hardly ever came over to Flick's place, always having to be at home for Libby when Ed was invariably working late, and Flick was aware, too, that she avoided visits to Georgie's. Was it just the chairs, or was it that she didn't relish the thought of being there when Ed came home and it was all Happy Families?

'So, do you reckon you can do it? The pole thing, I mean.'

Georgie took another sip and rested her head back against the wall. 'Well, how hard can it be? It's ages since I went to dancing college but it's like riding a bike, isn't it?'

'Poor choice of expression, if I might say so!'

Georgie looked confused for a moment, then threw her head back and laughed, and Flick realised she hadn't seen her do that in ages. 'I'll just try to think sex goddess. Shouldn't be hard for a girl like me!' Her eyes twinkled with laughter.

'Sex gnome, more like!'

Georgie slapped Flick's arm. 'Haven't had any complaints so

far, thank you very much. I'm no minger, me!' At that moment there was a draught as the front door opened and Ed let himself in.

'Hello, ladies,' he bent over to kiss his wife, then put a cold cheek against Flick's. He smelt of the outdoors and something sweet. Flick was never quite sure about aftershave, it being such a fine line between refined and utterly vile, and this fragrance was too floral on Ed. This evening he looked like Beethoven, his wiry hair made even more chaotic by the strong winds outside. He unwrapped the scarf from round his neck and shook off his long tweed coat, throwing it over the minimalist hatstand in the hallway.

'How's life with you, Flick?' Ed asked distractedly, rifling through the post he'd picked up from the hall table. 'Any advance on the love life?' He ran a thick finger under the flap of an envelope and pulled out the contents.

'Oh you know, usual thing. Everybody wants me—'

'And are they getting you?' he asked dryly under his breath, failing to be funny. Tosser. 'Oh, George.' Ed looked up from his letter. 'Coleman says he can do the new lighting for the bathroom at cost, so I've ordered two from him when he does the Milan fair.'

'Oh, right.' Georgie's brow furrowed. 'Will they really be that wonderful?'

Ed's hands dropped to his sides as if Georgie was being totally dense. 'Oh God, yes. They are stunning. They'll *make* that room. I'm trying to persuade some other clients to incorporate them too. Fantastic wash of light so, even though they aren't cheap, they'll be so worth it.' His face was excited like a small boy's.

Georgie smiled gently. 'I'm sure they'll be perfect.'

As Flick made her way home in the dark, peering through the wipers at the rain which had made gigantic puddles she couldn't resist driving through, she wondered why Georgie gave in so easily to Ed's bullying. Because that's what it was, giving Georgie no chink through which to make an objection to any of his ideas. The more Flick thought about it, the more convinced she became. Everything in that house was Ed's and there was barely any sign of Georgie's personality in it at all. Flick had never known Georgie in her former life, she had been introduced by a mutual friend at a girly supper when she was with Ed, so she had no idea what Georgie's style was exactly. She had a strong suspicion, though. On the odd occasion they'd been shopping together – usually a spontaneous affair when they'd been working close to an antiques market or some bijou south London shops – she'd seen Georgie make a bee-line for things that were pretty and delicate. A couple of years ago she'd agonised over a beautiful French mirror with ornate carving that they'd found in a junk shop in Southfields, then changed her mind with the excuse that it was too expensive.

Wouldn't pass the Ed test, more like. As she turned into her road, Flick mused on the joys of living alone with the freedom to decorate exactly as she wanted to. She let herself into the dark flat, and flicked on the lights. It felt chilly, despite the heating being on, and she pushed through into the kitchen, shoving the half-drunk, cold cup of coffee from this morning further back on the side, dumping a small bag of groceries in front of it. She turned the oven on for the lasagne she'd picked up from Sainsbury's and, going through to the sitting room, noticed the light on the answering machine wasn't flashing. Throwing off her jacket, she turned on the TV. There was bound to be something on she could watch later. She'd have a shower now. That would fill the time while the oven got up to temperature. Then perhaps she'd call her mother.

'You are, of course, joking? That is not funny in the slightest.'

'Swear to God I'm not. I was taking down the curtains at the Railton-Finches' to take to the dry-cleaners and the sodding stepladder slipped.'

'Have you broken it?'

'Don't think so. It's a bad sprain, I expect, but I'm at A&E and the queue of cripples waiting to be seen is hours' long. Libby's going back to a friend's and I should get back about five.'

Flick had sighed. 'We'll just have to ring the club man and make it another night.'

'Flick, we can't!' Georgie had wailed. 'For one, he was so reluctant, if we don't go tonight he'll probably never let us do it. And besides, we know Mr Jackson is going there tonight with his colleagues. His wife just called to confirm. It's our only chance. There's only one option. You'll just have to dance and I'll take the pictures.'

Flick had gasped. 'Now you are being utterly ridiculous.'

'What choice do we have? The club's a brilliant idea and the woman has paid half so we can't back out now. Besides, you're leggy and gorgeous and much more the pole-dancer type than me anyway.'

Flick looked at herself in her bedroom mirror. Sure the legs were long – but dancer she was not. According to her mother, she'd inherited her physique from her grandfather, who had been a navvy. So that was reassuring. Georgie's call from A&E had come in the early afternoon, and Flick now had an hour before she had to pick up Georgie and be at the club. His wife had said Jackson would be there about eleven. Flick's bedroom floor was strewn with beachwear and she was stood in a cheap two-piece she'd bought in Crete a couple of years back. It was vaguely attractive without being outrageously revealing. Her legs and bikini line looked blotchy from an emergency shave and some fake tan she'd found at the back of the cupboard and had slapped on in desperation. They now looked more American tan than fake tan, and her stomach resembled a doughy loaf before it went into the oven. She could only hope the lighting was dim and subtle in the club.

'Flick, old girl, you've let things slip 'cos there ain't a bloke to make an effort for,' she chided herself out loud. Then she groaned. 'Oh fuck – this is ridiculous. What the hell am I doing?' She grabbed some tracksuit bottoms and a top, throwing them on in haste and anger. 'It's too bloody late to be going out now. I just want to go to bed. Why can't this woman just tell her husband where to get off, the filthy bastard.'

She chucked some more make-up into a bag, and at the last minute put in a different bikini too. 'I bet she lives in bloody splendour with white sofas and flat-screen TVs and dinner parties and I bet their kids have a computer and a sodding Playstation in their room and everything they want and no discipline. And she's probably frigid and he's probably lousy in bed and—'. Pulling out a ghastly pair of silver stilettos from the back of the wardrobe that she'd bought for a friend's hen night – theme, WAGS – and never worn again after peeling them off her agonised feet at 4 a.m. after the party, she threw them in her bag too and headed out of the door, slamming it in rage behind her.

'Ouch! Oh thanks, love,' Georgie shifted on the sofa and took a grateful sip of the tea Ed had brought her.

Ed shook his head irritably. 'You should keep that ankle up. Going out is the last thing you should be doing.' He carefully lifted the pack of frozen peas, wrapped in a tea towel, and turned them over so the colder side was against her skin. 'Why can't Flick fend for herself for a change? I thought she was supposed to be Little Miss Independence, after all. Why does she need someone to hold her hand, all of a sudden?'

'It's not that,' Georgie sighed. 'It's just a two-person job, hanging pictures. I'll be sitting down the whole time, just telling her if they're straight or not.' She was amazed how easily the lie had come to her when Ed had started complaining. And he seemed to have swallowed it whole, although if he'd asked why a client should have such a desperate need to have their walls adorned late on a Wednesday night, she'd have been stuck for a convincing reply.

She did feel awful, telling Ed an outright lie. And he'd been so solicitous, picking Libby up from a friend's house after school where she'd had a jolly time while Georgie waited for an X-ray confirming that her ankle wasn't broken, merely badly sprained. When they'd finally arrived home and found her neat, criss-crossed bandage strapping up her swollen ankle, Libby had played nurse and Ed had rallied round and cooked some pasta, although at the last minute he'd stirred in chilli oil that meant Libby refused to eat it.

And now she was insisting on going out. But, no matter how painful the evening was going to be for Georgie, it was going to be far, far worse for Flick.

The club was rocking by the time Georgie and Flick arrived. In her ribcage Flick could feel the thwump thwump of the music that emanated through the doorway. It must be deafening inside, but there were no houses close by to disturb, just a street of flashing neon, ropey-looking shops and brightly lit restaurants disgorging clientele.

'You're absolutely sure he's going to be here tonight?'

Georgie was struggling to keep up with Flick's long strides. 'You've asked that five times at least and yes, according to the text I just got, they left the restaurant ten minutes ago and are due here any minute. Hang on – I can't go that fast.'

Flick slowed down to let peg-leg catch up. 'Sure you've got the Digicam?'

'Yesss,' Georgie sighed, 'though it took a bit of explaining to Ed why I needed it at a picture hanging.'

Flick wasn't listening. She could feel the blood pounding in her head. 'And what does he look like again?'

Georgie laughed. 'Don't you listen to a thing? About six two, balding, rotund, dark-blue shirt.'

'Like that'll make him stand out from the rest of the pervs.' Flick breathed deeply, her stomach churning. 'OK let's get on with it.'

Down in the bowels of the club, the drum 'n' base beat rattled their brains. It was dark, washed with red light, and a round stage in the centre of the room was lit, highlighting two empty poles. A few men sat around the skirt of the stage, chatting, and there were more at the bar that ran the length of the room. Bottles and glasses sparkled, and Flick was sorely tempted to order a double Scotch. Another group of men, with a couple of women, had followed them in and were noisily jostling for service, raising their voices to be heard above the music.

'Excuse me?' Flick shouted into the ear of a passing waitress. 'We're looking for Gary.'

'In the back.' The waitress jerked her head to indicate a door on the other side of the stage. Flick strode over to it, aware that Georgie was hobbling to keep up, and pushed through. So this was the engine room of a seedy pole-dancing club. Three poky little rooms. Through one door, Flick could see a half-dressed girl putting on make-up in a cracked mirror. The next room, more of a cupboard actually, was crammed with cases of wine, alcopops and spirits. Through the half-closed door of the last room Flick could make out a stocky man with his feet up on a small desk that was pushed against a peeling wall on which bits of paper had been stuck with sellotape. The desk was covered in empty paper cups of takeout coffee and papers. He was talking loudly down the phone and, catching Flick out the corner of his eye, turned and, unashamedly, appraised her from head to foot.

'Gotta go, mate. Give you a bell later.'

Lazily he lowered his feet to the floor and clicked off his phone. 'So you're the one who wants to pay to dance then? Is this some kind of *Jim'll Fix It* wish fulfilment?'

'Yeah, something like that,' mumbled Flick.

'It's a present from me for her birthday,' gushed Georgie, as if to make the story more plausible.

'Mmm, right,' he gently threw his phone onto the table. 'The dressing room's next door, Sharon will show you where to put your stuff. You're on from ten forty-five p.m.' He turned away, dismissing them.

'Can I take pictures?' Georgie asked innocently. 'For her album, I mean.'

'No, definitely not. The punters won't like that.'

Flick and Georgie both stopped. 'Right,' said Georgie and turned away.

'Now what?' hissed Flick.

'Leave it to me. I've watched enough *Cook Report*s.'

Half an hour and a quick briefing from the sullen Sharon later, Flick was perched on a broken chair in the dressing room, her hoody top wrapped tightly round her, not quite able to summon up enough courage to reveal her body yet. Sharon had no such qualms, and was smoking a fag and tottering around in her heels and a bikini that appeared to be made of hand-kerchiefs. With her back to Flick, she bent from the waist to rummage in her bag, giving Flick the view that had probably got her the job in the first place.

'You a dancer then?' Sharon asked eventually, as if she couldn't care less.

'Er, not really. I just always wanted to have a go at this.' Flick hoped she sounded convincing.

'Fuck, you must be mad. I do it 'cos it's better than stacking shelves. On Fridays and Saturdays I do Rodeo Joe's.'

'Which is ... ?'

'The lap-dancing club in Deptford. The tips are better.'

'Do they tip then?'

'On a good night. Depends what you let them do to ya.' Flick started to feel very sick indeed. 'Mean buggers here, though, and they're not allowed to touch ya, so tell Gary if they do.'

'You're on!' one of the waitresses shouted from the door. Sharon dropped her fag onto the floor, crushed it under the toe of her stilettos and, double-checking her make-up in the mirror, headed for the door. Flick scrambled to take off her hoody, tried not to glance in the mirror, winced and followed her as quickly as she could.

The seating round the bar and stage had filled whilst she'd been backstage and Flick squinted through the murk. There were a few women, which surprised her, but the majority were blokes, mainly middle-aged and all tanked-up by the expressions on their faces. She couldn't work out which was Jackson.

'I can't do this. I can't do this.' She scanned the room, or as much as she could see of it, to try and find Georgie but, with the lights in her eyes, the back of the room blended into darkness. She did her best to look nonchalant, like an old pro, as it were, adjusting her expression from squint to pouting and sultry.

Sharon, meanwhile, had morphed from fag-smoking slut to vamp, and sashayed up onto the stage. Flick tried to clamber up behind her as seamlessly as she could, but stumbled, grabbing the shoulder of the bloke standing by the steps for balance.

'Cor, darlin',' he roared, glancing at his friend. 'Look, she can't resist me already.'

Flick bolted before he could get his hand on her bum and, following Sharon's lead, curled herself round the other pole. There were whistles and roars of approval from the crowd, all well-oiled now, and Flick tried to mirror Sharon's moves, hoping it would appear as though they had choreographed it so she was supposed to be four beats behind. As she threw her head back wantonly, she tried to scan the rows of men again to see if she could differentiate one chubby, middle-aged punter from another. A task made even harder by the fact that she was doing it upside down. But out of the corner of her eye she spotted Georgie, waving frantically and mouthing at her, pointing downwards onto the head of the man in front of her.

'Very subtle, George,' Flick muttered. Standing upright again – the blood that had rushed to her head, making her see stars – she took a good look at Jackson, their prey. Indistinguishable. Dark shirt bulging over his belly. Pint of beer in his hand

and surrounded by work colleagues, including, Flick noticed, a younger woman in a white shirt and tight-black skirt who was flirting and laughing along with him at some joke. Flick wrapped her leg around the pole and, aware she must appear to be staring, directed her gaze somewhere else to a bloke to her left who, rather alarmingly, had his pint suspended halfway to his mouth and was unable to take his eyes off her. She spun round, intent on mimicking Sharon, but seeing her now thrusting her hips into the pole, changed her mind and, pathetically, wrapped her other leg round the pole, the toe of her insufferably uncomfortable shoes getting caught at the bottom and suddenly tipping her off-balance.

With a sweaty hand she just managed to hold on and, more out of relief than anything else, pulled herself towards the pole and held on as if her life depended on it, hoping it looked like she was seducing the damned thing.

She cast about again for Georgie, who she spotted a few people away from their prey this time, gripping her handbag under her arm and waving it in a suspiciously odd way, and was frantically indicating her watch in the hope of hurrying up Flick's progress towards him. But how could she? Sharon was still doing unmentionable things to her pole – the woman's imagination was immense – and Flick wasn't sure if it was permissible to leave your pole and sally forth propless. But how else was she going to get close enough for Georgie to get them both in shot?

The next track seemed to be endless and Flick was getting more and more bored and more and more frantic, gyrating and pulsating, then suddenly the mood of the music changed to something slower and sexier. Flick almost moaned with relief, Sharon let go of her pole and made her way to the edge of the stage, bending from the waist and displaying her cleavage to the man in front of her, and her backside to the blokes on the other side.

Flick followed suit, making her way across the stage and

carefully placing one foot in front of the other, as if she was on a catwalk, like she'd seen them do on the TV. So this was how you wiggle your bum. She homed in on her prey, who feigned alarm at her approach and then roared with approval as she came closer. Then, glancing over at Sharon, who was now jiggling her cantilevered breasts close to the face of the man beneath her, Flick gritted her teeth and did the same, hoping that her face showed some semblance of enjoyment. God, she wasn't being paid enough for this.

Nothing she could fake, though, could come close to the ecstasy of Jackson's face. He had lunged forward, egged on by his mates, and was now a centimetre away from having his nose buried in her cleavage. She could even feel his breath on her skin and smell the beer. You'd better be getting this shot, Georgie, because I'm not doing it again, Flick thought to herself.

In pain now from bending so low, Flick stood up to howls of disappointment and glanced over at Georgie, whose face was registering panic. She clearly hadn't got the shot and was trying to indicate to Flick, as surreptitiously as she could, to bend down again. Sharon had moved on to the next punter and was working her magic there so, rather than hang around and appear suspiciously attached to Jackson, Flick moved away, shook her cleavage again, hoping she wouldn't tumble out of her bikini top, turned and did an apology for a hip thrust in the face of someone else, sidestepping out of the way before he made a lunge for her ankle, then, aware the track was coming to an end, diverted as fast as she reasonably could back to target No.1.

Sideways on to him now, she put her hands on her hips and wiggled them as she lowered herself down slowly, feeling her knees creak and hoping she wouldn't land in his lap. She should have paid more attention to her gym membership. The effect seemed to work though and the chubby man was practically dribbling, pushed forward by his mates again to get closer. Flick turned and, aware that she was about to break the pole-dancing code of practice, jiggled so closely that he was in danger of suffocating. Get that, Georgie, or else.

To her relief the track ended and Sharon was making her way off-stage. It was all Flick could do not to sprint after her, but she managed to restrict herself to an undignified scuttle. It wasn't until she was in the safety of the dressing room, her heart pounding fit to burst, that she discovered someone had slipped a tenner into her bikini bottom.

Chapter Nine

'Right, what are we going to call the clip?' Georgie's fingers hovered over the keyboard.

'Wanker beware?' Flick replied laconically.

'Mmm, maybe not. What about: "Who's watching?"'

'That'll do.'

'OK, here goes.' Georgie squinted at the screen and clicked on 'upload'. A little window appeared, showing the progress of the video clip she'd recorded the night before. When it reached the end, she sat back in triumph. 'Ta da! You are now officially on YouTube, Mr Jackson. Now the world can see what you are up to.'

Flick groaned from the other side of the room. After a quick, horrified glance from between her fingers at the recording, she'd retreated to make some phone calls. 'You're sure no one would recognise me from that? You haven't got my face in the shot?'

Georgie leaned back and laughed, enjoying this rare moment of embarrassment from Flick. 'Well, it depends how people recognise you. If it's your face, I think you're pretty safe. I was concentrating on getting a good image of Jackson with his tongue hanging out. There are some parts of you in perfect focus, though. And pretty impressive they are too. It wasn't easy though, I'll have you know – aiming my handbag with the lens peeping out.'

'Not obvious at all,' laughed Flick sarcastically.

'Well – I did my best. I'll just have another look at it now it's loaded, then we can start sending the link to Jackson's colleagues.'

Georgie sat back and watched as the video loaded. Even though her ankle was throbbing like mad this morning, she wouldn't have missed Flick's performance for anything. After her initial hesitancy, she'd quite got into it, swinging round the pole and wiggling her arse in the absurdly skimpy bikini. Fortunately she hadn't attempted the 'kick-up invert' or any of the more advanced manoeuvres they'd gawped at on the internet. One of them in bandages was quite enough. It was when she'd made her way along the front of the raised platform, bumping and grinding for all she was worth, until she came crotch to face with Jackson that Flick had really come into her own. She was always complaining about her height, the width of her shoulders, and the size of her bum. Georgie had given up on reminding her that her height was largely due to the length of her legs. She'd never seen Flick naked – only a glimpse on the odd occasion they'd shared a changing room in a shop – but, at the club in her all-but-naked and faked-tanned glory, Flick had looked magnificent. A whole lot of woman, certainly, but beautifully proportioned and undeniably sexy. That slight air of disdain she carried around like a shield came over as provocative rather than aloof, as it sometimes did in everyday life, and the men in the audience, not just Jackson, looked mesmerised. Flick's face, visible for a fleeting moment, seemed wanton and confident, though that had to be far from the truth.

Georgie squinted at the screen. 'Flick, my dear,' she sighed. 'There's just no other way to put this. You look darned sexy here. If Domestic Angels ever falls on hard times, I think we can count on you for a new income stream.'

Flick rolled her eyes. 'Please, let us never mention this again. And, George, bear in mind you're the only other person in the whole world who knows about this. Tell anyone and I may have to kill you.'

Georgie laughed and, using the anonymous Hotmail account

she'd set up yesterday, went about sending the link to the raft of Mr Jackson's colleagues' email addresses his wife had supplied. That would give them something to chat about over the office water cooler. Ten minutes later, she stood up and tested her ankle. 'It's feeling a bit better already,' she said. 'You know, I think I'll risk going to the sorting office on my way home, then I'll stay off it for the rest of the day, if you're sure you don't need me here. Apparently I've got a parcel to pick up, and I've got to sign for it. If it's another one of those free washing power scoops, I think I'll shove it down the postie's throat.'

'Are you sure? I could collect it for you, if you like. I've got to go over that way later.'

Georgie pulled on her jacket. 'No thanks. I'll be fine. See you tonight for Operation Ben Houghton. Have you got everything planned?'

'Er, yuh. Everything sorted, thanks.'

Well, it obviously wasn't a washing powder measuring scoop. The parcel was large, squishy and addressed to her from a Central London postcode. Georgie tossed it onto the seat beside her and drove home gingerly, wincing every time she put her foot down on the clutch.

In the quiet of the house, Georgie limped into the kitchen and filled the kettle. From the stark white cupboards with the recessed handles that didn't spoil the refined line, she took out her flowery teapot and matching mug, both presents from Flick, hidden away so as not to spoil the carefully coordinated kitchen landscape. Also from her hidden cache, she selected a nice, strong teabag for her secret vice – builder's tea, lovely and strong. She'd had enough of Ed's green tea and lapsang souchong to last her the rest of her life. Alone, she could have what she wanted, and never mind the style. She turned back to the package and started to tear open the flap. Something dark. Something soft. Something that smelled unfamiliar. She pulled it out. A dark-grey cashmere sweater the colour of a storm cloud and with the name of a designer she'd read about, but would never dream of affording, or even entering his hallowed Bond Street portals. She shook it out and sniffed at it, puzzled. Not a perfume she recognised. Sweet and dark. Not the sort she'd ever wear.

And a note. Typewritten on the headed paper of a London boutique hotel. Georgie scanned it, a feeling of hollowness filling her head. Snippets of phrases came to her. 'Your recent stay ... hope you enjoyed ... chambermaid found this ... delighted to return it to you.'

The kettle clicked off. She looked around and picked up the sweater, squeezing it hard in her fists. A silly mistake, of course. She looked at the letter again. The dates they mentioned. Last week. She opened the drawer and checked the diary. The beautiful grey leather diary she'd bought Ed for Christmas. She turned the pages, noticing almost in surprise that her hands were trembling.

Then laughed in relief. Of course, that was when he'd been in Cardiff on that site visit. Everything was all right. They'd made a mistake. She made her tea and sat down, taking a first sip so hot it burned her lips. But say it wasn't all right. What then?

It wasn't until lunchtime that she called his office. His secretary, brisk and coolly efficient as ever, told Georgie he was out. She pretended to be disappointed, but she'd known he wouldn't be there. That was why she'd waited to call; so she wouldn't be put through to him.

'Perhaps you can help me then, Abi. I was just trying to remember something. The date of a thing that happened. Something to do with Libby. Erm, it was that last time he was in Cardiff. Can you remind me of that? When it was?'

There was a pause. 'Hmm, that is going back a bit. We signed that project off a couple of months ago.'

Georgie could hear herself breathing, shallow and fast. At the end of the phone, Abi was tapping the keyboard in front of her.

'Yes, here it is. In April. He was there on the 17th and 18th. Is there anything else?'

Somehow, Georgie managed to stammer a 'goodbye', then stumbled back into the kitchen. The diary was still where she'd left it. She flicked through the pages and saw his writing, bold and confident and lying. Days and nights when he'd carefully written in his invented stays in Cardiff.

With a single sweep of her arm, Georgie pushed it all onto the floor. The diary fell face up and the strong tea from the broken teapot soaked into its creamy, lying pages.

Chapter Ten

Alison Houghton had said she was fairly sure that the meeting at the hotel was at twelve, but it was ten past and there was still no sign of her husband. Flick and Georgie had settled themselves in a corner of the hotel lobby by the massive glass windows, and Flick was rather proud of the fact that, from this strategic position, she could see both who was arriving and who was already here in the foyer. Georgie would have preferred to cower behind one of the huge palms, but they'd agreed that was a bit too Inspector Clouseau. The waiter was already suspicious that they'd both ordered water when others around them were on champagne or cocktails.

'How the other half live, hey?' Georgie muttered.

'Mm, wouldn't it be nice to totter about Knightsbridge of a Tuesday, doing a bit of shopping then slipping in here for a glass of champers before a girly lunch?'

'Or a shag with someone else's husband.'

The venom in Georgie's tone startled Flick, but she couldn't read her expression because she'd turned her head away to look around at the elegant people milling about. An Asian gentleman had come in and was greeting two associates loudly and warmly with much handshaking and broad smiles.

'You never know with people, do you? They could be shop-keepers or here to discuss some multi-billion-dollar oil deal.'

Georgie didn't answer. In fact, she'd said very little since Flick had picked her up, which was unlike Georgie. That was the joy of her company for Flick, a constant lively banter about Libby, or a difficult client. She always made Flick laugh, and Flick had been expecting a bit more of a debrief on the ghastly club fiasco, but this morning she'd been taciturn, her eyes suspiciously red and swollen.

'None of my business, but have you two had a marital tiff? Did he leave the lid off the Marmite?' Flick had asked eventually, but Georgie hadn't replied immediately. In fact, they'd almost reached South Kensington before she'd muttered, 'No, no tiff.' Flick hadn't pursued it and, after battling to find a parking space, they'd walked across the park to the hotel without any comment from Georgie about how pretty everything looked and how she'd rather sit on the grass and eat an ice cream.

Flick hoped now that their silence didn't make them appear suspicious – two women drinking water and not talking – but the vibes emanating off Georgie were 'don't ask' so Flick backed off and watched the doorman through the glass as he greeted guests who'd arrived in taxis or limousines. Flick had heard that they earned enough fat tips to keep them very warm indeed in their braided coats and top hats, but she wasn't sure even that would entice her to want the job. Hotel staff must possess a charm gene which make them smile sweetly at even the trickiest customer. Flick was pretty sure if someone was rude to her she'd kick them in the shins. Mind you, who'd ever heard of a door-woman? Not a job any woman *she* knew would hanker for.

She was assessing so closely the petite foreign woman who'd just climbed elegantly out from the back of a Bentley, disgorging Louis Vuitton luggage of varying sizes, as well as a small dog onto which she held firmly, that she almost missed Ben Houghton's tall frame arriving through the doors of the hotel. He stopped as the doors slid shut behind him and did a recce of the people seated. Flick looked away hurriedly before he glanced their way.

'Psst, it's him,' Flick hissed to Georgie, who'd been flicking with disinterest through a glossy magazine. Georgie craned around and gave him the once-over.

'Is the tart here too?'

Flick thought she'd already done a good job of sussing out the other people sitting in the lobby. But as if from nowhere, a statuesque Middle Eastern-looking woman stepped forward from the right, close to the reception desk. She was shorter than Flick – who wasn't? – but her slim legs were made even more elegant by high black court shoes. She wore a cream suit and understated jewellery. Her hair, an immaculately coiffeured dark bob, framed an equally immaculately made-up face. She didn't seem the type to want to muss herself up with an afternoon of passion and debauchery but perhaps that was her secret. Underneath she might be all black lingerie and stockings. Flick felt vaguely uneasy at the thought. The woman strode over to Ben, her hand outstretched, revealing a large, clinking gold charm bracelet, and he smiled broadly as he spotted her, took her hand and kissed her on both cheeks.

'Very cool, Mr Houghton,' Flick said under her breath and, checking no one was looking, lifted her phone as nonchalantly as she could to take a picture of their embrace, but they had parted before she got a chance. 'Damn.'

'Come on, Flick. They're not going to snog right here in broad daylight, are they?' Georgie barely looked up from her magazine.

'I've got to get evidence, haven't I? Oh bugger, they're going into the restaurant. Come on, looks like we're going to have to follow them.'

After a brief and worrying moment when the maître d' fussed over his book, clucking that they didn't have a reservation – a detail which seemed entirely unnecessary in the vast, empty dining room – he finally minced ahead of them to a table which was thankfully not too close to Ben and his companion. Only six or seven other tables were occupied, mainly by businessmen, but the noise level, plus the compulsory muszak, was enough to make them less conspicuous.

'Have you the seen the bloody prices?' Georgie gasped. 'I'm not paying that just to observe her chase a lettuce leaf round the plate while she waits for him to slip his hand up her thigh.'

Flick scanned the menu quickly. What if Ben had the full three courses? How could they string out a Niçoise salad – the cheapest option by far. Did people really pay these prices at lunchtime?

'*Mesdames?*' The obsequious waiter sidled up to them, fussing about with their napkins as he took their order. Flick glanced over at the Ben and his companion, who'd closed their menus and were chatting now. She didn't look the type to polish off the Full Monty. In fact, with that figure she probably survived on an entirely liquid diet. And Ben, whose build was strong, appeared more the 'lunch is for wimps' type so, hoping she'd got it right, she risked it and ordered salads for her and Georgie.

As the waiter sidled off, they sat in silence and Flick, for want of anything else to do, pretended to fiddle with her phone, holding it up at an angle and taking shots of her target. Images that were entirely innocent. In fact, Ben had taken a file out of his briefcase and was discussing the contents of a piece of paper with his lunch companion.

'Oh come on mate, at least put your hand over hers,' she muttered.

'He will. Give him time,' replied Georgie looking in the other direction.

Flick pretended to gaze about the room nonchalantly too, taking in the Grecian pillars and absurd amount of curtaining at the windows, but her eyes kept returning to Ben Houghton. She hadn't been able to see properly in the dark from her car, but she could see now that he really was a ridiculously good-looking man. His face, under a mop of fair hair, was strong and interesting; his chin was square, and his forearms were shapely where they stuck out from his rolled-up sleeves. Compared to the suited and booted businessmen in the room, he looked distinctive and casual, almost like a cowboy in his shirt and jeans. Flick couldn't see his eyes though. Those were always the giveaway.

'You're staring,' said Georgie.

'Am I? Sorry. Just wanted to be able to make a full report.'

Their salads were undoubtedly worth the price and Flick was hungry. She also made short work of the bread, using Georgie's allocation to mop up the dressing at the bottom of her bowl. Georgie didn't want it, nor the salad, which she played with and teased with her fork.

'What's up?' Flick urged.

'I'm just not hungry. I feel a bit nauseous, to be honest. It must be something that didn't agree with me yesterday.' Georgie pushed her plate away and Flick dived in with her fork. 'I don't think you are supposed to do that in five-star hotels,' Georgie muttered, smiling slightly for the first time.

'Yeah, well, saves them throwing it away,' Flick's mouth was full. 'I bet loads gets left in places like this. And besides, it's too expensive to waste.'

Ben and his companion were finishing what looked like fish. The woman was doing most of the talking, throwing her head back to laugh occasionally. She gesticulated with long, thin hands as she talked, her bracelet rattling wildly, and Flick could see large gold rings on her wedding finger. Oddly, she didn't appear to have a handbag, which was strange for a woman and even stranger in one who was probably never more than an inch away from her lipstick at any given moment. The waiter came over to their table and she waved him away imperiously, after briefly consulting with Ben. She was clearly the dominatrix type. A brief vision of her, dressed in a black basque and stockings, astride Ben, popped into Flick's head and she batted it away quickly.

Suddenly they both rose from their seats and made their way to the door of the restaurant. Flick stumbled up to follow.

'Can you settle the bill?' She grabbed her bag and, fishing out a few tenners, pushed them into Georgie's hand and made for the door as nonchalantly as she could. She couldn't see them at first in the lobby and was beginning to panic that she had missed them, when she saw the back of Ben's head over by the lifts. There was no sign of his companion until Flick saw her walk towards him from the reception. She pressed the button to call the lift and as it opened, Flick, suppressing a vague feeling of disappointment, just had the wherewithal to take another picture on her phone.

'What did I tell you?' said Georgie cynically from behind her.

'Lies, lies, lies.' All the way home, Georgie's heart thumped in time with the single word that rattled round her head again and again. The journey back, she'd hardly noticed. She was miles away. Miles away in Cardiff, visions of Ed in a hotel going up in a lift like Ben Houghton had. Occasions and things he'd said. Had he been lying then too? She'd started to doubt everything. What could she believe any more? The sound of her key in the door gave her none of the usual pleasure. She ached all over and nausea gripped her again.

In the house, everything looked as she had left it. She had swept up the broken china and hidden away Ed's diary, as if, somehow, putting it away in the smoothly gliding drawer would make that whole mess just disappear. Nice and neat, just the way Ed always liked things. She prowled up and down the open-plan living area, tormenting herself with imagined details.

Had he kissed Georgie goodbye the morning he went to meet that woman? Had he kissed Libby? Had he worn his best suit? Had she brushed it off for him, thinking he was going to have to make a good impression at his meeting? Had he laughed with this woman, this woman who wore cashmere, at things Georgie had done when they met? Had he kissed her the way he kissed Georgie? How had they made love? Had he cried out when he came? Had he told her he loved her?

Vomit surged in the back of Georgie's throat and she had to run to the loo. Gasping and sweating, she clung onto the basin before emptying the contents of her stomach again and again until she was retching painfully and convulsively, her throat burning. She looked at herself in the mirror, red-faced, and open-mouthed. Panting for breath. Maybe this was what she looked like when they were having sex. Sex and vomit – maybe not so far apart after all.

She stood up slowly and stared at herself for a long time. Then, calmly and methodically, she wiped up the mess on the loo seat and flushed it all away. She rinsed her face with cold water and patted it dry with the soft white towel she had draped over the designer towel rail Ed had chosen. Ed. She stared at herself again and smoothed down her hair. Incredibly, she still looked like herself.

How had this happened? How could she not have realised that Ed was lying to her? This was something that happened to other people, not to her. Why had he done it? She knew she'd been preoccupied with her own work and with Libby's stuff – maybe Ed had felt excluded or that she was not really interested in him and his worries. Maybe that was it. That thing about the school fees the other day, for example. She'd had no idea that things were so bad for him. Perhaps it was sex. He'd hardly laid a hand on her in ages. Perhaps she'd let herself go and it was boring and domestic for him now. She let her head drop back and stared at the exquisite lights on the ceiling. Ed's care and hard work were evident in every detail of the house and she'd taken it all for granted, even trying to undermine it with her junk-shops buys. Perhaps he hated her taste. He'd teased her about it mercilessly when they were dating, but he didn't say much about it now, and she'd been relieved. She looked down at her beaded top with the velvet trim, the boot-leg jeans, the suede ankle boots which had seemed so practical and such fun this morning, and which now looked banal and unoriginal, taken without modification from the pages of a

Yummy Mummy mail-order catalogue. Georgie pulled herself up to her full height and challenged her reflection.

'You're going to put this right, Georgina Casey. You're going to put an end to – whatever is going on. You're not giving up without a fight. He's your husband and *that's* the way it's going to stay.' She walked into the kitchen. There on the side was a jug she'd bought from IKEA – a shop Ed referred to as 'The Aldi of interior design'. How cheap and tacky it now looked next to the glass sculpture Ed had bought in a gallery for her last birthday. Disgusted at herself, Georgie swept out her arm and the jug flew through the air, hit the wall and smashed onto the tile floor. At that she felt her face transform with ugly, noisy tears and she crumpled onto the ground, her body heaving with grief.

Chapter Eleven

'Has she gone?' Flick asked Joanna, when she came off the phone. Flick had dropped Georgie back at the office after they'd battled their way back across town, and had gone off to oversee a painter who was creating a *trompe l'oeil* of an Italian garden on the bathroom wall of a house in Balham. She was now way behind with the day's messages and jobs, but she felt uneasy that Georgie's desk was as ordered as she had left it this morning. She hadn't even moved the yellow Post-it note that Flick was sure had been stuck in the middle of her desk when they'd left for the hotel.

Joanna got up and stuck another Post-it note phone message beside it. 'No, she came in and then left again shortly after. She said she wasn't feeling great. I need her to sort out the flood damage from the overflowing bath at the Mouzykantskiis' before they get back from Grand Cayman on Thursday. I've already had madam on the phone twice this morning about it.'

Flick sighed, casting her eyes over the piles of messages she too would have to deal with.

Joanna paused for a moment. 'She didn't seem right, to be honest. Do you think she's OK?'

'Not sure.' Flick looked over at Georgie's desk again. 'Can you hold the fort a bit longer? I won't be long.' And before Joanna could complain, Flick grabbed her jacket and headed for the door.

It took a frustratingly long time to get to Georgie's, and even longer to find a parking space. Bloody London. The whole place was going to grind to a halt eventually and the entire population would be stuck in a log jam, unable to go forward or back. She knocked at the door, but there was no answer. Clambering over the bins at the front, Flick squinted through the bay window, holding her hand up against the glass to reduce the glare. The room inside looked as ordered as usual, the leather sofas, statuesque lamps and sculptured ornaments in regimental layout, except for a pair of blood-red little girl's shoes thrown aside on the floor.

It gave no clues as to where Georgie was and why she wasn't answering the door. Her car was here, parked slightly further up, and Flick peered up the street to see if she could see her. Perhaps she'd nipped to the corner shop for something? Flick sat on the steps up to the front door for a moment to wait, closing her eyes and absorbing the warm sunshine. It was ages since she'd done this and, for a moment, she let herself relax and drop her shoulders.

Ten minutes later, there was still no sign of Georgie. She could be anywhere. She could even have gone for a walk, though that was unlikely in the middle of the working day and, Flick glanced at her watch, it was still too early to collect Libby from school. Standing up and stretching, she peered through the window again and then, returning to the front door, banged even harder.

She was about to give up when she heard the latch being pulled back and it opened slowly to reveal Georgie as Flick had never seen her before. Her face was grey and she seemed a foot shorter than normal, bent and wizened. She squinted up at Flick in the sunlight as if she'd been asleep and had only just woken up.

'Christ, you look awful. Have you got a bug?'

Georgie didn't answer and turned away from the door, leaving it open for Flick to follow. Flick shut it behind her and followed Georgie as she shuffled into the kitchen.

'I was worried about you, old thing,' Flick chattered. 'Just wanted to check you were – oh bloody hell. What's happened?'

The floor was covered in shards of glass. Flick took it in, Georgie's face, the glass. 'What the hell's happened, George?'

'It's Ed. He's been having an affair.' She looked up at Flick, her eyes enormous like a child's. There was silence for a long time. Flick couldn't think of anything to say, or at least anything that didn't sound trite and stupid. Georgie seemed to be focused on putting on the kettle and preparing tea with intense concentration, suddenly swiping a pile of papers onto the floor to make room for the mugs. Feeling useless, Flick eventually headed for the cupboard under the sink, then couldn't work out how to open the door when there was no handle. Georgie, walking past, tapped it with her foot and it popped open noiselessly. As Flick had suspected, the inside was rammed with bottles of kitchen cleaner, cloths, dishwasher tablets – the integral elements of running a kitchen but at odds with a room that bore little resemblance to a kitchen at all – and, as she suspected, tucked behind a bottle of bleach, was the dustpan and brush.

Without daring to speak, Flick set about carefully sweeping up the shards of glass. The power of Georgie's throw had left a mark on the opposite wall and sent fragments flying across the room and it took Flick a good five minutes to locate all the pieces, a task made no easier by the papers Georgie had strewn all around.

'You'd better make sure Libby wears shoes in here for a while,' she said eventually. Georgie didn't reply. Instead she picked up the tray and headed out to the sitting room. Flick wrapped the lethal-looking pieces in a newspaper she found in the top of the bin and, putting the dustpan back, followed Georgie into the front room.

'So when did you find—'

'He's been telling me he's been in Cardiff overnight for

business,' Georgie interrupted, carefully stirring the tea as if she was entertaining the vicar, her voice full of tears, 'but I've just found out that the Cardiff job finished months ago. Then, guess what?'

She handed Flick her tea, which was woefully weak. Flick didn't dare to complain. 'Er, you did the old go-through-the-inbox-on-his-phone routine?'

'No, funnily enough, but perhaps I will. Now you come to mention it, he has been umbilically attached to it for ages, so perhaps I should have been suspicious. Silly me,' she added sarcastically, looking out of the window. 'There I was, thinking I could trust him. No, actually, and if it wasn't so tragic, it would be funny, I collected a parcel from the Post Office addressed to me and it was another woman's jumper that had been left at a hotel where he – they – had stayed. They'd obviously booked in as Mr and Mrs.' At this her face crumpled and Flick, leaving her tea, went to sit beside Georgie who turned instinctively into her arms and howled, her body heaving with the power of the sobs. Flick held her as if she was a child and let her cry until the front of her T-shirt was soaked. Spent, Georgie eventually looked up, wiping her face and her nose on her sleeve.

'Sorry ...' she sniffed.

'Forget it. What's a bit of snot between friends?' Flick fished a bit of rolled-up tissue from her pocket and handed it to her. 'I don't suppose calling him shithead, tosser, wanker helps?'

'Sort of.' Georgie blew loudly into the tissue. 'I don't think I even feel angry. I feel as though my insides have been pulled out. It's the lies I can't cope with, Flick. It makes such a mockery of everything. Such a lie. All the family things we've done, and the calls from him when he was actually somewhere else all the time.' The tears started to roll again, and she rocked backwards and forwards. 'And then he'd climb into our bed and he'd probably been ...'

'Woah, now,' Flick put her hand on Georgie's knee,

uncomfortable when she thought now of John and his returns home from London to his wife. 'Don't go there.'

Georgie looked up. 'I can't help it. How can I put that out of my mind? You know, we didn't really understand what these women who come to us have been getting at. Now I think I understand it.'

Flick didn't say anything for a moment, but sat back against the hard, cold sofa. Opposite was a bookshelf but instead of the well-thumbed holiday paperbacks that she'd crammed onto her shelves at home, this contained a handful of large, arty books on designers and architects, interspersed with a sculptured piece of glass in stunning reds and greens that Flick noticed matched the cover of the book beside it. All so controlled and contrived. Ed was a show-off really, wanting to be judged by what he displayed on the outside, and perhaps Georgie's simplicity and straightforwardness, her inner goodness, were not enough for him. He needed glamour and status to be someone. Tosser indeed.

'What do you want to do now?' she asked gently.

'I don't know really. It's all too soon. I can't absorb it all. I keep wondering if there are reasons, or if I've got it wrong somehow. You know, there's been some terrible mistake.' She looked up at Flick, who couldn't hide her own opinion from her face quickly enough. 'No, I'm not wrong, am I?'

'It doesn't sound like it, but you could challenge him?'

'Yes, I must.' She looked at her watch and sighed. 'I'd better go and wash my face. I have to get Libby.'

'Want me to fetch her?'

'No. Thank you. I need her with me, Flick. She's the only thing that makes sense.'

Flick left Georgie doing a damage limitation on the kitchen chaos before she headed off towards school, after assuring herself that her face didn't look too bad. She headed back to the office. Joanna's curiosity was assuaged with a story about Georgie having an upset stomach, and Flick got her head down to the increasing pile of enquiries and problems that was mounting up. As she dealt with invoices and paperwork, checking bank statements and trying to solve a discrepancy on the VAT return, her mind kept wandering back to Georgie and Ed and where they found themselves now. Could George go back from here? And how could she begin, when everything she had believed in had been shattered? Flick tried to remember when Georgie and Ed had ever had a major tiff, when George had ever come into work and ranted about him, as so many of Flick's friends did about their partners. She'd sat for hours in pubs and wine bars listening to tales of woe and selfishness, anniversaries forgotten and chores not shared. But this had never been the case with Georgie. They'd seemed solid.

Or had they? Flick mused. Perhaps there had been nothing there, like one of those cheap paper lampshades that you can push your finger through and there is nothing inside. A marriage based on nothing very much at all. How much safer not to commit, not to lay everything you value as precious out in the open for someone to come along and stamp all over.

On the dot of five Joanna switched off her computer and, waving goodbye, left the office. Flick switched the phone to answering machine, grateful for the peace, and turned her full attention to the spreadsheet on her screen. It was a good half an hour and some serious profanity before she could make the figures tally and, pleased with herself, she signed the cheque and slipped it into the envelope, sealing it with aplomb.

'There, HM Revenue and Sodding Customs. Take it all. Bloody pointless tax anyway.'

'Quite agree,' said a voice behind her and Flick turned round sharply.

Tim Rowlands stood in the doorway, which she hadn't heard open at all. 'Sorry, did I startle you?'

'A bit, yeah. I forgot to lock up.'

'I thought you two girls worked twenty-four-seven,' he laughed, his eyes crinkling.

'Sometimes I think we do.' She was pleased to see his friendly face. 'We are officially closed – it's the downside of having a shop front for an office – but valued customers are welcome to drop by. How are you? How's it all going with the refurb? I haven't been round there for a while – Georgie's been dealing with it.'

Tim glanced over at Georgie's desk. 'Has she? I was only passing, but I wanted to let you – her – know that I'm away to Stuttgart again next week and I wondered if you could oversee the painters? I've worked with them before and they can be a bit haphazard with their cleaning up.'

'Sure,' Flick bought up the schedule on her computer for the following week. 'What day are they in and when do you want us to go round?'

'I fly early Tuesday. Could you stick your head round the door on Wednesday and Thursday?'

'Of course.' She typed a note so Joanna and Georgie would see it.

'Oh, and if you're still willing, I'm about to start a big project near Battersea Park – major refurb of a mansion flat. I'd love your help liaising with the contractors. Nightmare of a client though!'

Flick straightened up and laughed. 'That's our stock in trade – tricky homeowners.'

'Great! Must dash.' Tim paused and looked over again at Georgie's desk. 'Ask her to call me on the mobile if there are any problems with my place, will you?' And he ducked out of the office.

Flick smiled. 'I was only passing ...' he'd said. Yeah right.

After Flick left, Georgie tidied the mess on the kitchen floor, secreted away the detritus of family life that had gathered around the house and grimly polished the uncompromising brushed steel, marble and granite until they gleamed, giving back a watered-down reflection of herself. She'd stared at it, turning this way and that, trying to make out a Georgie that Ed might have loved more. By the time she'd left to pick up Libby from school, the kitchen looked like a set for an upmarket design advertisement.

Libby, squirming in irritation at her mother's unusually tight and prolonged hug, had chattered all the way home, as she always did. Georgie listened more than she spoke, relieved that, for Libby, everything was still as it had always been. Never mind his wife. How could Ed have betrayed Libby that way? The knowledge of what might lie in the future for the little girl suddenly struck Georgie, and Libby squealed, 'Mummy, you're hurting my hand. Gerroff, will you? I can cross the road on my own, you know.'

They'd stopped at the florists on their way, Georgie determined that if she could adorn the house with something dramatic and sophisticated, Ed would realise how accomplished she really was. What a good wife she was, really. Georgie had stepped through the doorway into the jungly chill and looked round, Libby following her in, still talking. The florist had appeared from behind a large strelizia. 'Hello again, Mrs Casey. And how are you? Are you after some more of those tulips? They're nearly over now but I've got some lovely mixed bunches here – aren't they lovely and blousy? – or I've got some anemones, if you'd rather. Just in. Lovely deep reds.'

But this wasn't the Georgie of hand-tied bunches and meadow posies. Quite deliberately, she turned from the multi-coloured blooms with their sweet-shop colours toward the severity of some willow twigs and emerged from the shop, to the florist's obvious surprise, with a bunch, all stiff and sculptural. Everything had to be perfect.

Back at home, Libby had whistled as they entered. 'Cor, Mummy! Where's all our stuff?'

'Yours is in your room, where it should be,' Georgie laughed tightly. 'Mine and daddy's is all tucked away.'

'Daddy doesn't have any stuff, though. Only papers.'

Georgie flinched. So even Libby had noticed. 'Run upstairs and have a look. I'd forgotten what colour your carpet was underneath all those books and dolls.'

Libby had pouted. 'I like it that way. I can find everything when it's where *I* put it. Now I'll have to get it all out again. And I was right in the middle of a story.' She flounced off upstairs, leaving Georgie to pour her a glass of milk in the immaculate kitchen.

Libby was watching a DVD and their supper was underway when she heard Ed's key in the door, sometime after seven. Georgie tensed, then turned to face him, suddenly terribly anxious, but he seemed exactly as normal, kissing her briefly while she tried to remember how she'd normally respond.

He looked around and whistled. 'You've been busy. Not at work today?'

'Not this afternoon, no.'

Ed stared at the vase of willow twigs for a moment, then reached out and adjusted a couple so that they spread out further, then nodded and walked in to say hello to Libby. Georgie watched from the kitchen, her hands gripping the granite counter so hard she felt as though she could snap it like gingerbread. Libby glanced up at her father, almost disinterested, while Ed merely dropped a peck on her sleek little head. They exchanged a few words Georgie couldn't hear and he turned away. Libby had barely looked up from her film. He disappeared upstairs to change out of his suit and his handmade shoes and Georgie carefully put his David Mellor cutlery down on the table. Over dinner she couldn't stop staring at him, searching for something that would explain it all. It was the performance of a lifetime – for both of them, she thought wryly. Only Libby seemed her usual self – welcome proof that Georgie was keeping up her façade.

As Ed shovelled his way through a steak, baked potato and side salad with his favourite dressing (unacknowledged), their conversation followed what Georgie realised had become a pattern. Georgie asked Libby about her homework. Libby chattered a bit. Ed threw in the odd comment, usually a tease, and didn't really start to talk until Georgie asked him directly how *his* day had been.

She watched him closely, barely listening, following the movement of his fork as he gestured with it. Had she been such a terrible wife? Had she driven him to it? He wiped grease from his mouth and continued talking but it was like watching a silent film. Her eyes, unbidden, slid back towards Libby, mopping up juices from her plate with a piece of bread. Her and Libby. They'd been a little unit all this time, with Ed making the occasional appearance. Was that the problem? Had she shut him out? Perhaps she should make a plan that they do something together as a family. That's it – she'd cement them together and make him realise what he was missing. Georgie felt a lump of self-pity forming in her throat, and clenched her fists under the table. Her food congealed on the plate, almost untouched.

'How's the Cardiff project going?' she blurted, noting how rapidly he blinked before he answered.

'Oh well, you know. Nearing the end, of course, but there's always lots of snagging at this stage.'

'So you'll be going there again, will you? To Cardiff?'

He laughed dismissively, inappropriately. 'Yes, probably. Almost certainly, in fact. Why do you ask?'

Georgie looked at him as though for the first time. 'No reason,' she said. 'It's nothing. Nothing important. Libby, would you like some grapes?' And she turned away.

Later that night, with Libby tucked up safely in her bed, her room showing the first signs of her rebellion in the form of a pile of books on the floor, Georgie pottered about, not wanting to join Ed who was watching a documentary, his bare feet up on the ottoman. She eyed him dispassionately from the doorway, assessing the situation from the outside as if through a camera. She could say something now as he sat there. Blurt it out and everything would change in a moment. But she hadn't the courage.

'Ed?'

He glanced at her irritably. 'I'm trying to watch this.'

All it would take was one phrase. She paused. 'Right. Well, goodnight then. I'm a bit tired, so I'm going to bed.'

'Mmm. Night.'

She looked around the immaculate kitchen once more, the washing machine humming quietly behind a smooth blank panel, then walked quietly upstairs.

Chapter Twelve

Georgie jabbed the button on the phone, changed gear, then held it up to her ear. Flick answered almost instantly.

'Hi, Flick. It's me. Listen, are you busy?'

'No. Are you OK? You sound a bit weird.'

'Are you free to come out?'

'Erm, yeah. Want to meet somewhere?'

'Well, I'm just turning into your road.'

'Oh! Right. Well, I'm not dressed really so if you want to have a drink while you wait—'

'Not that kind of out. Look, I'll explain when I see you.'

Flick was at the door when she arrived, eyes wary. 'Are you OK?'

'No, I don't think I am.' She took a deep, shuddering breath. 'It's Ed. I think he's meeting her tonight.'

Georgie had buried the reality over the last two days and had wandered around in a bubble of disbelief, until earlier this evening when Ed had called on his mobile to say he wouldn't be home and had a meeting with clients over dinner. Georgie's stomach had clenched, and after pacing the house, she'd called his office and asked airily where he was eating. The receptionist, blissfully ignorant of the implications of what she was saying, revealed he'd asked her to reserve a table at a nice little French place in The City. Unable to concentrate on Libby and her chatter, by seven-thirty Georgie had commandeered the teenage babysitter from up the road, who had a coursework deadline, with a promise of double pay, and shaking, had jumped into her car.

Flick's face creased now in concern. 'Oh, babe. You must be gutted. Listen, why don't we have a drink here and we can talk about it.'

'No, you don't understand.' Georgie shook her head impatiently. 'I have to see for myself. I have to see him with her.'

'Oh.' Flick rubbed her face. 'Do you know where he is?'

'Sort of. Well, I know where he's booked into.' Georgie could feel tears threatening and stared hard at the floor.'

Flick led her gently over to the sofa. 'And where's that?'

'Le Comptoir Gascon. The one in the City. He goes there a lot for meetings and stuff. There's a sort of courtyard thing outside. It would be easy enough to see from there.'

'Hold on. You just want to go and wait there? Is that a good idea, George? Are you sure that's what you want – it could be very painful.'

'Yes, that's exactly what I want.' Georgie felt impatient. 'I *have* to know, Flick. And I'll go even if you don't come with me. Can't you see how important it is?'

Flick shrugged. 'Yes, of course I can. Whatever you want, you know I'll be there for you. I'm just trying to think this through. You've got a babysitter for Lib, I assume.'

'Of course I have!' Georgie replied indignantly. 'I'm not that distraught, for goodness sake.'

'OK, sorry. I was just thinking, maybe we should phone the restaurant and find out what time his reservation is for.'

Georgie stared at Flick in admiration. 'I never even thought to ask his receptionist.'

'Well, you're allowed to be not completely on the ball, under the circumstances. Hand me the phone book, would you?'

Flick found the number and dialled. 'Hello! Wonder if you can help me,' she crooned. 'Just meeting some friends later for a drink after their meal and wanted to check the time. It's Mr Casey. It'll be a table for two. Eight-thirty? That's what I thought. Thank you. Bye!'

She turned back to Georgie, looking almost regretful, and shrugged. 'Looks like you're absolutely right. I'm so sorry.'

Georgie stood up. 'Don't be nice to me, Flick, please. I won't be able to hold it together. Come on, let's go.'

'OK, but I'm driving.'

They parked on a meter in a side street off High Holborn and walked quickly in the direction of the looming Barbican towers. When they were opposite Smithfields, Georgie led Flick down a gloomy and unprepossessing alley which opened out into not so much a courtyard as a triangle, in one corner of which a restaurant, warmly lit and inviting, spilled out onto the quiet pavement.

Georgie took Flick by the arm and pulled her into the shadows. 'There – that's the place. I've been there a few times with Ed and his colleagues.' She shivered, although it wasn't that cold. 'I can't believe I'm doing this.'

'We don't *have* to. If you don't feel up to it, we can just go home.'

'No, Flick.' Georgie turned to her friend and saw the reflection of the moon in her eyes. 'I have to know. I have to see what I'm up against. I'll be able to tell if it's serious or not, I'm sure, as soon as I see them together.'

Flick held her watch up to catch the light. 'They might be in there already.'

'Doubt it. Ed's never very punctual. At least, not when he's with me.' It crossed Georgie's mind suddenly that perhaps they were late because they'd been at a hotel, or her place? She felt nausea rising within her.

From the alley that led out the other way, they heard voices. Georgie reached for Flick's hand in the darkness and she recognised Ed's laugh, intimate and teasing. And then, there they were. Just the two of them. Ed. Her Ed and some woman, taller than him in her high heels, walking along side by side. Not so close together. Not touching even. She was well groomed with some sort of dark wrap thing slung around her shoulders. Good legs. Shortish blonde hair. Quite sleek looking. She didn't look much younger than her. Maybe older, even. And, for a moment, Georgie thought it was all right. She felt herself start to relax. Then the woman wobbled on the uneven setts and rested her hand on Ed's shoulder for support. And he put his hand on her back to steady her. And Georgie felt such a stab of pain she thought she would die.

Then Flick was pulling her away. And she couldn't see because she was crying again. She felt she was suffocating, right there in the street.

Flick peered through the windscreen, concentrating hard on the road ahead. There was silence in the car and Georgie was staring fixedly ahead, not seeing anything. Blinded by the pain of witnessing Ed.

Flick couldn't think of anything to say. She'd virtually carried Georgie to the car but the right words wouldn't form themselves in her head. She wanted to wrap Georgie in a cocoon of safety and take away the agony of what she had witnessed. She wanted to confront Ed, though she feared for what she might do to him. And she wanted to wrench the plastic necklace from the women's neck – the necklace she had seen in Ed's hand in D'Alton's before Christmas – and strangle her with it. So he'd been seeing her that long at least.

But, worst of all, Flick wanted to ignore the shouting in her head. You hypocrite, it screamed at her. You hypocrite, because she too had been that woman on the arm of another woman's husband. She'd known John was married and she hadn't given the pain she might be causing some other woman a second's thought.

The journey back to Georgie's flew by. Every traffic light was green and Flick felt a rising panic that Georgie hadn't had time to recover sufficiently to put on a mask of normality and face Libby.

'Do you want to stop for a drink?' she asked eventually, as they passed the common.

Georgie's teeth were chattering now. 'No thanks,' she muttered and, as the car stopped and before Flick could ask if she wanted company, she opened the door and stumbled out, slamming it behind her. Flick watched as Georgie crept up the steps to the front door, hunched and vulnerable, fumbled with her key and then closed the door behind her.

Three days passed in a veneer of normality. They were so busy there was no time to talk in the day and Georgie left the office bang on five-thirty and, Flick noticed, left when she was on the phone, to avoid the possibility of any conversation. Flick didn't push it. She knew Georgie was on closedown. However, by day three, Flick knew things had to be confronted.

'Right,' she pulled on her jacket. 'Jo, hold the fort. Georgie, you're coming with me.' Georgie looked up, but seeing the expression on her friend's face, didn't argue.

They managed to get a table by the window. Flick carefully set down a cup of black tea in front of Georgie – the thought of coffee had made her nauseous today – and an espresso for herself, then darted back to the crowded counter. Through the assortment of customers, damp like them, and taking refuge from the sudden shower, Georgie watched Flick reach over the heads of two lads and take the two lemon poppy seed muffins she had ordered for them. Glancing round in surprise, the students openly ogled Flick who, Georgie saw, gave them a teasing smile and exchanged a few words with them, then sauntered back to their table, seemingly unaware of the admiring stares.

Flick was like that. Everywhere they went, she turned heads but seemed totally unaware of the fact. Even when there was a man around she was interested in, she never seemed to work terribly hard at attracting him. Or keeping him. In all the years they'd known each other – getting on for five now – she'd never had a relationship that had lasted more than six months. In fact, she didn't think there had been anyone on the scene since last year, and the last one had been a Wandsworth estate agent – another one in a long line of utter bastards that Flick had wasted her time on while Georgie had watched, with anxious but slightly smug disapproval, readying herself to offer muffins and sympathy once again.

And all the time she'd been cocooned in a false paradise of married bliss, thinking how lucky she was to have a devoted husband like Ed.

Georgie took a deep breath and consciously unclenched both her jaw and her fists. In the last few days, since she'd witnessed that scene outside the restaurant, she'd emptied herself of tears, or at least that's how it felt. Her disbelief had been replaced with an awful aching emptiness and a desperation to get life back on an even keel. The way it should be. And in a familiar setting like this, it seemed even more incomprehensible that her life had, effectively, come to an end while everyone else seemed to be going on as normal. It was so bizarre, in fact, that she even managed to smile, albeit a little weakly, at Flick as she plonked the plate down between them, then sat down with a contented sigh.

'Thanks. I needed this.' Georgie took a large sip and sat back in the leather bucket chair, aware that Flick was watching her closely.

'This is a bit of a role reversal for us, isn't it?'

Flick was right. 'Mmm. I was just thinking that myself.' She shook her head. 'All that advice I was doling out when really I was in more of a mess than you ever were.'

Flick took a sip of her bitter brew. 'Have you any idea when it started?'

'No, not really. I suppose it could have been going on for ages, though. He's had plenty of opportunity. And I never questioned him about where he was going or what he was doing. I don't even know who she is.' Georgie shook her head in disbelief. 'How can I have been such a fool?'

'But you weren't. You were only acting as you had every right to act. You're married, for goodness sake. That's what you're supposed to do – trust each other.' Flick sat back and looked down at her hands. 'You can't blame yourself for assuming he would keep his side of the bargain. You're the one person who's blameless in all this. You've been hurt enough. Don't make it worse by blaming yourself.'

Georgie nodded slowly. 'I suppose,' she shrugged. 'But looking at all his stuff, it's as if I haven't even known who he was, all this time. I just assumed he was the person I wanted him to be and didn't bother to think any more about it. I was so wrapped up in playing Happy Families, I didn't see the signs.'

Flick tutted loudly. 'Stop that now! You're doing it again, aren't you? Blaming yourself for everything. He's been lying to you, George. Maybe for years. How are you still managing to make it your fault? You're not responsible for everything that happens in your family, you know. It comes down to this: you kept your side of the bargain and he didn't. He's a cheat. Just like all those other blokes we've been getting revenge on. You never blamed any of the *wives* before, did you? You never thought any of our clients was at fault, so why treat yourself differently?'

Georgie picked up her tea again and breathed in the fragrant steam. She took another grateful gulp, enjoying the slight scalding sensation in her throat. 'You're right. I know that. You're absolutely right. It's just hard to keep remembering it.'

Flick didn't say anything for a while and they looked around the café, sipping their drinks. Finally Flick voiced her thoughts. 'Do you want to nail him?'

Georgie felt a shiver and shook her head. She didn't want revenge. She felt too hurt for that. She was filled with self-doubt. If she were to be confronted with Ed at this moment, would she even have the guts to tell him that she knew everything? Maybe this was why their new enterprise was doing so well. She and Flick were like a pair of avenging angels, detached from the everyday details of the cases they were dealing with, and able to carry out their, so far, petty revenges without feelings getting in the way.

'No. I want life back how it was.'

Chapter Thirteen

'Crikey Moses,' Flick gasped. She hadn't bothered to look on YouTube since Georgie had posted the pole-dancing video, partly because other more important things had cropped up but also because she didn't want to see herself gyrating again, thank you very much. But this evening, fortifying glass of wine in her hand and nothing much worth watching on TV except a three-part thriller that she'd missed parts one and two of, she'd started that dangerous game called Let's Look For Shoes on the internet. Already she'd come *that* close to buying a pair of Louboutins on eBay – if she didn't buy them then some trannie with equally huge feet would – so, to save herself and her credit card, she tentatively opened YouTube.

Four and a half thousand views. Flick flinched, recoiling at the idea that so many people had seen her in a bikini, thrusting her cleavage into the face of a chubby, middle-aged business-man. Then she chuckled. Good old Georgie. She'd certainly done her stuff, emailing everyone in Jackson's address book a link of the unfortunate clip. They in turn must have sent it on to everyone they knew. Oh, the wonders of the worldwide web. Tomorrow everyone would have forgotten it, no doubt, and would be viewing clips of puppies being cute or violent accidents in cars. Fickle world.

The phone shrilled and, clicking off the internet, Flick answered it.

'Hello, love.' Her mum sounded chipper this evening. 'Nice to hear your voice.'

'Yours too, Mum. How's the knee?' When she'd popped by at the weekend her mother had been hobbling, having turned it tripping over a pile of newspapers in the hallway.

'Fine. Now, listen. I wondered if you could drop me off somewhere on Friday evening?'

'Is the car at the garage again?' Flick sighed. It was a heap of rust and really ought to be scrapped.

'Not exactly.' Her mother sounded a bit sheepish. 'I'm off on a little holiday with Lydia.'

'Mum, that's great!' Flick was thrilled. Her mother rarely took time off. Cash was always tight on her derisory pension and the last trip she'd had that Flick could remember was the two nights they'd spent together in Woolacombe a couple of years before. Flick's idea of hell of course – what was the point of a holiday unless you were stuck to the deck chair with sun cream and had a thick chick-lit novel in your hand to tax your intellect? But her mum had loved the ice cream and wet sand element of it all, and as they'd sat eating fish and chips on the beach, Flick had had to admit to a wave of nostalgia.

'Where are you both off to? Somewhere exotic down the M4?'

'Malaga.'

'What!' Flick sat forward in her seat. 'You, on a plane? What about the carbon footprint, Mum?' she teased. 'Think of the environment! The fuel! All the good you've done recycling yoghurt pots all these years. Just to throw it all away!'

Her mother missed the irony entirely. 'Well, I've worked it out,' she said, her tone very serious. 'I calculated what the emissions would be if we drove anywhere, and set that against a short flight. And the flights were very cheap, and Lydia's sister has a little apartment so accommodation will be free …' her voice trailed off.

'Mum, I'm thrilled. Do you want me to take you to the airport?'

Her mother's voice was small and squeaky as she wrestled with her conscience. 'Could you?'

They made arrangements for Friday evening – clearly her mother had kept this gem of information until the last possible minute – and, still smiling, Flick put the phone down. How the mighty are fallen. She scooped up some papers, put her wine glass on the side in the kitchen and was just about to switch off the light above her computer, but she hesitated. The images she'd printed off of Ben Houghton at the hotel were piled up on top of the mess of bills and papers beneath, waiting for her to take to Alison Houghton tomorrow. Ben's frame filled the picture and he was standing, legs slightly apart, scanning the lobby for his – his what? Lover, mistress? His physique exuded an almost brazen confidence. No skulking around like Ed, like John, for dangerous liaisons here. Or the repulsive, drink-induced courage of Jackson at the club. Perhaps that was the secret. Do it with enough confidence and no one will believe you are being unfaithful. High fidelity infidelity.

The following evening she pulled up outside Alison Houghton's house at six-thirty, as arranged. It had been a long day in the office. Georgie was taciturn, going about her work in a very determined and businesslike way, and Joanna's attempts to jolly her along had begun to grate on them both by mid-afternoon. You couldn't fault the woman. At lunchtime she'd brought back cup cakes for them all, knowing they were Georgie's favourite, in an attempt to cheer her up. Georgie, however, had simply smiled weakly, picked the chocolate topping off, and left the rest in a crumby mess on her desk.

By five-thirty, Flick was glad to escape, but she would have loved to be the proverbial fly on the designer kitchen wall when Georgie got home. What the hell was the atmosphere like there? Clearly Georgie hadn't revealed to Ed all she knew, and Flick was prepared to lay odds that Georgie would, characteristically, be over-compensating, convinced his infidelity was *her* fault; Ed had been unfaithful due to some short-coming on *her* part.

The Houghton's house looked beautiful in the summer-evening sunshine. A climbing rose was in full orange bloom against the immaculate white render and Flick felt a surge of envy. A Have-Not faced with the riches of the Haves. Alison took her time to answer the door – for a moment Flick thought she'd got the time wrong – but she couldn't have done because Alison had assured her Ben would be away and not back until late, so the coast was clear. Alison said hello quietly as she opened the door and turned, clearly expecting Flick to close the door behind her. Flick followed the small, slim woman in her pink kaftan top and white trousers up the stairs. She was immaculate, petit and coiffeured, her pedicured toes peeping out of gold sandals, the toenails painted in a light-pink polish. Flick felt like an elephant.

Alison led her into the sitting room, and perched demurely on the edge of a white sofa, indicating for Flick to do the same. The room was as beautiful as Flick had guessed when she'd looked through the windows on the dark night of the stake-out. It was predominantly white, with splashes of colour in the form of two giant canvasses on the wall. Cosier than Georgie's house but, in every respect, more opulent. The real thing. It took Flick a while to realise what was missing, however, and then she got it – this was a showroom, the type of room that fools you in posh interiors magazines. Houses that are perfect in every way, like a set, because all the little touches of human life have been removed. No books half-read by the chair, yesterday's paper on the ottoman, no half-drunk cup of coffee. Here there weren't even photographs. Not even a wedding picture which, Flick imagined, would have been beautiful, had there been one. Flick tried to picture how this woman would cope if she were allowed to have the babies she so craved. Playdough and crayon smeared on the sofa fabric by some designer-dressed toddler? She thought not.

Flick realised suddenly that she must seem quite rude, staring, and focused back on Alison Houghton's perfect face. She was seated ram-rod straight, her small brown hands folded in her lap. Was that nose for real? Surely no one was allowed one that straight and cute?

'So, what have you found out?' Alison's voice was hesitant.

'Well, I – we – can confirm that he was at the hotel, as you said,' Flick swallowed. 'And I'm afraid that he did meet up with someone.'

'Someone?'

'Yes. A woman. Middle Eastern–looking.'

Alison nodded and looked down at her hands. 'And?' There was pain in her voice.

'They had a short lunch together.' Flick handed over the slightly grainy pictures she'd managed to capture in the restaurant.

'Then?'

'Well ...'

'Go on.' Alison prompted, her eyes big and round now.

'I have to tell you that they did go up in the lift together ...' Flick felt like an executioner. 'But it might have been nothing,' she said quickly. 'There is a bar on the roof terrace. It was a lovely afternoon so they might have gone up for coffee.'

'Mmmm. Perhaps. I think you are being naive, though. I know my husband. He wouldn't waste time drinking coffee when he could bed a beautiful woman.'

'Does he, I mean has he ... ?'

'Often.' A tear slid slowly down Alison's face and she wiped it away irritably. 'It's been the same since we were first married, even before, I think.' She sniffed. 'He whisked me off my feet – he was very charming and good-looking and I was so young and naive. I thought he was everything. I was right, but he was everything to everyone else too.'

'I'm so sorry. Perhaps this will be evidence enough for you to— ' They both started as they heard the front door close loudly downstairs. Flick's heart leaped and pounded violently in her chest and she could feel her face heat up. Alison, with impressive composure, handed the photographs back to Flick, who thrust them quickly into her bag.

'Is it him?' Flick mouthed, hoping she wasn't looking as panic-stricken as she felt. Alison only had time to nod before he was suddenly at the top of the stairs, filling the doorway. He glanced at his wife and then at Flick who, feeling even more vulnerable from her seated position, stood up, smoothing down her jeans nervously. Some ridiculous thought made her wish she'd brushed her hair before she'd arrived. She felt totally at odds in this beautiful room with this beautiful couple.

'Hello.' His voice was deeper than she'd expected, and she realised she hadn't really heard it at the hotel.

Alison had turned to face him across the room. 'You're back earlier than expected,' she said, her voice cool and controlled. Not a trace of the panic she must be feeling.

'Yes, I got an earlier flight.' He ran his hands through his hair.

'This is Flick.' Alison indicated her with an elegant arm outstretched. 'She popped over to talk about the garden landscaping.'

Flick tried not to look astonished. Did she look so awful that she looked as if she could lug patio slabs?

Ben frowned. 'Landscaping? You've only just had it done.'

Alison waved her hand. 'I'm not sure about that area at the back. They haven't got it quite right.'

Ben rubbed his face. He looked tired. 'Well they charged enough for it. Get them back.' He looked hard at Flick and she had to glance away at his gaze.

'We'll see. Can you get me a price, then?'

'Er yes, of course.' Flick picked up her bag, desperate now to get out of this room charged with atmosphere. 'I'll get something to you in the next couple of days.' She headed for the door and though Ben stepped out of the way, she brushed past his arm.

'I'll see myself out,' she threw over her shoulder as breezily as she could, and was down the stairs and out of the front door with unseemly haste, face hot with embarrassment.

Georgie was beginning to feel like Martha Stewart. She'd never baked so much in her life, in fact, even Libby asked why the pudding hadn't come from Sainsbury's. She'd lit the candles at the table on Saturday night and had rented a DVD so Libby was out of the way as she filled Ed with boeuf bourguignon and fascinating conversation. He'd responded to her questions about his dental appointment, work, the impending launch of the Atrium project near King's Cross and she had hung on his every word, paying avid attention. Ed had revealed how it had been nominated for an award from the prestigious *Concept* magazine and she'd gushed appropriately.

On Sunday morning she'd got gotten up early to make Scotch pancakes and fresh coffee, and when Ed emerged in his dressing gown, she was ready with her plan for a perfect day.

'How about a lovely trip to Kew together? We haven't been for ages and we can have lunch in the Orangery.'

Ed had rubbed his eyes at first, which was always a sign he wasn't onside, but he had relented after a bit of persuasion, not least from his daughter. It had been pleasant, if a little strained for Georgie, keeping up a pretence of family unity. A couple of times Ed had hung back and she had turned round surreptitiously to see him quickly pull his phone out of his pocket, though she hadn't heard the beep of a message. Whilst Libby ran on ahead through the glasshouse, she'd even slipped her hand in Ed's as he talked and he hadn't shaken her off.

Sunday night, though, was the greatest challenge. She'd come out of the bathroom in a new nightie and, slipping into bed beside him, had run her hand over his thigh. He'd responded efficiently enough, but as he entered her Georgie bit her lip hard to fight the images in her mind. Images of Ed and the other woman. Georgie then realised, as Ed lay snoring beside her and she'd pulled her new nightie down, that he hadn't even tried to make her come.

Monday brought the pressure of a new week, and Georgie busied herself over breakfast and packing Libby's PE bag, unsure that she could keep up the pretence of normality, and perversely relieved that Ed would soon be off to work.

'Here's that cheque for the phone bill,' Ed said, coming into the kitchen already wearing his coat, and handing over the paper with a perfunctory kiss on her cheek. 'Oh, and did I mention that I'll be in Cardiff tomorrow night? Bloody nuisance, but until it's all signed off it's got to be done.' He looked insufferably pleased with himself and, feeling nauseous, her hands shaking, Georgie mumbled an acknowledgement and emptied her half-eaten piece of toast into the bin.

Chapter Fourteen

Flick usually loved this time of year. Every few days she noticed another plant had burst out, in its urban way giving a snapshot of what must be happening in the countryside. The real world. A world of fêtes and gardening that she only really followed through the supplements in the weekend newspapers because she'd never had any truck with the countryside. Flick felt uneasy if she was too far away from a London cab or an underground station. She'd done the odd weekend away – including an interminable forty-eight hours with an old schoolfriend who'd married, spawned and been transplanted to somewhere near Norwich for a life of Crocs and organic veg boxes and an inability to talk about anything but lactation. But now Flick tended to stay close to home. Weekends in major European cities were acceptable, of course. The level of exhaust emissions was enough to make her feel at home, and the retail therapy more than made up for it.

Outside her flat a lilac was in full, blousy bloom and, ignoring the silly wives' tale about bad luck, she snapped off a couple of flowers and dunked them into a vase on the window sill, brushing off the storm bugs that had gathered there. The air was thick and muggy outside on the street, and more storm bugs stuck to her bare arms. It felt sticky already, though it was still only early, and she felt creased and uncomfortable in her summer dress. She hated it anyway, feeling much more at home in shorts and a vest, but Georgie had made it clear that they ought to look more professional at the office.

Georgie had also made it clear that she was a fool to have gone to Alison Houghton's house, and she was probably right. Flick wasn't sure why, but the last couple of days seemed to have hardened Georgie, and her hurt was manifesting itself in a very dogmatic attitude and little tolerance of anyone who did anything idiotic, whether it was other drivers, or agency clients who called more than once about something that they already had in hand.

'Why can't she just bloody trust us?' she'd snarled yesterday, slamming down the phone. 'There are some people around who *can* be trusted, you know!'

Joanna had been startled at her tone and there had been an awkward silence. Georgie had lost weight too. Her face looked tired and drawn. Flick had made tentative enquiries about the atmosphere at home, but Georgie had only muttered something about it being fake. Flick wanted to give her an embrace and show her she was feeling for her, but the aura she was giving off was not very conducive to that. Instead, on her way back from feeding the Finchs' guinea pig, Flick popped into one of her favourite shops and bought a tube of ludicrously expensive hand cream and slid it onto Georgie's desk as she walked past. A pathetic gesture, Flick knew, but Georgie had smiled tearily when she'd peeped into the bag and gave Flick a very warm hug of thanks.

Friday night saw Flick in her role as the sad single at an impromptu barbecue at her friend Sally's in Herne Hill. Flick liked Sally, though she wasn't mad about her boyfriend Martin, who could bore for England on most subjects but, Flick mused over a glass of chilled Prosecco, it was rare indeed to be friends with a couple and like both of them. At least, she thought she was the sad single until about nine-thirty when the sausages and kebabs were almost over, and a mate of Martin's arrived, carrying a peace-offering in the form of a bottle of wine wrapped in tissue from the off-licence on the corner. He was tall and moderately good-looking and, true to form, made a bee-line for Flick. She smiled and laughed at his jokes and searching questions about her job, but her heart wasn't really in it and, at midnight, assuring Martin's friend she was a big girl now and capable of getting home unaided, left with a sigh of relief. The night was as warm as the day and she drove home with the windows down, Faithless' *Insomnia* thumping out as loud as she dared. She turned it down as she pulled into her road and parked. The street was lit well enough, the sky a deep velvet-blue above her, as if night hadn't fallen properly, but for no reason she shivered. She knew she was walking faster than was necessary to her front door, but there seemed to be shadows everywhere. A cat shot out from under a car as she passed and she let out a little yelp of surprise. She fumbled with her keys, chastising herself for being ridiculous and, as her door gave way, she turned to scour the street behind her. Nothing there. But then why would there be?

As she made herself a cup of mint tea to take to bed, she made sure the blind in the kitchen was firmly closed, then couldn't help herself and lifted one of the slats with a finger to peep out onto the street again. There was no one about at this hour, naturally, and she chided herself and padded off to bed.

Half an hour later, she'd read the same page of her book three times and sighing, had thrown back the duvet, gone back into the kitchen, and slipping a carving knife out of the drawer, had taken it back to bed with her.

'Nice evening at Sally's?' her mother enquired the following morning as they sat at her kitchen table. They'd had the debrief on Malaga, which had been a roaring success, and Flick was now into her second cup of tea – safer than the politically correct coffee substitute – and was idly perusing the papers.

Flick groaned. 'Oh, usual thing – I was the Obvious Single until the Ubiquitous Bloke turned up. Why does everyone feel the urge to hitch me up? It's almost insulting.'

Her mother laughed, flicking through the *Guardian*. 'Just be glad they do. When you get to my age they either don't bother lining anyone up, or they don't invite you at all.'

'I bet you that out there is some lovely, single man of your age – widowed or divorced – who would just love you and your company.'

'Maybe.' Her mother took a sip of her drink and broke a biscuit in half on the plate in front of her. 'But I'm not so sure I want it now. I did once. I got very lonely. But if I met someone now it would bring all the baggage, guilt and revolting step-children and step in-laws to accommodate. And a widower – oh, that's worse. I'd be compared to the First One who would be perfect in every way. All too exhausting and I just can't be bothered.' She snorted with glee.

Flick ran her hand through her hair. 'Perhaps that's the problem. We're too fussy.'

'Well, that's something you inherited from me and not your father. He clearly had low standards.'

'After you, of course!' Flick said indignantly.

'Naturally! How could anyone compare?'

They sat in companionable silence for a moment. It was on the tip of Flick's tongue to tell her mother about the vengeance sideline, then she stopped herself. She wouldn't approve, Flick was sure. She could be old-fashioned about such things and would never have dreamed of seeking revenge on her errant ex-husband. Would Georgie stoop to such a thing?

'What do you—' Flick started tentatively. 'What is it, do you think, that makes men wander?'

'Wander?'

'Go off and have affairs.'

Her mother shrugged her shoulders, then rested her hand on her chin. 'Because some of them feel they have to prove themselves. It's something inherent in the species – though women aren't infallible. We're all animals really – match up, mate, spawn and wander off. Trouble is, it's often us women who get left looking after the babies and the blokes go off and preen and strut to impress some other pair of ovaries.'

'Nicely put, Mum! Thanks.'

Her mother went back to her paper. 'Well it's true, isn't it? You only have to sit with a man in a public place and they can't take their eyes off the bottom of every woman that goes past. Women really do have to keep on their toes to keep them interested.'

'But what about those couples you see who are truly content? You know, the ones that still hold hands at eighty, sit on the pier together and finish each other's sentences?'

'Like Uncle Brian and Auntie Jean, you mean?' Her mother's sister had been married for aeons and still lived in the same house in East Sheen that Uncle Brian had carried her over the threshold of all those years ago. 'That's 'cos the poor man didn't dare stray. She'd have hung his testicles out to dry.'

They both laughed, thinking about bossy Auntie Jean, who her mother likened to Hyacinth Bucket.

'But what about love?' Flick asked, not sure she'd ever discussed love with her mother, who'd been so badly hurt by her father's desertion for the Mare of Catford.

'Oh, that.' She licked her finger and turned the page of the paper, a habit which was one in a long list of reasons why Flick would never be able to live with her. 'It's pretty strong when it hits you.'

Flick's eyes shot to her mother's face. That was a response she hadn't been expecting. 'Is it?'

'You've clearly never been in love, if you don't know that.'

'Well ...' Flick wasn't so sure now. 'I was pretty smitten by Joe Fabbrino at school.' She had mooned about for weeks over the tall, dark boy in her class until her mother had lost patience with her. But he had been Flick's first kiss and the first boy she'd let touch her breasts, so that made him pretty unforgettable.

'He was a nice boy,' her mother nodded. 'He married a girl from up north, didn't he? Had a brood of little Italianos.' Her mother seemed to have lost interest in the love thing and Flick was relieved. She wasn't even sure why she'd mentioned it and she got up to put the kettle on again.

'You know you're truly in love because you can't think of anything, or anyone else, at all,' her mother said suddenly. 'Your head is full, and it hurts. Love can be very painful indeed. The secret is the transition from the infatuation to being comfortable and confident with each other. That was something your father just could not manage.'

At that, the phone jangled. 'Hello? Oh hello, darling! Didn't we have fun?' Her mother picked up her drink and moved next door to chat to her friend. Flick sighed, taking in what she had said. That was something Ed hadn't managed either. He hadn't made that transition and George and Libby were the casualties. She finished one section of the paper and her eyes flitted over the front of the business section disinterestedly. Big corporate mergers. CEOs who'd been headhunted. A different world. Then her eyes fell on a headline: Houghton Properties Picks Up Another Big Name. Flick read on. 'Houghton Properties, which has already acquired land in Canary Wharf to add to its increasingly impressive portfolio of property in the capital, has now added The Westborough, the prestigious five-star hotel in Lancaster Gate.'

The Westborough, with its grand lobby and over-priced dining room. Flick laughed quietly to herself. A bit radical, but maybe that was what Ben Houghton was about. To be on the safe side, he'd bought the hotel where he screwed his mistress. 'I liked it so much I bought the company'. Saved embarrassing questions from the staff, she supposed.

She knew it was ridiculous, but why did she feel so disappointed?

On Monday morning, even Georgie's reaction to the news of Ben Houghton's shopping spree was uncharacteristically cynical, 'How very convenient for him!'

'How was your weekend? Did you confront Ed?' Flick asked quietly.

'Same old, same old. We had the boys over so no chance to say anything, thank God. They really are rude little buggers, you know. They spend the whole time with their heads in the biscuit cupboard without even asking.'

I'm amazed they can find it, thought Flick. 'Perhaps you should take it as a compliment that they feel so at home there ... ?'

'Harrumph. They can do that in their own home. I made Ed take all three of them to the Natural History Museum. Naturally, the boys were bored stiff.'

'Naturally.' Flick went through the calls and emails that had come in over the weekend. There was the usual list of emergencies and the Sunday night ramblings from people who'd found time over the weekend to chat and make decisions about decorating or a new bathroom. Flick worked her way through them, allocating jobs where they needed to go. Then she opened the email from Alison Houghton. No preamble, just: 'He'll be at Stapley Park tomorrow at eight p.m. Please follow him. Usual fee, plus expenses.'

Chapter Fifteen

'Georgina Casey, surgery five, please.'

Georgie took a deep breath and stood up, leaving the dog-eared copy of *Country Life* on the seat. She looked around. She hadn't been here since Libby's last ear infection and the place seemed to have changed; there were more rooms, more corridors, and more health education posters on the wall. An older woman tugged at her cardigan sleeve and pointed. 'That way, love.'

Was her confusion that obvious? It seemed to have gradually become the norm for her in the last few weeks. Confusion and an awful grinding tiredness that made even the most mundane of tasks feel like scaling the foothills of the Andes. She nodded a quick thanks and made her way past closed doors, knocked on the one labelled five, and went in.

The doctor looked up and smiled reassuringly. 'Hello, what can I do for you?' she asked gently and her sympathy was almost too much. Georgie had to resist the urge to turn tail and run. But she had Libby to think of. Libby, who had shaken her awake on the sofa a few nights ago, indignant in her towelling robe after she'd had to bathe herself. Georgie had been mortified. This overwhelming tiredness was becoming too much and she started to talk.

'... and that's basically why I'm here.' Georgie took a deep breath out. She hadn't meant to blurt out quite so much. God, she'd even talked about the state of her marriage.

The doctor nodded and steepled her fingers together. 'Well,

let's deal with first things first. There are a number of things that could cause the tiredness you describe, apart from stress, but I need to ask you a few questions. Now, tell me, how long has it been since you last had intercourse with your husband? I was wondering ... is it possible you could be pregnant? When was your last period?'

Georgie blinked. The room had gone terribly cold. 'I can't remember,' she heard herself whisper. 'I can't be.'

The doctor looked sympathetically at her. 'Do you really mean that you *can't* be? Or do you mean that you don't want to be?'

Georgie's arms were icy cold. 'I don't know. But I think it's been a while.' She shook her head. 'I've maybe missed two, but I've always been a bit unpredictable.'

'Well, if there's any possibility that you might be, we can easily do some tests. We can do a urine test but if your last period was over ten weeks ago, I should be able to feel the height of your uterus manually, just by feeling your abdomen. I'll take your blood pressure at the same time.'

Georgie got up from the seat in a daze and followed the doctor's gesturing finger over to the black examination couch, but just stood beside it, her mind racing, while the doctor washed her hands. 'Can you hop up, please, and just undo your jeans. That's it. Cold hands, I'm afraid.'

When had it been, that time she'd risked it? It seemed an eternity ago. Another lifetime completely. When she'd been married and still believed in the future.

The doctor was probing gently. 'I think we'd better do a blood test. There's very little doubt in my mind that you're pregnant, about thirteen weeks, I'd guess. A lot of the tiredness probably stems from the hormonal changes your body is undergoing at the moment. It generally improves once the placenta takes over. But, of course, you must remember that from last time.' The doctor was back at her computer now but Georgie stayed lying down, staring at the ceiling. She felt herself start to shake and shrill laughter escaped her trembling lips.

'Mrs Casey? Come and sit down. This must be quite a surprise for you. Would you like a drink of water?'

Cooperative as ever, Georgie rearranged her top, pulling it out from her jeans, although there was nothing there to hide. 'I wanted this for so long,' she heard herself say out loud, although she hadn't meant to. 'But now ...'

The doctor looked up from the keyboard. 'Whatever you decide to do, we should still do the blood tests. Here.' She passed an envelope with a printed label on it to Georgie. 'Ask at reception and you can have it done straightaway. I'll also refer you for a scan as you should have had one by now. And, Mrs Casey, I think you need to talk to your husband.'

Georgie felt the room come into focus for the first time and she returned the doctor's steady gaze. 'Yes. Yes, I will.'

Flick wasn't sure why she didn't tell Georgie she was going to stake-out Ben Houghton again this evening. She had enough on her mind, Flick supposed, and wouldn't want to be bothered so, alone, she made her way up through the wilderness of north London towards leafy Hertfordshire and the idyllic grounds that were Stapley Park, the south-east's newest and chicest hotel. Flick had read about it in the papers as a favourite of WAGs and golfers, who flocked here for five-star pampering, but the car park alone was enough to give her a good idea of the quality of the clientele. You couldn't move for Bentley Continentals and pretty little sports cars. New money was oozing from every exhaust pipe.

Her filthy Jeep stuck out like a sore thumb – perhaps they'd think she was staff – so she hid it under a tree by a clump of bushes, as far away from the hotel entrance as she could, and made her way inside. She was greeted by an impeccably mannered doorman, clearly trained to welcome even the riff-raff with equanimity and, ordering a glass of wine, found herself a discreet little spot close enough to see the goings-on but far enough away to be slightly hidden.

By nine she was frankly bored. She'd eked out a glass of Pinot for as long as she could, had flicked through every paper available, and was now on water after repeated approaches from the waiter, who seemed to be getting a bit suspicious. The hotel was fairly busy and Flick was badly under-dressed and under-perma-tanned. Several groups and couples had ordered dinner over drinks and moved through to the restaurant, but there was no sign of Ben Houghton or any lascivious-looking women. Flick had even made a couple of detours on the pretext of going to the loo, via the entrance to the restaurant, to check she hadn't missed him, but she couldn't see his tall frame and thick head of hair anywhere.

Alison hadn't replied to her querying text and, by nine forty-five, Flick was losing the will to live. She was hungry and wanted to get home.

'Anything else, madam?' the waiter swooped on her glass again. 'Has your friend not arrived?'

'No.' Flick answered quickly. 'No, she must have got held up. Thanks anyway.' She gathered up her bag and headed out of thick glass, monogrammed doors into the car park and the darkness. Several of the cars had now gone, back to their neo-Georgian home-county mansions, no doubt, and she delved into her bag in search of her keys as she made her way to the clump of bushes where she'd left the Jeep. She couldn't feel them in the detritus at the bottom of her bag and, uneasy now in the gloom, began to search more frantically. She could make out lipsticks, her phone, loose change, but no sodding keys.

She heard a movement behind her and swung round, her heart pounding. There, standing about six feet away from her in the darkness, was the unmistakable figure of Ben Houghton. Flick gasped.

'Do you make a habit of hanging out in hotel lobbies?' he asked quietly. 'A strange pastime for a landscape gardener.'

Georgie had tried Flick's number a couple of times since she got home but was almost relieved she wasn't there. So much so, in fact, that she didn't even bother calling her on her mobile. She wasn't sure how, or even if, she'd tell her anyway, but the idea of trying to shout out her news so Flick could hear it above the clamour of some crowded bar was too appalling. She looked around the ordered blankness of her house then shivered and pulled her cardigan around her.

By chance, Libby was sleeping over at a friend's and she wasn't expecting Ed until much later. A glass of wine. That was what she needed. There was an open bottle of white in the fridge. But should she? Furious with herself, Georgie flung open the fridge door, making the bottles rattle. She stared in at the contents. Soft cheese. Pâté. Egg yolks in a cling-film-covered bowl, ready for making mayonnaise. She closed her eyes. She remembered how careful she'd been all the time she was pregnant with Libby and how Ed had laughed at her earnest study of those awful, preachy books.

How strange life was. All this time, she'd been longing, longing for another baby. Longing for her body to be taken over by a tiny invader. Longing for her life to be turned upside down. But not like this. Not like this. This was all wrong. And how could she have been so blind as to have missed the signs? She'd been sick as a dog with Libby, but perhaps this explained the nausea. It hadn't been just the result of thinking about Ed and that woman. She touched her breasts tentatively. With Libby they'd been sensitive from the word go, but nothing felt different to normal.

Ed's baby. This changed everything. Knowing that they had a child on the way, even unplanned, would pull him up short. This would make him realise how precious family life was.

Making herself a cup of tea instead, Georgie cast her mind back to Libby as a baby. How Ed had loved choosing her a new buggy – the best of course! – and how he'd marvelled over her tiny fingers. Taking her cup through to the living room, she opened the cupboard beside the fireplace and pulled out the photo album she'd put together so lovingly. There was the proof. Page after page of shots of Libby, from her first moments; pictures of Georgie, tired but elated in the delivery room; and later, pictures of Ed in the garden or out and about, Libby strapped to his chest in her papoose. Georgie touched her tummy. This baby would mend the chasm; mean a new start. Wouldn't it?

The scene was set. Georgie had cleaned and polished like a woman possessed; at the back of her mind the thought that she was preparing a haven for Ed, one that would surely convince him that the grass was actually greener on his side of the fence.

She smiled to herself as she moved quietly about the house. Since she'd found out, just a few hours ago now, Georgie had been ultra aware of every nuance of feeling in her body and she couldn't stop touching her stomach, trying to work out whether the slightly rounded shape was the baby or simply a few too many Jaffa Cakes. It didn't really matter. She felt good. She felt right. And now that the nausea and tiredness could be accounted for, she actually felt tremendously well.

Flick's mouth opened and closed like a fish. Her hand was still inserted into her bag and her fingers finally located her keys. She gripped her hand around them reassuringly and pulled them out.

'Er. Not usually,' she managed eventually. 'I was waiting for someone and ...'

'Same woman you were with at The Westborough?' Oh, bloody hell. She couldn't really see his face but his voice sounded quite harsh.

'No. Maybe.' Flick knew she sounded pathetic.

'I think we need to have a chat you and I, don't you? Shall we go back inside?' He didn't wait for an answer but turned abruptly and walked back towards the hotel entrance. For a moment Flick considered jumping into the car and screeching off but, like a lamb, followed him. The same waiter approached them in the lobby.

'Ah, Mr Houghton. You are back.' He looked over Ben's shoulder at Flick. 'It was Mr Houghton you were waiting for? You should have said, madam. I would have found him for you. Can I get you both a drink?'

'A coffee for me please, Greg. And the same for her.'

'I'd rather have tea,' Flick said defiantly. 'Darjeeling please.'

'Certainly.' The waiter backed away and Ben moved to sit on one of the lounge sofas, expecting her to follow. He was clearly angry. Thankfully there was no one about, though noise was permeating through from the restaurant, and Flick perched on the sofa opposite. Ben was leaning forward, his elbows resting on his knees as he looked at her intently. 'So, what's this all about?'

Flick had observed his face from a distance at The Westborough, and had tried not to look at him in his sitting room, so this was the first time she'd been able to see him properly. His eyes were a dark blue, she could see now, under dark brows, and his skin was quite tanned. Thick, dark hair was pushed off his face as if he'd run his hands through it. His nose was slightly hooked, which gave him a Romanesque profile, but his mouth was surprisingly soft. She tore her eyes away from his mouth and was irritated to see a mildly amused expression on his face.

'What's what all about?'

'What are you doing here on your own this evening? Who were you waiting for?'

Flick waved her hand airily. 'I told you. A girlfriend. But she couldn't get here. Babysitter problems.'

'I don't believe you.'

'Well,' Flick spluttered. 'You can choose to believe what you like.'

The waiter appeared at her shoulder with a tray. 'Darjeeling for you, madam.' He put down the pot and cup with a flourish. 'And filter coffee as usual, sir. Thank you.' He swanned off. There was a small plate of home-made biscuits and Flick was desperate to swoop on them. Her stomach was rumbling – her plan to stop for chips on the way back now scuppered.

'You're a long way from home.' It was a statement.

'Am I?' Her stomach began to feel uneasy and it wasn't just hunger. She fussed with the tea, spilling it in the saucer. Her hands were shaking.

'I don't believe you are here to meet a friend. And, judging by your window boxes, nor do I believe you are a landscape gardener.'

'Oh.' She put down the pot. 'Who am I, then?'

'Your name is Felicity Lane. You live at Flat 2, 57 Harbour Lane, SW11. You drive a very grubby Jeep, often too fast.'

Flick bristled, alarmed. Did that explain her unease the other night? Had he been watching her? 'You've done your home-work. That's very invasive of you. Knowing where I live.'

He carried on as if she hadn't spoken. 'It's not rocket science. You run Domestic Angels, also in SW11, with your partner. You make a habit of sitting in cars outside people's houses – mine specifically – and pretending to eat lunch in restaurants where I happen to be too.' Flick could feel her face burning now and she picked up her cup as a distraction. She and Georgie must have been so bloody obvious.

He leaned further forward and lowered his voice. 'You also look very good in a bikini.'

Flick's eyes shot up and she put the cup down hastily before she dropped it. 'What!'

'By coincidence, I happened to be on one of those irritating little mail loops that land in my PC virtually every day,' Ben was smiling smugly now. 'But this one came, uncharacteristic-ally, from a friend in the business so, rather than delete it, as I usually do, something made me look at it. And what a surprise!' He sat back in his seat now and observed her under his brows.

'There was this tall, leggy blonde I recognised in a very revealing bikini doing things to a very drunk man who my mate happened to know.' Flick turned her head and closed her eyes. 'Do you do that on the side, as well as the landscape gardening? You are a busy girl.'

There was a silence as he leaned forward and poured his coffee. 'So, Miss Lane. What's the story?'

Flick looked into Ben's face as he stirred in milk, then picked up a biscuit and popped it into his mouth. She was trapped now. Was there any point in trying to fib her way out of this one? She sighed and slumped back in her seat, looking anywhere else other than at Ben. 'I've been asked to follow you.'

'Well, that's obvious. And for a private detective you are pretty lousy, I might say. You need to brush up on your technique. Then you won't follow people in your car up one-way streets.'

'Oh,' she mumbled.

Ben sat back in his seat and observed her. Eventually she met his eyes and he held them there for a moment until she dragged them away and pretended to be fascinated by something over his shoulder.

'Who asked you?'

Flick searched his face again. He didn't seem angry any more, but his expression was intractable. She didn't think she'd get away with bluffing this and, besides, she wasn't sure he didn't know the answer already. He seemed to know everything else.

'Your wife.'

At this he looked down and started tapping his fingertips together distractedly, absorbing the information.

Flick felt compelled to explain. 'She came to see us a while ago. She was very upset.' Ben didn't look up at this. 'She thinks ... well, she believes that you are having an affair. Affairs. She wanted me to see what you were up to.' There was silence. Did this mean he was guilty? If so, what was he going to do now? Let her go, or beg her to pretend to Alison she'd seen nothing? That would be pathetic and suddenly Flick felt angry that she was involved in a marriage she knew nothing about. If he was playing away, she'd been put on the spot, made to feel awkward. Had he been with someone tonight? Was it the same woman he'd been with at The Westborough? Perhaps they'd had an early tryst tonight – a matinée performance – or perhaps she was waiting upstairs for him, all perfumed and ready. This made Flick feel angrier and felt an emotion she couldn't quite put a name to. 'So obviously I reported back about your lunch – that's what I was doing when you came back early the other night. She told me you'd be here tonight ... but well, obviously you were too clever this time.'

'You were too busy with your nose in the paper.' At this Ben smiled slightly. Flick felt stupid. 'I walked past you twice. I could have walked past you stark-naked right there in the lobby and I doubt you would have noticed.' Flick blushed deeply as an image popped into her head.

'Are you proud of what you are doing, then?' Flick bristled. 'I mean, you don't seem very contrite, considering what I saw. Doesn't it bother you that I had to go back and tell your wife that you were with a beautiful woman in a hotel and that you went up in the lift with her?'

Ben leaned forward again and took a sip of his coffee. Biding his time, no doubt. 'Does it bother *you*,' he said eventually, 'that you may have the whole thing wrong?'

Flick snorted. 'Well, you would say that, wouldn't you?'

Ben ignored her. 'That man you were – how shall I put it? – sharing your assets with in the YouTube video. Were you "seeing what he was up to" as well?'

Flick was about to tell him to mind his own business but he was holding her gaze again and she couldn't look away. What *was* it about this man? He made her feel confused and unable to think straight. Was this what Alison had meant about him being so clever?

'Actually – not that you have any right to know – but his wife knew he was a philanderer and asked us to embarrass him.'

Ben threw back his head and laughed. 'I see! You're running some kind of revenge set-up, are you? Hitting on "philanderers".'

Flick played with her sleeve. 'Maybe. Sort of.'

'Philanderer.' He shook his head, amused. 'How wonderfully old-fashioned you are, Felicity.'

'Flick,' she corrected.

'Flick.' His voice was soft. 'Well, you managed it with Mike Jackson. Anyone involved in property in the south-east has had your cleavage landing in their PC. If you fall on hard times with the revenge game, there will always be a job for you pole-dancing though, in my experience, I don't think you are supposed to get that close to the clients. That's lap-dancing.'

Flick's face was flaming red now. 'I know, but I had to get him in shot.' Why was she telling him this?

'He's a slimy creep, anyway,' Ben said unexpectedly. 'I don't suppose anyone felt sorry for him.'

'He deserved it.' Flick replied assertively. 'He *is* a creep and any man who behaves like that and upsets his wife, deserves to be humiliated!'

'Maybe. But you are setting yourselves up as judge and jury. The thing is, Flick, what happens if you get it wrong?'

'I don't think we have so far.'

'Yes you have.' Ben played with the teaspoon on his saucer. Flick's tea was going cold now. She hated Darjeeling anyway. 'I'm afraid you've got it very wrong. That woman you saw me with – her name's Nadin. Yes, she is very beautiful, but she is also very married to a good friend of mine.'

'That's never stopped anyone!' Flick laughed, too loudly.

'No. But I'm not the sort of man who does that kind of thing. However, more importantly, she also owns The Westborough Hotel. Or did. I own it now.'

'I know.'

The penny began to drop, very slowly, in Flick's head. 'I read about it in the Sunday papers.'

'So, Miss Detective, instead of *philandering* with her over lunch, we were actually discussing the details of the take-over and I went up in the lift with her, not to rip her clothes off, but to go to her office on the fourth floor. If you want verification, you can talk to her husband who arrived about ten minutes later to join us. Happy now?'

Flick didn't know what to say.

'And tonight I had a meeting with an architect who's working on a project I own just outside St Albans. He's called Charlie and he is very male.' Ben's eyes twinkled.

'OK, OK, but I was only doing what Alison asked me to do.' A thought occurred to Flick. 'And besides, she must have other reasons to suspect you might be having an affair, hey? She must have some grounds for her suspicions, mustn't she? Why else would she bother to employ us? And the fact that you've been following *me* makes me wonder what you've got to hide.'

Ben held her eyes again. 'I found out about you because I wanted to know who it was who was parked in my street in the dark.'

'How did you know where I lived?'

'Because I have ways of finding out these things – that don't involve stalking. And I don't rely on the newspapers to give me information after the event,' he said pointedly. 'Then you appeared at the hotel and I was intrigued as to why two women seemed so fascinated in my life.'

'Did you check out Georgie, too?'

'Of course. But it was you I was interested in, because it was you who was parked in the street and who followed my car. Then I recognised your … face on the video. Lo and behold, you appear in my sitting room posing as a landscape gardener, and then here too. I couldn't believe my eyes when I saw you engrossed in the paper out here.'

'And Alison? What about that?' Flick pressed.

Ben put his hands on his thighs and tapped out a rhythm gently, almost nervously. 'I really don't know,' he said eventually, 'and I'm not sure that I want to discuss it with you. I think you should just be content with the fact that I am not having an affair and we'll leave it at that. Incidentally, if I was, I'd be a bloody sight more discreet than to have lunch with a mistress in a major London hotel for anyone to see.'

Somehow, Flick knew he was right. That wouldn't be his style at all. She picked up her bag, wanting to go home and get away from him. She'd been rumbled and she felt ludicrous and embarrassed, all at the same time.

'OK, I'm off now. I'm sorry I've been on your tail. I won't bother you again. I'll tell Alison that we've finished with this.' Flick stood up and slung her bag over her shoulder. 'Thanks for the tea.'

Ben didn't stand up, but looked up at her. 'Pleasure.' And as she walked away, she glanced back over her shoulder. He had slumped back in his chair and put both hands pensively to his lips.

Georgie stood up and stretched, put away the albums and, looking at her watch, was halfway upstairs to run a bath when she heard his key in the lock. Her heart was pounding.

'Hello there.'

Ed gave a start and looked up at her. 'Oh, hello. Thought you'd be in bed by now.'

She came downstairs and stood in front of him. 'No, no. Lib's staying at a friend's and I thought it would give us some time together. You know, to talk.'

'Right.'

He turned away and hung up his coat, then pushed his hair back.

'Shall I get you a drink?' she asked brightly.

'Hmm, yes please. OK if I go and sit down?'

'Oh, but supper's ready.'

He came into the kitchen. 'I'm sure I said. I've eaten already.' He looked at the table, carefully set with candles ready to light.

'Oh. Sorry. But I'm stuffed. Look, can't you plate it up and stick it in the fridge? I'll have it heated up tomorrow.'

Georgie felt the situation starting to slip away. This was not how she'd planned it. 'But I haven't eaten.'

'So have it now. I'll just go and watch *Newsnight*, OK?'

He turned to walk out.

'Ed, we need to talk,' Georgie blurted out.

He paused and she could see him set his shoulders before he turned round. There was a wariness in his eyes. Did he know what was coming? Not all of it, he didn't.

Georgie rubbed her face. 'Ed, sit down please.' She started to clear away the plates while she thought of what to say. He settled heavily into a seat and sighed.

She turned to face him, aware of the pounding of her pulse in her ears. This was one of those moments when everything was going to change and she felt as though she was about to dive into icy water. 'Ed, I know you've been ... seeing someone. A woman.' Her mouth was moving, but she couldn't believe she was actually saying the words.

Although his expression didn't change, something in his demeanour did. Georgie paused, wondering if he was going to speak. But after seconds stretched out agonisingly, she went on.

'A parcel came. I had to pick it up from the post office. It was a jumper, cashmere. A hotel had sent it. They'd found it in the room where you'd been staying.'

'Hang on,' he said, his voice puzzled. 'A parcel from a hotel? Is this what this is all about? Let me see it. Hotels do have a lot of people staying, you know. Didn't it occur to you it might be a mistake?'

She hesitated. He did seem genuinely surprised. Then she thought of the restaurant. 'It's not just that. It's Cardiff. You haven't been going there, really. Have you? It's been over for ages. Months.'

He laughed, but did she sense a hint of anxiety? 'How do you know that?'

'Ed, I called your office and they told me.' She took a deep breath. 'Look, there's no point trying to argue this. I know you've been seeing someone. You've got to tell me the truth. You owe me that, at least.'

He sat back and stared first at her, then down at his hands. There was a long pause and he jiggled his leg. 'Oh God, darling, I'm so sorry. Yes, there has been somebody. But it's not what you think.' He looked up pleadingly. 'I hate myself for not telling you.'

Georgie swallowed. 'Who is she?'

He shrugged. 'She's just someone I met at a gallery. We were the only people there and we got talking. When I said what I did, she asked for my card and I gave it to her. She called and said she wanted to retain an architect. She said she was converting a place in Hammersmith. An old church. It was going to be used as a restaurant.'

'So she wanted to employ you?'

'That's what I thought, at first.' Ed refilled his glass. 'She kept calling, arranging meetings at lunch, then dinner. I was going along with it because I thought if I could bring her in as a client, you know, for the practice, it would look good. But she kept stringing me along and then – well, it got a bit embarrassing, and she was all over me.' He glanced up at her again, briefly. 'I was stupid and naive. Flattered, maybe.'

Georgie paused, almost reluctant to ask. 'What's her name?'

Ed looked down. 'Lynn. I'm sorry.'

Georgie gazed at him, his expression so penitent and ashamed and her heart swelled. 'And have you seen her since?'

'I'll be perfectly straight with you, George. I finished it the other night. Told her she'd have to contact the practice directly if she wanted any more help – although I'm not sure she really took it in.' He sighed heavily. 'I'd be surprised if I hear from her again.'

'Is it honestly over, Ed?'

He reached over and took her hand, looking deep into her eyes. 'Truly, love. I wouldn't lie to you about a thing like this. I didn't want to tell you – well, because it didn't mean anything. And I felt so stupid, being taken in by her and everything. But I'm relieved now that it's out in the open. I don't want there to be secrets between us.'

Georgie felt herself relax. She should be angrier, she knew. But at one level it was less awful than she'd expected. And at least she knew, now, that he was telling the truth, because he'd actually confessed about going out for dinner, which she hadn't even mentioned. If he'd covered up about that, she'd have known it was still going on. It was a very good sign. But one more thing was bothering her.

'Ed, what I don't understand is why you did it in the first place? I mean, Libby and me, aren't we good enough for you? Weren't we enough to keep you happy?'

He sighed. 'Of course you are. You are both so important to me. I was just stupid and vain, maybe. One thing led to another. I never meant for it to happen ...'

She squeezed his hand. 'Right, well – I can't say I'm not terribly hurt but ... I mean, maybe I'm to blame too, in a way. I know I get too wrapped up in Libby and her stuff – maybe it's because it's only her and I obsess a little bit – but I'm going to focus much more on you now, Ed. And on us, because ...' She adjusted her cardigan. 'I've got something to tell you too.'

'Oh, really?' Ed's expression was interested. 'What's that then?'

She could feel the smile growing on her face. 'It's so amazing, Ed. And I know it's not what we planned but I think it's come at exactly the right time. It's like it was meant to be.'

'What are you on about, love? Don't keep me in suspense!'

'Oh, Ed, I'm pregnant!' she blurted out. 'I didn't even realise I was, but I went to see the doctor because I was feeling ropey – and I thought it might be stress, you know, because of what

I'd found out about you – but it turned out to be just the most wonderful news!'

She gazed at him, a rapturous smile on her face, but he didn't respond at all. He seemed frozen.

'Fuck.' He looked away. 'You can't be.'

'That's exactly what I said to the doctor,' Georgie laughed. 'I must have slipped up or something with my cap.' She crossed her fingers in her lap. 'I know this must be a shock, and I know you didn't really want to have any more but, really, if you think about it, a new baby won't make much difference to our finances. I've thought it all out – with Lib going to the Academy we won't have any more fees, and I've kept loads of stuff from first time round. And Flick will help out, covering for me at work and everything—'

Ed stood up. 'You've told Flick already? How long have you known about this? You seem to have it all planned out!'

'No, of course not,' she continued, confused. 'I haven't seen her since I went to the doctor's. I'll tell her tomorrow or something. But the exciting thing is, I'm going for a scan after we get back from holiday in Brittany. I've got the date here somewhere. And maybe you can get time off to come with me, like last time. Do you remember?'

Ed rubbed his face and turned away for a moment. Georgie felt a sense of growing discomfort and straightened her back, as if she could dispel it somehow. He turned round again, slowly, and the look on his face was closed and cold.

'Listen, Georgie. I accept I was in the wrong with this – business – but I'm prepared to put it behind me now and I want to commit fully to our marriage. That's why I've been completely honest with you. But this was never part of our plan, was it?' He sighed heavily. 'I knew you wanted another baby. Christ knows, you've gone on about it enough. But I didn't think you'd take it upon yourself to decide for both of us.'

'But, Ed,' Georgie said, her voice sounding plaintive and whiney, even to her, 'You know what they say, "babies bring their own love with them". I really believe that this is what we need, both of us. And Lib too. After what you've done with this – woman – you have to agree. You owe me this, Ed. This will cement our marriage, believe me.'

He shrugged. 'I'd like to believe you, Georgie. I really would. But I never wanted any more children. I thought I'd always made that clear.' He shrugged helplessly. 'I just don't know what to say.' He turned and left the room. She heard the music signalling the start of *Newsnight* and the creak of leather as he shifted his weight on the hard, unyielding sofa.

Chapter Sixteen

Georgie woke with a terrible sense of despondency. She'd sat in the kitchen for hours after she'd heard Ed go upstairs and then, from some weird sense of self-pity, had orgied on the contents of the fridge which had ended, predictably, with her throwing up violently, her stomach cramping and her throat burnt by the bitter torrent of vomit. The morning dawned cool and overcast, and she and Ed shadow-boxed, careful not to look at each other and speaking only about things that were necessary, about a bill or the bins that needed putting out. He pecked her on the cheek briefly and left, shutting the door firmly behind him.

In the office, Flick glanced up in greeting, then stared, appalled. 'You're white as a sheet. What's up? Sit down and I'll get you a cup of tea. Jo's at the dentist.'

'Would you? That would be great. I, er, must have eaten something dodgy last night.'

Flick stirred a well-brewed concoction before setting it in front of Georgie. 'Don't tell me *you* accidentally ate the steak with rat poison instead of giving it to Ed?'

Georgie attempted a feeble laugh but gave up and slurped her tea instead. She glanced guiltily at Flick. She really should tell her. And she would, eventually. She'd have to. But not yet. Not after last night. It was lucky, really, that Flick's complete inexperience with all things baby-related meant she hadn't even guessed. Although, she thought bitterly as she dunked one of the biscuits Flick had shoved towards her, Georgie had thought she was a bit of an expert and *she* hadn't even realised.

'Ooh, that feels a bit better,' she sighed as the nausea faded. 'Right, what's on today, then?'

Flick sat up and peered at her over the computers. 'Yes, your colour's back to normal now. Well—' And she proceeded to list the jobs for the day. 'Dog collection for the Bates. We've got to find another ironing service in SW17, Maria's done her back in. The Colemans – we need to check that bloke has cleared their gutters. Oh, and I wondered if you could drop off some swatches on your way to Tim's house to let in the carpet-layer.'

'I thought he was back from Stuttgart this week,' Georgie struggled to concentrate on her notebook as Flick rattled on.

'He is, but he was going up to Scotland for a few days and he's expecting the carpet people in to measure up. Can you be there at two o'clock?'

Georgie nodded sleepily. 'There was something I meant to ask you. What was it again? Oh, I remember. What's the score with Alison Houghton? What does she want us to do next about that husband of hers?'

Flick got up from her desk, ready to leave. 'Oh, I'll fill you in on that later. I have to call her first. She was a bit undecided.'

'Really? She didn't seem the undecided type. How strange. Maybe she wasn't sufficiently impressed with those photos from the hotel. Do you want me to give her a ring while you're out?'

'No, no. It's all right,' Flick said quickly. 'I remember now. She said she'd call here later, when she was sure Ben wasn't going to be around.'

Georgie yawned and stretched. 'Whatever. As long as—'

But Flick had already left, closing the door unusually quietly behind her.

The phone kept Georgie awake for the rest of the morning. If it hadn't been for the fairly constant stream of calls – mostly existing clients panicking before they left on holiday – she'd have been tempted to curl up under her desk and have a nap. Bloody-mindedness played a part too, though. She was determined not to give in to the effects of this pregnancy. She wouldn't show weakness to Ed. Their holiday in France, booked months ago, now presented an ordeal Georgie was dreading. It seemed, though, that she was becoming expert at blanking out parts of her life that weren't going according to plan.

Between calls, during which she dealt with a query about bikini waxes and how to request a 'landing strip' in France ('billet de metro', she ascertained by texting a friend in Paris), and ordered a hamper stuffed with deli delights to be sent down to a holiday cottage in Polzeath, she forced herself to get up and march round the office, swinging her arms and breathing deeply, in an effort to energise herself. And as a way of avoiding having to think too much. All she achieved, though, was to stimulate her appetite, and she left the office a little earlier than she really needed to for Tim Rowlands's house, before Flick had even returned, partly because she wasn't sure she could resist the biscuit tin any longer, partly because she wasn't sure she could resist confiding in her friend.

The sun had broken through and was now quite intense, and Georgie's car was roasting as she slipped in behind the wheel, the upholstery sticking to the backs of her legs, bare where she'd hitched the full cotton skirt up above her knees. She wound down her window and inclined her head towards the slight, but welcome, breeze as she crawled through the lunchtime traffic. She'd pick up a snack on the way to Tim's house. Something light and bland, after last night's excesses. Maybe some fruit or a smoothie. She pulled in on a single yellow and dodged into a deli she knew for a mango lassi, then continued on her way, steadying the plastic takeaway cup with one hand.

In Tim's street, she parked a little further down than normal, but under a plane tree, grateful for the shade. She whistled to herself as she strolled back towards number sixteen, now familiar to her and always welcoming, even with the stairs still covered in sawdust.

But the sawdust was gone, replaced by a carpet runner. Odd.

But there it undeniably was, exuding that new carpet smell that made her hold her breath. She closed the door behind her and walked through to the kitchen, to see if there was a note from Tim. It wasn't like him to get his wires crossed. But there was no note and no indication that he was there, although she could trace a faint scent of his trademark lime and basil cologne. The fridge gave no sign of having been used recently. Georgie called the office, but the answerphone was still on, so she shrugged. Perhaps the carpet fitters had done half a job and were due back. So she settled herself in the leather chair in the corner of the kitchen and sipped at her lassi. It was as quiet as ever. Through the closed windows, she could vaguely make out the sounds of the children playing in the school beyond the garden. She sighed in contentment and put her empty cup down on the floor beside her. It really was very ...

Georgie opened her eyes. Then blinked hard. She must have fallen asleep, here, in Tim Rowlands's kitchen. She sat up, feeling panicky for a moment. A quick glance at her watch reassured her, though, that she still had plenty of time before she had to pick up Libby from school so, after a moment's hesitation, she stretched luxuriously and rested her cheek back on the cool pillow under her head. Then froze. Pillow? She heard footsteps on the stairs and, before she could stand up, Tim appeared, carrying a stack of books.

'Oh, did I wake you?' he smiled teasingly. 'I'm sorry. You looked so peaceful, I just stopped your head from lolling and left you to get on with it.'

Georgie yawned but tried to stifle it quickly. She felt terribly embarrassed at her unprofessional behaviour and felt impelled to explain. 'The thing is, I'm pregnant and it makes me so tired.'

'Oh, congratulations,' he said, looking slightly surprised and she felt embarrassed that she'd revealed it to him of all people. 'I remember it with my wife. She was permanently knocked-out in the early months. I'm so sorry you had a wasted journey. The carpet layers called this morning and asked if they could come a bit early. I tried to call you from the office about an hour ago, but your answerphone was on. Cup of tea?'

Georgie sat, blinking stupidly. She felt refreshed and relaxed. 'Not wasted at all – I needed the kip! Thanks, yes, I'd love a cup.'

'No, don't get up. I'll bring it over to you. I haven't got anything fancy, I'm afraid. I'm a bit staid when it comes to tea. It's got to be hot, strong, dark brown and in a mug. That suit you?'

'Hmmm, lovely.' The situation was so peculiar, Georgie just allowed herself to go along with it and took the mug gratefully.

Tim sat backwards on a dining chair looking at her calmly as he drank his tea. 'Want a biscuit?' he enquired pleasantly.

'Er, yes. I think I would.'

He unfolded himself from the chair and opened a few cupboard doors at random. 'I haven't got a system yet,' he admitted. 'I'm quite sure there are some in here, somewhere. Unless you've been coming in and eating them, of course!'

Georgie struggled to sit up straight. 'Oh no. I really haven't. This is absolutely the first time, I promise. I just had a bit of a bad night's sleep and it's so hot and everything, I just couldn't help it.'

Tim withdrew his head from the cupboard and smiled at her. 'Teasing. Sorry. It's a bad habit of mine. I've got a stack of brothers and sisters and it's how we all function.'

Georgie laughed. 'I can relate to that. Teasing when we weren't actually trying to draw blood or kill each other.'

'Anyway, look! I've found them.' He extended an already open pack of chocolate HobNobs, and then took a couple himself. Georgie nibbled at hers as she watched him padding round the kitchen, arranging things and attaching papers to the front of the fridge using a magnet in the shape of the Empire State Building. He feet were bare and strong, and he looked relaxed in jeans and an untucked shirt. It was unbuttoned at the bottom and as he moved she caught a flash of flat stomach and a thin line of dark hair leading down from his navel. She felt an unexpected whoosh of lust. Hot and raw. My god. She'd forgotten the power of pregnancy hormones.

'You must be almost finished here now,' she ventured, hoping she wasn't blushing.

'What? Er, yes, probably. The bathrooms are all but done. I've got to get some more bed linen and towels. Lamps. That kind of thing. I might need to have them delivered to your office, if that's OK – unless you want to have them delivered here so you can pop over for a little nap!'

Georgie stood up, anxious to redeem herself. 'I don't normally do this kind of thing you know!'

'Georgie,' he said gently, smiling. 'I'm quite sure you don't. But make sure you get enough rest, won't you? You need to look after yourself.'

There was an awkward silence, and Georgie looked down at the floor. Tim's kind words had made her eyes fill with tears and she daren't look at him. She would be too early to pick up Lib but she suddenly felt she had to leave. Get away from this house and this man, both of which felt much too comfortable.

By the time Flick got back to the office – later than she'd hoped – Joanna was back at her desk. She filled in Flick on the details of her dental appointment and they fell into a busy silence, their fingers tapping on their keyboards.

Flick was well into drafting a letter to their database persuading them why an increase in membership fees was inevitable – 'the pressures of the market, blah blah blah' – when the phone shrilled. Without taking her eyes off the screen, she picked it up. 'Hello? Domestic Angels. Flick Lane speaking.'

There was silence at the other end, then the phone went dead. She put it back onto her desk and carried on. Ten minutes later it rang again. 'Hello, Domestic Angels. Flick here.' Again there was nothing. She put it down.

'No one there?' Joanna asked over her shoulder.

Flick carried on typing. 'Probably a mobile out of range or something. They'll call back when they can.'

'Maybe.' Joanna replied. 'It's odd though 'cos it's happened a few times recently. When I try 1471, it's always "number withheld".'

'Pah. Ignore it,' Flick said, keen to crack the wording of the letter. 'Probably some perv who gets off on hearing our voices!'

Life with Ed certainly didn't feel comfortable, and the couple of weeks leading up to their holiday was polite and unnatural. Thank goodness for the maelstrom of the end of term and the packing, which filled awkward moments and gave them something to focus on. They discussed everything politely except the elephant in the corner. Georgie even winced at a story about a miracle baby which came on the news one evening. Ed was suddenly very engrossed in his paper and Georgie dared not look at him. The topic of babies seemed to be everywhere, capped off by an emotional phone call one evening from Georgie's younger brother announcing that Giselle, his wife, was pregnant at last, after years of IVF treatment. Ed, who took the call, congratulated him gruffly, then handed the phone to Georgie. After saying goodbye, she'd gone to hide in the bathroom to let the cascade of tears she'd been holding back fall without comment.

Any references Ed made to her wellbeing were brief and rare, but nonetheless she seized upon them, welcoming his overtures and seeing them as a promising sign. He'd come round. She was his wife.

The cottage was one that a colleague of Ed's had recommended. In the heart of Brittany, it certainly wasn't like any of the *gîtes rurales* that Georgie remembered from her childhood, with uneven floors, gruesome wallpaper and a permanent smell of damp. The photos Ed had shown her, from the pages of a design magazine of course, showed a large, bright space with light wood floors and beautifully arching ceilings, plus the very latest in bathroom gadgetry. It looked wonderful. Barefoot luxury concealed within a sensitively renovated shell. As they made their way along smaller and smaller roads, following the typed directions Georgie held clenched in her lap, she couldn't help thinking that being tucked away, far from London, could be the best thing possible. Ed's irritation, when she got them lost in the side streets of Josselin and he stopped the car, wordlessly holding out his hand for the instructions, his lips thin and censorious, was nothing more sinister than usual. She never could read maps, and she knew he'd be more relaxed when they finally reached their destination.

Georgie's mood lifted even further when they arrived at the house, which really was everything Ed had promised – and more. Libby clattered from room to room, exclaiming with delight at every new discovery – the bunk beds, the little niches in the stone walls that would provide a perfect place for her toy cat to sit, the snooker table, the breakfast bar already set for three and the basket of croissants on the long kitchen table. Following at a more sedate rate, Georgie clocked up her own list of treats – the underfloor heating in the slate-lined wet room, the comfortable, brown-cord sofas, long enough to lie on full length, with pendant standard lamps at each end, so you could read there at night; the skylights through which she could see swallows swooping about the house. It was modern and streamlined, yet warm and welcoming and eminently liveable. And it reminded her of something ... somewhere. She nodded in satisfaction as she looked round. Yes, it was lovely. Perhaps the holiday wouldn't be so bad after all. She'd take Lib and pop down to the boulangerie she'd seen in the nearby village, once Ed had unloaded the car. Or maybe they could see if there were any bikes to rent nearby. She could really make it fun for Lib.

'Mummy, I'm going to sleep in the top bunk tonight and the bottom one tomorrow,' Libby called down.

The joy at discovering the house and the surroundings

carried on throughout the rest of the day. Georgie quashed a feeling of disquiet though when Ed came in from outside and his 'exploration of the garden', mobile in hand, delighted to report he could get coverage.

'Does it matter, darling?' she asked brightly. 'We're on holiday after all.'

'Well,' Ed replied airily. 'Just in case the office need to get hold of me, you know.'

That evening they walked to a little pizza restaurant in the local village and came back merry and relaxed.

Libby, ensconced in her bunk, dropped off in seconds and Georgie, seizing the moment, determinedly took a bottle of wine out of the fridge, pulled Ed up from the sofa where he was flicking through a novel that he'd found on a bookshelf, and led him wordlessly up the stairs. Turning the lights of their bedroom low, she turned to him and slipped her hands under his shirt and ran them gently up and down the skin of his back. He didn't respond at first so, undeterred, she began to undo his belt. She heard him groan and could feel an encouraging response under her hand. She began to undo the buttons on her top and lifted it over her head while Ed kicked off his jeans. She felt his hands touch her now tender breasts and she tried not to flinch. He turned her to the bed and pushed her back gently, straddling her as he pulled his shirt over his head. She tried to pull him down beside her, wanting to feel his lips on hers, hoping it would put her more in the mood, but he wouldn't meet her eyes. He slipped off his boxers as she quickly took off her knickers. The sheets were cold and felt a little damp, but it felt important to get this done, to set a seal on the new course she was determined their relationship would take.

Under the covers, he pulled her towards him again and reached down to touch her, delving vaguely in a way that wasn't particularly comfortable. She wriggled towards him and kissed his neck. He stopped, took hold of her hand, and pushed it down inside the bed. He had an abstracted air, as if he was thinking about something else. She caressed his thighs teasingly, but there was little response. She stopped, mildly discouraged. Maybe this called for more drastic action. Wordlessly, she slipped down between the sheets, kissing and licking his chest and stomach as she went, then took him into her mouth. For a moment, he stiffened, but after a while he gently took hold of her shoulders and pulled her up beside him again. He shrugged sheepishly. 'Sorry, love. I'm just too tired after the drive.'

'Never mind, darling,' Georgie lied. 'We've got plenty of time.' She rolled onto her back and lay there thinking until she heard his breathing soften.

Chapter Seventeen

'All right, all right, I'll fix it, Mrs Holstein. I'm sure the plumbers didn't do it intentionally. Perhaps the instructions – yes, I'm sure we were to blame, too – but perhaps the instructions weren't clear.

Mrs Holstein's voice rose even further at the end of the phone and Flick held it away from her ear. Funny how people all over the world have to tolerate the most immense discomfort, living in shanty towns or in bombed-out buildings, yet Mrs Holstein of 145 Caveye Road, couldn't put up with the wrong loo seat.

It had been a long old morning for Flick – from a 4.30 a.m. early awakening when Dolce had bought in a bird as a gift for her and deposited it on her bed. Then there was the rain, rain, rain, that had punctuated the last few days and which seemed to have made up more of the summer than sunshine so far. Joanna glanced over and smiled. With Georgie away on who-knew-what kind of holiday, Joanna and Flick were flat-out fielding calls and having to do holiday-cover, feeding hamsters, gerbils and other revolting pet duties. Flick wasn't going to admit that a couple of times she'd given various vermin two days' worth of food and hoped they wouldn't have died of obesity before her next visit. The responsibility of looking after other people's pets was immense, but they'd lost only one in the whole time the agency had been in business, and that had been a goldfish who had been looking peaky before its owners had left for Spain, so they weren't entirely to blame.

'Oh God, is it really only three-thirty?' Flick groaned,

looking at her watch, finally getting shot of Mrs Holstein with promises that the great loo seat crisis would be resolved as soon as humanly possible. She made a mental note that when they hit their revenue target for members of the agency, there were some that would not be allowed to renew their membership. The two Mrs Hs were at the top of the list, nothing but trouble since the day they'd paid their first subs, and they'd been on the phone ever since.

'Are you going to be able to help with this wedding on Friday?' Flick asked Joanna who was, like an angel, making her way towards the kettle.

'Sure, four hundred balloons be all right?'

'Yup, and I've asked ...'

The phone jangled again. Joanna was the nearest so she picked up the extension on Georgie's empty desk.

'Domestic Angels? Yes, certainly, I'll put you through.' She muted the call. 'It's Alison.'

Flick's heart sank. She'd known she would have to call Alison eventually, but had been hoping she could leave it until Joanna went home.

'Can I call her back later?' she asked.

Joanna made the call live again. 'Can she call you a bit later this afternoon, she's a bit tied up.' Flick winced. She thought she'd got Joanna out of the habit of using that ridiculous expression; as if they were all in the corner gagged and bound.

'Right. I'll see.' Joanna turned to Flick again and raised an eyebrow. 'She's very insistent that later is highly inconvenient.'

'OK,' Flick sighed and indicated for Joanna to transfer the call.

'Alison? How are you?'

'Fine,' she answered, quite abruptly, as if she was in too much of a hurry to bother with niceties. 'What have you found out?'

'Weeell,' Flick said slowly, trying to buy time while she thought what to say and wondering if she could word it obtusely enough so that Joanna wouldn't get suspicious. She prayed the other line would ring so Joanna would have to concentrate on that, but it stayed obstinately silent.

'I'm afraid I couldn't determine anything.'

'Determine? What does that mean?'

'Well, he wasn't with anyone.'

'What was he doing then?' Alison pressed, her voice becoming uncharacteristically high and waspish.

'To be honest, I didn't see him with anyone … he was on his own.' Flick watched as Joanna opened her desk drawer and unwrapped a packet of Polo mints with studied nonchalance. Her ears were practically twitching like antennae.

There was a silence. 'Oh.'

'And,' Flick continued, swivelling in her chair so her back was to Joanna. 'I have subsequently found out that the woman he was with at The Westborough is the owner and I understand they were discussing the sale.'

'That means nothing.' Alison brushed off the information impatiently. Flick wasn't quite sure how to react to this sudden change in her manner. 'He's been overfriendly with her for years; it's just an excuse. And she's staying on the management team as a consultant.'

'Right. I could still find no evidence to suggest they are … lovers.' Flick could almost sense Joanna stiffen and lean at an angle in her chair, earwigging. Alison made a 'pah' noise. Suddenly Flick felt a wave of fatigue. She really couldn't be bothered with this any more, nor did she really care what Joanna heard now. This situation was all too weird. 'Alison, you seem determined to believe the worst of your husband. I can find nothing to suggest your suspicions are justified.'

'That's because you haven't looked hard enough.' Alison's voice was shrill and she was clearly on the verge of tears. 'I know what he does. He never spends any time here with me. He's always at the bloody office or off with some whore, no doubt.'

Flick held the phone slightly away from her ear to avoid

being deafened. This was not the woman who had come into their office tearful and vulnerable. There had been a seismic shift in her demeanour and Flick suspected her current behaviour might just be closer to the real Alison.

'You are clearly not up to the job. I shan't be paying you for this last fiasco,' Alison was now saying.

'No. No, perhaps you shouldn't,' Flick waded in, interrupting her. 'In fact, we don't wish to be involved in this case any more. Perhaps you should find someone else to take it over and try to catch out your husband because I can't see any reason to hound him. Thanks for your custom and we'd be delighted to recommend a very reliable landscape gardener should you decide to go ahead with remodelling your garden ... again.' At that, Flick slammed down the phone.

The silence in the office was deafening and she looked round to see Joanna staring at her and Tim standing beside Joanna's desk.

'Right.' Joanna said eventually.

'Right,' said Flick, adrenaline making her heart beat hard.

'Interesting,' smiled Tim slowly. 'Is this a new service you are offering?'

Flick slumped back in her seat and tapped her pen on her pad. She wasn't sure how much Tim had heard, but it was obviously enough. 'Hello, Tim,' she smiled sheepishly.

'I just came by to drop off details of another job, but it sounds like you have your hands full. I didn't realise that Domestic Angels was so diverse.'

'Neither did I,' Joanna replied dryly. 'Anyone want a cuppa?'

'Don't mind if I do.' Tim perched himself on the side of her desk and Joanna got up to do the honours. The demand for an explanation hung in the air. Flick sighed.

'I'll explain, but if you breathe a word I'll fire you Joanna and Tim, I'll smash every Italian tile in your precious new bathroom.'

'Sounds fair enough,' Tim laughed. What a nice man he was.

'A while ago Georgie and I were approached by a woman who wanted us to play a trick on her cheating husband. We did – it was a bit of fun, just a prank, really, and it worked – and she must have told someone else and they came to us and it went on for – I don't know, a few months now.'

Joanna raised an eyebrow again and put mugs down in front of them both. 'So that explains the secret top-level meetings in the broom cupboard.'

'Yes it does, and I'm sorry that we didn't involve you, Jo. We're not really very proud of what we were doing but it seemed harmless enough.'

'That call didn't sound very harmless,' Tim offered.

'No.' Alison's attitude was bothering her. Had she missed something? Had she been taken in by Ben's charm, though he hadn't been exactly charming to her. She could imagine what it would be like to be on the receiving end of a charm offensive. His smile would have most women keeling over and begging for mercy. 'No, this one's been a bit different. His wife seems convinced that he is – well, that he's had lovers. Maybe he has, but I can't seem to nail him.'

'Flick,' Tim sipped his tea. 'I think you've stepped over the line a bit here.'

'How do you mean?'

'It sounds, from what you've said, that up until now you've been getting revenge in a fairly gentle way. Dishing out just desserts. But this sounds like a different thing altogether. This is private dick country. You know, the type of people who sit in cars all night with a long lens, trying to get a shot of the errant husband *in flagrante delicto*.'

'In what?' Joanna asked.

'At it.' Flick and Tim said simultaneously and laughed.

'Well, why didn't you say that?' Joanna asked, confused.

'Perhaps you're right. She seems so upset, that's the thing

though. She says he's a bastard and that he's never allowed her to have children, and I feel quite sorry for her.'

'You didn't sound it on the phone.' Joanna snorted and turned back to her computer.

Tim slid from his perch and came over to Flick's desk. 'People have lots of reasons for doing things that are deep and complicated,' he said quietly, draining his mug. 'I think you are probably best out of this one, Flick. See you soon and take care of yourself. I'll collect my keys when I get back.' He left his mug on her desk, thanked Joanna for the tea and left the office.

The evening was warm now, after the afternoon's downpour, and Flick decided to leave her car and walk back home across the common. People were playing football and couples were lying side by side on rugs, murmuring quietly to each other and kissing. Flick slipped off her cardigan and slung it loosely over her shoulders, the breeze cooling her skin. It was good to be outside. She needed a holiday and she wondered again how Georgie was getting on. A brief text earlier in the day, in response to an enquiry about the weather, had said that it was lousy and Flick was pretty sure Georgie wasn't just referring to the rain.

What was Flick's holiday going to be? A mate had mentioned a girls' trip to Turkey but Flick hadn't fancied it. She'd sooner drink ink. All they'd do was talk about men and money and take hours to get ready to go out in the evening. Flick couldn't bear the thought of it. Perhaps she should take her mum away somewhere, but that would be just sad.

She turned into her street, her pace speeded on by the thought of a chilled glass of wine. She could almost taste the cool Pinot on her tongue. She noticed that the window boxes Ben had been so rude about needed watering. As she slipped her key in the door, she heard a car rev up behind her and screech out of a space and off down the road. She turned, too late to get a number plate but, despite her sketchy knowledge of cars, she was fairly sure it was a dark-blue BMW.

*

Even before she opened her eyes, even before she woke up, Georgie knew it was raining, again. Why would it do anything else? It had rained almost constantly since the moment they had arrived. How many days had it been? Only four, yet it was beginning to feel like an eternity. What had started with such high hopes was beginning to become a nightmare. She couldn't bear the tension of another breakfast with Ed asking her what they were going to do that day, as though she really ought to have it all planned out. She'd run out of cathedrals, the beach was out of the question, and none of them could stick another trip to the doll museum. They were all crêped out, and neither she nor Ed drank cider. The only thing left, according to the leaflets of local attractions she'd found in a drawer in the kitchen, was a glass-blowing studio. For God's sake.

Ed's voice broke into her thoughts. 'I was thinking, perhaps we ought to think about setting off early and seeing if we can get a crossing today. What do you think?'

At once, Georgie felt a surge of relief. They hadn't repeated the lovemaking fiasco of that first night, but the failure hung between them. All Georgie wanted was to be back in England, at home, where life could go on as normal. 'Yes, that would be a very good idea. I'll start packing now, before Lib wakes up.'

As she piled clothes back into cases, shoes first as always, she thought about the first time she had come to France with Ed. It had been her birthday and he'd been so evasive about what they were going to do for it, she'd actually got quite annoyed with him. Then, just when she was seriously beginning to wonder if they actually had a future together, since he seemed incapable of responding to her heavy hints – no matter how heavy – he'd called her at work, while she was trying to catch up on some admin for a new dance class starting after Easter.

'Oh hi,' she'd said, a bit shortly. 'Look, I'm rather busy at the moment. Can it wait?'

'No, not really. Thing is – this weekend. I know we were

thinking about going out for supper for your birthday at that new place by the river, but I just don't think I'm going to be able to make it.'

She remembered actually counting to ten before she answered. 'I see. Well, in that case...'

'And I don't think you're going to be able to make it either.'

'What?' she'd answered, really irritated now.

'I know – but there's no way we're going to be able to get back from Paris, just to go out for supper in Richmond, is there?'

'What?'

'I mean, we could if you really wanted, but we'd have to cancel the tickets for the opera.'

'What?'

'Well, not the opera exactly. The Opera House. The New York City Ballet.'

Georgie had lost all power of speech by then, but she remembered his low chuckle as she'd gasped incoherently into the phone. It had been a passing comment, no more, several months ago about the NYCB tour and how she'd love to see them. And he'd remembered.

'Yes,' he continued, and she could hear the smile in his voice. 'I kind of wanted it to be a surprise, but you'll have to pack for it so ... if I pick you up on Friday at about six, we should have plenty of time to get to the airport. OK?'

Finally, she'd got her breath back. 'Oh, Ed, I can't believe it. I'd never have been able to keep it secret even this long. I *do* love you,' she'd sighed. 'Thank you so much. I can't *wait*!'

And their weekend had been everything she'd hoped for, and more. Ed, who knew Paris well, took care of everything, showing her the very best views, buying her the very best ice creams, taking her to the very chicest café where they'd people-watched for hours over steamy cups of coffee. At the opera she was ultra aware of him next to her, watching not the ballet but her face the whole time as she feasted her eyes on the raw energy of the performers, enthralled by every move. And when they got back to the hotel, a beautiful, elegant establishment in the Marais, he'd made slow and languorous love to her, brushing her hands aside as she'd tried to pull him to her, admiring and caressing her as if she were a work of art.

And now here they were. How had they come to this? She'd barely noticed the change, but the contrast with what they'd once had was too painful to think about. Sighing deeply, she snapped the suitcase shut and lowered it to the floor.

Chapter Eighteen

'What *is* it?' Flick hissed, once Joanna had closed the door behind her and left the office. 'You can't come back from holiday early and not tell me why!'

'Give me a chance! We've been flat-out all morning and – well, it's all a bit complicated.'

Flick sat back in her chair. 'Well, it's obvious it wasn't a holiday in paradise.'

'The house was lovely but the weather was lousy and the atmosphere was worse.'

'Oh?'

Georgie took a deep breath. 'Well, there's no easy way to tell you this, Flick. I'm pregnant.'

Flick's face cantered through a range of expressions, starting with shock, then pleasure, then worry, and ended up, after several others that Georgie couldn't begin to identify, watchful and concerned. 'I see. A holiday souvenir?'

'Er, no – a bit longer ago than that.'

'Surprise?' Flick was clearly trying to find out if it was planned.

'Yup. It came as a bit of a shock actually.'

There was a long pause. 'Have you told Ed?'

'Yes. Straight after I told him I knew about the affair, as a matter of fact.'

Flick's eyebrows shot up. 'Christ – no wonder you came home early.'

'Actually, I told him before we went.' And Georgie went on to explain Ed's version of events.

'Mmm,' Flick was clearly trying to cover her scepticism, 'but what about the baby?'

'That is the sticking point. He wants to rebuild our marriage but he's still in shock about the baby. I'm not going to push it – just give him time. I know he'll come round.' Georgie paused. If only she was as confident as she sounded. The trip back from France had been long and silent, broken up only by Libby's chatter, and any conversation was normal on the surface. But they seemed to both be thinking before they spoke. Everything since she'd told him about the baby was out of kilter. 'This should be a time for celebration,' she said eventually.

Flick jumped up and gave Georgie an awkward hug in her seat. 'George, it *is* wonderful news. I'm so pleased for you.'

'I'm glad *you* are,' Georgie smiled tearfully. 'The thing is, I was wondering ... I've got a scan booked and I don't want Ed to come ...' Her voice started to shake and she took several quick breaths.

Flick was at her side in an instant. 'Of course I'll come with you. For the scan and ... I'll be there whenever you need me.'

Georgie nodded quickly, not trusting herself to say anything more.

'What time?'

She tried to smile. 'At ten to twelve, at St George's. It's where I had Lib.'

She felt Flick's hand close round her arm. 'I'm going to call Joanna on her mobile and tell her she needs to cover for us. I'll just make a few calls, change some appointments, then we'll go. All right?'

She nodded and closed her eyes.

Flick handed her another paper cup of water and Georgie took it. She made a quick tally of the number of women who might be going in ahead of her before she took a sip. A full bladder was one thing, but she wasn't sure her pelvic floor was up to this. She glanced at her watch. At the rate they were going she'd be lucky to be seen before one o'clock and by then there might be a splash down.

The waiting room was the same one she came to when she was having Lib. Little more than a corridor, it had no natural light, just fluorescent strips that made everyone look pale and tired. Flick was pretending to read a dog-eared copy of *Hello!* and not even trying to make conversation, bless her. Georgie didn't think she could bear the pretence of small talk. She looked down at her hands, and tried very hard not to think.

'Georgina Casey.' She got up and was aware of Flick at her side but didn't turn to look at her. In the dark of the scanning room, though, she felt her hand lightly rub hers as she slipped off her shoes and lay on the couch.

Baring her stomach and tucking the tissues over her clothes to protect them from the gel, she glanced briefly at Flick while answering the woman's questions. With the screen turned away from them both, Georgie submitted to the insistent movement of the probe over her stomach while the radiographer recorded whatever she needed to record. Her bladder was complaining and she flinched a couple of times, aware that Flick was following her every movement.

'You OK?'

'Yeah. Just desperate for a pee. It can't be much longer, though. I mean, with Lib ...'

The radiographer spoke now, cool and professional. 'I'm going to turn the screen round now so you can see.' A shoal of silvery dots darted across the screen, then coalesced into a blob. 'This is your baby's head. It's a normal size for your probable dates. So I'm just moving across. This is the right shoulder.'

Beside her, Georgie felt Flick sit bolt upright in her seat and she could hear her own heart beating loudly in her ears.

'This is the right arm. These are the ribs and you can see the heart beating here. And you can see the chambers of the heart.

This is all fine. Baby is on the move. Oh look, here's the spine. Are you all right, Mrs Casey?'

Georgie could hear sobbing, but she wasn't sure if it was Flick or her until she realised she couldn't see the screen any more.

'Here you are, dear.' The radiographer handed her a wodge of tissues. 'Don't worry. It takes a lot of people that way. Oh, here are some for you too.'

Now Georgie was quite certain. They were both crying.

'Shall I carry on?'

'Yes, yes please.'

'We can see the kidneys, too, here. And here is the femur, the thigh bone. Looks like your baby is going to be tall. The legs are crossed here.'

'It's incredible,' Georgie breathed.

'Ah, look, baby's turned round again, you can see the eye orbits and the mouth.'

Flick's face was right next to hers now as they gazed at the screen together. Georgie reached out and felt her friend grasp her hand hard.

'This baby, Georgie. It's *your* baby. It's in you.'

Georgie felt a huge release as tears poured down her face again. She'd been so focused on the fact that this was half Ed's, conceived during his deceit and infidelity, that she had forgotten that it was her baby too. Her longed-for baby and a miracle. For the first time since she'd found out, she was actually happy, accepting the reality at last. 'I know. I know. I can't believe it. I've wanted this for so long. I just didn't want it to be like this.'

'This is special. It's so special. I never realised.' Flick breathed in amazement.

The radiographer cleared her throat. 'I'm going to take some images now for you to take away with you, all right?'

'It's my baby, Flick. Mine. You know, it doesn't even matter what Ed thinks. It may be our baby but I'll do it on my own if I have to—'

'No you bloody well won't,' Flick sniffed. ''Cos I'm here.

And listen, you mustn't worry about anything now. Do you hear me, George? You're going to love this baby. You're going to love it so much. And I'll help you. I'll be with you every step.'

'I know, Flick. You're the best. My darling little baby.' She touched her hand gently to her stomach, sliding her fingers over the gel. 'Hello there. I'm your mummy.'

Chapter Nineteen

Flick felt restless and not in the mood for work, even though she knew she had a pile of things to do. The most significant was a request from a client that she find an entertainer prepared to recreate a party based around the entire theme of *Shrek*. Pity the poor child who was picked to play the ogre or the lovely but fatally flawed Princess Fiona. That would be one to live down and it was unlikely to be the spoiled birthday girl who was selected. The agency had a meagre database of top-notch party entertainers, and this might stretch even the most imaginative of them. They were more used to re-enacting fairy tales, though one had manfully gritted her teeth though an army party with thirty small boys pretending to be Andy McNab and blowing each other to smithereens with replica machine guns. That, combined with lashings of Coke, meant she'd had to peel them off the ceiling at the end.

Why couldn't parents say 'No' sometimes, Flick mused. And what had happened to Musical Chairs and Pass the Parcel? She'd been happy with that as a theme as a child, hadn't she?

But Flick had to admit that, after her appointment with Georgie, she felt a little closer to understanding why parents give their children the world. And then more. That moment in the hospital when the sea-horse of a baby had appeared on the screen moved Flick more than she cared to admit. At first it had seemed disassociated from anything that was inside Georgie. Like watching TV. Then, as the radiographer had explained the various parts, the link was made. This small life, its heart beating frantically, its hands up to its tadpole-like face, was a baby. A future. And for the first time in her life Flick could understand the urge to fulfil the most basic role for women: to reproduce. She even felt a wave of anger that people should be allowed this most amazing of achievements and then submit their children to violence and cruelty, fast food and broken homes. She was even beginning to admit to herself a growing desire to do it herself.

As she filed through the handwritten list of demands from *Shrek*-Mummy for the party on Friday, Alison popped into her head. She might be an hysteric, but no wonder she was so distressed that Ben had denied her children. Flick was only at the foothills of broodiness. Alison was sitting on the summit waiting for the green light. What if she had duped him into it – forgotten to take her pill or ravished him without protection? Would he have come round then, once he witnessed what Flick had this morning? Who could fail to be moved?

The idea of ravishing Ben Houghton didn't seem like a chore to her. She raised her eyes from the paperwork. The truth was that, for right or wrong, she fancied the pants off him. Not a cor-he's-not-half-bad sort of fancying that would make her and her girlfriends shriek with delight when they spotted someone in a club. She felt a fascination for him. He was bright and intelligent, with a presence that was irresistible. Nothing about him seemed to square with how Alison had portrayed him. Throughout their meeting at the hotel she'd explored his face and watched how he moved his hands when he talked. She was mesmerised by the way he walked and the way his jeans fitted on his bum. But who could tell? Oh God, it was all very, very wrong.

'What about Pin the Tail on Donkey?' Joanna offered, dragging Flick back to *Shrek*-reality.

'Genius,' Flick laughed, 'if those spoilt brats can cope with anything so gloriously basic. I know, what about a meal of swamp food? Chocolate meringue-mess pudding and sausages that look like worms?'

'Fantastic. I'll speak to the caterer.'

Flick sighed. 'Sometimes I think we're wasted waiting in for plumbers and feeding gerbils. We ought to do kids parties full time.'

Joanna was running her finger through her Rolodex. 'You'd have to double my wages, mate, if that's your plan. I only suffer small children if paid handsomely or very drunk.'

Flick smiled. Joanna was one of those women who was resolutely childless, despite being married to Derek for more than twenty-five years. She'd never mentioned any plans they might have had for kids. Georgie and Flick had never really discussed it with her – why would they? – and she always came up with presents for Libby on birthdays and Christmas that were well-intentioned, if off the mark.

'Jo, can I ask you something?'

Joanna was looking at the list in front of her. 'Yup,' she murmured distractedly. 'So long as it's not to ask me to dress up as Lord Do-Da, the poofy one who wants to be King. I know I'm short, but that would be an insult.'

Flick smiled. 'Now, I hadn't thought of that! No – it's a personal question and you can tell me to bugger off if you like.'

Joanna turned to look at her. 'Try me.'

'I just wondered if you had ever wanted a family.'

Joanna focused on her carefully and paused for a long time before replying. 'You're right, it is a personal question.'

'I'm sorry. Don't answer if you don't want to.'

'If you must know, it was never an option. Derek and I tried it all, even the adoption route, but then they decided we were too old so ...' She turned back to her desk.

'Sorry, Jo, I shouldn't have asked.'

'It's OK. We went through the pain barrier years ago and we've moved to a different place now.'

So it *had* all been a front. Flick knew *she* was guilty of sneering at the cutesy, Croc-wearing, *über*-pram-pushing south London parents because babies, for her, were becoming an increasingly unlikely option. Perhaps that was Joanna's way of handling a childless-life too. There was silence as they both got on with their work, though it was loaded.

'The only side of it that still frightens me though,' said Jo quietly after a while, 'is that there will be no one there for me in my old age.'

Flick couldn't reply. A least there's a fighting chance you'll have Derek, she thought, and put her head down to hide the welling tears.

The days became hotter and the nights sticky and long. Flick slept badly, waking with a start from a bad dream and finding herself wrapped in the duvet, sweating. Her head pounded and, unable to sleep any longer, she'd gotten up early – too early even to pick up a coffee at Nino's – and was at the office by seven where there were fans to cool her skin. She realised too that she was working longer hours, consciously taking on more clients for Tim, and some of Georgie's work, too, though she hadn't asked her to, covering her holiday pet-feeding rota so she could get home, even if she didn't particularly want to be there.

The *Shrek* party was a triumph – the caterer having taken up the challenge brilliantly, and produced a dragon-shaped cake and buns that looked like onions – and now the back-to-school-related enquiries were coming in, which was how Flick found herself in a children's shoe department on a poundingly hot Thursday afternoon just before the Bank Holiday. She had come in to collect a pair ordered by the client, but there was fat chance of attracting the attention of a sales assistant, all of whom were completely occupied with trying to persuade hot, bored, difficult children that pink shoes with bows were not suitable for school. Somehow the whole experience was worsened by indulgent parents who were revelling in the hundred per cent attention of the assistants to whom they had delegated the welfare of their children's precious feet.

Flick sighed in despair, took a ticket, the number on which seemed light years away from the number they were serving, and wandered along the shelves. She tried to recall buying school shoes with her mum, but couldn't. They had usually been hand-me-downs from her cousin Mandy and any spare money Flick's mum had was used to buy what she called 'treats'. 'Money's short enough as it is,' she'd say, the seeds of recycling already sown, 'so let's not waste what we have on boring stuff.' The memory of a pair of gorgeous patent-leather party shoes – an expensive birthday gift – came into Flick's mind and even though her feet had been huge even then, she had loved them to bits, keeping them in their box and stroking them lovingly. So she had her mother to blame for her shoe fetish.

Now she found herself in front of the toddler shoes, and, without meaning to, she put her hand out and took one down slowly. She wasn't sure she had even held a child's shoe before. It was barely as long as the palm of her hand, exquisite and miniature, with little straps to hold in tiny, pudgy feet. Flick examined them as if they were works of art until she felt something grab her leg. Looking up at her was a little girl of no more than two with spiky blonde hair, using Flick's leg for balance, a new pair of shoes on her feet.

'Hello, little one,' Flick smiled down and received a wide, gummy grin and a fascinated stare in reply until the child was scooped up by an apologetic and flustered mother.

'I'm so sorry. They're trouble once they can get about. She's like lightning,' she said, planting a huge kiss on her daughter's chubby cheek, nuzzling her with her nose. Flick's heart leaped.

To make amends for the stupid emotion that had come over her, Flick promptly arranged a night out with some other single girlfriends – the clan that hadn't gone away. They'd all been delighted by her call – relieved that someone else was not being feeble and had taken the initiative. They arranged to meet at a brasserie Flick loved, and a favourite haunt of them all.

At first it was easy – except for the usual nonsense when they ordered, with everyone waiting to hear what everyone else was going to order first so they didn't embarrass themselves by appearing greedy. Flick was starving as usual and, ignoring their simpering about 'having two starters instead of a main course', plumped for a burger and chips. As much as she tried to steer the conversation to shoes and the rather adorable skirt she'd recently seen in Selfridges, the chat veered inevitably towards men. Blokes and relationships. Blokes who wouldn't take the hint and propose. Blokes who were happy to share a mortgage but wouldn't commit to putting a ring on your finger. Blokes who hogged the remote control and farted in front of *Match of the Day*. Each of her friends around the table berated their boyfriends – all fast approaching forty now so clinging on to the 'boyfriend' soubriquet for grim death – but, Flick sighed, all they really wanted was to nab them and have them down at B&Q at weekends. She helped herself to another large glass of Prosecco from the bottle.

'What about you, Flick?' prodded Gill, an old schoolmate who had ditched husband number one and was bringing up two small children alone. She was made up to the nines this evening, perspiring gently under a layer of orange foundation. 'You've been fairly quiet on the bloke front recently. Nothing doing?'

'Nope,' Flick answered curtly, hugging her glass. 'Totally fine on my own thanks. It's easier just me and the cats.'

'You could have anyone, you could,' shrieked Sharon, currently in a destructively tempestuous relationship with a short, stocky policeman from Seven Sisters whose shifts and adoration for Spurs was doing nothing to ease the passage of true love. 'I'd give anything to look like you, I would. My Terry fancies the pants off you.'

Flick groaned inwardly. Men always had a fantasy about tall women, which was all the weirder considering Terry was so vertically challenged.

Eventually she couldn't take any more. Making her excuses about an early start the following morning, she picked up her bag, was enveloped in a fragrant collision of Issey Miyake and Thierry Mugler's Angel, and bolted for the door. 'Sure you're gonna be OK, babes,' Sharon asked, wobbling slightly.

'Yeah. No one messes with six foot two girls in stilettos.'

'You take care. Love you.' Sharon sat down again, hard, before she fell.

Flick relished the evening air, still warm, but a welcome relief from the heat of the restaurant. Slinging her bag over her shoulder, she strolled down the road, stopping every now and then to look in the window of the brightly lit shops. All were displaying sales, desperate to get rid of summer stock before the full arrival of the autumn ranges that were already beginning to take up floor space, their grey wool and winter coats at odds with the heat of the days. Flick stopped in front of the window of Cantaloupe, a favourite haunt of her's and run by her mate Susie who had managed to create a delicious emporium of pretty dresses and accessories, shoes and bags. On display was a pair of salmon-pink sling-backs, reduced to seventy pounds. The minx, smiled Flick, I bet she knows they'd fit me and she's put them there to tempt me. She fished out her phone and sent Susie a message insisting she put them to one side tomorrow until Flick had a chance to try them.

She moved on, smiling at people as they wandered past, some holding hands and window shopping, just as she was. A noisy group of lads came towards her, one of them walking backwards in front of the group, all of them dressed in T-shirts with jeans hanging off their bums.

'Oi, what's the weather like up there?' one yelled, just as she'd passed them. Such an original joke.

'Ho ho. You'd need a ladder to find out,' she called over her shoulder and walked on, leaving them to work it out for themselves.

The streets were less well lit as she turned into her road, and she walked faster as she always did, a habit developed from years of walking home alone. She had her keys ready as she approached her door and, as she turned into her gateway she spotted something on the doorstep. As she got closer she saw it was a carrier bag and she thought someone must have left a package for her or the man in the flat below. Gingerly she opened it and leaped back. Lying on its side, its mouth open and bloody, was an enormous dead rat.

Behind her an engine started up and a car screeched out of a parking space. Heart pounding, Flick could see clearly this time that it was the same BMW. Flick frowned, disquiet rising inside her. Had she got something very wrong? Had Ben lied to her after all?

Chapter Twenty

'Come on, Lib. That's enough. *Top Cat* will still be there in the morning.'

Libby stared at the screen, unmoved. 'Yes, but I just want to see this one. There aren't many, and I want to see them all tonight. And I haven't got school tomorrow ...'

This stubbornness was new. Georgie hesitated. It didn't really matter, in the great scheme of things, whether Lib went to bed now or in ten minutes time. It was Saturday after all. But before too long, Georgie would be having to cope with an increasingly adolescent Lib and a new baby, and how much help would Ed be? Time to get tough. 'Lib,' she stated firmly. 'It's up to you. If you stop now, you can carry on watching tomorrow after you've finished your homework. If you don't stop, you won't be using the computer again this week.'

Libby paused, glanced up at her mother, then turned back to the screen. 'Let me think. Are you saying that I can't use the computer at all if I don't stop now?'

'No, no. That's not what I'm saying at all. If you don't stop now, you won't go on again this week, that's all.'

The little girl bit her lip, still staring intently at the screen. 'Well, what do you mean by "this week"? Do you just mean until Friday? Or is it the whole of next weekend too? 'Cos that would be really mean.'

Georgie sighed. 'Friday, I suppose.'

'Is that including Friday?' Lib's eyes were still fixed on Officer Dibble and Benny.

'Yes! Including Friday. For goodness sake, Lib, what's with the third degree?'

With a triumphant grin, Libby closed the window. 'There! I've finished anyway. So does that mean I can go back on tomorrow?'

'Oh, you little monkey! Were you asking all those questions just to grab a bit more time?'

'Yes, and it worked, didn't it? I just distracted you until the video was finished. Can I have some orange juice before I go to bed?'

'No! I've been fooled once already by you. Don't push it, or there'll be no more Mrs Nice-Mummy! Honestly, how am I going to manage you and the new baby?'

Libby giggled and came up close to Georgie, bending down a little so her face was on a level with her mother's tiny bump. 'Baby, I'm going to teach you *all* about getting what you want from Mummy. But you have to be nice too and not cry all the time.'

She peeped up, a mischievous smile on her face. 'See, I'll be a very good big sister. And I'll teach the baby to read and everything. Don't you worry.'

Georgie hugged her quickly before she could dodge away. She'd been so worried about Lib's reaction when she'd told her the news earlier in the day, but her face had broken into an enormous grin. But then she had been going on for ages about not wanting to be an only child. And it helped that the mother of her best friend, Caitlin, had recently announced a pregnancy. Libby couldn't wait to get back to school now and announce it to the class.

Ed sauntered into the room and stroked Georgie's back as he came to stand behind her. Libby took the opportunity to wriggle free but called over her shoulder, 'And you can teach the baby to draw, Daddy. Mummy will teach her to dance and how to cook. She'll be the cleverest baby in the world.'

Ed scowled comically at her. 'And you can teach it how to be bossy. Then heaven help us, being ordered around by two little monsters!'

Georgie smiled, encouraged by the joke. 'God help us when she's a teenager ... mind you, she seems to be starting already!'

Ed chuckled. 'It'll get worse before it gets better. And I've got a double dose of it with the boys tomorrow, so spare me it at home.'

'Where are you taking them?'

'Ross is going to one of those God-awful paintball parties. Liquid testosterone.'

Georgie rested her head on his shoulder and was surprised and pleased when he put an arm around her. 'Not really your thing, getting mucky, is it? At least he'll come back looking like a walking Jackson Pollock.'

'Perhaps I'll frame his overalls then. Sell them at auction. Leave the computer on – I've some stuff I need to do, then I'll come and kiss Lib goodnight.'

Half an hour later, Libby was tucked up in bed, her stuffed pig clutched tightly in her arms. Georgie kissed her forehead one more time and padded out, closing the door gently behind her, leaving Ed reading the last page of *Pippi Longstocking* to her. Alone in the corridor, she gently rubbed her stomach and smiled.

She was making herself a cup of tea when he came down, yawned and declared he was done in and needed to get to bed before his early start tomorrow. He kissed her on the mouth and made his way upstairs. Steaming cup in hand, she padded through to the study where the computer was still on, though slumbering. Pleased to be permitted five minutes uninterrupted access to it – Lib tended to dominate the machine when she was home – Georgie clicked onto her account and logged in, pulling up YouTube. She hadn't checked on the clip of Flick dancing in the club for ages. Last time she'd looked, there had been a few thousand hits and several comments, mostly from friends and colleagues of Jackson, who must have clicked on the link they'd been sent. Fairly ribald, they'd mocked him mercilessly, and one or two had said that, whatever he'd paid that girl in the bikini, it hadn't been enough. There had been no feedback from his wife, Sara, because they'd been out when she'd dropped off the balance of the money. Was she satisfied with what they'd done? How did she feel about seeing her husband with his nose in another woman's cleavage? Georgie hadn't been entirely sure their prank had achieved the desired effect. None of the commentators had thought any the worse of Mike Jackson. On the contrary, they seemed to regard him as a good ol' boy – one of the lads. Perhaps it had even worked in his favour, Georgie tutted. The page loaded and the video began to play, Flick gyrating and Jackson salivating. Georgie winced a bit at the moment when you could see Flick's face clearly. She'd tried so hard to keep anything recognisable out of it, but it was hard with all the movement going on and Georgie's arm had been jogged a couple of times. It probably didn't matter. There were thousands, millions of videos on YouTube.

Then she scrolled down the page and stared. Over ten thousand views. And well over a hundred comments. She scrolled down further.

'Could seriously give her one. Where is this club? Anyone know?'

'Look at that tosser. He doesn't know what to do with her.'

'She is crap, tho. That other girl is way better.'

Then another. 'She's gonna get what she's asking for. Bitch.'

Georgie frowned and stared. The screen name, 'hardman127', didn't give anything away. She scrolled down. There he was again. 'Slags get what slags deserve. This one is no exception.' She swallowed, her mouth suddenly dry. This was different to the rest of the comments. On the next page, there he was again. 'Dirty skank. Pricktease. She'd better watch out she doesn't get more than she bargained for.'

Should she delete it? Contact YouTube? Georgie was pretty

sure Flick hadn't seen it. She couldn't have. She probably should. Georgie rubbed her forehead, feeling uneasy. There was no one she could ask – certainly not Ed. It was probably just some spotty teenager acting tough. She'd tell Flick about it tomorrow. But still.

Yawning, Georgie looked at the time and closed the browser window, and the log-off screen appeared. Ed's was still open – he'd obviously forgotten to close it down before he came up to read to Lib – and Georgie clicked on his icon to log him off too. His email account was still active. She hovered the mouse over the cross at the corner of the page. Then stopped. The messages were there on the page, and a couple of new ones cascaded down as she looked. There were business ones from people she'd never heard of. There were details of appointments made and changed. But there, dominating the whole page, were messages from Lynn, replied to and replied to again, all sent and received within the last few weeks. And these weren't even messages of regret. These were messages of love and lust and passion. Memories of trysts only last week and plans for meetings to come 'when I can get away'. The most recent one received and replied to was just an hour ago.

Georgie didn't know how long she had been staring at the screensaver but her tea was cold by the time she finally moved and closed down the computer. The pounding in her heart had finally begun to subside but her head ached. Out of the window, the curtains left open, she could see cars moving and street lights, but it was the only piece of normality. Everything she'd been holding out for had gone. Her eyes scanned the room as she searched for something to cling onto. Something that was honest and that reminded her of who she was. But there was nothing of her here. Ed's severe minimalism threatened to engulf them all. Where was she in this? He'd even drawn the line at cards or photos, she realised, regardless of how tasteful the frames. The professional one of Libby she'd had taken a couple of years ago had been smiled over and then disappeared, never to be displayed on a table or sideboard. Even Libby's little paintings from school had been banished – except for one that looked a bit like a Rothko, that he'd had framed and had hung in the kitchen. Where other families had home-made cards and invitations, this was a contrived tablescape, agonised over and positioned carefully. By Ed.

As the shock of what she had read, the little intimacies between Ed and his lover, receded, it was replaced with a cold, hard core of anger. Fucking bastard. 'This is not my home.' Her voice sounded harsh and rough in the silence, and she hadn't even realised she had spoken out loud. 'This is not me.' From the centre of the perfect, cold, hostile room she slowly looked round, then stood up and went upstairs to Ed's dressing room – the little vanity he'd sneaked in at the expense of a spare room for her parents to come and stay. It was far enough away from their bedroom that she wouldn't disturb him, but who cared if she did?

This was solidly his domain and she realised that she barely even went in there, except to vacuum. It even smelled of him. She turned to the built-in wardrobes, set so flush with their maple doors you would hardly know they were there. She pressed one and allowed it to release, then slid it smoothly aside. His clothes were neatly folded onto shelves and hanging from racks on either side – a sea of black and charcoal with shoes neatly paired on sloping metal racks. He had always been fanatically tidy, liking his things 'just so', and even handled his own dry-cleaning. She'd thought it endearing. Once.

Tentatively at first, Georgie reached into the pockets of his jackets, not encountering much. A parking ticket, apparently unpaid. She frowned. That wasn't like Ed. Then she caught herself. What *was* like Ed? She had thought she knew him through and through. She replaced the chequered envelope, then tried another pocket. A receipt for dinner at a restaurant she'd never been to, dated months before. A napkin from a cocktail bar in the West End. Normally, she'd have dismissed it as unimportant, but now she scoured it for detail. Lipstick? Perfume? Phone number? It was disappointingly blank.

Breathing fast, but with icy calm, Georgie picked up Ed's shoes and shook them. What was she expecting to find? Scorpions? Rolled up bundles of fivers? After the first few pairs, she gave up. She recognised that it was unlikely that someone as controlled as Ed would leave anything truly incriminating for her to find. She started to feel foolish. This temple to Ed's high-minded design mission wasn't going to yield anything, yet she couldn't stop. She clicked another door open. And gasped.

It was crammed full of ... stuff. Every one of the deep shelves was full to bursting. She almost laughed. So this was where he hid what the rest of us have on show. All kinds of detritus – papers, shoe boxes, clear-sided containers with clothes crammed inside, folders, loose photographs. It was as if she had found the anti-Ed. She started pulling out a shoe box at random. Letters and postcards, school reports for the boys, bills and counterfoils, information about courses or special offers. Even thumbed holiday paperbacks she'd thought had gone in the bin. Inside a Hackett shoe box were old phone chargers and cassette boxes, now obsolete, and CDs without covers. There were even Barbie shoes – odd ones that had disappeared off the floor – and rubber bands with fluff on them.

Fascinated now, she withdrew another box of odd scraps of paper. More bills, but for clothes and artwork this time. For shoes like the ones she'd just been admiring. Handmade in Jermyn Street, and costing hundreds of pounds a pair. She swallowed hard – so this was why funds were tight.

She slumped down on the chair in the corner of the room. So was this her husband – a fraud? Suddenly he seemed like one of those buildings he so admired. All glass and steel on the outside, *über*-designed and contemporary, reflecting back what people wanted to see, but behind it was the normal chaos of everyday real life. But Ed, it seemed, didn't want real life. He hadn't betrayed her with the woman with the spicy sweet perfume. He hadn't betrayed Georgie at all because he'd never really been honest about who he was, hiding it behind maple doors.

From where she was sitting she could see the back of the bottom shelf, and there, behind a pair of old trainers, was the scruffy little overnight bag that she recognised immediately but couldn't remember when she'd last seen it. She slowly unzipped it, knowing exactly what she'd find. Pastel stretch-towelling babygros in pinks and yellows, daisies and ducks, teddies and bumble bees. Tiny socks and muslins. The scent of Fairy Non-Bio still clinging to them wafted up to Georgie's nose and she was lost, sobs wrenching from her throat. Libby's baby things, carefully folded up by her and stored in the little holdall she'd used for a hospital bag. For the next time she might need them. And here they were, shoved unceremoniously at the very back of this cupboard full of lies and secrets, not treasured as they should be. Out of Georgie's sight to make the idea of another baby be out of her mind.

Georgie started to tremble uncontrollably. What did she feel? A tsunami of sadness and regret. She'd fooled herself that things would be OK and yet he had deceived her again. He didn't deserve the love she'd thrown away on him. He didn't deserve his beautiful little girl. Or the baby that was, even now, growing inside her.

Chapter Twenty-One

Flick squinted in the dark at the clock again. It had only moved on about twenty minutes and she sighed. This was pointless. Her sheets were crumpled and she couldn't find a comfortable position.

Perhaps she should give up trying to sleep and make another stab at the novel she was trying to get into – a very heavy-going account of the trials of an impoverished Irish family – but she wasn't sure she could be bothered with someone else's guilt and misery. She had enough of her own.

Ten minutes later – time she'd spent trying to bore herself back to sleep by going though the company accounts in her head – she admitted defeat and slid out of bed, her feet enjoying the wonderful coolness of the floor. She stuck her head in the fridge to absorb the cold on her skin and, pouring the dregs of a carton of orange juice into a glass, flopped onto the sofa, the light from the street outside strong enough for her to see the shapes in the room clearly enough.

A BMW. Could it have been Ben parked out in the road? Surely not when he'd said stalking really wasn't his style. But then, doesn't everyone say one thing and do another? Flick knew she was far more cynical than she was attractive, but she also knew that scepticism and caution were a very effective shield against hurt. If you don't show your heart, then no one can break it.

So why did she want to believe so badly that Ben was what he said he was? Why should it even matter – especially when he was someone else's husband.

Flick rested her head back against a cushion. Because, she realised, she was tired of playing games; of living half a life because she was afraid of the consequences if she ever lost control.

Georgie pretended to stay asleep when Ed got up and ignored the cup of tea he left beside her bed. In fact she'd been awake for hours, running everything through her head like a tape, her resolve hardening with every re-run, as she matched up his lies with the weight of evidence.

Libby climbed sleepily into his space as he left the house and they cuddled for a while before Libby's incessant questions about some banality drove her into the shower. Ed would be away for the whole day; she'd spend this glorious, sunny day with her daughter. They'd have a bacon sandwich at the Parkview Café – maybe get an ice cream – and she'd buy Lib that expensive backpack she'd been nagging about. Why the hell not? Ed had asked her to pick up some new socks for him, but she'd forget. Instead, they'd browse in the bookshop, feed the ducks and maybe pick up something nice for her and Lib for tea.

Ed, Ed, Ed. Her footsteps drummed out his name as they walked down the street. Libby chatted, holding firmly onto her mother's hand and skipping every now and then. Georgie felt indulgent and steeped in love for her daughter. Then Libby stopped in front of the windows of a downmarket department store, the display cluttered with colourful plastic.

'Look, Mum,' she squealed. 'Chantelle at school's got that dressing table. It's lush, isn't it?'

Georgie peered in at the purple heart-shaped piece of furniture, deliciously spangled and enticingly discounted. Ed would hate it. Ed would hate it!

Perfect. And Sara Jackson's cash could pay for it. Pulling her astonished daughter by the hand, they entered through the swing doors, the scent of pick'n'mix welcoming them. They moved towards the back of the store, past the plastic dolls dressed like hookers and accessorised with irresistible little bags and shoes that seemed, grotesquely, to have feet already in them. She picked one up. Libby looked at her wide-eyed.

Basket over her arm now and deep in the recesses of the store, they found more delights. The CDs and games consoles Georgie ignored completely. They had a hi-tech look that Ed might even have approved of. But the mirror surrounded with a fringe of pink feathers was a must, and there was the purple plastic dressing table with film-star lights round the outside. The fact that they could pick it all up by car from the back entrance sealed the deal.

'I think we need something to go with it, don't you?' Georgie smiled down at her daughter, trying not to look frighteningly manic, like Jack Nicholson in *The Shining*. Posters, pink and glittery, a Disney-print quilt cover and pillowcase, a pink waste-paper bin – in they went. A heart-shaped rug, a basket full of fluffy toy kittens with a very cross-eyed mother, a wallpaper frieze with large cartoon daisies in pink and orange. This was looking very good indeed. Back and forth to the till they went, stacking up their finds until the manager, unable to believe his luck, assigned an assistant to help her.

Georgie was giddy with triumph, finally adding a pink, glittery stationery set to the pile, on top of the light-up doll's house that housed not dolls but little bears! Exquisite.

Sara Jackson's cash wouldn't cover it all so, with glee, she topped it up with their joint credit card and threw in some novelty socks for Ed. Well, he said he needed socks. Snatching up her receipt, they rushed from the store with a promise that they'd be back to collect it all in fifteen minutes.

Libby sang the whole way home, and Georgie watched her in the rear-view mirror, stroking the plush cushions and smiling seraphically.

At four o'clock, sated on fish-finger sandwiches with ketchup, they completed the transformation of Libby's room. Georgie looked round in delight. At last Libby had a little girl's room.

She'd replaced the stark white waffle-weave duvet she'd had before with the Disney-print one and arranged her cushions along the wall to turn her bed into a cosy reading alcove. The rug was covering up a good part of the charcoal carpet that covered the entire upper floor, and she'd put up the posters. The tasteful white steel bookends that had confined the small collection of pristine hardbacks she'd been allowed to display had been dumped unceremoniously on the floor, and a heap of much-loved and dog-eared paperbacks with garish covers had been emptied from the cupboard alongside them.

She'd never seen Libby so happy. Georgie blinked hard as a wave of guilt swept through her. She should have asserted herself earlier. What had she allowed herself to become? Georgie could only be thankful that the thrill of being allowed to use drawing pins to put up her new posters had distracted Libby from her mother's red nose and eyes. And once they started, she felt a kind of fierce glee – quite reprehensible but oh, so pleasurable – in piercing the immaculate pale walls. This must be, she realised with a wild cackle that set Libby laughing helplessly along with her, what it felt like to stick pins into a voodoo doll. Take that, Ed. And that. And that.

They stopped and looked around the transformed room in astonished triumph. 'Yesssss!' Libby hissed. 'This is how I want my room to be for ever and ever.'

And Georgie, too, gazing at the jumbled, colourful walls, the creative muddle of stationery on the purple dressing table, and the cosy, inviting and utterly tasteless cushions mounded on the bed, had a similar thought. This is how I want my *life* to be for ever and ever. They hugged gleefully, then Georgie left her to enjoy her new domain while she got started on supper.

Ed didn't come through the door until seven, by which time she'd prepared herself for seeing him again. She almost squealed with guilty excitement but instead turned to him with a sweet smile, amazed by her capacity for dissembling. 'Hello there. Good day with the boys?' and proffered her face for a kiss of greeting that landed on her cheek. Everything was normal, until Libby came hurtling downstairs.

'Daddy! Daddy! You're late! I've been waiting and waiting. Me and Mummy went shopping. Come and look at my room. It's so beautiful.'

Ed disentangled himself from his daughter's hug and ruffled her hair. 'Shopping, eh? Well, you'd better show me.' He allowed himself to be dragged upstairs. 'Pour me a Scotch, will you? There's a love,' he called over his shoulder before he disappeared.

Oh yes, Georgie smiled. I think you're going to need one. She positioned herself, glass in hand, at the bottom of the stairs. And waited.

An indistinct roar floated down to her, followed by Libby's crystal tones, scandalised. 'Daddy! Mummy said you should never say that word.'

Georgie felt a broad smile spread across her face. Whatever came next, it would be totally worth it. She took a tiny sip of his Scotch and waited.

Chapter Twenty-Two

Flick sat on the tree stump on the common, nursing the cold bottle of water in her hand and occasionally rubbing it along her neck, which was sticky and hot. She felt stupid for having done it but she'd scanned the grassy area before she sat down, peering right over into the clump of trees beyond, just to reassure herself that there was no one suspicious watching her. But it was late morning on a Monday, the road in front was nose to tail with cars waiting for the traffic lights to change, and the sun was bright and hot in the sky – hardly a scene from *Silence of the Lambs*.

However the screech-off on Saturday night was bothering her more than she'd initially realised. Her neck ached from the headache she seemed to have been suffering since Sunday morning and she wasn't sure she'd slept for more than a few hours at all. She'd spent Sunday with her mother who'd had plans and had sounded a little confused and put out that her daughter was so insistent on coming over to help in the garden.

'But I wasn't really planning to do anything with that border this weekend,' she'd said helplessly when Flick had called her, suggesting she came over, 'but if you insist.'

Flick had been in the car by nine, having been awake since five-thirty, telling herself firmly that she was just being a dutiful daughter and heading over to Mitcham at some ungodly hour on a Sunday morning had nothing whatsoever to do with the fact that she didn't want to be at home. She had almost suggested she stay overnight, but her mother was going to meet a friend for a walk by the river and a light supper and, besides, as Flick hadn't stayed the night with her since she was about seventeen, she might have had doubts about her daughter's sanity.

Flick was having doubts about it herself now. She felt tense and dizzy. What the hell was going on? There was only one person she could think of who had a reason to park in her road and leave vile things on her doorstep and that was Ben Houghton. So why was he intimidating her? Hadn't they talked it through at the hotel? Flick had racked her brains to think why he would be following her, but had drawn a blank.

Standing up, she brushed off the bum of her trousers and kicked back a ball that some lads had sent astray and which had landed at her feet. What a mess. She knew she ought to be talking to Georgie about this, but she shouldn't have staked out Ben at Stapley Park and she should have come clean about everything already. And besides, Georgie had enough to think about right now and, more importantly, she was happy. Content with her pregnancy.

She wandered back towards the road. What niggled at the back of her mind were the details Ben had revealed he knew about her. Obviously he knew where she lived – any fool could find that out – but it unnerved her that he also knew her full name, her job and the agency, even the contents of her window boxes. He knew about the YouTube video too. She stopped. Who could have posted those vile comments Georgie had quickly told her about this morning when she'd come into the office before the phones kicked off? 'Skank.' 'Prick-tease.' Is that how men saw her? Had she read Ben terribly wrong? Had he fooled her by being oh-so honest and rational?

Flick raised her hand in thanks to the woman who stopped to let her cross the line of traffic and headed up the road back towards the office. Her mind was racing. Had she and Georgie made an awful mistake in getting involved with these women and their problems? Had they gone too far and put themselves in danger with men they didn't know or understand?

Joanna was still out on lunch. 'Have a nice walk?' Georgie looked up when Flick walked back in and frowned. 'You look a bit washed-out. Is it the YouTube thing?'

'No, I'm fine,' Flick smiled back weakly. 'You don't look much better. Perhaps we both need a holiday.'

Georgie opened her mouth as if to say something, but was interrupted by the phone and, by the time she had finished, Flick had made a decision. 'Actually, I think I might just pop home for a while if you don't mind. I didn't get much sleep last night – the cats were being a pain – and I'm going to grab some shut-eye. Perhaps I'm having an sympathetic pregnancy!'

Georgie's expression was searching. Flick knew her admission of tiredness was very out of character, but Georgie didn't pursue it. 'Sure. We'll cope. See ya.'

Flick had planned to head straight home, but, to cheer herself up, she diverted via Cantaloupe and tried on the luscious shoes she'd earmarked in the window. Susie, as gushing and absurdly flattering as usual, clinched the deal.

'It's a no-brainer, darling,' she pronounced as if the decision was not Flick's to make. 'They make your legs look longer than ever and I hate you for it.'

'And I hate you for persuading me with your sales bullshit,' Flick laughed and watched as Susie whisked them away and wrapped them in pink tissue before tucking them back into the box and scanning the bar code. Flick slipped her pumps on again and glanced around the shop as Susie rummaged for a carrier. On a shelf next to the counter she'd put together a display of baby gifts – hats and little scarves, bowls and mugs (though Flick couldn't imagine why anyone would give a toddler china to eat from). And there, peeping out from behind, a minute pair of knitted booties in greens, pinks and pale yellow with ribbons around the top to secure on to small, chubby legs. Flick lifted them off and inspected them.

'Gorgeous, aren't they?' Susie laughed. 'Anything you should be telling me?'

'God no – just a friend who's pregnant. Do you think they'd do for a girl or a boy?'

'I think they are beautiful enough to hang on the mantelpiece as an ornament.'

Flick handed them over to Susie quickly and fished out her debit card. She wasn't sure Georgie was ready for something so emotive just yet, but she'd have them ready when she was.

Picking up some juice and a bag of salad from a shop for later – her appetite had deserted her – she headed home and found a parking space easily, the majority of the street being out at work. But even the shoes hadn't managed to get rid of her headache. Her shoulders ached too and she winced as she pulled the crisp Cantaloupe bag out of her car. Dumping it in the hallway and greeting the cats, she kicked off her shoes, threw open the sitting room windows, and headed for the kitchen to pour herself a glass of ice-cold water. Tossing back a couple of paracetamol, she turned off the phone and, in her bedroom, slipped off her skirt so she was just in a vest and knickers. She opened the windows wide open in here, too, then flopped, exhausted onto the cool sheets. A faint breeze moved the blinds and they clacked gently against the window frame. Outside she could hear children playing in the distance and traffic humming. It reminded her of being home, sick from school and listening as everyone else went about their day. Stretching out like a starfish she let sleep overtake her and surrendered to it willingly.

The crashing noise in the sitting room made her sit bolt upright. She felt disorientated and squinted at the bedside clock. She'd only been out for about twenty minutes at most. Bloody cats. Swinging her legs off the bed, she padded through to investigate and there, smashed to pieces and strewn all over the wooden floor in front of the window, was her tall table lamp. Perhaps it was the wind, though surely it couldn't have been strong enough. Neither Dolce nor Gabanna were anywhere to be seen.

Something wasn't right. She froze.

A dull thud and movement in the hallway made her start and her skin prickled with fear. Completely alert now, forgetting she was dressed just in her underwear, Flick picked up a discarded trainer from the floor and peered round the corner.

Just as the front door slammed shut, and through the glass she could make out the blurred outline of a figure moving away, fast.

'Oh fuck, oh fuck,' Flick said out loud, glancing about, not sure what to do and where to put herself. Somewhere between abject fear and anger, she stomped to the bathroom, throwing open the door to reassure herself there was no one there. There were no other rooms, there was nowhere else to hide, but regardless, she pulled open her wardrobe and looked under the bed. She hopped on one leg pulling on her trousers again, and grabbed a cardigan from the drawer.

'You bloody, bloody bastard,' she snarled to herself, suddenly very afraid it had to be something to do with Ben. An intimidation technique. Some kind of deranged campaign to get her off his tail. Yet still clinging to the hope that it wasn't him at all. He couldn't be capable of this. Could he?

Locking the windows, her hands shaking, she checked the flat one more time, then slammed the door shut behind her. She turned the deadlock and ran for her car.

She wasn't even sure where his office was – though Alison had mentioned Chelsea Harbour – and as she negotiated the traffic, she tangled with her earpiece and called directory enquiries to get a number.

'Houghton Properties?'

'Yes. Is Mr Houghton in, please?'

'He's been out at a meeting but I believe he is on his way back to the office.' The voice was crisp and efficient. 'Can I ask who's calling?'

'No.' Flick snapped back. 'No, it's nothing. Can you give me your address? I have a parcel to deliver.' Making a mental note of the number, Flick clicked off the phone and charged like a bull into the traffic, cutting people up aggressively and dodging round buses.

Of course it was impossible to park – it would be, wouldn't it? – and her mood wasn't helped by a torrential summer downpour that arrived without warning and left the air steamy, the stench of the streets heightened by the rain. Flick wound down the window and tried to catch a breeze, but she was moving so slowly trying to undertake other vehicles to find a space, it was negligible. She banged her hand on the shelf on the door. Buggeration. He probably wouldn't be there when she arrived, anyway, or he'd have gone into some top-level meeting in his beautifully air-conditioned office overlooking the serenity of the Thames to negotiate the sale of some prime plot of land for a cool twenty million.

She was right about the air-conditioning. The blast of chilly air that hit her skin as the lift slid open noiselessly made her shiver. The colour scheme of the offices was cool too. Light-coloured sofas set about a low coffee table on which stood an unusual sculpture, the meaning of which Flick couldn't determine. She was wrong, however, about him being in a meeting. As she approached the reception desk she could see Ben through the glass wall. He had his back to her and was on the phone, looking out of the huge windows as he talked. She couldn't hear what he was saying, of course, but his body was alert and he had one hand on his hip.

'Can I help?'

The receptionist was small and blonde but seemed very casually dressed for the office of a property magnate. She must be a PA too, as there was no one else about. She smiled broadly and put her head to one side as she waited for an answer. Flick was out of breath and felt scruffy and tall, towering over the desk.

'I've come to see Mr Houghton.'

The girl glanced at the screen on her desk. 'Is he expecting you? I don't have any appointments booked in.'

'No. No, he's not. I just wanted to catch him on the off-chance ...' She tailed off.

'If I could take your name?'

'Flick.'

'Right, Flick. He's just on a call to Dubai at the moment, but as soon as he comes off, I'll let him know you are here. If you could take a seat? Would you like a cup of coffee?'

Flick could have murdered one, but if she got too cosy it might take the edge off her anger and she was very angry indeed.

'No thanks. I'm fine.' She perched on the sofa and the girl resumed her tapping on the keyboard, probably typing up some property contract with Sheik Do-Dah. Perhaps Ben had bought the Sahara and was planning to tarmac it over for a premier league football club. Flick was aware she was jiggling her leg up and down, something she did when she was keyed up and something Georgie always pulled her up on. To divert herself she studied the sculpture in front of her more closely, peering round it to try and work out what the shape meant. It was bold and chunky, made of some sort of smooth, gold-flecked stone, the shape soft and rounded. As she craned, it revealed itself. It was a mother cradling a child.

'Ben?' Flick looked up as the receptionist spoke informally into the phone. 'There's someone called Flick here to see you?'

Flick could see Ben turn abruptly, phone to his ear. He was looking at her, hard, through the glass. His mouth moved in reply.

'Sure.' The receptionist replied and put down the phone. 'You can go in.'

Flick stood up and pushed through the door, entering his silent box. He was about to speak but she barged in first. 'What the bloody hell is going on?'

'Pardon?' He put both hands on his hips but, for some reason, he didn't look as intimidated as she'd have liked him to be.

'I thought this had stopped.'

'What had stopped?'

'I told your wife that I was off the case and that I wouldn't follow you any more.'

'And?' He crossed his arms over his chest. Flick hoisted her bag further up her shoulder. She was crap at arguing and all the great sentences that she had rehearsed in her head on the way over evaporated.

'Well, I haven't been following you, but it seems that you are following me.'

'Following you?' he asked patiently.

'Parking in my street and waiting until I get home late, leaving revolting things on my doorstep and—'

'I have been doing no such thing, Flick. I've told you before. I've got better things to do than stake-out houses late at night. Besides, I thought *you* were following *me*.'

Flick stopped short, her mouth still open. 'What?'

'The bloke parked over the road in the Vauxhall Astra.' Ben jerked his head towards the window. 'Isn't that something to do with you and your private dick business?'

Flick walked over and looked down at the street below. A man was sitting in a row of parked cars, the car window was open and his arm was resting on the door shelf. Ben came to stand beside her. 'He's been there for the last few days. He follows me wherever I go and he's becoming a pain in the arse.'

'I have no idea who he is.' Flick's brain was racing. What the hell was going on? 'I haven't been near you since that night at the hotel. But you drive a BMW, don't you? It had to be you parked outside my house.'

'Flick,' Ben smiled, his eyes crinkling. 'I don't own the only BMW in London.' Flick felt stupid and could sense her face redden.

'No, of course not. It just seemed too much of a coincidence. So,' she was beginning to feel really frightened now. 'So, just now. That was nothing to do with you?'

His brow furrowed. 'Just now?'

'There was someone in my flat.' Ben's eyes widened. 'I came back to the flat from work because ... well, I haven't been sleeping too well since the rat incident—'

'Rat?'

'On my doorstep on Saturday night. In a Tesco bag.' He clearly knew nothing about it. 'Anyway, I fell asleep but someone must have got in through the window.' She looked at him and she could tell by his expression that his shock was genuine.

'Did you see them?'

'No, they scarpered through the front door. It was ...' She could feel her eyes welling with tears and turned away quickly before he saw them. That wouldn't do at all.

She felt his hands on her arms as he turned her towards him and she sniffed and fixed her gaze firmly out of the window. He was too close and she could feel the warmth of his hands.

'Flick, listen to me. This isn't funny. I promise I don't know anything about today. In fact, I think I knew really that Mr Vauxhall Astra was nothing to do with you, but that's my problem to sort out. People climbing into your flat, though, is a different matter. Did you call the police?'

'No. I was too angry. Too sure it was you.' Even as she said it, Flick knew she'd never really believed it was him.

'Do you live on your own?'

'Yup,' she blinked, trying not to show how vulnerable and scared she was feeling.

'Could you stay somewhere else?'

Flick shrugged. 'I suppose so. I could go to my mum's, though that would be a bit of a nightmare,' she smiled weakly.

Ben dropped his hands. 'Give me a minute.' He left the office and went over to talk to the receptionist. Flick couldn't hear what they were saying, but they consulted the computer screen together and the girl nodded at something. Ben said something to her again and came back into the office, shutting the glass door behind him.

'I've got a flat in a development – it's the show flat and it's empty until a sale is completed. You could stay there?'

'That's ridiculous,' Flick laughed, touched by his concern. 'I'll be fine. They won't come back, I'm sure, and I'll keep a baseball bat under my bed.'

Ben shrugged. 'It's up to you but I think it might be a good idea not to be there for a while, don't you? Can you get some things together? You can stay at this flat straightaway – Claire's sorting it out with the building manager.'

Flick's mind raced. It was unorthodox. In fact, it was downright odd. But the thought of going home swayed it. 'I'll have to go back to my place to get things and sort out my cats ...'

Ben looked at his watch. 'I'll take you back there – just in case. The flat's not far from here so we could leave your car here – and pick it up later?'

He seemed to have it all sorted out and as much as she fought it, Flick couldn't help feeling relieved that someone else was taking over. 'OK, and ... thanks,' she replied eventually.

On Ben's instruction, she put her car in his packing space when he'd pulled out, and slipped into the passenger seat beside him. He looked over at her as she folded her legs into the space.

'Other BMWs are available,' he laughed and she smiled back.

'I'm sorry. I just assumed. I'm crap at recognising cars. I've even lost my own in car parks before now.'

'Probably best lost,' he commented dryly and shot her an amused glance.

They pulled out into the traffic and Flick was thrown backwards slightly as the car sped forward, then Ben made a sudden turn into a side road, leaving a bus behind him, blocking any chance of another car following him. The leather of the seats was cool under her hands, and she could smell Ben beside her, a faint tinge of aftershave combined with the scent of the leather. Air-conditioning played cool air over her face and, for the first time in days, she felt her shoulders relax. She must have sighed.

'This has really got to you, hasn't it?' He asked as they began to cross over the river.

'Yes it has.' Flick looked out of the window. 'I'm trying to rack my brains as to who it could be. Who the hell would want to follow me – to put the fear of God into me?'

'You've probably pissed off a lot of men, Flick.' Ben said quietly. 'I know they probably deserved what you and your partner did, but they would still have been angry that they'd been rumbled – and no, I'm not including myself in that. You would be the obvious target for any retribution.'

Flick sighed. 'I suppose.'

'Has your colleague – has she had any trouble too?'

'No, I don't think so. She hasn't mentioned it and I think I'd know.'

He glanced at her. 'Haven't you told her anything?' he sounded surprised.

'Er, no. She's got stuff on her plate at the moment – real problems, and I didn't want to bother her with it. Anyway,' she hurried on, ignoring his raised eyebrow. 'This seems very much directed at me.' There was silence in the car for a while as they drove through the streets.

'It seems to me it might be someone who thinks you are the only one involved, or who saw you close-up.'

'Most of our hits were kind of remote, you know.'

'Except the pole-dancing. That was very close-up.'

Flick turned to Ben sharply. 'Yes.' Realisation began to dawn. 'Yes, of course. Jackson.'

'I don't know the man, but there are some pretty vile comments on that video, you know.' They were at traffic lights and he turned his head to her. His gaze was very deep.

Flick smiled nervously. How did he know? Had he gone back to look at the site? She blushed. 'I know. I thought at first that you might have put them there.'

His car phone interrupted before he could reply. 'Hi, Claire?'

'Ben, Richard says that's fine.' Her voice came over the speaker. 'Reception will have the keys. I've said to expect you later.'

'Thanks. Can you postpone my three-thirty?'

'Will do. Bye.' Claire clicked off the phone, and they pulled up outside Flick's flat. She scanned the road but everything seemed quiet. Her neighbour two doors down came out of her house with her two West Highland terriers, who tottered ahead of her, and the trees that pushed through the pavement were moving slightly in the light breeze.

'You wait here and I'll grab some things.'

'I don't think so. I'm coming in with you.' He climbed out of the car and followed her to the door.

The flat felt stuffy already with the windows shut, but Flick pulled down the blinds even further, and scooped up the remains of the broken light, then went through to her bedroom. 'Would you like some coffee or a cold drink?' she called. 'I think there's some juice in the fridge. Help yourself.'

It seemed odd to have Ben in her flat and she hurriedly threw together some clothes so they could leave as soon as possible. When she came back through, clutching a holdall, he was standing looking at her bookshelf and the photographs of her mum on the shelves above. She was aware the place was a mess, so different from his and Alison's bijou Chelsea pad. Silly cards stuck out from behind her collection of china pigs that filled a whole shelf haphazardly, and she was horrified to notice a mug of coffee that she'd put up there days ago and forgotten about.

'I'm sorry about the carnage. I'll just put out some food for the cats and then I'll be with you.'

'No hurry.' He didn't turn around. 'An interesting choice of reading you have here,' he said, and pulled out a novel from the top shelf. Thankfully it was one of the more serious ones she'd read, wedged between the bonkbusters covered in sun-tan oil stains that she took on holiday to relax with.

'What did you think of this?'

Flick emptied some dried food into Dolce and Gabbana's bowl and they made a bee-line for it. She'd have to arrange for someone to come and feed them until – well, until she thought it was safe to come back. 'I loved it. It was the first one of his I've read. I've re-read it twice since, and all the rest of his stuff.'

'Me too.'

She stopped and looked at him. How incongruous – a tragic love story. Hardly reading fodder for a property developer.

'Don't look so surprised,' he laughed. 'I do have feelings you know.'

Suddenly unnerved that the mood was becoming a little more personal than was comfortable, she stuffed a couple of last-minute things into the bag and picked up her keys. 'Shall we?'

Ben slipped the book back onto the shelf. 'Yeah,' he replied hesitantly. 'Yeah, sure.'

Georgie got up and eased her back. The mini-fridge they'd bought was stocked with cartons of juice and bottles of water and she poured herself a generous shot of cranberry juice. 'One for you, Jo?'

Joanna glanced up and stretched. 'Can I have pomegranate and sparkling, please?'

With the blinds drawn against the glare, the office had taken on a somnolent atmosphere. Even without Flick to help, she and Joanna had managed the rest of the day's business without too much effort.

It was hard to believe that the new school year was about to start. Georgie didn't want to think too hard about what the end of the year would bring. She needed all her strength to cope with what lay ahead and the anger it brought with it.

Mercifully, this morning Libby had been packed off to Devon to stay with Georgie's younger brother, Tris, his wife and their brood. Hopefully she'd have a carefree few days, making dams in the stream that ran though their garden, playing on the beach with her cousins, camping and picnicking daily. Georgie and Ed were, theoretically, free to go out to dinner; spend cosy nights in. But that would have been ridiculous. Instead Ed kept his distance, deflected by a chilliness Georgie didn't even attempt to conceal. Oddly, he didn't even question it, and the only thing that made her smile was watching him wince as he passed Libby's room. Tonight Georgie would sleep beneath Libby's new purple duvet, on the pretext that his snoring disturbed her and the pregnancy was keeping her awake. It was like being separated whilst still living together.

She'd lain awake again last night, running it all through her head. Where did her discoveries leave her now? Ed had always joked he couldn't afford another divorce – did that explain why he'd lied so convincingly? She knew that she would be better to confront him about the fact that he was so obviously still having a relationship with Lynn, but if she did, what would be his response? More assurances? More pap? For the first time, she could understand the hunger for revenge she'd seen in the women who'd taken on Flick and her services. She'd always thought it was a bit of a joke, until now. She'd thought that infidelity always brings heartbreak for the wounded one, and the passionate desire to have everything back the way it had been before. And hadn't she been guilty of making concessions to Ed the first time, in a desperate attempt to win him back?

Now, lodged somewhere between the baby and her heart was a core of anger which, like indigestion, burned away. It was anger mixed with something very close to hate. By keeping quiet, it gave her time to think how she was going to handle the next step.

She placed Joanna's drink at her elbow and returned to her own chair, passing Flick's desk on the way. Flick. She hadn't seemed quite right when she'd left. Georgie had assumed it was the stupid comments on YouTube that had thrown her off balance – although that would be out of character. On previous experience it took more than that to worry Flick. But maybe Georgie shouldn't have told her what she'd seen. She took a sip of juice and picked up the phone. 'Just calling Flick,' she said quickly to Joanna. 'Thought she was looking a bit peaky. Did you?'

Joanna shrugged. 'She said something about not sleeping, but I assumed it was the heat. She was rather quiet, though. And that's definitely not Flick!'

Georgie laughed, but her sense of unease rose as the phone rang on until the answerphone picked up. 'She's probably out buying shoes. I'll try her mobile.'

But that, too, clicked straight through to the answerphone. Something didn't feel right. 'Hi, Flick, it's only me. Just calling to make sure you're …' – what, exactly? Why had she called? To make sure her mate was all right. Georgie rubbed her forehead. She realised too that she wanted to talk to Flick, to spill out to her all about Ed and Lynn and what she'd found on his email. '… At home because, er, I thought I might drop by later. Gimme a call when you get this, will you? Ta.'

Going to see Flick would also be a good idea, because it would mean she wouldn't be at home when Ed got in. The only conversation they'd had this morning had been exclusively details about the imminent launch party for the Atrium project near King's Cross. The awful atmosphere couldn't stop his going on about it; how the design had been nominated for an architecture prize; how Lord Rogers might be there; how, even though he wasn't the lead architect, this was bound to get his name noticed by the big-cheese developers. Her lack of interest or response in no way seemed to dissuade him from banging on about it. Perhaps Ed just thought it was a neutral subject that wouldn't lead to any nasty confrontations. Or perhaps he was just so up himself, he didn't care whether she was interested or not. Georgie shook her head slowly. That was probably closer to the mark.

Joanna left the office and, just after five, Georgie, having tried both Flick's numbers for most of the afternoon, was by now genuinely worried. She tried one more time, then left in her turn, locking up behind her and heading for the car. It was the worst time of day to get through the streets of south London and she drummed her fingers irritably on the roof of the car, her elbow resting on the opened window. Her mobile was lying on the seat beside her, in case Flick returned her call. She hadn't left any further messages – perhaps she was asleep and had turned everything off – but the caller ID would show how many times she'd tried. Surely Flick would call her back straightaway when she saw?

Flick's street was pretty much full by the time Georgie arrived. Georgie found a space around the corner and walked back briskly, looking forward to being able to put on the kettle and have a chat about Ed and everything else. She rang the bell and stepped back, squinting as the low sun shone into her eyes. She listened, as best she could, for sounds of footsteps on the stairs. Flick always took them at a run before flinging the door open. Nothing. She tried again, looking up and down the street and wondering if she looked as shifty as she felt. Some small boys were taking turns on a skateboard, laughing and squealing with excitement. Further along, a woman appeared with two little white dogs, straining at the leash, looking anxious to get home. Still nothing. Georgie called Flick's landline and could hear it ringing inside the flat. Where *was* she?

Georgie jumped as the woman with the dogs cleared her throat. 'She went out, dear. Earlier this afternoon. I saw her. They got into a big car and off they went.'

'They? Did you recognise who she was with?'

'No. A fella. Big fella.' The woman laughed wheezily.

'Well, what did he look like?' Georgie felt herself gripped with a fear – but of what, she wasn't sure.

'Oh, very nice. Good-looking. Looked very – what do you call it? – protective. Like he was looking after her. Mind you, big girl like her can probably take care of herself, can't she?'

'I hope so,' Georgie muttered. 'So you didn't speak to her? She didn't say when she'd be back?'

'No, love. I don't like to pry. But she had a big bag with her. Not a suitcase exactly. What do you call those things?'

'A holdall?'

'That's it. Holdall. Overnight sort of thing. Don't expect she'll be back till the morning!' More wheezy cackling.

Georgie smiled weakly. 'And the man? Would you recognise him again?'

The woman looked suddenly suspicious. 'What do you take me for? I'm no busybody. Tall – that's what he was like. Tall and dark. That's all I saw. Must have a few bob, with a car like that. Big, shiny one. Dunno what sort. They sort of rushed off, though. Looked like they were in a hurry.' She went on her way, tugged on by the dogs, leaving Georgie alone and thoughtful on the doorstep.

Flick felt like one of those smug women you see in property ads in the Sunday newspapers. She'd always envied the owners of these sort of developments as she drove over the river and now here she was, standing on the balcony, gazing out over the Thames, which sparkled in the sunlight, and watching the river traffic going about its business.

It all seemed a bit surreal. After a song and dance to shake off the man in the Vauxhall, Ben had led the way from his office, driving slowly so she could keep up in her car. He'd then left her in the nearly completed car park – two spaces per apartment apparently – and handed her over to Richard, the building manager, as he had to leave for his postponed meeting. Richard, a very affable thirty-something, had led her through the sliding-glass doors into a giant, naturally lit space with super-sized plants – trees almost – and giant windows that looked out over the river from ground-floor level. Flick had been too amazed to ask many questions, so Richard had filled her in anyway, explaining how almost all of the flats were sold and that she would be in the show flat, which was fully furnished. He didn't seem to question why his boss had delivered an emergency tenant at a moment's notice and behaved as if it was something that happened all the time.

'I'm sorry about all this,' Flick smiled at Richard as the external lift whisked them up smoothly. She tried not to peer down as the ground was left behind. She felt vaguely queasy. 'It must seem a bit odd, you know, me turning up …' She tailed off.

'No trouble at all.' Richard selected a key from the bunch in his hand and had it ready when the lift came to a silent and smooth standstill.

Only two doors led off from the landing, and Flick's suspicion was confirmed – these apartments took up half the building's floor space each. Richard unlocked the door on the left and opened it wide, letting Flick go through first. What faced her took her breath away. Like something out of a James Bond movie, an enormous lounge with a pale wooden floor and deep-red sofas looked out through floor-to-ceiling glass over the London skyline. Richard tried to show her the kitchen area and the doorways through to the bedrooms but Flick ignored him, sliding open the balcony doors and absorbing what lay in front of her. This was her idea of heaven – modern and light, like coming up from being submerged underwater. She felt she could breathe and, best of all, she felt safe here. She felt safe with Ben.

Richard came out onto the balcony. 'Good view, isn't it?'

'Wonderful. Almost makes you forget what a shit-pit the city is!'

'I know what you mean.'

'It really gives you a sense of superiority, being up here. I might get above myself! I envy whoever's going to buy it.'

'We've got lots of people interested but – between you and

me – I think the boss would love it. He seems to come up here whenever he can and he oversaw all the decoration. Anyway, here's the key, with the external entrance key. There's a code – I've left it on a piece of paper on the side in the kitchen. I'm here till six and I'm back in at nine tomorrow. Give me a call if you need anything. My mobile's on that note as well.'

'Thanks so much, Richard. I'll just stand here all night!'

He smiled and waved as he left the apartment. After a while Flick explored – opening and shutting the kitchen units and cupboards – all empty, of course, except for a skeleton selection of beautiful crockery, glasses and cutlery to show unimaginative prospective buyers what a plate might look like in a cupboard. The two bedrooms were roughly the size of her flat with beds made up with thick duvets, pillows and throws that would sleep a small family. The space was bathed in afternoon sunlight which also filtered through the long bathroom window with its wet room shower and limestone egg-shaped bath. How Georgie would have laughed at this – and Ed would be green with envy at the spec. Yet somehow it was friendlier than Georgie's house, with warmer colours and wood that begged to be touched. Even the door handles were big, sexy and curved, and Flick ran her hands over them, absorbing the coolness of the metal.

She itched to tell Georgie where she was but she knew she couldn't. She'd be mad as hell that she'd let things get out of hand. To pacify her and throw her off the scent though, she would send her a text, so she fished out her phone from her bag. The screen told her she'd missed loads of calls. Most were from Georgie, with a couple from her mother, and Flick felt a surge of guilt. She texted them both – 'I'm feeling better but I'm going over to my mum's' to Georgie, and 'Sorry, my phone's been off. I'm at Georgie's and will call tomorrow' to her mum. Throwing her phone back into her bag, she stretched languidly, and, strolling through to the bedroom again, lay down on the bed, letting the sunshine warm her face and her body.

Flick blinked hard and rubbed her eyes, trying to focus on

her watch. She had to look twice to register it said seven o'clock. She'd been so tired sleep must have enveloped her immediately and deeply. She felt disorientated. The sun had dropped lower, its evening rays catching the top of buildings and church towers which reflected back in gold. Her tummy rumbled and she realised she hadn't eaten for hours but she felt groggy. First a bath – why not, when that huge tub was waiting to be experienced? – then she'd go and grab something to eat.

Half an hour later and she was eyeball-deep in fragrant bubbles (the Acqua di Parma bottles on the side were for real, not empty fakes just for show, as she'd suspected). She let the warm water embrace her and watched the sun sinking further in the sky, letting her head rest against the smooth stone of the bath. She was just beginning to think she had missed a vocation as a Hollywood A-lister when the doorbell rang. Could it be Richard saying goodbye before he left? But he'd have gone by now. Wrapping a towel around her head and another round her body – too short as usual – she padded to the door anxiously, trying not to drip on the smooth wooden floor. Through the spyhole she could make out Ben Houghton.

She opened the door and peered round. 'Oh, hello.'

'Hello.' In one hand was a carrier bag, in another a bottle of wine. 'I realised that you can't have any provisions in so I …' He lifted the bags with a look of apology. 'I took the liberty of getting you some supper.'

Flick could feel her face break into a spontaneous smile. 'Oh, you saviour! I was going to go out in a minute.' She realised he was still standing on the landing and opened the door wider. 'Come on in, I'll just—'

He came through the door and for a moment they both stood there, Ben looking at her with an expression she couldn't read. She pulled the towel further round her and backed away, muttering something about changing.

She realised she was shaking as she dried and put on the jeans and the T-shirt she'd stuffed into her bag. It was creased and had a rather embarrassing girl-power logo on the front. She towel-dried her hair as best she could and, with no hair drier, let it fall loose around her shoulders.

By the time she padded back into the kitchen area in bare feet, Ben had poured a glass of wine for her and was unpacking his carrier bag. On the side was crusty bread, cheese and olives, sun-dried tomatoes and what looked like hummus. Her stomach rumbled even louder.

'That looks good!' Flick said and he turned his head to look at her. 'I hope you're having a glass of wine too?'

'Well,' he hesitated. 'I hadn't really thought about it. I was just going to drop this off and go home.'

'The least I can do is offer you a glass of your own wine!' Flick took out another glass from the cupboard. 'I'm afraid it's going to have to be a tumbler. The developer didn't think to put the right type of glasses in the cupboards.' She looked at him sidelong and was rewarded with a broad smile.

'Pah! I wouldn't buy a place with that sort of lack of attention to detail!'

Flick picked up her glass and the large plate that he had put the food onto haphazardly, and walked over to the balcony. 'Shall we make the best of the dregs of the sunshine?'

Ben followed her out with his glass and the bottle, and they sat at the table. For a moment they both gazed at the river in silence. How odd to be hundreds of feet up above London with Ben Houghton. If it had been him who had been intimidating her, this would be the perfect opportunity to push her over the balcony railing!

'This is really lovely, Ben,' she said eventually, taking a sip of the cold wine. 'I am very grateful, you know.'

Ben shrugged. 'It made sense.'

'Have you ever been up the London Eye?' she asked, knowing it sounded random.

'Yes, I have actually,' he sounded surprised at himself. 'Alison never wanted to, but one day I found myself on the South Bank and I bought a ticket spontaneously and took a flight – isn't that what they call it?'

'It's cool, isn't it?'

'Yes, it's very cool. The sun was setting like it is now and the city was lighting up. I love London – I find it really exciting. I was bought up in Cumbria but it didn't suit me. All those hills!' He took a swig from his glass and Flick realised that he was embarrassed, as if he'd said something too revealing.

'Oh, me too! I was brought up in the suburbs but I'm a city girl through and through. Georgie – well, she's from the sticks. Lincolnshire or somewhere up north—' She realised she was gabbling. 'She always said I go wobbly when I see a field. Do you develop stuff here mainly or … ?'

'No – all over the place. All over the world actually. I've just bought a plot of land in Houston, in fact. I'm going over there soon to meet the contractors. I've even built a shopping development in Lincolnshire!'

Flick smiled and picked idly at the bread and cheese. She pushed the plate wordlessly over to Ben and he too dipped some bread in the hummus. There was something very intimate about it – surrounded as they were by the hum of traffic, yet suspended high above it all.

'Did the Vauxhall man follow you?' she asked after a while, remembering the reality of why she was here.

'No, I don't think so. I managed to lose him at some traffic lights and I did a bit of a duck and dive, just to make sure he really was lost.'

She searched his face to check she could ask her next question. 'Why *is* there someone on your tail?'

For a moment he stared back at her, then, taking an olive stone from his mouth, lobbed it over the balcony. 'It's Alison's doing. She isn't going to let it rest.' His expression was nonchalant.

'Don't you think that's a bit odd? You know, her having you followed – still – and then going home to her at night? Don't you discuss it? I mean, you're very cool about it all.'

Ben leaned forward and rested his arms on his knees. 'Flick, you need to understand something. Alison and I haven't had what you might call a marriage for years. At the risk of sounding like the my-wife-doesn't-understand-me brigade, we have grown apart and rarely spend much time together. I travel a lot and she holidays with friends that she has all over the world. They aren't the kind of holidays that I enjoy – sitting on a beach.'

'Right,' said Flick. He wouldn't want to holiday with me then, she thought. 'But why the tail?'

'Because,' he leaned back in his chair and sighed. There was a long silence and Flick began to wonder if he had forgotten what they were discussing. 'Because Alison is a very complicated woman. She won't be happy with a straightforward divorce. She wants to nail me for adultery, which will give her leverage to take as much of what I've earned as she can and Flick, I'm not having that. I worked for it. She has never worked, and I don't see why she should walk off with it all. I'd see she was more than comfortable, but I don't buy into this belief that wives have a right to everything that you've worked your nuts off for.'

He frowned and Flick didn't reply for a moment. 'And has she got ... you know, grounds?' Flick couldn't explain why it hurt to ask this.

He shook his head. 'No, Flick, she doesn't. God knows, I've been tempted at times – sometimes just out of spite – but no. Besides, I don't want to give her the ammunition.'

Flick chewed a crust of bread thoughtfully. 'That's not how she put it to us, you know. About wanting to nail you.'

'No, I bet it wasn't.' He didn't sound bitter, just resigned.

'No, she talked about you being – well, to be frank, she said you had been hell to live with.'

Ben threw his head back in despair. 'Christ, how could she? I bet she gave you some sob story about children too.'

Flick was surprised. 'Well, yes actually ...'

'And she said I didn't want any, I'll bet?'

'Yes.'

He leaned forward again. 'It's Alison who doesn't want children, and she's never wanted them. That was apparent from the moment we married. She's far too selfish to give her love to a child. Anything that might cramp her style, crease her Armani, or stop her going to Cape Cod when she feels like it.'

Flick was beginning to understand just how many lies Alison had woven. Somehow the next question was important. 'And you? Do you want them?'

This time Ben lost the expression of disinterest and he jiggled his leg unconsciously. 'I desperately wanted a family. It was the ultimate sticking point between us but she was intractable.'

'Didn't you – I mean, isn't it something you discussed before you got married?'

Ben ran his hands through his hair, messing it up. 'I suppose we talked the usual codswallop that people talk about when they can't think further than next week. She was always ambitious, which is odd when she has only achieved a life of luxury through marriage. But whenever I raised the subject, she'd deflect it by making a plan to move house or buy a little *gîte* in the Dordogne.' He fixed his gaze into the middle distance.

'Oh,' said Flick quietly, taken aback by this outpouring.

'The thing is that if either of us has grounds for ending this farce of a marriage then it's me.' He looked out over the skyline and Flick waited for him to continue. 'Ha!' He laughed briefly without mirth. 'Let's just say that living with Alison is a challenge.' He then collected himself. 'I'm sorry. I don't know why I'm talking to you about it. It's something I've never really discussed, to be honest.' He smiled apologetically. 'It's a bit odd it should be you I'm discussing it with.'

'It's part of our service,' Flick said lightly, smiling back.

'Quite an agency you run there!'

233

'Have you ever tried giving her an ultimatum about the children issue?'

He looked wry. 'No point now. She was sterilised without telling me.'

'Oh, Ben.' Flick blurted.

He shrugged. 'She did it in New York. I thought she'd gone there to go shopping and stay with friends. She didn't let on for months.' Flick didn't know what to say. She thought about Georgie and the baby. Conceived because she wanted another child so badly, but in such sad circumstances. What a complicated mess.

'Anyway—' he topped up her glass, clearly trying to lighten the tone – 'That's for me to sort out. As it happens, I am talking to my lawyers about it all – it's just a question of getting the timing and the settlement right. Alison having me tailed is all part of some race she imagines we're in, to be the first to the divorce post. But enough of that – let's talk about you and why *you* are being followed.'

He looked uncomfortable and Flick followed his diversion. 'Oh, 'cos we've been stupid and naive, I suppose. I guess we thought that if Jackson was made a fool of, then he'd go back to his wife, tail between his legs, and it would all be forgotten. What I didn't realise is that sometimes a man humiliated is a man who'll get very angry indeed. I haven't got enough to go to the police with, have I? What I can't understand is how he discovered where I live.'

'The club? Did you give the manger your name?'

''Course not – that was far too risky.' She bit her lip, thinking hard.

'What about his wife – might he have pressed her for information?'

Flick tried to remember Sara Jackson's visit to the agency. What had happened when she came? 'Oh, fuck.'

'Sorry?'

'I've just remembered,' she said slowly. 'We gave her a card

234

and I stupidly crossed out the "Domestic" of Domestic Angels and put Avenging, just for a joke. He must have found it or something. Stupid, stupid, stupid.'

'Perhaps he followed you home from the office.'

Flick shivered, horrified at the idea that someone had watched her every move and she'd been oblivious. 'It's odd,' she ran her finger around the top of her glass nervously. 'Most of the hits we've done – if you can call them that – have been fun, an irritation, and they've had the desired effect. You wouldn't believe how pleased the wives who've come to us have been. The thing is, they don't seem to want to *get rid of* their husbands, whatever they've done or however badly they've behaved. They just wanted a shot across the bows. But this one has been different.' She paused. 'Tell me, why do men have affairs?'

Ben picked up another olive. 'Because men need sex. They need to prove their manhood, I suppose. We're programmed to respond to an attractive woman.' Flick thought back to her mother's similar remarks. 'Women do too though,' he went on. 'You can't just blame us. There has to be a woman somewhere in the dynamic.'

Flick thought about John. 'Oh, I know.'

Ben glanced at her and she avoided his eyes.

'It can be more than just a quick shag though.'

'Meaning?'

He threw another stone over the balcony.

'That might hit terminal velocity by the time it reaches the ground and you'll kill someone!'

Ben laughed and picked up another olive, nibbling it between his teeth. 'It can happen when you think you are happy, content. Life's bobbing along and then wham! You meet someone who pulls the rug out from under you. That's when an affair is something much more dangerous.'

There was an awkward silence. Flick wasn't sure what to say and gazed out over the skyline to avoid his eyes.

'Well,' Ben said quietly after a moment, 'I'd better go before I *do* kill someone passing by below.' He stood up and moved through the sliding doors, back into the apartment. Flick followed and was behind him as he turned towards her at the front door.

'Goodnight, Flick,' he said. 'I think you'll be OK here.' Then he leaned forward and gently kissed her on the edge of her mouth.

The door closed behind him and Flick went back to stand on the balcony and watch his car pull out of the car park below. She could still feel his lips where he had kissed her. Rugs out from under you? What she was feeling seemed more like the whole bloody carpet.

Chapter Twenty-Three

The door opened and Georgie's head snapped up. It was Flick at last. Joanna looked from one to the other, and quietly made her exit to the broom cupboard and the kettle. Georgie couldn't blame her. When Joanna arrived at nine, Georgie had been in the office, wild-eyed and tense after a sleepless night during which she'd swung between trying to think rationally, and panicking that Flick had been abducted by force.

And here Flick was. Looking, if anything, quietly pleased with herself. A glance at Georgie's pale, shadowy-eyed face must have dispelled that in an instant.

'George, what is it? Are you OK? Nothing's happened, has it? With the baby, I mean.'

Georgie was torn between wanting to throw her arms round Flick and wanting to shake her. 'I'm fine, but where have *you* been? I've been frantic here.'

Flick stopped short. 'Oh! Oh I never thought. Were you trying to get hold of me?' She asked, wide-eyed and innocent.

'Yes, of course I was. And I went round to your house, and you didn't answer your mobile, and that woman said you'd gone off with some man, and I thought—' Georgie angrily dashed away the tears that were starting to spill down her cheeks. Flick crossed the room in long, rapid strides and hugged the now sobbing Georgie who, nonetheless, was still talking. 'And I know you weren't at your mother's 'cos I called her and she thought you were with me. And I had to make up some story so she wouldn't worry. And,' she sniffed, 'I was frantic.'

'Look, have a good blow.' Flick handed Georgie a wodge of tissues from the box on the desk. 'I'll make us both a cup of tea and ... well, I've got quite a bit to tell you, actually. Maybe later when ...' She jerked her head in the direction of the broom cupboard.

'What?' Joanna appeared from round the corner and stared from one to the other, her hands on her hips. 'When I'm not here?' She shook her head slowly. 'It sounds to me as if you've both got quite a bit to tell me.' She stared hard at Georgie. 'Baby, eh? Well, that explains a lot. Thought you were just getting fat. And you, Flick? It sounds like you've been keeping both of us in the dark. If I'm going to go on working here, I want in.' She stared at them challengingly. 'On everything!'

Georgie and Flick exchanged a quick glance, but there was no escape. Joanna was crucial to their everyday operations and, if the price of her staying was admitting what they'd been up to, then they had to come clean. 'OK, Jo,' Flick nodded. 'If you make the tea, we'll spill the beans.'

An hour later, they were on their third cup. Joanna had insisted on seeing the YouTube video. Flick had winced as Jo leaned forward to stare as Jackson slipped a couple of notes into her bikini bottoms. 'Honestly,' she'd sighed. 'What would your mother say?'

Flick's faltering admission about Ben and her botched stakeouts had both Georgie and Jo tutting, but when she finally admitted to them about the threats and the break-in, Georgie had jumped to her feet. 'But how can you be sure it's *not* Ben? And after all Alison said. You went off with him without even telling me! Flick, you want your head looking at.'

'It's not like that, though,' Flick said gently. 'You haven't spoken to him, not like I have. He's not like Alison says, Georgie, honestly. She made it all up because she wants to – I don't know, get a better divorce settlement, or something. He's good and he's kind.'

'And you're in love with him, aren't you?' Joanna broke in abruptly.

Silence. Flick looked down at her hands, an unfamiliar flush creeping up over her neck.

Georgie snorted. 'Well, looks like you've chosen another slimeball.'

Flick raised her head and stared back at her. 'Honestly, Georgie,' she said quietly. 'I don't think he is. He's different.'

It was deadlock. Georgie could feel the cynical sneer on her face, could see how her attitude was hurting Flick, who suddenly looked vulnerable, and hated herself for it. But the hard, cold resentment that had settled in the pit of her stomach wouldn't go away. 'Flick, love, take it from me. All men are bastards.'

'You don't really mean that. You're giving Ed another chance.'

Joanna looked as though she was trying to keep up. Georgie snorted. 'Actually, Flick, he's blown it already. It turns out he's still seeing that woman. He's still lying and he never stopped. I reckon he's just telling me what he thinks I want to hear so he doesn't have to stump up more maintenance.'

By this time Joanna's eyebrows were up near her hairline, and Georgie had to stop and fill her in on the details, including what she'd seen on his email. 'He probably thinks that I'll be so busy lactating, he can carry on shagging this woman without me noticing. So,' she could hear the hardness in her own voice, 'You'll excuse me if I'm not really big on trust at the moment. I'll take some convincing that your Ben really is different.'

Neither spoke for a while and it was Joanna who broke the deadlock. 'Well, this is quite a turnaround. I never thought I'd see the day when you two swapped places. Ever since I've been here, you've both been going along, each quite sure that you were right. Georgie, you let that husband of yours have it all his own way and pandered to him non-stop. In fact, you've made a right doormat of yourself. And all in the name of love. Flick, you've been hard as nails – or so you thought – never giving any man who was halfway decent a chance of getting close to you. And laughing it all off, as if you were one of the boys.'

Georgie and Flick gaped at her. 'Don't hold back, will you, Jo,' Georgie said drily, at last. 'Say exactly what you think.'

Jo leaned back in her chair and surveyed them both coolly. 'I think you've both been mugs. There are some good people out there. And some bad. But you can tell, deep down, whether a man cares for you. It's in everything he does and everything he says. The good ones,' she turned to look at Flick. 'Well, they're keepers. But the bad ones, the ones who lie and cheat and still expect you to be there for them, keeping everything nice and comfy at home, they're the ones who deserve everything they get.'

Flick turned to Georgie. 'Look, I'm sorry about last night and, well, everything, really. Not telling you about Ben and stuff. But I'd really like you to meet him. Because I know you'd like him. I don't know what I feel about him. I don't have any idea what he feels about me. Probably nothing. But he's a kind, kind man and I hope he'll become a good friend. He's arranged this safe house for me and if we take down the YouTube thing now, that'll pacify—'

She stopped short, and Georgie realised that Flick knew who was behind the campaign of harassment and intimidation.

'Pacify who?' she snapped.

Flick looked at her with big eyes. 'I think it's Jackson.'

'Oh God, of course. It's obvious. The comments must have been from him.'

'And he's the only one who'd be able to find out where I lived. Ben and I talked it through last night.'

'What if Jackson doesn't drop it – the following and intimidating you?' Georgie said slowly, trying to think through the implications.

'Then we go to his wife, I suppose. What else can we do?'

Joanna stood up. 'I'll make another cup of tea, then we can decide the other thing on the agenda.'

Flick and Georgie both turned to her in surprise. 'What?'

'What colour wool I should use for the bootees I'm going to start knitting.'

Chapter Twenty-Four

The next few days fell into a pattern of sorts. Flick worked as normal during the day, then would head back to her flat to feed the disgruntled cats, pick up the post, collect clean clothes and air the place for a while, then she would lock up and head towards Ben's apartment. Ben had told her to take different routes each time and to keep an eye on the rear-view mirror, and she'd taken to parking away from the development and walking a circuitous route so as to shake off anyone who might be following.

It all seemed vaguely ridiculous, especially when the sky was denim blue and the city was as busy and disinterested as ever. Besides, there was no sign of anything untoward at the flat – no more dead vermin or smashed ornaments – but Flick was aware that each time she put the key in the lock she could feel her anxiety levels rising and she didn't dawdle for long, only really breathing out when she was back in her car heading towards the river.

Even though her make-up was now spread all over the bathroom and her clothes strewn on the bedroom chair, she still felt as if she was camping, but every time she walked into the apartment and saw the river through the gigantic windows, her heart lifted. It lifted too when her phone showed a message from Ben or he called. He dropped in for a quick drink each night, not staying long, but on the fourth evening he seemed in less of a hurry to go and was uneasy, as if he had something to ask her.

'I've got to go to Bath tomorrow to look at a possible project.'

'Nice place. Haven't been there for ages,' Flick replied over her shoulder as she opened the fridge, hoping to find the makings of supper. 'Great shopping too, but I don't suppose you'll have time for that.'

'No. I doubt it.'

Flick turned to look at him, not quite sure what relevance this topic of conversation had. He was lightly drumming his fingers on the back of a chair.

'I wondered if you'd like to come with me?'

Her stomach leapt but she tried to stay composed and cool. 'Oh.'

'That's if you can spare a day away and if you'd like to, of course. Perhaps you can explore the great shopping whilst I have my meeting and—'

'I'd love to,' Flick replied, sounding too keen. 'I mean, I'll have to check with Georgie, of course, but I'm sure they can cover for me.'

Ben stretched and smiled. 'Good. Great. Right. I'll collect you about eight-thirty, if that's OK?'

Flick didn't give Georgie much of an opportunity to object, using the 'I haven't had a proper day off for months' excuse and ignoring her friend's pointed remarks about spending time with married men.

'I'm only going to spend the day in Bath,' Flick whined back.

'Whatever. Bring me back a pressie.' There was a smile in Georgie's voice as she rang off.

Ben was at the door, his hair still damp from the shower, on the dot, and by nine-thirty they had made good headway out of town and down the motorway. There didn't seem a huge reason to chat and, being with him now out of context and out of her milieu, Flick felt shy and awkward. Ben must have sensed it, or was wondering why she seemed fascinated by everything outside of the passenger window, because as the traffic thinned out and he put his foot down, he relaxed, put on a CD and offered her a piece of chewing gum. Taking it from him emphasised their proximity and she fumbled as she took it from the proffered packet, dropping it down the side of the seat.

'Oops!' she laughed, stupidly, and slipped her hand down to find it. Feeling about, her fingers fell on a pencil and she pulled it out. 'Do you want this?' She held it out and then realised it was a Mac lipliner pencil. Suddenly Alison was there in the car with them, as a third presence, and Flick experienced a wave of what felt horribly like subversive guilt.

Ben, however, showed no emotion, even if he felt it. 'I don't wear that colour generally. It doesn't match my lipstick.' He smiled cheekily. Flick relaxed. They weren't doing anything wrong, were they, and she fished her hand down again, located the chewing gum and, blowing off the fluff, popped it in her mouth.

'So how did you start working with Georgie?' he asked after a while.

'We were introduced by friends – someone I know who had a child in the same school. I liked her straightaway – she's hard not to like – and we met for coffee. I worked in a really dull job then for a local estate agent – one in a long line of dull jobs actually – and the only talent I have is quite a good knowledge of south London. Georgie was looking for something to do now that her daughter, Libby, was at school, and we sort of hit on the idea of people who are cash-rich, time-poor needing help running their domestic lives.'

'It's a very good idea.'

'Well, it seems to have caught on – run away with us a bit, actually – but Jo's our Girl Friday and we're just getting to the stage where we can be a bit fussier about who we take on as members. Some are a nightmare.'

Ben smiled. 'So why the sideline?'

Flick looked out of the window and thought about it. What had driven them? 'I'm not sure I remember now. The office rent had just gone up when we were approached the first time, and I can't say having some crisp tenners pushed into our hands hasn't been a bonus ... maybe it was also a way of helping people who had a genuine grievance.' She shrugged.

Ben didn't pursue it and the chat moved to traffic, books, favourite music and live gigs they'd been to. She asked him about where he'd grown up and he painted a picture of grammar school and college in Kendal; a mother who was a schoolteacher and a dad who was an architectural technician.

'Are they proud of you?'

'I think so,' he answered, glancing at her as if he'd never really considered it. 'My brothers are a doctor and a solicitor respectively, which I think my parents consider respectable professions, whereas I think they have me down as a raving capitalist – but on the odd occasion I can lure them down here and I've shown them a project, they grudgingly admire it – in the way the older generation do. "Don't get above yourself, son!"'

'Do you see them often?'

'Not enough. They don't ... well, Alison doesn't really get on with them and it can make it awkward.' They covered the next few miles in silence.

'Did you want to be an architect?' Flick asked as they pulled off at the Bath junction.

'I wanted to be a graphic designer really, but I'm lumbered with too much of a commercial head – I love the challenge of the figures and making it all work, so I'd be no good at the drawing board.'

Ben stopped talking as they negotiated their way through the traffic, then he dropped her on George Street in the centre of the city and headed off to his meeting, waving and smiling as he went. Flick loved the rest of the day and, for the first time in ages, spent two hours browsing through shops, buying a novel and trying on shoes she didn't need. Off the high street, she found a luscious place selling handmade chocolates and bought a box of four Florentines wrapped in cellophane and ribbon for George and Jo, and, just before she paid, added a small gift box of truffles for Ben. By way of a thank you.

He called her just as her stomach was beginning to rumble and they arranged where he'd pick her up. She started to admire the contemporary paintings in a gallery window whilst she waited, but he was there, pulling up to the kerb, right on time. He took her to a little French restaurant and made her try snails (which she hated) and they talked over a glass of wine. She regaled him with some of the most extreme behaviour of their clients – hamming up the Mrs Halliman hamster story shamefully – and he told about the plans he had for future developments.

'God, you're all over the world!' Flick gasped, feeling small. 'I don't even go north of the Thames unless I'm forced to!'

At four they headed back down the motorway, every mile making her feel more depressed – couldn't they get a flat tyre or something? – and she spent the companionable silence trying to think of excuses why he might stay and have a drink when he dropped her off.

'Would you like to come up to your place for a cuppa?' she asked, laughing nervously when they pulled into the car park.

'I'd love to, but we're out for dinner tonight and I really ought to get back.'

We're out for dinner. 'Oh. Anywhere nice?'

'Regent's Park. My wife's cousin. Business really.'

'I see. Well, thanks for a lovely day.' She slipped out of the car.

'Thanks for coming,' he smiled and drove off.

Chapter Twenty-Five

'Well, regard it as an opportunity for personal growth, Ed,' Georgie snapped finally, brushing her hair vigorously. 'You really spend very little time actually looking after Libby, so there's no point acting so hard-done-by. She'll finish tennis tomorrow at four, but she's going home with Annabel afterwards. I'll give you the address. So, if you pick her up by six-thirty at the latest, you can be home by seven, I'll leave the lasagne to defrost and all you'll have to do is pop it in the microwave. I'll even put the timings on a Post-it so you won't have to dedicate even one brain cell to remembering how to cook it.'

Ed scowled. 'It's all very well you acting so flippant, but the launch—'

'Yes, yes. The launch – I do know it's in less than two weeks. But I don't think it's too much to expect you to dedicate a single evening to your family. And I do have to devote more time to my work now, since yours isn't paying enough.'

Ed shifted uncomfortably and Georgie eyed him with bitter amusement. She could see him struggling with himself. He had to comply because it's what he would do if he were sincere about all the gumph he'd talked, instead of being the lying bastard he actually was. If it weren't so indescribably awful, it would actually be quite funny, watching him squirm like this in an effort to have his cake and eat it. Georgie smiled quietly to herself and turned to face him.

He was staring at her expanding waist and didn't quite hide his expression in time. His lip was curled in a look of distaste and, in spite of everything, she felt herself flinch. Had he been like that when she was pregnant with Libby? No, he'd been proud and fond. How far apart they'd grown since then.

He must have sensed her uncertainty, and followed it up. 'You've put on more weight this time, I think. I don't remember you looking like that before. Perhaps it's being that bit older?'

It hurt. Georgie took a deep breath. She'd never thought marriage was a power struggle before – now she knew better – but she forced herself not to respond. The last thing she wanted was a slanging match when he would repeat how much he didn't want this pregnancy. He had always been better at arguing than her and she needed to be ready. She needed to be in control.

She felt even less in control later, as she watched her car being towed to the garage on the back of an AA truck. A radiator leak was in danger of messing up all her plans. By the time she got to Tim's, ridiculously late, the tiler that needed paying had already left. Now she had to work out how to get to Flick's and she opened her mobile to call one of the minicab firms they dealt with. 'Can I have a cab to Chelsea Harbour, please?' She heard a key in the door and, unaccountably, felt a sense of – what – anticipation?

'Hello!' Tim called and she heard his footsteps coming straight for the kitchen where she stood, negotiating with the minicab firm. She waved and mouthed a silent hello, and he smiled in response, miming raising a mug to his lips with a questioning lift of his eyebrows. She shook her head, but felt warmed by his thoughtfulness. He picked up the kettle, filled it from a filter jug that Georgie had picked up for him a few days earlier, and took the red spotty teapot down from a cupboard that, she noted, was now starting to fill up with food.

'Well, I need to be there for seven,' she said. 'So can you send someone to pick me up here at six-thirty? Yes, I'll give you the address.'

Suddenly Tim was gesticulating, shaking his head vigorously and pointing to himself. 'I'll take you,' he mouthed.

'Oh, hang on a moment.' Georgie covered the mouthpiece. 'No, it's fine. I'm just ordering a minicab.'

'I'm not having you take a cab. Certainly not. I'm free this evening. Cancel the cab. I'll take you. Really, I mean it.'

She hesitated. 'Are you sure, Tim? It's on the river at Wandsworth.' He nodded emphatically. Georgie thought it would be nice to travel in a vehicle that didn't have one of those little pine tree things dangling from the mirror and as the phone squawked at her, she hurriedly put it to her ear. 'Sorry, there's been a change of plan, I don't need a cab now. Thanks. Bye.'

'Well,' Tim smiled, glancing at his watch. 'Looks like we have time for a cup of tea. Would you like one?'

Georgie thought. 'Do you know, I really would. It's terribly kind of you to offer me a lift. Are you sure it's not too much trouble?'

'I wouldn't have offered if it was. Earl Grey or builders'?'

'Ooh, builders' please,' Georgie sighed. 'My radiator sprang a leak this morning and it's messed everything up.'

'Sounds nasty. Is that a pregnancy euphemism?' His eyes twinkled and she laughed. 'Isn't your husband around?' Tim busied himself with the tea, giving Georgie a quick sideways look.

'Yes. Well, no. I mean, he's picking up our daughter from a friend's house and I'm going to Flick's place.'

'On the river? The revenge business must be lucrative.'

Georgie took the mug of tea and helped herself from the plate of biscuits he'd put out. 'Oh yes, I'd forgotten you knew about that. Well, actually that's the whole problem. We bit off more than we could chew, I'm afraid.' And Georgie explained their suspicions about Jackson and the situation with Ben Houghton while Tim listened intently.

'I know half the story. I heard Flick talking to Houghton's

wife and she told me the details, but I didn't know anything about Flick and pole-dancing. Surely that was above and beyond?'

'Yup, on reflection, it was and things were looking a bit unpleasant, but I think it's OK, now that she's been able to disappear for a bit. But I don't know this Houghton bloke. He might be as bad as the rest.'

'I don't know him personally, but I know people who do and I've never heard anything bad. Rich as Croesus, apparently.' Tim drained his tea and looked at his watch. 'Time to go, I think. Have you got everything?'

'Uh-huh. Could I just use your loo, though, before we go.'

'Is it that radiator again?' Georgie pretended to bat at him but he moved away swiftly. 'Help yourself. You know where everything is. I'll get the car round so you won't have to walk so far.'

Moments later, Georgie locked the front door behind her and turned round at the sound of a purring engine. And couldn't prevent a huge smile spreading across her face. Tim was waiting in a soft-top Beetle – the original kind – painted a ludicrous shade of orange. It was the kind of car you couldn't help but have fun with. And she couldn't wait to get in. Tim jumped out and opened her door, then jumped back in and pulled away, the warm evening air blowing his dark hair back. He turned to smile at her, then opened the glove box and offered her a pair of sunglasses identical to the ones he was wearing. 'Never mind the hair,' he said, glancing sideways at her as she quickly tied it back with a scrunchie from her bag. 'Getting a bug in your eye isn't so much fun.'

Georgie settled back and gazed around, enjoying the warm air and the unexpected turn this evening had taken. She didn't feel any pressing need to make conversation. It wasn't like that with Tim. But she did feel intrigued by him. 'So what takes you abroad so much? Is it work?'

'Partly,' he said, indicating left and slowing at a junction.

'I'm winding up my business there but my ex-wife is German and she and my son still live there.'

'Oh, I see. I'm sorry.'

Tim shrugged. 'There's no need. It's a perfectly amicable situation. We get on pretty much as well as we ever did – by which I mean we're still good friends. We've known each other since we were kids and we probably shouldn't have married really, because we certainly weren't in love or anything. It had to happen one day, I suppose.'

'What had to?'

'Well, one of us falling in love for real.'

'Right,' Georgie said slowly, studying his profile. 'So, er ...'

'Well, she met a bloke at work and it changed everything. It was obvious she'd fallen hard and it was nothing like what we felt for each other. She really suffered at first. But then it became clear that he felt the same and I wasn't going to stand in their way.'

'How – strange!'

'Do you think so? I don't know really. I suppose we were just open about how we felt – she didn't try to hide it from me or anything. She's not like that, Sabine. You'll like her, I'm sure.'

Georgie had turned round in her seat to look at Tim's face as he drove. She felt strangely moved by this story, so unlike her own. He turned to smile briefly at her as they drew to a halt in the traffic beside the common, then looked around. 'What a lovely evening. Look at those birds, going home to roost, I suppose.'

Above them a surging flock of birds swooped as one across the sky and on the grass people were playing a game of cricket in the evening sunshine. The towers of the Royal Patriotic Building poked out above the trees, looking almost like a fairytale castle. She felt completely contented.

'London can be gorgeous sometimes, can't it?'

'Oh yes,' Tim agreed. 'That's one thing that is definitely better now. Sabine wanted to be close to her family, and that kept me in Stuttgart. I missed my family tremendously and I was always sorry that Anton – that's our son – didn't spend more time with his cousins. But now, when he comes to stay at Christmas, we'll go up to Derbyshire and it'll be just like when I was growing up. Fantastic!'

Georgie felt a sudden wave of envy for the unknown Sabine, with an adoring new husband and a lovely, devoted ex. She looked out of the window. 'Your ex-wife is very lucky.'

'Yes,' Tim nodded. 'I suppose she is. I used to envy her, in a way. You know, having found someone she felt so strongly about. Loved – you know. I suppose I envied her that, because what we'd had was more like a mutual respect. We were in "like" with each other. But I've realised love is so much more.'

Georgie's thoughts flashed back to home and Ed and now. 'And it can be so much less.'

There was a long silence. She turned to look at him and he quickly turned back to the road as the traffic started to move once more. They didn't speak again until Tim pulled up in front of the steel and glass building where Flick was staying. Georgie looked up at the façade, studded with balconies, winking in the setting sun, then turned to look at Tim. 'Wow. This is flash!'

He too was looking up at the building. Suddenly Georgie felt a surge of independence. She didn't want this to end. 'Come in with me,' she blurted before she could persuade herself otherwise. 'Please. If you've got time, I mean. I know Flick would be delighted, and we were only going to order in pizza. We could just get one more in for you.'

He hesitated, but she saw the pleasure in his eyes. 'Well, if you're sure. I'd love to.' Georgie waited on the pavement and smiled as she watched him put the roof up on the little orange car.

Flick turned back from the fridge where she'd cooled another bottle of wine and took in the curious tableau in front of her. Somehow she'd gone from the same-old, same-old existence of work, drinks with friends and nights on her own in front of the TV, to this: a temporary stop-over in a penthouse flat overlooking the Thames and an evening with Georgie and her deliciously rounding tummy, a man who wasn't Georgie's husband but who, any fool could see, was besotted with her, and Ben Houghton. And what was he to her, exactly?

Ben had called earlier to see how she was and, on impulse, she'd asked him if he'd like to come over, feeling a frisson of delight when he'd said, 'Why not?' Now he was deep in conversation with the other two and Flick took the opportunity to study him. His profile was strong and, as he talked, he unconsciously gesticulated with his hands, or ran them through his hair – a habit she'd noticed he had when he was thinking about something challenging. He was wearing glasses tonight, which she hadn't seen before, but then she knew so little about him. She liked his shirt, casual but well-made and in a shade of sea blue. In fact, she admitted, unscrewing the top of the wine bottle, she liked it all; his hands, the strong thighs that strained against his jeans, the way he rested his foot across his knee when he was relaxed, the way he moved.

The way he moved. She swallowed. This man made her feel something she'd never felt before with anyone. It was sexual, but deeper than sexual. When she was near him, it made every fibre of her respond. It was almost animal. It felt like that moment when you wade out to sea and suddenly find you're out of your depth and the current lifts your body. She shook her head. She had no idea how he felt, despite the friendly kiss he'd given her on his arrival this evening and, besides, he was someone else's husband and, worse, she was the one who'd been sent to catch him out. That put him right out of bounds. And yet ...

She made her way back to the table, strewn with the remnants of takeout pizza, and put the bottle down. Ben looked up at her and smiled.

'It's not quite cool enough, I'm afraid,' she said apologetically, for something to say.

'You just can't get the service these days,' he teased, quietly, and she topped up his glass.

'That was delicious.' Tim stretched and rubbed his tummy. 'I shall make sure that I have Giovanni's Pizza Palace cater all my dinner parties in future!'

'It was wonderful,' Georgie rubbed her tummy as well and laughed. 'Augustus enjoyed it too.'

'Augustus? Crikey, that would be a yoke to go through life with.'

'I think you need to go for something much more *Hello!* magazine,' Tim interjected enthusiastically. 'Like Apple, or Zoro.' Ben laughed.

'There's a couple of girls at Libby's school called Eunique and Destiny.'

Tim threw his head back with glee. 'Love it! Let's hope Eunique doesn't end up being an ugly frump.'

Flick watched as they laughed together. She'd never seen Georgie and Ed interact like this. She hadn't had time to brief Ben on the situation and she saw him look from one to the other. 'Are you two hoping for a boy this time?' he asked tentatively. 'That seems to be the pattern – one of each.'

Georgie blushed. 'Oh, Ben. I'm sorry, I thought you realised. Tim and I, we're not ... I mean, my husband isn't here tonight.'

'Oh, right.' Ben looked a bit perplexed.

'Tim's a friend.' Georgie turned to him. 'You're a good friend, aren't you? And, for the record,' she said quietly, her eyes big and round, 'I don't think my husband's bothered either way.'

'Oh, I see. I'm sorry.'

'I'm not.'

Ben glanced at Flick as if asking for help, and Flick looked at Georgie for approval that she had the go-ahead to say something. Georgie shrugged, and smiled wryly.

'Georgie and her husband Ed are ... well, they're having problems. This baby was not planned and well, it turns out he's been having an affair. Still is, actually.' There was an awkward silence around the table; the bubble of pleasure they'd felt whilst munching through pizza had been popped.

'Bit ironic really, isn't it?' Georgie said bravely, fiddling with the ties on her wrap-round cardigan. 'There were Flick and I, taking the moral high ground, dishing out punishment to men with a wandering eye and lo and behold, it was going on right under my nose.'

'Fuck,' said Tim eloquently.

'Fuck, indeed.' Georgie smiled at him.

'What are you going to do?' Tim had leaned forward and was leaning his elbows on the table. His face wore an expression of genuine concern; a desire to help her with this shattering blow. Flick's heart warmed to him.

'I don't really know, to be honest. I haven't confronted him yet – well, not this time anyway. I did when I found out initially and he promised to give her up. I think he's hoping that I'll be so busy with the baby that he'll have free rein.' Georgie paused. 'To be honest, I am so angry that I'm frightened I might run him through with the Sabatier.'

'Has he asked for a divorce?' Tim prodded gently.

'Hah!' Georgie laughed dryly. 'Another divorce for Ed? He's too worried about the expense of another ex-Mrs Casey. He just wants to have his cake and eat it – but he doesn't want to pay for it.'

There was silence for a while, and Flick nervously topped up her glass.

'Casey. Is that your surname?' Ben asked into the silence.

'Yes.'

'Ed Casey. I don't suppose he's an architect? Does he work for Fulbrook, Nathan and Hughes?'

'Yes. God, do you know him?'

Ben smiled. 'I've worked with them on lots of occasions. Not necessarily Ed – he wouldn't know me – but I did a project in the City with them a while back. It's a good outfit. They do mainly London work, don't they?'

'And Cardiff,' said Flick and Georgie simultaneously and burst out laughing.

Georgie was aware of the two men looking at her, Ben with curiosity, Tim with something altogether harder to read – pity maybe? She hoped not, but the laughter of a moment ago died away and Georgie fiddled with her glass.

'So?' Tim asked.

'Well, it's obvious, isn't it?' Ben went on. 'At least, it is to me. You've been getting revenge for the wronged women of south London for the last six months or so. What are you going to do to Ed? I mean, he deserves it more than most.'

Flick nodded. 'You're right. Of all the cases we've taken on, this is by far the worst.'

Georgie shrugged. 'It doesn't show me in a terribly good light, does it? The gullible doormat.'

Tim whistled. 'That's pretty harsh,' he said quietly. 'Sounds like you're blaming yourself.'

Ben nodded. 'It's amazing, though, what you'll put up with to keep a marriage going. It's not like it happens all at once, either, is it? It's so gradual – at least it was with me and my wife – that you don't realise at first what's going on. You don't understand how much you're compromising yourself and who you are.'

'Exactly!' Georgie looked at him, grateful that he understood. Her judgement of him had changed totally over the course of the evening. He'd turned up whilst they were having a glass of wine on the balcony, looking over the river while Flick was hamming it up being Châtelaine. He'd been unfazed by the two invaders into what was, effectively, his apartment. But what astonished Georgie more, was the change in Flick when he came through the door. She seemed to light up.

Ben was particularly attentive towards her and, throughout the evening, she responded in a way Georgie had never seen

256

before, her face open and her eyes following him as he moved around the table, filling their glasses and serving more slices of the giant pizza they'd had delivered.

Georgie shook her head and went on, relieved to be able to share her feelings at last. 'You know, if someone had told me, when Ed and I first got married, what I'd end up accepting, I wouldn't have believed it. I'd have ended it there and then rather than compromise myself so much.'

Tim reached over and squeezed her hand quickly in a brotherly way, then released it. 'I think I've been unusually lucky in the break-up of my marriage. And – this is going to sound weird – but in a way, I envy you both. It was only easy because Sabine and I were never crazy in love with each other. Maybe you only feel this angry and hurt now because of how much you loved Ed. Maybe that's where the desire for revenge comes from. It's as deep as the love you once felt.'

There was a companionable silence as the other three thought about Tim's suggestion. Flick spoke first, unusually hesitantly. 'I'm not sure that's even it, Tim. I think it's more to do with how the other person has treated you. And what they've put you through. I mean, look at Mike Jackson. He didn't even know I existed until that night but, somehow, he blames me for what he's experienced and for making a fool of him, and he's been determined to make me suffer for it.'

Georgie intercepted a look of such concern from Ben towards Flick, sitting with her head bowed at the end of the table, that she almost gasped.

'Jackson's a nutter, Flick,' Ben said. 'He was full of anger – probably towards women in general – and he focused it on you. But he's not typical. And that kind of revenge isn't what you've been involved in at all.'

Georgie picked up a pizza crust and gnawed at it. 'Some people say that the best revenge is living well, but I don't subscribe to that. Not any more.'

'Why is that then?' asked Tim, reaching forward to fill her glass with water.

'Well, even before I found out what Ed had been up to, I could see that the women coming to us needed to take some kind of action, but they just didn't know what. In most cases, it was a question of regaining their self-respect. Just "living well" sounds far too passive for what those women wanted.'

Flick laughed scornfully. 'Judging by the clothes they wore, they were living pretty well already. I think the desire for revenge is a really basic one. You know, an eye for and eye, and all that.'

Georgie laughed, bitterly. 'To be honest, at the moment I wouldn't be satisfied with an eye or a tooth. I'd be looking much more for one of Ed's testicles. Removed with a pair of rusty secateurs.'

Both men winced and Flick chuckled. Georgie shrugged apologetically.

'We didn't do anything that really hurt anyone, did we?' Flick went on, 'At first, I mean, it was more like pranks. The Jackson thing was probably the worst, but that was just to show him up.'

Georgie agreed. 'I suppose we tried to make the punishment fit the crime – like that bloke with the phone numbers in the public loos, right back at the beginning.'

Ben and Tim exchanged bewildered looks and, taking it in turns to prompt each other, Georgie and Flick told them about their choicest revenge capers. 'The point was also to hit them where it hurts,' Flick went on, getting into her stride. 'Now, what could we do to Ed? I can see that taking the scissors to his suits would be pretty satisfying, but it would lack finesse. And besides, hasn't that been done already? The least he deserves is originality '

Georgie smiled weakly. 'I can't let him get way with how he's treated me.'

Tim smiled. 'It's trite, I know, but I did hear a lovely story the other day about a woman who "borrowed" her errant husband's Ferrari and wrote it off by driving it around town in first gear. The engine set alight.'

'Fabulous!' Georgie smiled broadly. 'Shame we've only got a sodding Toyota Prius.' Georgie thought for a moment. 'I think we ought to go for his Achilles heel.'

'Not the Philippe Starck lemon squeezer?' Flick asked with wide-eyed irony.

'I'd shove that where the sun don't shine,' Georgie twinkled. 'No, it's got to be his work. Bloody work. Let's get him where it hurts. I just want to make him look an idiot, I don't want to destroy him. He isn't worth the bother. And, besides,' she gave a mischievous grin, 'I'm going to need him for child maintenance.'

They chatted a while longer until Georgie yawned and Tim, noticing how tired she was, stood up and announced he was taking her home.

'Good idea,' said Flick. 'Take care of her,' she added.

'Oh, I will,' he said quietly as he kissed Flick goodnight and the two of them left. Georgie looked small and vulnerable as she stood beside him in the lift before the doors closed.

Ben was standing in the kitchen when Flick went back into the apartment and, for a moment, it was as if they were a couple who'd been entertaining for the evening. Flick was suddenly very aware that they were alone and she felt awkward.

'Nice man,' said Ben as he rinsed out the glasses. 'Have you both known him long?'

'He's an agency client.' Flick busied herself clearing up the pizza boxes. 'But we're doing quite a lot of work with him now. I like him a lot and I like the way he is with Georgie. She needs some tender loving care.'

As they tidied up, she told Ben more about Ed and he listened in silence.

'I can imagine,' he'd said, which surprised her. 'I only met him the once, but I thought he was jumped-up and full of self-importance. But I didn't want to say that to Georgie – you have to be so careful speaking your mind with break-ups, because sometimes they end up back together and you're well and truly off the Christmas card list after that! I have to say, I'm not convinced by the revenge thing in general, but I'd make an exception in his case.' He paused. 'I'd better go now.'

They stood in front of each other in silence and, for want of anything else to do, she put her hands in the pocket of her jeans.

'Right.'

Then Ben stepped forward and putting his hand on the back of her neck, lifting up her hair, he pulled her gently towards him. She felt her breath catch in her throat and then his lips on hers, searchingly. Before she was even aware of it, she put her hands on his shoulders and he pulled her close. He tasted so good and Flick held herself against his body, hungry for him. They pulled apart breathlessly, both shocked by their passion.

'Goodnight, lovely woman,' he said eventually, and closed the door behind him.

Chapter Twenty-Six

'Ben's got the swishest flat!' Georgie was enthusing to Jo when Flick arrived the next morning.

Flick waved a hand airily. 'I can't imagine how I'm going to lower myself to your pathetic level now, darlings!'

'Get you, Ms Fancy Pants,' muttered Jo, pretending to be disgruntled. 'Just to bring you back down to earth, the Settons' sewer manhole is overflowing into their conservatory, and I can't get hold of Clive.'

Flick checked her book and groaned. 'He's round at the Hambletts'. He'll be there all day – she's terribly difficult and demanding and will have him polishing the taps before he leaves. Can you call Manny? He might be able to pull off the Kinghams.'

'Ooh er, Mrs!' laughed Georgie, her eyes scanning the day's schedule on the screen. The phone jangled again, as it had almost non-stop, and Jo picked it up. 'Flick,' Georgie continued, 'Can you coordinate the Streatham washing machine repair let-in with this pick-up in Croydon?'

'What pick-up is that?' Flick threw her coat over the chair. She felt good this morning. Every nerve in her body tingled and she'd revisited that kiss all through the night.

'It's come as an email from a member we haven't done much for, actually. It's to pick up curtains from the maker in Fendale Road. Number thirty-nine. There's a footnote to say park in the Hayes Street multi-storey and it's two minutes from there.

They have to be collected at three apparently – not convenient before or after.'

'That's helpful. OK, I'll do that this afternoon.'

They worked on together, and filled the busy morning so fast that Flick looked at her watch when Jo stood up and asked if anyone wanted a sandwich.

'God, is that the time already? Can you get me one of those tuna and mayo ones and a smoothie?'

Jo left with their orders and, for the first time that day, Flick had a chance to grill George about last night.

'He's lovely, George.'

'Which one?' Georgie smiled back.

'*Tim*. Kind, funny, supportive – and that's a novelty in most men.'

'Sounds too good to be true.' Georgie was crouched over her keyboard and Flick could tell she was trying very hard not to sound enthusiastic.

'Come on,' Flick pressed. 'Don't be cynical. You told me once that there are good men out there, and I think Tim is gold-dust.'

Georgie finally leaned back in her chair and fiddled with the bracelet on her wrist. Flick noted it wasn't the one that Ed had given her last Christmas. 'I'm not jumping out of the frying pan into the inferno, Flick. I do happen to think he's lovely – we talked quite a bit in the car and he filled me in on his ex-wife and things. But it all gets so complicated with baggage, doesn't it? I married someone with baggage and that's caused enough problems. And, more to the point, I'm still married and I'm not in the market – or in the mood – to get involved. Apart from anything else, I'm pregnant.'

'I know.' Flick realised she shouldn't pursue it; her enthusiasm that Ed might finally be out of Georgie's life was getting the better of her. 'Just don't push him away. You've got real support there, for whatever reason, and he's worth holding on to.'

Georgie smiled. 'Yes, I know. He's a real friend.'

'And a pretty scrumptious one at that.'

Georgie sighed 'How very complicated life is!'

'Meaning?'

'I've got myself into a situation whereby my husband is sleep-ing with someone else – it still hurts to say that – and you've fallen for a man who is still married.'

'I have not!'

Georgie snorted and picked up her pen. 'Flick, old girl, I think I know you quite well by now and I've seen you in all sorts of situations, but I have never seen you like you were last night.'

Flick winced. 'Oh God, was I that obvious?'

'No, to be fair, you were cool. You didn't actually dribble, but I could see it in your eyes.' Flick blushed. Had Ben noticed? That wouldn't do at all. She looked sheepishly at Georgie.

'I have to admit I find him quite magnetic.' Flick looked at her watch, stood up, slipped on her coat, and made her way to the door. 'See you later.'

She just heard Georgie say, 'Take care' as the door shut behind her.

Georgie had been on the phone for ten minutes, pressing the numbers when asked to, and listening to the hits of the Carpenters down her ear while she waited. It wasn't until Joanna cleared her throat ostentatiously that she realised she must have been singing along. She needed a wee, but there was no way she was going to hang up before she'd sorted out when she could collect her car. And if she had to start all over again, it would be another hour, at this rate, before she got through.

Besides, she had things to think about. Although Georgie had dismissed with a laugh Flick's comments about Tim, they'd struck home, but probably not in the way she'd intended. Tim was kind and thoughtful, it was true. And relaxing company. And good-looking. In fact, he was almost perfect in every way – for someone *not* in Georgie's situation. Married, albeit not for very much longer, pregnant and with an adorable little girl who deserved all the attention Georgie could give.

She understood where Flick was coming from. She'd seen it before with girlfriends. Hell, she'd probably done it herself. Now that Flick had fallen in love, she wanted everyone else to be fixed up too. But Georgie had gone through all that and was now out the other side. For a moment, she felt old, sad, deserted and cynical. She stabbed at another number with the end of her pencil, and was told, once again, that her call could be recorded for training purposes. 'That is, if I ever get to speak to someone who needs training,' she growled.

Then, suddenly, her attention shifted and she caught her breath. Inside, deep inside, she felt a tiny flutter. A subtle shift that was almost like a caress, and a smile started to slowly spread across her face. She plopped the phone back into its cradle and placed both hands on her stomach. This was all the love she needed, and she couldn't, simply couldn't, ask for more.

Flick put the radio on as she drove, and opened the window a little way to let in the fresh air. The trees that ran alongside Tooting Common were turning now, curling at the edges and tinged with yellow. The year had flown by, but what changes it had brought! Not least for Georgie, whose Christmas this year would be so different from last. New Year would bring a new baby and a future on her own. Flick thought about her encounter with Ed in the shop last Christmas when she'd found him choosing a necklace. Had he meant that one for Georgie or had she caught him choosing something for his mistress?

Paul, the washing machine repair man, was on time, as always. Despite being a shameless flirt who was the *roi* of *double entendre*, he was one of the agency's most long-serving and reliable contractors. Flick and Georgie had long ago decided that he was their desert islander of choice in case they needed anything mended, even if it meant tolerating the banter.

'You look foxy today, Mrs,' he leered up at her from his five foot six inches as she let him into the client's house. 'If I could reach you and if I wasn't a married man—'

'Don't suppose that would stop you!' She looked down at her short skirt and boots. Too foxy? It probably was a bit, but she felt tingly and sexy today and had wanted to look it.

'Can you drop the keys back at the office, Paul? And the usual thing about this client – not a speck of dust out of place.'

Paul made a mock salute. 'Wilco, Roger. And you watch what you're doing with those legs. You should have a licence for 'em!'

Laughing, Flick jumped back into the car. Time was marching on to get to the curtain-makers in Croydon and she crossed her fingers that the traffic wasn't too bad and she'd make the three o'clock deadline. She'd have to go back to her flat at some point later to get clean knickers and check that the cats were OK, but she should be fine in daylight. She let her shoulders drop, admitting to herself that she would be completely safe back there now, but something was making her want to stay at Ben's apartment. Well, someone, actually.

As if on cue, her phone went and she slipped in her earpiece. It was The Someone.

'Hi,' she tried to keep the smile out of her voice.

'Hi, yourself.' Ben's voice sounded warm and friendly. 'Just thought I'd see how you are and to thank you for entertaining me last night at … er, my place!'

'It was a pleasure.' She swung past a slow Citroën that was dawdling at the lights. There was silence for a moment. Was he thinking about their parting kiss too?

'Are you on your way to stalk someone else or have you resumed your day job now?' he teased lightly.

'Nope – business as usual today. I'm off to sunny Croydon to collect some curtains. Actually, I haven't got a clue where I'm going.'

'And I don't suppose you have sat nav, do you?'

'God no – what's wrong with a good old *A–Z*? It can't be that hard.'

'What's the address? Unlike you, I *am* clued up enough to have the technology.'

'Naturally.' Flick smiled and looked at the scrap of paper on the passenger seat beside her. 'Hayes Street multi-storey?'

There was silence for a moment. 'Got it. Just off Coombe Road, it looks like. Bit of a wiggle. Do they make curtains in the car park?'

'Probably. No, the client suggested I park there. Come to think of it, I don't recognise this client's name so I hope they're reliable with their information.'

There was silence again and she wondered if his phone had lost coverage, then she heard him say, 'Is that the normal sort of thing you do?'

'Well, it's a bit odd to go this far out, and we usually only collect from makers we've recommended, but this member hasn't used us much and it's all part of the service, you know.'

'Right. Look, better go. Speak later.'

She liked the sound of that. 'Sure.' She clicked off the phone.

He was right about the wiggle and it was five to three before she found the entrance to the car park, tucked away down a rat-run of streets. She had to ask two pedestrians before she actually located it and turned into the narrow entrance and down the slope into its bowels. It was small and dark, with litter strewn around the entrance. Weeds grew tall from between the pavings. What a dump, Flick thought, negotiating her car around the tight turnings between the concrete pillars.

It wasn't full, by any means, and some cars looked almost as if they had been abandoned. There was a pay and display machine on the far side of the basement level and she pulled up into a space close to it. No point in walking too far. She had to fumble around the bottom of her bag to find some change in amongst the odd Polo mint now covered in fluff. She couldn't believe this was high priority on the parking warden patrol, but she didn't want to risk it. She put in the change, sticking the ticket to the inside of her windscreen. Emerging out of the back of the car park into the bright daylight it wasn't clear which way she should head, so, spotting a gap in the fence, she climbed through onto the road beyond. It was empty, with gates leading into gardens. Walking to the end, it became apparent that the next road was much the same. Flick looked around, lost now, trying to find someone to ask. At this rate she'd miss the curtain-maker.

She must have walked for ten minutes before she came across a middle-aged man in a brown jacket walking a large mastiff down the road. Flooded with relief, she hurried towards him.

'I'm sorry to bother you, but I'm a bit lost. Can you tell me where Fendale Road is?'

He looked up, an expression of incomprehension on his face. Oh bugger. She'd found the local half-wit.

'Fendale Road?'

'Yes,' she replied patiently. 'It's just around here, apparently.'

He gave Flick the once-over appreciatively. 'Turn right just round there, sweetheart,' he smiled suggestively and watched her as she scurried off. Fendale Road looked a bit more hopeful, but the house numbers were hard to see. She'd expected the curtain-maker to have a shop front, but all sorts of people worked from home these days, so, peering at doors, she worked her way down the street. Thirty-seven looked derelict and number thirty-nine, oddly, had a plaque for a dental practice. Flick fished out her phone and called the office.

'George, it's me. Number thirty-nine can't be right. It's a dentist's.'

'Hang on. I'll check and call you back.'

Flick kicked about some leaves on the pavement while she waited. The day was warmer than she'd anticipated and she felt sticky now in her skirt and boots. Eventually her phone rang again.

'Hi. All a bit odd. I got hold of the member – a Mrs Jellicoe – and she says she never emailed and doesn't have any curtains to collect. Sounds like someone has given us the wrong member number. Sorry, love, you'll have to abandon that one.'

'Oh bollocks,' Flick sighed. 'What a bloody waste of time. See you in a bit.' And, snapping her phone shut, she began to stomp back to the car. Now her feet hurt and she'd have murdered a cuppa. Her phone rang again. It was her mother, so she shared her frustration with her.

Georgie stared ahead of her without really seeing. The delight she'd felt earlier had given way to nagging worry about Flick. Nothing about this errand tied up and she called up the email to check it, one more time. Either this was nothing – just a silly mistake – or it was something awful. The email request hadn't seemed unreasonable – it was the kind of thing they dealt with all the time. But the email address it had come from was a Hotmail one, without a recognisable name attached. On impulse, she called Flick back, but the call went straight to answerphone. Well, that could have been for loads of reasons, all of them quite innocent. She tried a text. 'R u ok? On yr way back?' and pressed 'send'.

She blew out a long breath, puffing out her cheeks, and tried to relax her shoulders. If Flick didn't call back in, say, five minutes she'd ... what? She stood up, then sat down again. Her phone was still mute and she pressed a random button to check she had a good signal. Five bars. She tried calling again but the answerphone clicked on straightaway. Georgie rubbed her eyes, then clicked on the computer screen and looked up the number of Ben's office. She sighed with relief when the receptionist answered. 'I'm afraid he's just left the office. Can I take a message?'

Where the hell was everybody?

By the time Flick climbed back through the fence, her head

hurt. The sun had gone behind a dark cloud and the air felt close and heavy. She stumbled over some stones and rubble in the scrap of land near the car-park entrance and she cursed, trying to find her car keys in the mêlée at the bottom of her bag. Her heels clicked loudly on the concrete floor and echoed around the empty space. As she turned the corner of a pillar, her fingers felt her keyring.

'Well, if it isn't the tart from the club.'

Flick stopped and looked around, not sure where the voice had come from.

'Been out whoring, have you, or do you only work nights?'

Now she knew he was behind her, perhaps ten metres away, his voice calm and controlled. She didn't turn, but persuaded her legs to carry her towards her car, pulling her keys as she walked. The keyring caught on a piece of thread on the edge of the zip and wouldn't budge as she pulled.

'Oi, I'm talking to you,' he shouted. Flick ignored him and pulled harder, fear rising now in her chest. But it was mid-afternoon. What was there to fear?

She heard his footsteps now coming towards her, speeding up. She turned to face him.

It was Mike Jackson, bigger than she remembered, and this time in a T-shirt and jeans, his belly pushing out against the fabric as if he were pregnant. In his hand he gripped what looked suspiciously like a baseball bat.

'What are you doing here?' she asked, trying not to let her voice shake. She realised how stupid it must sound – like small talk – and how obvious the answer must be.

'Now, what do you think?' He spoke quietly this time, almost calmly, as a teacher might to a dim-witted pupil.

'I have no idea.' Flick tried to sound brave, almost haughty, grappling to get the upper hand. 'I would like to know, though, why you are following me?'

Her mobile shrilled and she moved her hand to get it from her bag.

'Leave it,' he shouted. She let her hand drop.

'Because you, you little tart, have ruined my life.'

She put her weight on one leg and sighed. 'Don't be ridiculous,' she said, trying a tolerant smile this time. 'How can I have done that?'

He walked slowly towards her and she had to hold steady so she didn't back away. Only inches away from her now, she was eye to eye with him, and was grateful for her heels. She could feel his breath and see his pock-marked skin and the blackheads on his nose.

'Because every bugger I've ever met seems to have witnessed your little pricktease act, you bitch.' She felt his spittle on her face. Pricktease. So it had been Jackson's comments on YouTube.

'What makes you so sure this has anything to do with me?' Flick tried to pull back from him without actually moving.

'Because my silly, silly wife happened to leave your business card lying about and so I found out where your office was. Hardly Inspector Morse stuff really, was it?' He pushed his face in towards hers and gently tapped her leg with the baseball bat.

Flick's fear rose and she knew she had to move away now. She turned and, crab-like, made her way towards her car without actually turning her back on him. 'I think that it's not really my problem,' she said, sticking her hand into her bag again and miraculously feeling her keys immediately beneath her fingers. With renewed strength borne from panic, she pulled them hard and felt the thread that had caught the keyring snap. 'I think you need to talk to your silly, silly wife about why you were filmed in the first place.'

The moment the words were out of her mouth she knew she shouldn't have said them, and in four or five paces he was beside her. 'Don't fuck with me!' he shouted and lifted the baseball bat above his head. Flick flinched away as he brought it down, shattering the windscreen of her car. 'I've lost my job—'

Down it came again. 'Lost any fucking respect I might have had!' This time it was the side window, the glass shattering into a thousand pieces and cascading in onto the driver's seat. 'You have no idea what you've done, you bitch.' His face was red now, his eyes popping with rage. Spittle ran down his lip and onto his chin as he spluttered out the words. 'Shaking your tits, thinking you were having a laugh.'

Flick couldn't have spoken if she had wanted to. He stepped towards her and shoved the end of the baseball bat under her chin, forcing her head painfully upwards. 'Do you want to know what it really feels like to be shafted?' he asked, more quietly now, pushing her so her back was up against the side of the car. 'You're asking for it with those boots on, aren't you? Is that what your boyfriend likes? Is that why you haven't been at home?'

She could feel his other hand on her thigh now.

'Stop it,' she tried to swallow. 'Don't touch me.'

'I bet you don't say that to him, do you?' This time his hand went under her skirt and he ripped at her tights, the force of his fingers making a hole. 'Does he do this then?' She could feel his hand on her skin and the touch of it galvanised her suddenly. With as much strength as she could muster, she brought up her knee as hard as she could and then kicked him. She heard him wince at the same moment that she heard the screech of tyres and a car career down the slope into the car park, its lights on full.

For a terrifying moment, she thought it might be someone Jackson knew; someone timed to arrive so he could shove her into the car. Then she saw it was a blue BMW.

Ben seemed to get from the driver's seat to Jackson without actually moving, but the force of the punch he landed on the side of Jackson's head sent the stocky man reeling away from Flick and towards the wall of the car park. Ben was in front of him by the time he had steadied himself.

'What the hell do you think you are doing?' Flick could hear

Ben's voice, not loud but incontrovertible. The two men were eye to eye now. Though much the same height, Jackson was broader and larger, and Flick worried that one retaliation from him and Ben would be laid-out.

'None of your goddam business.'

'That's where you're wrong, you tosser. I don't really like people who intimidate, follow people around, go into their flats in broad daylight. That's the kind of thing that cowards do.'

Jackson pulled himself up tall, and Flick moved around to the back of her car, using it as protection, casting about the empty car park for someone, anyone. Through the grills in the walls she could see that the sky had darkened to a deep purple and rain was hammering down now onto the road. Her heart pounded and she felt sick with panic.

'And it's OK for that tart to go flashing her tits in people's faces and then putting it up for the world to see, is it?' He lunged into Ben's face. *'Is it?'*

Ben held steady and before Jackson could respond, he wrenched the baseball bat from his hand. 'When the idiot deserves it, yes. Now,' he said, walking away towards Flick, 'What's it to be? Are you going to back off and never come near her again, or are we going report you for criminal damage, attempted rape and breaking and entering?'

'Ben!' Flick just managed to shout as Jackson lunged at Ben's back, almost knocking him off his feet. Ben, in a knee-jerk response, swung his body round and sent the man slamming onto the floor. Then he bent over him, anger contorting his face, his hand gripping the fabric of Jackson's T-shirt and his knee pinning him to the ground. Very slowly and deliberately he spoke into his face, 'Don't-ever-do-that-again!' Then he stood up, leaving the man lying panting on the floor, and slowly walked back to Flick's car.

'Is there anything in there you need?' he asked gently.

'My cardigan,' she stuttered. He leaned in through the broken window, retrieved her cardigan and shook the glass off it then, taking Flick's hand, led her to his car, the engine of which she now realised was still running. He opened the passenger door and, wordlessly, she slipped into the seat. He shut it firmly behind her and walked round, getting into the driver's seat and throwing the baseball bat into the back. His face was expressionless and she looked from him to Jackson, who was now sitting upright on the concrete floor, his arms resting on his knees, eyes fixed down at the ground. Ben let off the handbrake and they drove off.

It must have been ten minutes before Flick could control her breathing and she started to shake. She couldn't stop herself, her body was taken over by involuntary spasms. Ben, who hadn't yet spoken, reached his arm over onto the back seat and passed her a jacket which she slipped around her shoulders. She could smell him on the fabric and she pulled it around herself like a cocoon.

'Are you OK?' he asked quietly, eventually, concentrating on the road ahead and the traffic.

'No,' she replied.

'Did he hurt you?'

Flick pulled her skirt up her thigh a little way to inspect her skin through the gaping hole in her tights. The flesh was livid and red where his hands had been. 'It's OK.'

'Did he—'

'No.'

There was silence as they headed towards the river. Flick couldn't focus on where they were but the rain had passed over and mercifully there seemed to be little traffic. She knew she ought to think about what to do now, but all she could do was re-run in her head the events of the last hour. He had set her up and she had fallen right into the trap. If it had been Georgie who'd done the so-called pick-up, what then? What would ... she started to rock at the thought of it ... what would have happened if Ben hadn't turned up?

'How did you know?'

Ben's face was tense and his mouth was set and tight-lipped. 'Because what you said didn't sound right. Thank God I knew where you were going.' Flick's phone rang again. It was Georgie.

'Flick.' She sounded breathless. 'Where are you? Are you OK?'

'I'm OK.' Even she knew her voice sounded shaky.

'It wasn't a curtain pick-up, was it?'

'No. No, George, it wasn't. It was Jackson.'

Flick could hear Georgie's intake of breath. 'Oh God, I'm so sorry. I should have noticed it didn't sound right – the client and stuff. I tried to call. I was frantic. Where are you now?'

'It's OK – I'm with Ben. He arrived when … well, things got a bit messy and—' she could feel the tears welling up in her eyes.

'Are you safe? Where's Jackson now?' Georgie's voice was getting shrill with panic.

'George, it's OK, darling. I'm OK. I'm in Ben's car and we're nearly …' She could see the apartment block up ahead. '… home.'

'Thank God. Are you going to go to the Police?'

'I don't know yet. Look, I'm a bit wobbly. Can I call you in a bit?' Her hands were shaking.

Georgie let out a breath. 'Of course, I'm just glad you're OK. That you're with Ben. Call me later.' And she clicked off.

All Flick wanted to do was get back to the safety of the apartment and, pulling Ben's jacket around her, she headed for the lift. He was right beside her, only inches away, but without touching her. Thankfully no one was around and they headed up in the lift. She handed Ben the keys and he opened the apartment door, letting her through and shutting it firmly behind them. It was that sound which seemed to cut the rope of control that was holding everything in place and she crumpled onto the floor, her head in her hands, tears pouring down her face.

He left her there for a moment as he dropped the keys on the side then, taking her bag from her shoulders, very gently he put his hands under her arms and lifted her up so she was standing in front of him, supported by him.

'I'm so sorry.'

'What are you sorry for?'

'For being stupid,' she sniffed, her body still shaking, 'and for getting you involved in all this mess and for putting you in danger ...'

Amazingly, she saw him smile slightly. 'Well, it's not the sort of thing I do normally.'

'I've been so stupid, so naive that we wouldn't end up in trouble,' she couldn't get the words out quick enough. 'And I didn't know what to do, and he had that bat and his hands, and I thought he was going to ... and then you were there and ...' She could feel her mouth contorting with the agony. 'What would I have done if you hadn't—'

His face was very close to hers now and his voice was urgent. 'You weren't to know that he'd be there but, the important thing is, I *was* there.' He put his hand up and brushed the hair away from her face. 'I was there because I knew you were in trouble. That's what matters. It's over now, it's over and you're safe.' And with that, his mouth came down on hers with an urgency, a hunger, as if he wanted to consume her. He took her face in his hands and she responded to him with the same urgency, finding safety in his kiss and knowing that it was really all she wanted to do.

'Oh God, Flick,' he said against her mouth. She didn't respond, just slipped her hands up to his head, burying her fingers in his hair and pulling his mouth harder towards hers. She wasn't sure if he groaned or if it was her, but they cleaved to each other with a desperation. A desperation mixed with lust that they couldn't and didn't want to control. She wasn't even sure which one of them led the way into the bedroom but, as they went, they pulled at each other's clothes until she was standing there in front of him, her bra discarded on the floor, her ripped tights still there. For a moment she felt embarrassed but as he reached down to take a nipple in his mouth she gasped and, very gently, he pulled off her tights, casting them aside, erasing what had happened in the car park. His touch was firm and gentle at the same time and, in her wonder and anticipation, she explored his body, running her hands over his bare skin. They lay back together, his naked body on top of hers, and, without needing to agree, and with his eyes never leaving her face, she opened up to him and he pushed into her.

'Jesus, Flick,' he gasped, and she could feel him filling her completely. 'I've wanted you so badly. This. Your body. Can you feel me? Can you feel how much?'

Lifting her head, Flick kissed him and, as the kiss deepened, they moved together until she felt every sinew in his body tense, and the tears poured down her face.

Chapter Twenty-Seven

In the days since the car park ambush, Joanna and Georgie had treated Flick with the kind of care normally reserved for minor royalty or the feeble-minded. And it was finally beginning to grate.

'For goodness sake, George, will you let me make the tea for a change. I'm perfectly fine. Really!'

But Georgie couldn't let it lie. 'But I can't help feeling it was my fault,' she wailed. 'All of it, from my ankle onwards.'

'Oh give over. Look – there's not a scratch on me. I'm perfectly fine.'

'But if Ben hadn't turned up. What then?' Georgie shuddered. 'You could have been ...'

'Well, I wasn't, so chill,' Flick said abruptly. 'And with the CCTV footage of Jackson doing my car in, I don't think we're going to hear from him again in a very long time. His poor wife. It's her I really feel sorry for. I don't think she had any idea he could be like that. And she was so apologetic about the business card.' Flick gestured at the huge bouquet propped up in a bucket of cold water. 'Those flowers she sent are gorgeous.'

Georgie subsided and allowed Flick to make a drink for the first time in days. She certainly looked fine. If anything, she seemed to have a kind of glow about her. More confirmation, if any were needed, that she had fallen for Ben big time. But oddly, whenever Georgie mentioned him, Flick went quiet. Georgie didn't want to probe too deeply.

Besides, she was too absorbed thinking about her and Ed.

She'd even got around to seeing a solicitor about filing for divorce, but she'd noticed something rather odd. Having spoken about nothing else other than the Atrium launch for about two months, and now it was just round the corner, Ed had gone very quiet about it.

She mentioned it to Flick, later that day, before she left to collect Libby from another play date. 'I don't want to ask, for fear of starting him off again, but it does seem odd, don't you think? It must be coming up soon and I'll have to get something to wear. I can't go looking like this,' she gestured down at herself and the outfit she'd cobbled together – a long-line, stretchy wrap-top over what had once been pyjama bottoms. 'Y'know, I think Ed's right. I have put on more weight this time.'

Flick peered around the side of her computer. 'Well, I still have to lean to see you from where I'm sitting, you'll be pleased to know. When you show on both sides of the desk, that's when to start worrying. Oh come on, George. You're pregnant and you're supposed to be larger than normal. I think you look lovely, if that's any comfort. Just right. But if you want to go shopping, count me in. I need some new stuff too.'

'Great. Jo, do you fancy a mooch round the shops anytime soon?'

'Maybe. When are you thinking?'

Georgie looked at the planner. 'I wish I could remember the date of that ruddy launch. I think I kind of blanked it out because I was so peed off at Ed, but I'm going to go to it and have my glass of free champagne. I think I deserve it, don't you?'

'Why don't you phone him now,' Flick suggested. 'And we can arrange a shopping day just before. We can't have you growing out of whatever you end up buying.'

Georgie expertly pinged an elastic band at Flick's head, then picked up the phone and dialled Ed's office number. 'Oh hi, is that Sukie? Hi, yes, it's Georgie Casey here. Fine thanks, growing all the time, you know how it is … er … yes, I'm pregnant ... about six months. Oh! Didn't Ed mention it? Oh right.' Georgie felt herself stammering. 'He must have been too excited about the launch. No, don't disturb him. I was just calling up to check on the timings and everything. What's the date, again? ... Oh ... right. Did he? When did he tell you that? Right. Well, I was just checking. Don't bother to tell him I called, will you. It doesn't matter. It really doesn't matter. Thanks. Thanks a lot.'

She took a deep breath to settle the churning in her stomach then put the phone down heavily and stared at Flick and Jo. 'Well, how about this? Not only has he not told anyone I'm pregnant, he's actually told everyone that I'm away for the launch – which is the day after tomorrow.'

There was a lengthy silence. 'You're kidding?' Jo asked at last.

'I only wish I was,' Georgie replied in a low voice. 'The bastard's trying to edit me out of his life. I'm an embarrassment, it seems, as well as an inconvenience.'

Flick was on her feet in an instant and at Georgie's side. 'Well, *be* an embarrassment, then. Turn up to his bloody launch. Turn up in the biggest, preggiest dress ever and stand right at the front where everyone will see you.'

A germ of an idea started to form in Georgie's mind. 'Do you know what – I do believe I will. And I think I may need back-up. I'd like this launch to be very memorable for Ed. Unforgettable, in fact!'

Georgie's idea for revenge had been far too tame at first, but after ten minutes and half a packet of biscuits, Jo and Flick had upped the ante to a level that would leave Ed in no doubt that he should have kept his discretion inside his trousers.

Flick thought the plan over as she headed back to her own flat that evening. She'd moved her stuff out of Ben's the day after the confrontation with Jackson. Ben had flown off to Texas first thing in the morning and, as she had no need for a safe house any more, she had spent the morning clearing up the small amount of things she had, polishing the place to within an inch of its life, and shipping out. She'd found the bag with the truffles she'd bought in Bath and, meagre offering though it was, she left them with a note to Ben saying thank you for all he had done. It had taken her three goes to get the right tone for the note and she was quite pleased with the result – personal, without sounding needy or anything. Richard, who was downstairs in the lobby talking to a maintenance contractor, had been very surprised when she came out of the lift with her holdall.

'I thought you would be here longer – or at least Ben talked about things as if you would be,' he said, opening the big glass doors for her.

'No, I don't think I need to be here any more. Things have been sorted out and I really ought to get home to my cats and real life,' she smiled. 'But if ever you need any house-sitting then please call me. It would be a chore to look at that view and wallow in such luxury, but I think I could cope!' Richard laughed and Flick walked to her car without daring to glance back at the building.

For once she wasn't in any need to get home, and she relaxed as the traffic crawled south, savouring every moment that delayed her return to normality. Every inch that didn't take her further away from Ben. She shivered, a wave of longing surging through her, as she thought about yesterday. They had lain in each other's arms afterwards, not speaking, his head resting on her shoulder and her arms around him, until she had been forced to move as his weight became too much. He rolled onto his side and they had looked at each other. He'd touched her face, running his fingers over her skin and tracing her mouth, but they hadn't spoken until he'd broken the silence.

'I wanted to do that so much.'

She'd merely nodded, unable to say anything and not wanting to break the moment, and after a while he had got up and slowly dressed. She'd made a cup of tea for them both and he'd drunk his, but the process had happened without touching and without speaking more than was necessary, until he'd picked up his keys to leave. She knew he couldn't stay. She knew he had to return to Alison and that what they had done was wrong and hypocritical, but everything in her had wanted to shout that he mustn't go, not after what they had experienced. And yet she couldn't move, standing helpless as he kissed her mouth gently and went to the door.

'Bye, Flick. I think you'll be OK now.'

She'd sat on the balcony after that, watching the evening progress over the city, wrapping a fleece around her as the temperature went down with the daylight, and worked her way through a bottle of wine. Now she knew what her mother had meant when she talked about pain. How could she have fallen so hard for someone who was so unavailable? He said he'd never been unfaithful. So he'd succumbed, finally given in to temptation. Now he'd go back to being beyond Alison's reproach. Perhaps Flick had been too accessible, too accommodating, so easy that he couldn't resist. Worse, perhaps it had been a pity fuck. Catharsis to help her get over Jackson's violation. What difference did it make – as ever, Flick had been screwed and left behind.

She had no reason to hear from him again. Instead she'd thrown herself into work, and Georgie's vengeance mission to dish out what Ed truly deserved. And, when the day's work was done, she let herself into her flat, the air stale with her absence, felt the cats rub themselves around her legs, and changed into some old tracksuit bottoms and a T-shirt. But instead of curling up in front of the TV, relishing the delicious selfishness of being on her own, she found herself picking at her meal for one before dropping it in the bin and going to bed, lying awake for hours, staring at the ceiling.

Chapter Twenty-Eight

As Georgie came into the kitchen, Ed quickly clicked on the corner of the screen to close the computer window, but not before Georgie noticed that he'd been working on a PowerPoint presentation, presumably for the Atrium launch tomorrow. In front of him on the laptop now was a letter that he ostentatiously pretended to amend.

'Oh dear, do you have to work tonight?' Georgie sighed with exaggerated sympathy. 'Honestly, Ed, you seem to be working every hour of the day at the moment, what with this and all the dinners and overnight stays. You must be exhausted.'

She saw his eyes flick nervously to her and then back at his laptop and he blinked rapidly. 'Well, yes, I have been pretty busy lately. But, er, with junior on the way I need to be putting in plenty of time at work and so on. Earn brownie points, you know.'

Georgie clenched her hands tightly behind her back. The skunk! Using the baby as an excuse for the long hours he was putting in at 'work'! A cold but almost pleasurable anger uncoiled within her.

'Oh, Ed,' she went on. 'I was meaning to ask, what's happened about the Atrium launch? You were so excited about it only last week. It must be any day now.'

There was an almost imperceptible pause. 'Oh, that,' he replied dismissively, not taking his eyes from the screen. 'That's all been put on hold. Delayed indefinitely, you know. They haven't got a new date yet, but I don't expect it'll be until autumn now.'

Georgie had to stop her chin hitting the floor at his audacity. Did he think she was a complete fool? 'What a shame!' she laid an apparently sympathetic hand on his shoulder. 'That was going to be your big moment, wasn't it? How disappointing for you. Well, for me too. 'Cos I'd have loved to be there with you. Sharing the glory, and all that.'

Ed squirmed a little and dislodged her hand, clearing his throat. Good, thought Georgie. At least he's still got enough conscience to feel uncomfortable about it. She went on. 'Especially after everything we've been through. With your, erm, with that business with that woman. I want everyone to see how committed you are, we are, to each other.' Ed appeared to be shrinking into the padded leather chair.

'Oh well!' She ruffled his carefully casually pushed-back hair, something she knew he hated. 'Maybe by the time they get around to it, I'll be able to bring the baby along in a sling.' She walked away and looked over her shoulder in time to catch his horrified expression.

Supper – which Libby had helped prepare – was a particularly garlicky affair; bouillabaisse with garlic bread and a spinach, bacon and walnut salad with garlic dressing. She watched him hesitate then, pressed by Libby, he took a small helping, then a larger one. It really was very good, and she'd known he wouldn't be able to resist it. They finished with raspberries and cream and he rubbed his stomach in satisfaction, then discreetly checked his breath by blowing into his hand. But garlic is always in the nose of the beholder and Georgie smiled quietly to herself.

Later, once Libby was tucked up and the kitchen was tidy, she watched out of the corner of her eye as Ed put his laptop carefully away in its case. 'Oh, I forgot to mention,' he said casually. 'I've got a meeting tomorrow night, but I'll pop home first to get changed.'

'Oh, what a shame! Lib's got a lovely evening lined up. She's going to a film with Sophie and they're having a sleep-over afterwards. I was hoping we could go out to dinner together.'

He shrugged. 'Sorry, should have mentioned it before. It's ... it's a last-minute thing.'

'Well, we can go out some other time. I'll have the evening to myself. Maybe I'll go out somewhere with friends.'

Ed didn't seem to have anything much else to say and he clapped his hands together awkwardly. 'Think I'll have a bath. You coming up?' he asked.

Georgie eased her back. 'No, not yet. I'm feeling quite energetic so I think I'll clear out some cupboards. You know, I was looking for that bag of Libby's little romper suits. Can't find it anywhere. Any ideas?'

He looked at her blankly before turning to go upstairs. 'No, can't say I have.'

Georgie listened for the sound of the water filling the bath, then carefully took his laptop out of its carrying case, plugged it in and switched it on. She loaded the PowerPoint presentation he'd been working on and flicked through it, an expression of grim satisfaction on her face. Now, who could help? She tapped her fingers on the desk then smiled, picking up the phone.

'Tim,' she whispered. 'Is that you?'

'Er, yes,' he replied. 'Georgie? I can't hear you very well. Can you speak up?'

'Yes, it's me, but no, I can't really talk any louder. Let me explain ...'

She could hear the smile in his voice when he realised it was her – a smile that became a deep chuckle when he heard what she wanted.

'Right,' he whispered back. 'I think I can help with that. Here's what you need to do ...'

'Just one thing though,' she interrupted.

'Yep? What?'

'Why are you whispering too?'

He paused and continued in a whisper, 'I don't really know. Fun, isn't it?'

'Yes,' she giggled. 'Yes, it is!'

284

'You're lucky you caught me, actually. I'm off to Germany tomorrow morning and I was just wondering about trying to get an earlier flight. Tell me all about it when I get back.'

Following his instructions, Georgie made all the changes and saved them, then said goodnight and rang off. As an afterthought, she had a quick look again at the emails Lynn had sent Ed, some that very day, and clicked on the ones with attachments. The photos were a bit grainy, probably taken with a mobile phone, but perfectly clear. She had to steel herself to look, and the pain of what was in front of her – Lynn and Ed in bed together – made her want to retch. She clicked on the images and saved them, then added them to the presentation.

By the time she went to bed, she had calmed herself and was feeling quite relaxed. In fact, she slept long and well, the fragrance of Ed's bath oil mixing not unpleasantly with the garlic on his breath.

Chapter Twenty-Nine

Georgie was early into the office the next day, refreshed and determined, and ready to fill Flick in on the details of her plan.

'I couldn't believe he was just standing there and telling me a bare-faced lie about the launch, so I took matters into my own hands. Tim helped, of course.'

Flick shook her head. 'What? Tim came round?'

'No, silly. I called him when Ed went up to have a bath. He talked me through it, 'cos he is a bit of a whiz on computers, you know.'

'Hmmm!' Flick smiled knowingly. 'He's an all-round ideal man, I reckon.'

'Oh, go on with you. You're just a recent convert to the concept of decent men and you're trying to convince everyone else.' She turned to look at Flick, and was surprised by the expression of sadness on her face. 'Er, anyway. Enough about me. Have you seen Ben since you moved out?'

Flick turned away with suspicious speed and busied herself with a pile of papers. 'No, he's in Texas, but there again, there's not really any reason to see him, is there? The whole thing is over, so ...'

Georgie looked at her appraisingly. 'Right,' she said slowly. 'So you don't have any plans to see him?'

'No, why should I? Honestly, Georgie, you're always trying to pair people up. What about you? Ben's married, remember?'

'Yeah,' Georgie flopped back in her chair. 'I can't really believe we're having this conversation. At one time it would have been me going on about the importance of marriage and you having no scruples when it came to relationships. What's happened to us?'

Flick shrugged sadly. 'I don't know. But I'm not sure there's any going back now, is there?'

The door opened and they both turned round. Tim strode in and planted himself in front of Georgie's desk.

'What are you doing here?' she stammered. 'You're supposed to be in Germany.'

'I know, but I'm not, am I?'

'Er, no.'

'That's because I'm here.'

'Er, yes.'

'Anton's got chickenpox so I'm not going over until next week.'

'Oh dear. Poor Anton.'

Tim smiled. 'He sounded all right on the phone. Quite cheerful, actually. But I was thinking, maybe I could come along to the launch with you? Or at least, drive you there. You know, moral support and all that.'

Georgie stood up because she didn't know what else to do. 'Oh, that would be ... yes, please.'

'And I was just passing a shop and they had ... well ... I was just thinking. They're a nice colour. You might hate them. You can always take them back.'

He thrust a paper bag into her hands, then quickly stepped backwards. She reached inside and pulled out a pair of pale blue and lilac striped bed-socks in the softest, softest cashmere. She blinked and looked up at him. Behind her, she was aware of Flick coughing meaningfully, but ignored it. The thoughtfulness of the awkward gesture was more touching than she could express, so she stepped forward and took his hand. 'Thank you, Tim. I mean it. I absolutely love them, and I'll think about you when I'm wearing them.' She blushed deeply. 'I mean ... I don't mean ...'

Tim looked at the ground. 'Well, look. I'm really glad you like them. They'll keep your toes warm. 'Cos you don't want to get cold feet, now do you? I'll, er, pick you up later then, shall I? Call me and tell me when. OK?'

And he backed out of the door.

Flick laughed slowly. 'Smooth. Really smooth.'

'Yes, Yes, I'll be there by six-thirty,' Flick was taking off her shoes, hopping on one leg, the phone tucked under her chin. It was the second call in about half an hour, with Georgie getting more and more fretful. 'I know it's five now but it won't take me long to change, then I'll head off.'

That wasn't enough for Georgie. 'Are you taking the tube?' she hissed. 'Just be careful if you are – you don't want people getting the wrong idea and after—'

'I'll be fine! Now, listen. Pour yourself a small glass of wine – I read somewhere that it can even benefit babies, a small glass of Pinot Grigio – and that'll give you a bit of Dutch courage. Has Ed left?'

'Not yet. Any minute.'

Flick was trying to undo her jeans with one hand. 'All going to plan so far?'

Georgie giggled nervously. 'Perfect. Oh, I'm afraid something's going to go wrong!'

'Have faith – you'll be fine. We're experts at this, remember?'

Flick pacified her again that everything was in place then, clicking off the phone, threw it on the sofa and headed for the shower. It felt small, poky and plasticy after the limestone luxury of Ben's place and she wasn't sure the fragrance of the shower gel she'd half-inched from there was helping her forget. She washed her hair as vigorously as she could, trying to focus on the evening ahead.

Georgie had been jumpy all day and she'd gasped in horror when Flick showed her the dress she'd bought for that evening.

'I can't wear that!' Georgie gasped.

'You bloody well can, my girl,' said Jo. 'Slip it on because I need to make some adjustments.'

Demands from agency members coming in throughout the day had been dealt with swiftly or put off until tomorrow, and Jo had spent her time stitching. Neither Flick nor Georgie had realised that she had such a talent for it, but Jo had merely waved a hand airily and talked about the values of Domestic Science at school.

'I only learned to boil an egg,' said Flick.

'That's obvious,' Georgie replied and got a ball of paper lobbed at her for her troubles.

Flick threw open her wardrobe and surveyed the contents. The obvious choice were the suede salmon-pink stilettos she'd bought from Cantaloupe and which she hadn't had a chance to air yet. She lifted them out of the box, almost salivating as she unwrapped them from their tissue paper. There, she thought, lifting them up and surveying them. Every girl should be armed with a drop-dead pair of heels when she has an impression to make.

Half an hour later she surveyed the results in the mirror. Her hair had taken ages, but, she thought, turning this way and that, it had been worth the trouble. She looked around for her phone to text Georgie and say she was leaving, but she couldn't find it. By the time she located it in her car, the battery was completely flat and if she went back to charge it she'd be late, so she threw it into her bag and headed for the tube.

Chapter Thirty

Georgie finished loading the dish-washer, turned it on, rubbed her hands together in satisfaction, then went to stand at the bottom of the stairs to listen. She could hear rummaging, then muffled expletives, then Ed's hurried footsteps along the corridor and back down the stairs, and she went back over to pretending to read the paper at the kitchen table.

'George, have you seen my black suit?'

'Hmmm, which one's that again? They're all black, aren't they?'

'You know, my best one. I left it out on a chair in my dressing room.'

'Nope, sorry, darling. That's not ringing any bells. They all look the same to me.'

He screeched. 'The Prada one I got when I went to Milan.'

'Gosh, Prada? That must have been awfully expensive. No, I'm sure I'd have remembered seeing something like that.'

'But it was there, just this morning. It can't just have disappeared. Have you been in the dressing room?'

Georgie fought the desire to laugh. 'No, of course not, darling. It's all your stuff. There's nothing of mine in there at all. Why on earth would I go in there?' She heard him hesitate at the door, obviously torn between wanting to quiz her and not wanting to raise her suspicions.

'Do you need it for something special?'

There was a long pause. 'No, it's nothing. Er, no, nevermind.'

He was halfway up the stairs again when she called out. 'Oh, actually I was in there the other day. I was taking a look at your shoes and, do you know, you do walk heavily on them. The soles of almost all of them were worn on the inside. I expect it's because they're leather. Well, that's what the repair man said, anyway.'

He came slowly back down. 'Repair man?'

'Yes, darling. That little man you used to always use off Balham High Street. He said the shoes were lovely quality, you'll be pleased to hear. I asked him to put on nice non-slip rubber soles so they'd be ready for the winter. I knew you'd be pleased. Actually, I was wanting to get them all done up for your launch but since you hadn't mentioned it lately, I haven't bothered to go and collect them. You've still got your comfy old ones, though. I'll pick the other ones up after the weekend, since there's no hurry.'

A strange gurgling sound came from Ed's throat and Georgie turned and said brightly, 'No need to thank me, love. What's a wife for, eh?' and calmly went back to her paper.

She got dressed up as soon as Ed had rushed off, obviously running late, thanks to her having edited the clothes he'd so carefully laid out. The Prada suit was safe and sound in her little overstuffed wardrobe, of course, and the shoes were in the loft. Childish, she knew, but it had been more than worth it to see the look on his face. She'd heard him on the phone just before he went, snarling at someone to have the screen ready and he'd plug in his laptop as soon as he arrived. No time now for a rehearsal. He'd left, clutching his precious computer for dear life and screeched away, actually burning rubber as he accelerated. If only he got a speeding ticket, that would be the icing on the cake!

The Atrium Building was hard to miss, with light flooding out from its doors and the acres of glass that made up its structure. For the launch, floodlights poured light up from the pavement in front and lasers danced from the roof like wartime search-lights. Flick, delighted to be out of the tube and the object of every leer from Clapham northward, admired it from the opposite side of the street. She knew Ed hadn't been involved in the design – he'd been the project manager, apparently – but it was an impressive piece of architecture that fitted well into the cacophony of differing periods and designs of the buildings that surrounded it.

As the doors opened and shut with people entering for the launch party, she could hear music – a jazz band – the chink of glasses and chatter. She glanced at her watch. These architecture types must be prompt because she was only ten minutes late and already it sounded as though the party was in full swing. Quashing her nerves, and self-consciously brushing down her dress in the hope it would grow a couple of inches longer, she crossed the road.

'May I have your invitation please, madam?' said the man on the door, his eyes wide as he took in Flick's outfit. She looked down at him from an advantage of at least four inches.

'I'm a guest of Edward Casey,' she said, as imperiously as she could. 'I'm afraid I left my invitation at home but he's knows me of old.' She laughed her best tinkling laugh. 'Always forgetting things.'

The doorman, not wanting to argue with a woman armed with salmon-pink stilettos, simply cowered and opened the door. The building was even more magical inside, illuminated by three giant contemporary chandeliers – a cascade of LED lights – that hung as high as a house from the steel framework of the ceiling. From between each chandelier was suspended white rope and a trapeze, and from each trapeze, dressed head to toe in silver jump suits, were black gymnasts, their muscles rippling as they performed contortions in perfect synchronicity above the heads of the guests.

And there were plenty of them. Most were still in work clothes, sensible and expensively cut suits, little black dresses

– the uniform of the minted and the successful. Flick, as intended, stuck out like a sore thumb, and she watched with pleasure, mixed with nerve-racking vulnerability, as people paused mid-conversation and watched her proceed towards the centre of the space, her blonde bouffant hair and the bright, flowery mini-dress that stuck to her like a second skin, a gash of colour in this mêlée of controlled sartorial elegance.

Thankfully, a waiter spun towards her with a tray of champagne and it was all she could do not to take two. Taking a large gulp that sent bubbles up her nose, she cast about the room trying to locate Georgie with a rising sense of panic. Where was she? Had she got cold feet? There wasn't a single person she recognised, then, just as she was about to bolt for the safety of the ladies, she tuned into the voice of the man behind her.

'The inspiration for the roof structure came from the neo-Gothic architecture of the railway stations of the glorious age of steam,' he was explaining painstakingly, 'brought up to date by imposing a twenty-first century dynamic.'

'Fascinating,' came the reply, in a voice laced with boredom. Flick grasped her moment.

'Ed!' she gushed, grabbing Ed by the arm and swinging him round. She lunged forward into an air kiss. Mwah, mwah. 'What a lovely little place, you must be so proud.' She pinched his cheek and watched with pleasure as his face turned from surprise to purple, incandescent embarrassment. She thrust out her hand to the gentleman Ed was regaling. 'Hi there, I'm Flick, an old friend of Ed's, aren't I, Ed?'

'Enchanted,' he replied, taking in her legs and hair combo. 'Derek Finch, editor of *Concept* magazine.'

'What's that?' Hoping she wasn't going overboard, she popped her gum.

'Only the most cutting-edge publication on the market today,' Ed squealed. 'Wonderful,' he continued, steering Flick out of the way. The *Concept* honcho turned to speak to someone who took his arm. 'What the fu—' Ed hissed.

'Oh sorry, Georgie said it would be OK to pop by on your big night,' she said loudly.

'Georgie's coming?' Ed gasped.

Flick ignored him. 'You've done awwwfully well!' She took another large slug of champagne. 'I must say, those trousers are a wee bit tight,' she giggled in a stage whisper. 'You don't leave much to the imagination, sweetie!'

'You have no right to be here,' Ed fumed, any pretence at friendliness evaporating. You graceless pillock, Flick thought. 'You didn't get an invitation and this is strictly invitation only. And you look like a vamp. Everyone is staring. How does that make me look?' Stupid? Flick was about to reply when Ed's face turned from an irritated frown into a beatific smile. Flick followed his gaze and, to her horror, she could see Ben coming towards them through the crowd.

'Ben Houghton,' Ed purred, putting out his hand. 'How delightful to see you and thank you so much for coming.' Ben tore his eyes from Flick and looked down at Ed as if he wasn't sure who was speaking. 'Might I say how much I admire your Dubai project – an inspired piece of development. Now, let me introduce you to some people I know want to speak to you.'

Ben looked down at Ed's hand, still suspended in mid-air, and shook it back. 'I'd like to talk to Flick please, if you don't mind.'

Ed looked quizzically from one to the other, not understanding. 'But—'

'If you could give us a moment?' Ben said, more forcefully, and Ed backed away, almost careering into a waiter with a tray of designer canapés behind him.

Ben didn't say anything for a while, then his gaze ran down the length of her. He didn't look very amused. 'You certainly brush up well.'

Flick flushed. 'It's all part of the project to piss off Ed,' she explained weakly.

'Well, you've certainly got them all talking.'

'How was Texas?'

'Fine thanks.' He paused. 'I've been trying to call you.'

Her heart leaped, but nothing in his expression gave any indication he was pleased to see her. 'My phone. The battery's dead.'

'I rang the office earlier and Joanna said you would be here.'

'You came here to find me?' Flick dared not smile.

'I was invited,' Ben said shortly and Flick looked down. Of course. Stupid. He was the property developer everyone in London would want a project commissioned from.

'I—' he started.

'Flick! Thank God!' Georgie was breathless at her side. 'Ben! How lovely to see you!' She reached up and he kissed her on the cheek. 'The ruddy traffic was appalling, then there was a road closed and a diversion. We had to go all around the houses.'

'We?' Ben asked.

'Yes, Tim brought me. He's trying to find a parking space.' Georgie smiled. 'His eyes are still popping out of his head!'

'I'm not surprised,' said Ben. 'You look radiant – and quite a bit larger, if I might say so!'

Georgie certainly did. The black jersey wrap-around dress Flick had bought her made her look sexy as hell, it was clingy whilst still being flattering, and it had a deep, plunging cleavage. On her ears were diamanté drop earrings which sparkled through her fluffed-up curls and, for once, she was wearing serious heels. Joanna had done miracles with the padded 'bump' she'd spent the day honing from an old cushion Flick had found on the market.

'Have you skipped forward a few weeks?' Ben laughed.

Georgie rubbed her bump affectionately. 'I think I look about ten months! But it's worked.' She moved closer, conspiratorially. 'I just saw Colin, a colleague of Ed's. His eyes nearly popped out of his head when he saw me – I think he's called out for warm water and towels, just in case I drop it here!'

'Have you seen Ed yet?' Flick whispered.

Georgie peered around. 'No, he was deep in conversation with someone, brown-nosing, no doubt.' A waiter proffered some champagne. 'Should I? I've had a glass of wine already at home.'

'Might as well get the little chap used to the high-life!' Flick laughed, aware of Ben next to her and all that was unsaid.

Georgie took a long-stemmed glass guiltily and took a sip.

'Brian,' came a loud voice behind them. 'May I introduce you to Lynn.' Flick and Georgie froze, Georgie with the glass in mid-air. 'Lynn and Ed have been working together on a major waterside redevelopment in Cardiff.'

Georgie's mind was racing in time with her heart. Only her body, it seemed, was moving in slow motion but Flick, bless her, swiftly moved round and away from Ben to look over Georgie's head at the conversation going on behind her. The male voice Georgie recognised as belonging to one of the senior partners, the unseen Brian could be any one of three people she could think of. But surely there could only be one Lynn. So that was yet another lie Ed had notched up. Not some chance meeting in a gallery. She had worked with him on the Cardiff project.

The look on Flick's face confirmed it. She returned Georgie's questioning gaze and nodded once, then a look of steely determination entered her eyes and she slipped past Georgie and exclaimed, 'Hello! Lynn, isn't it? I'm sure I recognise you. Sorry, Brian. Did I knock your drink? How clumsy of me. Well, there's plenty more over – well, everywhere, really. This lot certainly know how to throw a party, or so Ed Casey always says.'

Georgie remained rooted to the spot, but Ben, who had obviously worked out what was going on, moved closer and squeezed her shoulder kindly. He too was looking over at the conversation now in full, if rather stilted, flow between Flick and Lynn, who was sounding polite but baffled. Ben's face, though, was unreadable as he stared at Flick. He couldn't take his eyes off her; she looked like an exotic flower in this room full of designery black and charcoal, her legs film-star long in those gorgeous salmon-pink suede stilettos.

Flick was really doing a number on Lynn. It was as if she was a chat-show host with a bashful interviewee. 'So, do you know absolutely *everyone* here?' she asked innocently.

'Well, not everyone, but most of the senior people, of course.' Georgie listened with morbid fascination, her heartbeat gradually returning to normal. What an ugly voice Lynn had, hard and clipped.

'Riiiight, so does that mean you're rather important? You *look* terrifically important, I must say.'

Pause. 'Well, let's say I'm a decision-maker. I'm not without influence.'

Ben leaned over and whispered in Georgie's ear. 'But, sadly, without any sense of humour, it seems.'

Georgie's giggle was arrested by Flick's next comment. 'Actually, I know a few decision-makers here too. I'd love you to meet them.' Georgie felt a light tap on her shoulder and turned to look straight into the eyes of a blonde woman, expensively dressed in a dark, severely cut dress with a modern brown and orange plastic necklace nestled in her breast. This close, Georgie could see she was slightly over made-up and perhaps only a couple of years younger but slightly haggard looking. Not the invincible rival she'd imagined.

'I'm sure you know Ben Houghton,' Flick continued. 'He's a decision-maker too. Guys, this is Lynn. She's been involved in the Cardiff *affair*. You know, the one that Ed Casey's been working on.'

Georgie, who had just taken another tiny sip of champagne, coughed and Lynn breathed in sharply. Beside her, she could feel Ben chuckle. But Flick hadn't finished. 'Are you – what do you call it – a sleeping partner in that one, Lynn?'

A movement near the raised platform in the centre of the atrium indicated that the presentation was about to start. Flick mischievously pointed towards Georgie and said, in a stage whisper, 'Sorry, Lynn. I didn't have time to introduce you properly. This is Georgie. Ed Casey's *wife*. I don't believe you've met.'

Lynn, who had extended her hand in greeting, snatched it back as though she'd been bitten, then stared down at Georgie's huge belly in horror.

Georgie rubbed the cushion happily. 'Not long now,' she sighed, somehow finding strength from somewhere in this nightmare. 'Ed's terribly potent, you know. He's got two lovely boys already, and this will be our second too. He hardly needs to look at a woman and she's banged up. He's told me it's his ambition to have ten, but this is enough for me, so he'll have to try his luck somewhere else for the next six.' And she elbowed Lynn hard in the ribs and winked at her broadly.

Lynn, pale now, receded into the crowd and, seeing Ed up on the plinth, Georgie made her way to the front, propelled by Flick who was shamelessly tapping people on the shoulder and pointing to Georgie's very prominent stomach. Most stepped aside quickly, possibly fearing for their shoes and Georgie soon found herself at the very front where she sidled up to the senior partner and smiled engagingly at him. He did a double-take when he saw past her cleavage to her belly, and he turned to stare at Ed with a look of consternation on his face. This would undoubtedly make the most marvellous gossip in the office tomorrow.

Ed didn't look entirely comfortable in the suit he'd eventually found. It looked quite a bit too small and his black polo shirt was covered in white hairs, thanks to the neighbour's cat. She could tell, from the way he was using his handkerchief, that his nose was already itching. He was wearing the brown suede loafers he'd had on earlier – well, they probably looked better than his bedroom slippers, which were the only other footwear

Georgie had left out – apart from his Crocs, of course. Still, he had a look of quiet pride on his face as the music started up and he looked round at the crowd.

Then he stopped and stared, horrified. Georgie raised her hand and gave him a friendly little wave. He looked from her to the senior partner, standing right beside her; Flick, looking like Carmen Miranda behind her, and Tim smiling down at Georgie protectively. He swallowed hard, then turned his attention back to the laptop on a table beside him.

Georgie returned Tim's smile. 'This should be good,' she whispered.

'A development like the Atrium Building is a once-in-a-life-time opportunity to shape the skyline of the greatest city in the world,' Ed began and tapped a key, to reveal a stunning photograph of the finished building bathed in evening light. 'This has been a world-leading project, of which we are very proud.' He tapped again, to show another gorgeous angle of the completed building, and there was a ripple of applause.

'Of course,' Ed continued smugly, clicking to reveal an aerial shot of the project, 'none of this would have been possible with-out our world-leading team.' He clicked again and the image changed, filling the screen with one of a group of chimpanzees exposing their bottoms. The laughter made his head snap round and he tapped quickly on the keyboard again. 'As I was saying, the team …' A picture of the Bee Gees in lycra and sequins filled the screen. 'I – er—' He clicked on, and the image gave way to a picture of Bill and Ben the Flowerpot Men, followed by one of Andrew Lloyd Webber, followed by a donkey in a sombrero. 'I'm terribly sorry, there seems to be …'

By now the audience were hysterical. Georgie could feel a big smile spread across her face and Tim bent down to whisper in her ear. 'Do you know, I almost feel sorry for him. Almost, but not quite.'

Ed's face was an interesting shade of purple and he flicked on through the images, of kittens with amusing captions, exploding pipelines, a woman suggestively licking a vibrator, a bowl of ice cream … and the laughter started to build. Finally, another image – a line-drawing of the Atrium appeared.

'That's more like it,' Ed tried to laugh. 'Someone's obviously been *monkeying* around with my presentation.' There was a vague titter from the room. 'Well, I hope you enjoyed my impromptu slide show; we can continue now. As I was saying, from its first inception, when our amazing clients gave us carte blanche to create something unforgettable, a new London landmark, we knew that …' But the relief was short-lived. The next image was one from his emails, a photograph presumably taken by Lynn – Ed reclining on a rumpled hotel bed. The next was of her in the same room. A murmur started to build up around the Atrium and the senior partner looked, horror-struck, at Georgie. 'My dear Georgie,' he gasped. 'I had no idea, this is terrible.'

In an instant, he was up on the stage. 'Turn this off, please. There's obviously been some awful mix-up.' He turned to Ed and quietly, but very firmly, spoke just a few words that had him scurrying from the podium. 'Now, it's wonderful to see you all here tonight at the launch of the Atrium building. Of course, a building of this calibre really needs no presentation at all, particularly not one like that! It speaks for itself and for the talent of the design team, who I'd like to invite to join me here now.'

The team, conspicuously without its project manager, assembled to wild applause. The slide show seemed to have broken the ice somewhat, and the launch went on.

Chapter Thirty-One

Georgie found Ed leaning against a pillar, far away from the chattering, drinking crowd. He was staring blankly in front of him and for a moment she stood and simply assessed him. Despite their years together and all that linked them, he looked like a stranger. He must have felt her presence because he slowly turned towards her and, wordlessly, returned her gaze.

'How did you know?' he asked finally, his voice quiet.

'You didn't really make it difficult, did you?'

'And did you do this – all this, to pay me back?'

Georgie paused. There was no point in anything but total honesty now. 'Yes, Ed. Yes, I did. The way you treated me – all of us, really – me, Lib, your baby, was just unspeakable. And you've lied and lied.' The indignation and hurt started to rise in her throat, making it hard to speak.

Ed looked down, evading her eyes. 'It was nothing. Just a work thing. We were together and I was lonely and—'

'Don't!' She spat the words at him. 'Don't lie to me any more. If it was nothing, then why did you carry on? If it was nothing, why did you lie to me? If it was nothing, why did you risk losing me? If you were prepared to risk all that for "nothing", then I must be less than nothing to you. And can you even begin to imagine how that feels, Ed?'

'I'll give her up, if that's what you want. You only had to say. You didn't need to do all this,' he gestured towards the slowly emptying vestibule. 'All this. You've ruined my reputation here, you know that.'

Georgie took a deep breath. 'You don't get it, Ed, do you? I did ask, and you had your chance. And you blew it. You showed me just how unimportant me and our home and our family is to you. And now it's over. And do you know, you took something away from me – my trust, my belief – and I can never get that back. But getting my own back on you here – that helps, you know. You may think it was just stupid or vindictive – but I don't really care what you think. It helped me feel like myself again. For once, *I* was in control.'

He tutted petulantly. 'I don't know what you're talking about. You run everything. All I do is pay for it all.'

'No, you don't see it at all. You've controlled everything about our home since the word go. There's nothing of me in that house – except Libby.'

'And Libby's room,' he grunted.

Georgie had to stop herself from grabbing his arm to drive home her point. 'Yes, that's exactly it. That was me striking back – trying to get your attention.' She felt herself slump. 'But it was already too late.'

A tall man wandered past, a glass in his hand. 'Where are the loos in this place? Oh – you ought to know! You were the project manager weren't you – together with your team of chimpanzees. Nice presentation!' He laughed and strolled away.

'You see? You see what you've done?' Ed was suddenly furious. 'I'm a laughing stock. If you're counting on me to keep you and Libby and the baby, you're going to be out of luck.'

Georgie shook her head sadly. 'Whatever you think, Ed, this is not just about money. It's about respect and honesty.' She smiled a little to herself. 'Maybe you'll have to stop buying handmade shoes. Just a thought. I've seen a solicitor, by the way. I'm not short of grounds.' She laughed mirthlessly. 'I've even got the pictures.'

'So it's over, then?'

Georgie started to walk away. 'Yes. I'm going to make my way home now. Goodbye, Ed.'

By the time Flick emerged from the tube at Clapham South, all she wanted to do was take off her shoes and walk barefoot. No wonder they were in the sale. She might donate them to a terrorist group for torture purposes. She wrapped her cardigan around her shoulders against the autumn chill. The evening had gone even better than Georgie had planned. When she'd escaped, leaving with the crowds of guests who had scarpered early, keen to get out of the mayhem and hysterical laughter that filled the Atrium to the roof, she'd overheard comments which were just as she and Georgie had hoped for.

'What a fool!' one man guffawed. 'Not sure the senior partners are going to be too chuffed.'

'I always thought he was an arse,' his colleague concurred.

Flick wondered what the fall-out would be from Georgie's confrontation with him. When Flick had left, Georgie certainly looked six feet taller.

However, for Flick, things had gone badly wrong. As the presentation descended into farce, Ben had seemed to melt away into the crowd and, when she'd tried to see if she could find him above the heads of the other guests, she'd failed.

It was now only eight-thirty but dark already, and she picked up a loaf of bread and a bottle of wine from the corner shop and let herself into the flat. It felt cool and she flicked on the central heating for the first time since May, eased the shoes off her feet and headed for the bedroom. She peeled off the dress and slipped on some grey trackie bottoms and a hoody. She pinned her carefully curled and waved hair up on top of her head and headed for a wine glass and the corkscrew, then texted Georgie a quick 'congrats' message, though she wasn't sure that was the right word. For all the hilarity – and Lord knows, Ed deserved humiliation after all his deceit and pomposity – Flick was left with a sour taste. Was there ever any glory in revenge? Would Georgie be any better off now because of it? Flick curled up on the sofa and turned the TV on. She doubted it. She'd still be left with Libby and the new baby to raise herself and, added to that, the stress of bringing Ed on side to support his children. Flick went through the channels, nothing inspiring her, and settled on a comedy on Channel 4.

The doorbell rang and she put down her glass. Perhaps it was Georgie, over for a debrief, she thought, heading for the door.

Ben was standing on the step.

'Where did you go?' he asked without preamble.

'I left, of course, along with everyone else. It didn't seem right to stay to the bitter end and watch the vultures pick over the bones of Ed's reputation.'

'I tried to find you.'

'Oh. I tried to find you too.'

'Can I come in?' She realised she hadn't moved.

'Sure.' Flick opened the door wider, hoping he couldn't see how much she was shaking. 'I've just opened a bottle of wine. Would you like a glass?' She led the way into the sitting room and switched off the TV. It was a mistake because now they stood in silence.

'Was that all it deserved?' Ben asked, an expression of incomprehension on his face.

'What do you mean "it"?'

'Us.' He held out his hands expressively, then let them drop to his side. 'A note and a box of truffles?'

Flick searched his face. 'They were posh truffles,' she said pathetically.

'Very posh.' Did she detect the trace of a smile? 'Come on, Flick, you can do better than that.'

'I'm sorry — I wanted to say thank you for everything, but you'd gone away and there didn't seem to be any need for me to stay there any more. And you had to – well, you're ...'

'Married.'

'Yes, and even though I'm not Miss Morals or anything, you said yourself you'd not been unfaithful, despite everything, so what we did was wrong.'

'What we did was wonderful,' Ben said quietly. 'I haven't thought about much else since.'

Flick could feel something that felt like warmth fill her stomach. 'Yes, but it was still wrong.'

There was silence and, to fill it, she got another glass, poured wine into it and handed it to him. He took it and looked down into it before he spoke.

'Flick, I didn't get back from the States until this morning. I went round to the apartment and found your note. Richard said you'd left, but that was pretty obvious. I called the office but you were out so I didn't leave a message.' The expression on his face was very intense and he looked tired. She wanted to touch his skin and trace the shadows under his eyes. 'Instead, I went to see Alison.' He stopped.

She didn't understand. 'And?'

'And I told her I wanted a divorce.'

Flick's eyes shot up to meet his. 'She'll fleece you.'

'No she won't, because I've told her she won't. She can have the apartment in Paris and the house in London and I'll make sure she's well provided for. She won't be wanting for Armani.'

Dared she ask? 'What made you do that?'

'Well,' he put down his glass and moved a bit closer to her. 'Flights to and from the US are very boring and I had lots of time to think, and all I could think about was you and how much I wanted to be with you. How much I like being with you. That day in Bath – I haven't felt so relaxed in years and I couldn't get out of my meeting quick enough so I could get back to you. And when I drove round the corner and ...' He reached up and unclipped her hair. 'You were standing there, looking at something, I just knew everything about you was right.' He touched her mouth. 'I'm in love with you, Flick.'

Flick could only stare at him. She thought about how her mother had described the sensation and she was in absolutely no doubt that she felt the same way.

'And,' he put his hand on her cheek, 'I thought about how making love with you was perfect and how I want to do it again.' He kissed her mouth, 'And again. And again.'

Flick dared to let a small smile play over her lips. 'That's just 'cos you haven't had it for ages …'

'Yes, and I've got a lot of making up to do.'

'Ben,' Flick stepped back a moment, needing to be sure. 'I'm not an Armani type of girl. I do trash – charity shops and tarty shoes.' She indicated the flat. 'I'm not Chelsea cottages and designer labels. I was bought up in Sarf London, I've only ever been on a plane on a holiday package. I'm not at all posh and—' Ben bought a finger up to her lips.

'I know. You are *real*, Flick. You are funny, and warm, and – real. That's all I need.' And he kissed her harder this time and she responded because it was all she wanted to do.

Then, taking her hand to lead her through to the bedroom, he stopped and turned to her. 'About the trash bit. Would you mind wearing that dress again …?'

Epilogue

The spring sunshine poured in through the office windows. Jo had plonked a vase of narcissi on Georgie's desk, and Flick picked up the scent of them on the breeze that came through the open window. The office was blissfully quiet, with both Jo and Georgie out, and she had a few precious moments of peace to concentrate on the screen in front of her. The only noise to interrupt her was the occasional snuffling of the baby sleeping on her chest.

Between bouts of awkward typing with one hand, she kissed the top of his head, marvelling at its warmth and the softness of his downy hair. His long, dark eyelashes rested in his cheeks and his mouth was slightly open, the Cupid's bow of his lips utterly perfect.

She was just wondering how she could make herself a cup of tea without waking him when the door burst open and Libby tumbled in, school bag over her shoulder and socks round her ankles.

'Hello, sweetheart, how was your day?' Flick smiled up at the little girl who seemed to have grown a foot taller in the last few months

'Boring. I was pants at rounders and Gemma Foster was a cow.'

'Oh.' Flick tried to sound as serious as she could. 'Mum's just popped out, but she won't be long.'

Libby dumped her bag and leaned forward to kiss her baby brother on the head. 'Hello, yummy.' She then stroked his hair gently. 'I hope he doesn't get hungry before Mum gets back.'

'She fed him before she left,' Flick explained. 'Do you want to hold him while I put the kettle on?' Libby sat in Georgie's chair and held her arms out. Jack barely stirred as Flick placed him in her lap.

'I miss him when I'm at school,' Libby said as Flick dropped a tea bag into a mug. 'I've got lots of pictures on him on my phone, but it's not the same as having him around.'

'You're a lucky girl,' Flick replied. 'I so wanted a brother or sister when I was younger that I even asked my mum to steal one from our neighbour up the road.'

Libby looked up and smiled proudly. 'Ross and Charlie don't count really, do they, because they're not real brothers. Jack's my real brother.'

Flick faltered a moment. The last few months, since Ed had moved out, had been tense and Flick knew that Georgie had been treading on eggshells with Libby, working overtime to make everything right for her. She could tell from the way Libby spoke that she was seeking reassurance; trying to work out some sort of pattern for her fractured family. She didn't speak, waiting for Libby to speak next.

'Even though Dad's not living with us any more, he's still my Daddy, isn't he?'

'Oh, of course he is!' Flick answered quickly.

Libby ran a finger across Jack's forehead gently. 'It wasn't my fault, was it? Daddy leaving, I mean?' She didn't look up as she spoke and, leaving her mug of tea, Flick crouched down in front of her.

'No, Libby, it was nothing to do with you at all. Your mummy and daddy love you very much. Did you know that my mum and dad didn't live together either?'

Libby glanced up at her, and Flick could see she was computing the information.

'And, do you know, I used to lie in bed every night blaming

myself. I never dared ask my parents – I don't know why – but I know now that they could have explained it all to me. And it wasn't until I was a bit older that I realised that they still loved me very much.' She paused, hoping Libby couldn't read her fib. She was quite sure her father didn't love her, and she still felt a pang of pain as she thought it. 'It was just that *they* couldn't live together. That happens to quite a lot of grown-ups – they change and realise that they're better off away from each other. It's a bit like you and Gemma Foster. You just make each other cross. And, after all, a happy mummy is a much better mummy.' She felt a pain in her throat. Don't cry, Flick, don't cry.

'I think Mummy is happy, don't you?'

Flick smiled, getting a hold on herself again. 'I know she is – and who wouldn't be, with you two gorgeous ones to love?'

At that moment the door opened and Georgie and Joanna walked back in.

'Hi, darling!' Georgie dumped her bag on the desk and, taking her daughter's face in her hands, kissed her on the cheek. 'Good day?'

Libby looked up at Flick. 'It's been OK,' she said, and Flick winked at her.

'What time's Tim picking you all up?' Flick asked, going to rescue her tea.

Georgie glanced at the clock on the wall. 'Five-thirty.' She smiled. 'He's having supper with us tonight, as a matter of fact.'

Libby smiled too as Georgie lifted the baby from her and she climbed off the chair. 'Oh, goody. He's funny. Do you think he'll bring some ice cream like last time?' She went to take a proffered biscuit from Joanna.

Flick and Georgie exchanged amused glances. 'The way to a little girl's heart ...' Flick muttered.

'And a big one's too!' Georgie laughed and caught the expression in her friend's eye. 'OK, OK, don't you dare say anything. It's early days and I've got enough to think about.'

Flick held her hands up in submission. 'My lips are sealed. In the immortal words of Ms Diana Ross, you can't hurry love. God knows, it's taken *me* long enough to find Mr Right.'

Libby came back with crumbs around her mouth. 'Tim's house is fab, Flick.' She licked the chocolate from her fingers. 'Have you *seen* his bathroom?' Her eyes were wide. 'It's even posher than yours and Ben's.'

'Yeah,' replied Flick, with mock petulance, 'but we've got a better view. And the bath's bigger. You can get two people in it.'

'And I expect you often do,' Georgie replied under her breath.

'You can bet on it, honey!' Flick replied. 'No point in wasting water!'

Libby wrinkled her nose. 'Yuck, fancy sharing bathwater.'

The last hour of the day was spent in companionable silence, with Libby helping Joanna stick stamps on envelopes addressed to clients containing letters announcing an increase in membership subscriptions. Then, at five-thirty, Georgie switched off her computer and stood up. 'Come on, Lib, enough sticking for today. Let's pack up, ready for Tim.'

They were busy shrugging on coats and picking up bags, the baby strapped safely to Georgie's chest, when the office door opened and a tall, elegant woman came in.

'Sorry to bother you so late.' Flick, Georgie and Joanna looked at her expectantly. 'Only, I heard about you via a friend of mine.'

Flick had a sense of foreboding. 'Not Caroline Knightly?' she asked slowly.

'Yes, how did you know? It's a rather delicate matter, actually.' She glanced at the little girl and mouthed theatrically: 'I gather you do *anything*.'

'Wrong,' said Georgie emphatically.

'And,' added Flick quickly, 'certainly not *that*.'

And all three of them burst out laughing.

Acknowledgements

In the best stories the baddies get their come-uppance. Perhaps there's a dark side to all of us to which the idea of revenge appeals hugely. Of course we'd never do it – yet, at the same time, it would be so satisfying to nail someone who deserved it! We had lots of fun finding out people's stories whilst researching this book, but of course we couldn't possibly reveal their names. Thanks, however, to the following for their professional help and support: Dr Kate Crocker, Tim and Moira Sara, and, of course, Sara O'Keeffe and all at Orion for their unswerving confidence. Thanks also to Mary Pachnos, as ever.

Library Link Issues (For Staff Use Only)

1	2	3	4	5	6	7	8	9
		314A						